ALSO BY
DARCY COATES

The Haunting of Ashburn House
The Haunting of Blackwood House
The House Next Door
Craven Manor
The Haunting of Rookward House
The Carrow Haunt
Hunted
The Folcroft Ghosts
The Haunting of Gillespie House
Dead Lake
Parasite
Quarter to Midnight
Small Horrors

House of Shadows
House of Shadows
House of Secrets

Black Winter
Voices in the Snow
Secrets in the Dark
Whispers in the Mist

PARASITE

DARCY COATES

Poisoned Pen
PRESS

Published by Poisoned Pen Press, an imprint of Sourcebooks
P.O. Box 4410, Naperville, Illinois 60567-4410
(630) 961-3900
sourcebooks.com

Originally self-published in 2016 by Black Owl Books.

Library of Congress Cataloging-in-Publication Data

Names: Coates, Darcy, author.
Title: Parasite / Darcy Coates.
Description: Naperville, IL : Poisoned Pen Press, [2020]
Identifiers: LCCN 2019059650 | (trade paperback)
Subjects: GSAFD: Science fiction. | Horror fiction.
Classification: LCC PR9619.4.C628 P37 2020 | DDC 823/.92--dc23
LC record available at https://lccn.loc.gov/2019059650

Printed and bound in Canada.
MBP 10 9 8 7 6 5 4 3 2 1

PART 1

STATION 331

CHAPTER 1

JEN SNAPPED HER HELMET into place, enjoying the quiet hiss and click that told her it was locked. A lot of outpost staff complained about having to wear the thick suits during routine patrols, but Jen liked them. They made her feel secure, as though nothing could get to her.

Carly locked her gloves into place. She wiggled her fingers experimentally then shot Jen a grin through the tinted glass of her helmet. "Damn, but I've been looking forward to getting out of this joint."

Jen had never asked exactly what Carly had done to get herself condemned to their tiny station on Perros's second moon, and Carly hadn't volunteered the information—but it must have been bad. People didn't end up on Station 331 by accident, and out of the three of them, Carly was the least suited to endure the isolation and monotony.

Jen checked her wrist controls to ensure everything was airtight. Carly was already at the door, hopping from foot to foot and swinging her arms. "C'mon, let's do this already."

A quiet voice buzzed through the helmet's speakers. "Jen, I'm ready for your all clear."

Jen turned toward the plexiglass window. Alessicka stood behind it and leaned over the control panel, her delicate face tensed in concentration. She was the only one of their three-woman team who kept her hair long, and it fell like a sheet down one side of her thin neck to brush over the panel.

"All clear," Jen said, shooting her two thumbs up as added reassurance.

Alessicka gave Jen a small smile then looked toward her companion. "Carly, how are you doing?"

"If I were any more ready, I'd explode." Carly swiveled in a semicircle to face the window. Her eyes were huge, and the need to be free was etched into every line of her face.

There was a pause.

"Carly, your monitor says your helmet isn't locked properly."

There was a tremor in Alessicka's voice. She hated arguing with Carly, but Jen knew her too well to think she would overlook any problem she found, no matter how minor. It was both a blessing and a curse; they were sometimes stuck in the air lock for an hour or more as she troubleshot problems...but at least Jen knew she wasn't going to be sent out in substandard conditions.

Jen's partner didn't share her view. Carly let out a string of curses and kicked at the air lock doors. "We've been over this before. A half dozen times. It's a problem in the feedback or whatever. I promise you, the helmet is locked."

Alessicka stared at the readings on the screen. Jen could see sweat beading on her face as she braced herself. "I'd like to run some diagnostics on…on…it." She trailed off at the murderous look on Carly's face.

"I swear, Lessi, you delay this patrol for another minute, and I'll murder you in your sleep tonight."

Alessicka's face blanched, and Jen decided it was time to intervene. "That's enough, Carly. Don't make jokes like that."

"Who said I was joking?"

Jen held up a hand to quiet her partner then turned to the woman behind the console. "Lessi, I'm going to override you this time. We've checked out the helmet before, and you said it was probably a feedback glitch. Besides, it's been months since we've seen anything more exciting than sludge. I doubt Carly's going to need to test her helmet's seal today."

Alessicka gave a small nod and began pressing buttons on the console. "Prepare for gate unlock in twenty seconds."

"*Finally*," Carly groaned.

Jen stepped up to join her partner beside the door. They each took one of the stingers from the rack bolted to the wall and turned them on. Stingers were their main weapon against what lived outside the station. They looked like rifles with extended barrels, but the tip was shaped into a large metal needle. The idea was to push the needle into any unwanted creatures they found on their moon and pull the trigger. The stingers released a shot

5

of neurotoxins directly into the life-form's body, killing it within seconds.

That was one of their jobs on Station 331: keep the moon clean of hostile beings that came off comets or space debris. Some of the newer stations got more exciting infestations of aggressive creatures like parydonas and crawling Helens and had to call for backup from their ward planets, but even though Station 331 was on a remote moon near the edge of the system, the staff rarely had to deal with anything worse than poppers and sludge.

"External gate unlocking," Alessicka said through the helmet, and the metal doors in front of them hissed and parted.

"Yes," Carly moaned as she sprinted as quickly as her bulky suit would allow onto the surface of the moon. She took three steps then kicked the powdery ground, sending herself flying nearly ten feet into the air before gliding down to land in a billow of red dust. Jen followed at a slower pace, enjoying the sensation of weightlessness from the lower gravity outside the station.

The moon wasn't ugly, but it *was* dull. Its uneven surface was pocked after millennia of being beaten by asteroids and space rubble. Composed of four small living rooms, one air lock, and one control room, the station had been built into a sheltered indent. Red rock surrounded it on three sides, so it got only four hours of natural sunlight each day.

Carly was sprinting ahead, stinger held in both hands, as she searched for a target to unleash her pent-up frustration on. She disappeared over the lip of a crater, and a moment later, Jen heard a sharp pop through her headset, followed by a cackle of delight. Carly had found her first victim.

Jen went in the opposite direction and circled around the back of the base. Before long, she found a target of her own; a sludge was clinging to a rock formation just meters from the front door. The human-sized clump of coal-black slime undulated as its organs worked to convert the moon's minerals into nutrients.

Sludges weren't dangerous, but they could be a nuisance if they got out of control. They would clog doorways, damage equipment, and given enough time, even eat through metal. Jen forced the tip of her stinger through the sludge's leathery skin, flicked the safety lock, and pulled the trigger. The gun kicked into her shoulder as it injected its poison, and she stepped back to watch as the sludge writhed and coiled in on itself.

Scientists said the sludges were no more intelligent than a plant, but Jen still hated seeing the creature thrash as its flesh bubbled and split. She stood with it until it was completely still, then she unclipped one of the hooks from her belt and snagged a corner of the sludge's frothing flesh.

She dragged it back to the waste disposal unit behind their station—low gravity had its benefits—and while she was feeding it through the slot, she heard another crack in her headset as Carly bagged her second target.

"Jen, Carly," Alessicka's voice said, "I'm getting a reading of a living shape by the weather vane. It looks like a sludge, but it's a big one."

"On it." Carly sounded breathless, but Jen couldn't tell if it was from excitement or overexertion.

Jen scouted around the perimeter of the station, making sure it was clean, before widening her loop. She could hear Carly humming as she made her way to the weather vane, which was located on an outcropping a kilometer away from the base. Twice, Carly stopped to use her stinger on creatures she found along the way, and once, she swore loudly, apparently having stubbed her toe on a rock. Jen started to tune her out as she focused on her job—injecting another sludge and a couple of thick, veiny plants that were struggling to survive on the barren moon—so she almost didn't hear Carly say her name.

"What's up?" Jen asked, clipping a sludge to her cable and beginning to pull it toward the waste disposal.

"This thing by the weather vane—it's not a sludge. It's… Hell, I have no idea what this is."

"Describe it," Alessicka said.

"It's…like…big. Maybe four times as large as I am. Black and lumpy, with red veins running all over its body."

"Red veins?" Alessicka asked. "Not yellow, like a creeping Helen?"

"No, definitely red. They're pulsing. And there are these… tendril things coming out at its base. Like roots. I think they're moving, but very slowly."

There was a pause, and Jen could hear Alessicka typing. "I haven't heard of a creature like that," she said, "and the system isn't bringing up any matches. Should I call Perros, Jen?"

Calling Perros, their ward planet, essentially meant asking for backup. Technically, that was the correct protocol for when they found an unidentifiable alien life-form, but hardly any station followed it.

"Aw, hell no," Carly said. "It looks harmless. It's actually managing to move less than a sludge. I'll just inject it real quick, and then we can get back to our damn jobs."

Alessicka's voice was tight with anxiety when she replied, "Don't proceed. You don't have clearance." She hesitated then added, "She…she doesn't have clearance. Does she, Jen?"

Jen sighed. Calling Perros was a huge inconvenience for everyone involved. Support wouldn't reach them for nearly twenty-eight hours, and if Carly was right and the life-form was vegetation or low risk, they wouldn't be happy about having their time wasted.

"Stay where you are, Carly. I'll come to you, and we can deal with it together."

"Sure you don't want me to get it now? It's an ugly son of a—"

"No." Jen unclipped the sludge from her belt. "Just stay put."

"Fine," Carly huffed, and Jen thought she heard a relieved sigh from Alessicka in the background.

Jen bounded across the moon's surface, her boots kicking up puffs of dust with each step. Perros rose over the horizon to her left, and she could see one of their sister moons, 384, to the right. There wasn't any proper *day* or *night* on 331, so the moon felt perpetually suspended in twilight; the atmosphere cast a red glow over the already-bronze landscape, dimming the sun's light and casting strange, leaping shadows.

Jen was still a few minutes from the weather vane when she heard Carly inhale sharply.

"What happened?" she asked at the same moment Alessicka said, "Carly?"

Carly laughed. "Oh, wow. I didn't expect that. I poked it, and it started moving."

"Moving?"

"Yeah, these tendril, vine-like things are stretching out and waving all over the place. Are you sure we have to kill it? It's the most interesting thing we've had on this moon in months."

Jen kicked against the ground to leap over a rocky ridge. "Damn it, Carly. Stay away from it until I get there. We don't know how dangerous it is."

"Relax," Carly drawled. "It can't reach me. I don't even think it can see. It's—" She gasped sharply.

Jen heard scraping and rustling, then Carly shrieked.

"Carly?" Jen called. She increased her jog to a run, moving her legs as fast as the thick suit and low gravity would let her. "What happened?"

"Damn it," Carly said over more scuffling. "It's got me, Jen. I dropped my stinger, and I can't get it off—" She grunted in pain then yelled something incoherent.

Fear spiked through Jen as she raced for the weather vane. She could hear Carly panting, interspersed with snapping noises. "I'm about two minutes away, Carly. Hang on."

Then Carly's screams filled Jen's helmet, drowning her in the rawness of the other woman's terror. Jen called to her, but Carly either didn't hear or couldn't respond; she kept screaming and screaming. The shriek's pitch rose...

Then there was silence.

CHAPTER 2

"CARLY?" JEN PANTED INTO the stillness. "Carly, can you hear me? Carly!"

"Her...her helmet's disconnected." Alessicka's voice was thin with horror. "Audio's g-gone completely."

"Damn it!" Jen couldn't move fast enough, as if she were stuck in a nightmare where no matter how hard she ran, she couldn't move any closer. Then she cleared a ridge and finally saw Carly's monster.

Clinging to the rocks at the base of a crater was a massive mess of black tendrils with pulsing red rivulets running down them. They were probing outward, feeling along the ground, seeking something to grip. Jen stopped well out of their reach and started sidestepping the creature, searching for the white suit that held her partner. She couldn't see it.

"Lessi, can you tell me anything? Do you have any reading on Carly?"

"No." She sounded as if she were hyperventilating, but her fingers were hitting the keyboard at an incredible speed. "I-it's like her helmet has been separated from the suit. I can't get any stats at all."

"Okay." Jen's pulse pounded in her head as she weighed up her options. "I'm going to try to sting it. If anything...*goes wrong*, don't come after me, but send a message to Perros immediately."

Alessicka made a strangled sort of noise. "Don't. Please, Jen. Please don't—"

The creature's limbs were tapping at the ground and seeking contact, but they seemed to be slowing their pace.

"I've got to try to find Carly. Under no circumstances are you to leave the base. That's a direct order, Lessi. Do you copy?"

"C-copy."

"Okay."

Jen began sliding down the incline that led to the life-form. Two of the tendrils stretched toward her, apparently sensing the motion. Jen hoped that if she could sting it and get enough neurotoxins in it to kill it, she might still be able to find Carly. She didn't want to think about the state the other woman would be in, though; the air on 331 was toxic. *If she lost her helmet...*

One of the arms shot out at an impossible speed and snagged Jen's ankle. She gasped and tried to jump back, but the creature was too fast. Before she could understand what was happening, she was in the air, held upside down, while another tendril wrapped around her chest.

She swung her stinger toward the nearest tendril. It missed

its mark. A new arm came up and wrapped around Jen's helmet, blinding her. She heard cracking noises as the black pulsing limb strained to separate the helmet from its suit.

Is this what it did to Carly?

She could feel the creature becoming frustrated. She had only seconds before it tried a new method of killing her; she aimed blindly, felt the stinger's steel needle puncture something resistant, and pulled the trigger.

A horrific wailing noise rose around her, and Jen found herself plummeting to the ground. She twisted around in midair in time to see she was headed for a crop of jagged rock, which would certainly puncture her suit, but at the last second, one of the thrashing arms batted her aside. She skidded over a dusty patch of ground and rolled to a stop.

The creature had gone wild. Its limbs waved in every direction, as though it were trying to fight an invisible attacker, and the bestial wailing noise filled her head. The arms seemed able to stretch to impossible lengths, and Jen realized she wasn't safe where she was. She began scrambling backward, up the incline of the crater, not daring to take her eyes off the waving, slapping arms until she was over the top of the lip and running for the base.

The terrible noise followed her. The poison had hurt the life-form, but it wasn't dead; a single injection probably wasn't enough for a beast that size, and there was no way Jen was going back to have another go at it—especially now that she knew for certain Carly couldn't have survived. The creature had tried to pop Jen's helmet off, just as it must have done to Carly. Jen's had only stayed on because it wasn't faulty.

Tears stung her eyes, and she blinked them back furiously. The guilt was crushing; she'd used her power as the team leader to override Alessicka when she'd tried to do her job, and now her partner was dead. *This is what you get for cutting corners. This is what happens when you don't take your job seriously.*

She squinted and ran faster. All she wanted, more than anything else, was to be inside the safety of the double-walled metal station. She would never complain about how small it was again.

"Jen?" Alessicka breathed in her ear. She sounded terrified. "A-are you th-there?"

In her rush to get away from the monster, Jen had forgotten to tell her remaining partner that she was okay. Alessicka had heard the fight, but nothing afterward, and Jen had left her hanging in terrible suspense.

"I'm here," Jen said, fortifying her voice. "I'm fine, and I'm coming back now. Carly...isn't."

"Okay" was the only thing Alessicka managed to say. She sobbed quietly and discreetly the entire time Jen was jogging back to base. She was young, and Jen didn't think she'd ever lost a team member before.

Relief spread across Jen's chest when the hulking metal structure came into view. She approached the air lock doors and asked Alessicka to open them. The girl must have been waiting with her hand poised over the button; they drew apart immediately, and Jen entered the air lock.

They looked at each other through the thick plexiglass screen that separated the air lock from the control room. Alessicka's face was pale and covered in tear tracks, but she kept her voice from breaking as she stepped Jen through the protocol they'd followed so often that it was like second nature. This time was different, though. This time, Jen stood alone as she waited for the chamber to be filled with breathable air, stepped out of her suit, and stored her equipment.

"Central doors unlocking," Alessicka said at last as the metal doors separating them parted. Jen stepped into the control room, and Alessicka threw herself onto Jen. Trembling, she hugged her fiercely, and Jen patted her hair until she pulled back. The girl's red eyes searched Jen's face, and for a moment, Jen was frightened Alessicka would blame her—tell her it was all her fault for ignoring the warning about Carly's helmet—but instead, she said, "What do I need to do?"

Ignoring the guilt and the pain had been easier when she had a purpose, so Jen latched on to Alessicka's opening and led her to the command board. "We need to get a message to Perros. Explain about the life-form we found. Explain about…Carly. Ask for assistance."

They would also need to request a replacement team member, but they could do that after the creature was dealt with and Carly's death was confirmed.

Jen watched over Alessicka's shoulder as she typed the message. Because of the location of their outpost, communication with Perros was difficult. Their ward planet would receive the message, but it wasn't likely they would send a reply. Any discussions would have to wait until the backup arrived.

"Sent." Alessicka swiveled in her chair to look up at her leader. "What else should I do?"

She needed work to keep her mind off Carly just as badly as Jen did. Unfortunately, work was one thing they were low on: the patrols usually took most of the day, so they'd finished all of their regular chores that morning.

Jen opened her mouth to suggest they go over inventory again, but a sharp noise interrupted her. They both jumped and looked through the plexiglass window into the air lock. Something large and dark was pressed against the outside door.

It's the monster from the weather vane. It's followed me back to base, Jen thought with a spike of panic, but as the shape moved and she realized what it really was, she somehow felt even more horrified.

"Carly!" Alessicka shrieked.

Their missing team member stood outside the base. She wasn't wearing a helmet, and her crop of curly black hair was stuck to her forehead with sweat. Her dark eyes bored into them intently, desperately, as she banged a fist on the door.

Alessicka slammed her hand on the button that opened the air lock, and Carly stumbled inside. Jen stared at her, shocked that she had survived the unbreathable air long enough to get back to base, let alone lived through having her helmet ripped off. Alessicka was talking rapidly over the speaker as she changed the settings on her control panel.

"Hang on, Carly. I'm depressurizing the air lock—filtering in oxygen—stabilizing the seal. Just a moment, and we'll have you back in the base."

Jen couldn't take her eyes off Carly as the woman leaned against one of the walls, panting and shivering. It seemed incredible that she could have made it back. *More than incredible, actually. Impossible.*

"Carly?" Jen asked. "Are you hurt?"

Carly was unzipping what remained of her thick suit. Jen saw tears in it; one arm had been shredded completely, and Jen thought she saw a splash of red on the inside as Carly shimmied out of it. "A few bruises," she said, flashing them a shaky smile, "but I'm alive and in one piece, so I guess I can't complain."

"Thank goodness," Alessicka said. She was adjusting the levels in the air lock to filter out the planet's toxic air before she opened to doors to their base. "We thought—"

"Yeah, I thought that for a moment, too," Carly said. "I heard you come for me, Jen, but it had me pinned, and I couldn't help. I'm glad you got away okay."

"Me too," Jen said automatically, raking the woman over with her eyes. She looked fine, completely fine, and that terrified her.

"It's dead, by the way." Carly took one of the towels from the storage closet and rubbed at her sweaty face. "The monster. Life-form. Thing. Once you stung it, it let me go, and I was able to get my own stinger and finish it off."

"I see."

Alessicka looked ready to cry again, but a wide smile spread over her face. "Okay, Carly, central doors unlocking."

"Wait." Jen grabbed Alessicka's wrist to stop her from opening the metal doors that separated them from Carly.

The girl blinked up at her in confusion. "Did I do something wrong?"

"No. Uh, Carly, I'm sorry about this, but you need to stay in the air lock. Quarantine."

Carly's jaw dropped. She walked toward the plexiglass window. "Is this a joke? Because it's really sucky timing. I want a shower, damn it."

"I'm sorry, Carly, but you were exposed to that thing. We don't know what it was or if it infected you with anything. You need to stay in there until the team from Perros arrives."

Carly swore at her. "This is ridiculous! Let me back in, Jen!"

"Surely…surely she's fine," Alessicka said, offering a weak smile.

Jen let go of her wrist. "We can't take that chance. It's only twenty-eight hours, Carly, then we can decontaminate and release you."

Carly stared pure hatred at her leader, and Jen felt her resolve slipping. *Maybe I am being overcautious. We were told the air was poisonous, but not* how *poisonous. Maybe someone could survive in it for short amounts of time. Maybe it isn't so unbelievable that she's still alive.*

But then Jen looked at the torn, helmetless suit crumpled on the floor, and she knew, with complete certainty, that she wanted to keep the doors closed.

"Alessicka," Jen said, "could you bring Carly some food and water?"

The young woman still looked shocked that they were keeping their partner inside the air lock, but she nodded and got up. Carly slouched away from the window to sit against the back wall, scowling. As Alessicka's footsteps faded down the hallway, Jen said, "Carly, you know why I have to do this, right?"

"I'm your friend," she spat. "We've been stuck on this forsaken lump of rock for three years. Don't you trust me?"

Not at this moment I don't.

CHAPTER 3

THE DAY PASSED SLOWLY. Alessicka and Jen stayed at the control panel. Carly refused to touch the bottles of water and peach-flavored slurry packets they'd cautiously tossed through the door, but sat in her corner and sulked. After trying to make small talk for a few minutes, Alessicka gave up and joined them in silence.

When the clock ticked over to the third quarter of the day, Jen turned to Alessicka. "You'd better get some rest."

She looked ghastly. Her doe-like eyes were bloodshot from crying, and her face was pale, but she still smiled. "I'm fine, Jen."

Jen sighed. "No, you really need sleep. I'll stay here with Carly. Go on."

Alessicka obediently got up and waved goodbye to Carly, who flashed a grin back at her. Jen waited until she heard the bedroom door close before speaking.

"You haven't touched your food."

"Not hungry."

"So you're going to starve yourself until we let you out?"

Her only reply was a very slow blink.

"Carly," Jen said, choosing her phrasing carefully. "I don't believe you escaped from that creature."

The other woman didn't say anything.

"I felt how strong it was. It would have torn me in half if I'd given it another minute."

"I'm sure it would have."

Something about how she said that—almost with a hint of arrogance—made Jen pause. Carly was watching her through half-closed lids, a smirk hovering around her mouth.

"You don't have so much as a scratch on you."

"I was lucky, wasn't I?"

"The air isn't breathable."

"Are you sure about that? I swallowed it. It was fine."

"So you think the scientists lied to us when they said it was toxic?"

"Yes." Another slow, languid blink followed.

Jen pursed her lips. She had always gotten along reasonably well with Carly, but at that moment, she would have been glad to never see the other woman again. "I'm going to get some sleep too."

"Do you know why I was condemned to this hellscape?" Carly asked, and Jen froze halfway out of her chair. Carly's smile widened, but it wasn't a pleasant expression. "I know you've seen my work history. I'm beyond overqualified for a place like this.

You probably think I did something really bad to end up here, don't you?"

Now it was Jen's turn to play the silence game.

"You'd be right." Carly was speaking so quietly that Jen had difficulty hearing her. "Before this, I was in charge of a mineral processing plant. Big place, dozens of people under me. There was this one conveyer belt that was designed to crush rocks into gravel, and I took a walkway above it every morning on the way to my office."

She glanced to the side, and her eyes went hazy as she relived the memory. "One man there—I don't remember his name; Jon or James or something—tried to talk to me every morning about this idea he had. A way to streamline the plant. He'd follow me from the front door until I locked myself in my office. Tried to corral me every lunchtime too. His plans were flawed and wouldn't have worked in a million years, but no matter how often I told him that, he'd keep on, like a fly you can't catch, chasing me every morning. And eventually, I couldn't stand it any longer."

Jen swore under her breath, and Carly smiled, her dark eyes flicking back to watch her companion's face with relish. "You can guess what happened, can't you? He was still alive when he hit the conveyer belt, but the crushers took care of that pretty quickly. He painted the floor red." She laughed and licked her lips. "I told them he slipped. No one saw me push him, so they couldn't accuse me, but they guessed. And they punished me in the most effective way they could: they sent me here."

"Enough," Jen said. She was shaking.

Carly had never spoken like that before. She was sometimes brash, rude, or reckless, but Jen had never seen such maliciousness come from her.

"Just thought you'd like to know," Carly said sweetly before closing her eyes and pretending to sleep.

Jen turned on her heel and marched toward the bedroom. Her head was throbbing from stress and frustration. *I need some downtime. A chance to center myself, away from Carly.*

The bedroom was dark and cool. She paused in the doorway, listening to Alessicka's breathing from the bed at the back of the room, using the sound to reassure herself. She didn't bother changing—she didn't expect to sleep more than a few hours—so she crawled into her bed fully clothed.

Jen didn't fall asleep for a long time. Images of the black pulsing creature kept drifting across her closed eyelids. She saw Carly, too bold for her own good, snatched into the air. Then the tendrils latched onto and tore off her faulty helmet. Jen heard her scream. She was running toward her, but the faster she tried to move, the less progress she seemed to make. A tendril forced itself into Carly's mouth; she struggled against it then bit it, and ink-like blood burst from it to coat her face.

A loud bang pulled Jen out of the nightmare, and she sat up in bed, drawing in thick, ragged breaths. Sweat coated her body as though she'd just finished running a marathon, and her blanket had fallen to the floor. As she sat still, trying to rein in her thundering heart, she realized something was wrong: she couldn't hear Alessicka's breathing anymore.

CHAPTER 4

A SECOND BANG AND a drawn-out scraping noise came from the main part of building. Jen launched herself to her feet. Alessicka's bed was empty, the sheets pushed neatly back into place. Jen ran for the hallway.

"Please no," she muttered as she ran. "Please don't be in there. Don't be in there. Please."

The noise had quieted; the rooms were so still that she could have been the only living person in Station 331 as she rounded the corner and opened the door to the control room.

The air lock door was open, and Alessicka was inside, slumped on the ground with her back to Jen, while Carly knelt in front of her. Jen froze as Carly looked up, a wide, unnatural smile stretched across her face. Their gazes met for a second before Carly's eyes flicked to the open door.

They moved at the same time. Carly dashed toward freedom,

and Jen lunged for the control panel. Jen was a second faster; her hand hit the flashing red button, and the air lock doors slid closed just in time for Carly to hit them.

"Damn it, Jen!" she yelled.

Jen pulled back from the panel, feeling terror and nausea rush through her. Alessicka sat crumpled on the ground, looking like a doll that had been propped up into an imitation of a sitting pose.

"What did you do to her?" Jen called. Her mind raced, fighting to think of a way to get the girl out, desperately hoping she wasn't too late.

"She's *fiiine*, Jen," Carly said. She'd reverted to a complacent drawl as she paced back into view. "Aren't you, Lessi?"

As if on cue, Alessicka's body jerked. Slowly, like a puppet being pulled by strings, she began to twitch herself upright. It looked so unnatural that Jen wanted to scream.

"Lessi?" Jen asked as the girl rotated to face the window.

Alessicka's face was slack, and her eyes were blank as she stared at a space somewhere behind Jen's shoulder. Then she blinked, and her whole body shuddered. Her hands twitched up, her neck straightened, her back aligned itself, and a look of awareness returned to her face.

"Jen!" She clasped her hands in front of her chest, blinking quickly and giving the worried look she wore whenever she thought she was in trouble. "I'm sorry, Jen. I opened the door to give her some food, and we sat down to talk. I must have fallen asleep, and… Did you lock the doors?"

"Yes," Jen's lips moved to say, but no noise escaped her.

Alessicka looked normal again. Completely normal. Yet Jen couldn't erase the memory of her body, crumpled on the ground, as if the life had been sucked out of her…

"You can let me out now," Alessicka said, hurrying to the plexiglass window and giving Jen a sweet, apologetic smile as she pressed her hand to it. "I'm really sorry. I know I should have asked you before going in, but she said she was hungry, and…I'm so sorry. Please let me out."

"No." Jen wanted to cry as she said the words. "You're in quarantine now too."

Something flashed over Alessicka's face—anger or maybe resentment—and was covered over so quickly that Jen doubted she'd seen anything. "Oh, Jen," the girl said, her voice a tremulous whisper, "please don't be mad at me. I was just trying to do the right thing."

Jen turned away from the console so Alessicka wouldn't see how badly her words had cut.

On the day Alessicka had arrived on Station 331 to complete their three-woman team, Jen had realized the girl was too gentle and too young for a job that would entail years of isolation. As Alessicka examined the console station she would be in charge of, Jen had watched the woman's hands flutter above the buttons with the anxious motions of someone who'd never been outside a simulation room before. She'd made up her mind to watch over her newest ward carefully. She'd told herself she could shelter her, protect her, and guide her until her contract was up. Then she could usher her into an easier, more enjoyable job on Perros.

She'd failed. Whatever had happened to Carly had taken over Alessicka, and Jen hadn't been able to stop it.

"Jen?" Alessicka called, and she sounded so much like herself that it was agony for Jen to leave the doors closed. "I'm sorry, Jen. I didn't mean to upset you."

Jen grimaced then turned back to the window. Alessicka stared back, her smile apologetic, her doe eyes begging for forgiveness. Carly was near the back of the room, standing beside the shelves holding the equipment. She kept her eyes averted, seemingly trying to blend into the background, almost as though she hoped Jen would forget she was there.

Jen couldn't let Alessicka out…but she didn't want to leave her alone either. She sat in front of the console, ignoring the girl's curious gaze, and turned off the intercom. If she couldn't hear her, she wouldn't be so tempted.

As soon as she saw Jen wasn't going to open the doors, Alessicka turned away and joined Carly near the back of the room. They sat together, Carly's arm around her friend's shoulders, in the same pose Jen had once sat with Alessicka when she'd been crying from homesickness. Jen ignored them.

The console recorded and stored audio for up to forty-eight hours. Normally, it was Alessicka's job to retrieve it if they needed to check any of their patrol data, but Jen knew enough about the machine to fumble her way through it. She rewound it to a point just a few minutes before the door had been opened and pressed Play.

"Hi, Lessi," Carly's tinny voice said. "Couldn't sleep?"

"No."

"Neither could I."

A few minutes of silence was punctuated by rustling noises. Jen imagined Alessicka sitting in front of the desk and Carly moving toward the window.

"Lessi, I can trust you, can't I?"

"Yeah, of course you can."

She heard Carly sigh. "There's something wrong with Jen."

"Wha… In what way?"

"The creature didn't attack me, Lessi. It snagged my ankle and tripped me, but it wasn't dangerous. It was Jen who pulled my helmet off."

Alessicka was silent.

"I didn't want to say anything in front of her, in case it panicked her and she tried to hurt you too…but I think she wanted me to die out there. She pulled the faulty helmet off and left me to suffocate. I guess she thought the plant would be a very convenient explanation."

There was a thin sound; Jen thought it must be Alessicka trying not to cry.

"I'm so sorry, Lessi." Carly's voice was low and anxious. "I don't know what to do. She's locked me in here to divide us. Quarantine is just an excuse. Why would I need quarantining, anyway? I'm not hurt, and I'm not sick."

Alessicka mumbled something Jen couldn't make out.

"No. The creature was harmless. It was Jen all along. She doesn't want me working here. She wanted to get rid of me. I can prove it to you; she left a bruise on my neck—come in, and I'll show you."

Alessicka mumbled again. It was a wonder Carly had been able to understand her.

"No, it's okay. Just come in, and I'll show you. Then we can figure out what to do. We'll find a way to help Jen, I promise, but we'll need to work together. We'll need to be able to trust each other. You do trust me, don't you, Lessi?"

The squeak of a chair being vacated was followed by the slick *whoosh* of doors being opened, silence for a moment, then the loud bang that had broken through Jen's sleep. She heard a whimper, followed by another bang and a dragging sound. Then footsteps—her footsteps—raced into the console room.

Jen turned off the recording. She'd been so engrossed in it that she hadn't noticed Alessicka and Carly had moved. They stood in front of the window, equally calm faces holding tranquil eyes that stared down at her. Carly raised her hand and rapped on the plexiglass. Knowing what she wanted, Jen turned on the intercom with trembling fingers.

"You don't remember, do you, Jen?" Carly asked.

"What?" her mouth was dry. Their stares were almost hypnotic.

"You don't remember attacking me."

"Because I didn't! The plant—"

"The plant was harmless. It tangled around my legs, and while I was trying to pull myself free, you grabbed me from behind. I screamed, and you pulled my helmet off, disconnecting the audio so I couldn't get any word back to Lessi."

"No!" Jen shouted, launching herself out of the chair to face them. "That's a lie!"

"You've been acting strange for weeks," Alessicka murmured. "I confronted you about it yesterday. Don't you remember? You've been mumbling in your sleep and refusing to talk to us."

"That's…not true," Jen stammered.

Alessicka's gaze held her, mesmerizing her.

"It is true," Carly continued. "We've been so worried about you, Jen. It's this place. This station. It's too small and too remote for someone as strong as you. You've been gradually losing your mind for months."

"No…"

"Yes," Alessicka said. "And you finally snapped yesterday. You knew how wrong it was, how terrible what you were doing was, so your mind built a fantasy. A fantasy about a monster that tried to kill Carly…but it was you all along."

Jen pressed a hand to her cheek and found it was wet. Her body was shivering. They were lying to her, she knew, trying to chip away at her resolve and make her doubt herself.

"Do you remember what you did to be sent to this station?" Carly asked. Her lids were half-closed, and her voice was a low, comforting murmur. "Do you remember?"

"I-I talked back to a superior—"

"No, Jen, you tried to strangle your superior. You always protested your innocence. Your mind washed over it. You couldn't stand to think of yourself as a killer."

"No…no…"

"What will the relief unit from Perros think when they arrive and find you've locked both of your team members in a room with no food or water?"

"But I haven't," Jen managed. "We gave you food."

Carly waved her hand at the room. "No you didn't. It's just your mind telling you that you did."

Jen stared at the ground, the shelves, and the boxes, trying to find the packets of food and bottles of water she'd passed through the door. *We did give Carly food, didn't we?*

"You see?" Carly said, her voice a sweet song in Jen's ears, her eyes drawing the other woman back to drown in them. "You can't trust your mind. But you *can* trust us. We want to help you, Jen. Let us out before the relief team arrives, and we can protect you, look after you…make sure no one hurts you."

"Let us help," Alessicka whispered. She was standing so close to the glass that her breath fogged it. "We want to help you."

"It's okay, Jen. Just open the doors."

"Open them, Jen."

"It's okay."

"You can trust us."

Jen found her hand hovering over the red button that would unseal the air lock. Her body was shaking, and her head was foggy. Tears dripped off her chin as she stared at her teammates, the two people she'd relied on, cared for, and watched over for nearly three years. They smiled at her so warmly and so kindly that she knew denying them would be insanity.

Her hand pressed the button. The doors drew open with a

gentle *whoosh*, and it felt good to give in, to stop resisting, and to stop fighting her friends. That's what they were—friends. They walked through the doorway, came to her with open arms, and embraced her. The women held her still as she cried, stroked her hair, and told her she'd done the right thing.

Then Jen looked at Alessicka and saw a hairline fracture running down from her scalp, between her eyes, down her nose, and over her lips, chin, and neck before disappearing behind her shirt's collar. Jen frowned at it, confused and mesmerized. It began to part, splitting open, peeling the girl's smiling face back to show the pulsing, black mass inside her. Jen tried to pull away, but they held her firmly. She looked at Carly and saw she'd mimicked her partner; her skin was coiling back in on itself as the black tendrils reached out of their shell, tasting the air and stretching toward Jen's face…

CHAPTER 5

JEN STOOD IN FRONT of her station, suited up to protect against the toxic air, as she watched the ship from Perros land. It kicked up huge clouds of red soil as it touched down, and even though she was wearing a helmet, she raised her arm reflexively to shield her face.

The ship's doors opened, and three suited figures jumped out. Jen waved them over and led them into the air lock.

As soon as breathable oxygen had replaced the toxic air, they unlocked their suits. "Thanks so much for coming," Jen said as soon as her helmet was off.

"That's our job," the team's leader, a tall and wiry man, said. "What's the problem?"

Jen watched as they unsuited. Their team was composed of two men and a woman; they all looked tough and capable—exactly what she needed. "Long story," she said as they hung up their suits, "but it's been pretty crazy down here. Come in, and I'll explain everything."

The doors slid open, and they entered the main part of the station. Jen turned to smile at the assistance team as Alessicka and Carly, as quiet as shadows, appeared behind them. Jen didn't need to give any signal; they all knew what needed to be done.

"We've made some changes on this station. Want to see them?" she asked, beaming at the three newest additions to their small colony as her sisters shed their human skins.

PART 2

STATION 332

CHAPTER 6

"DIAMONDS, HUH?" CHARLES WATCHED the glittery sand-like shards rise in a flurry around their landing ship.

"Yeah, they're pretty sure," Jay said from the seat opposite her.

"I hate diamonds."

Jay twisted to look at her, a delighted grin spreading over his stubbled face. "What, really? A girl as pretty as you doesn't like diamonds? You continue to surprise me, Charlie."

"Screw you," she spat back. "They're ugly, overpriced lumps of carbon. And please, keep calling me *Charlie*. I'd love an excuse to force-feed you your own genitals."

Jay was wise enough not to retort, though his grin widened further, exposing more of his large white teeth. *Horse's teeth,* Charles thought to herself as she flashed him her middle finger.

Their ship hit the swirling surface, its landing struts digging deep into the bed of clear dust. The engines powered down, and

Charles unhooked her safety belt, stood up, and stretched with a relieved sigh. The moon had made for a difficult landing, and her muscles were sore from being held in the seat for two hours.

The door leading to the pilot's quarters opened, and Robin jumped out, her face looking even more haggard than normal. She tied her steel-gray hair in a short ponytail as she glanced between her two team members. "Suit up. We're going to do this job quick, okay? Get in, and get out. If they ask us to stay for tea, you have my permission to punch their faces."

Charles laughed as she pulled her suit out of the overhead compartment and started shimmying into it. She'd first met Commander Robin an hour before boarding their ship, and she thought it was a damn shame she hadn't known her longer. The older woman hated her job with an intensity that Charles could only respect.

They were on a routine response mission. The station they were visiting, Station 332, had sent a distress signal nearly a week prior. A week stuck with Jay and Robin on the cramped ship had sent Charles half-insane—and she certainly wasn't looking forward to the trip back—but she enjoyed visiting different stations, even if the moon's surface was made out of stupid diamonds.

"Okay," Robin said, checking their suits' signals on her monitor, "you guys know the drill. Play it cautious. If you need to use your weapons, keep their safety locks on, yadda, yadda, yadda. Let's get this over with."

They sealed their helmets in place then crowded into the

ship's tiny air lock. Jay gave Charles's butt a playful slap, and she jabbed her elbow into his stomach in response, even though both of their suits were too heavily padded for either of them to feel much. Charles couldn't see it through the tinted helmet, but she could easily imagine Robin's eye roll as the older woman began stabbing at the buttons on the console to release the air lock and open the outer doors.

They spilled out into the powdery diamonds. Charles sank up to her knees and wobbled, trying to keep her balance in the shifting surface.

"It's like snow!" Jay's voice came through her helmet's communication unit. He sounded delighted, and Charles glanced behind herself to see him flat on his back, swinging his arms and legs to make a snow angel.

"Get up, ass," Robin snapped. She was already five paces ahead of them, stomping toward a large, dark shape a dozen meters away. "If you slow me down, I'll be delighted to ditch you here."

Charles raised her eyebrows at Jay then jogged after her leader. The diamonds were dense, and by the time they'd reached the front doors of Station 332, they were both panting.

"Why haven't they opened them already?" Robin groused. She pressed the flashing red light beside the doors, requesting entrance. They waited in silence, but the light didn't turn green, and the doors didn't open.

"They know we're here, right?" Charles asked.

"I sent an alert when we were an hour out. They damn well better not have fallen asleep."

Jay finally caught up to them, stray diamonds falling off his suit. He glanced at the two women then at the door. "Want me to manually open it?"

"No, I think I'd rather stand here for a few hours first," Robin said, her voice dripping with scorn. "Idiot."

Jay chuckled and pulled a tiny square kit out of one of his suit's pouches. He extracted a screwdriver and began working the top off the gray access box.

They often didn't know what sort of situation they were responding to. Central's communication system was frustratingly crude. It used localized wormholes and refracted light to send messages across light years in a matter of minutes, but that limited messages to a very small selection of presets: *supplies low*, *assessment requested*, and *emergency assistance required*.

Supplies low meant exactly what it sounded like: the station's crew was going to run out of food, water, oxygen, or mechanical supplies before the scheduled bimonthly restocking. In response to this message, one of the refueling ships would be dispatched to drop off whatever they needed.

Assessment requested was used when one of the crew was requesting a transfer or if the station was deteriorating beyond what the assigned team could repair and they wanted approval for a renovation. Two council delegates would be sent to assess and approve those requests.

Emergency assistance required was the least-frequently used signal, but it was also the most difficult to prepare for. It could mean almost anything: one of the crew had been injured, a life-form beyond what the assigned team could handle had landed on the planet after hitching a ride on an asteroid or space junk, one of the crew members had gone insane from the solitude, or any other dangerous problem that the crew needed outside help to deal with.

Normally, Central tried to send highly skilled and efficient teams who had a history of working well together to respond to emergency assistance requests, but Charles suspected Central had been scraping the bottom of the barrel when they'd dispatched her. An abnormally high number of assistance requests had come in during the previous week, and all of the reliable response teams were already halfway across the known system.

Charles had never worked with her companions before, but she'd been told Jay was their mechanic—as she watched him fumble to remove the access box's protective cover, she had to wonder just how much experience he had. Robin was their pilot, leader, and medic. Charles had a background in defense, so she supposed Central had sent her as a fighter, even though she'd had only twelve weeks of active duty before being reassigned. The team was far from ideal.

The box's lid popped off, exposing a mess of multicolored wires and circuits. Jay began tracing one of the black wires, gave up on it partway along, and tugged on a red wire instead.

"Any time this decade will be fine," Robin said.

"Yeah, yeah, calm down, princess," Jay said fondly. "This part can't be rushed, but feel free to heckle me into electrocuting myself if it makes you feel better."

Jay finished tracing one of the green wires and pulled its end out of the socket. He then plugged it into the vacant gap next to it, and the thick metal doors slid aside with a quiet *whoosh*.

"You're welcome," he said as the women filed past him and into the station's air lock.

The small room had only two doors: one leading to the outside and one that would grant them access to the station. Shelves to their left held the equipment the station's team needed to maintain their moon, and a large plexiglass window would have let them see into the control room if the station lights had been on.

"Ha, you were right. They fell asleep," Charles said.

Jay had closed the doors behind them and was already working on the panel beside the interior doors. Without a reply, Robin stepped up to the plexiglass window and pressed her helmet against it.

Charles shifted uneasily as she waited. With the exterior doors closed, the only available light came from the backup lamp set in the wall behind her. It cast a strange greenish glow over the room. The more she thought about it, the more their situation unsettled her. Though it wasn't unheard of for a station's crew to sync their sleep schedules, it *was* against protocol…not that every station followed protocol, of course. But the station's team would have known when to expect their response crew, and she would have thought at least *someone* could have waited up for them.

"Air lock pressurizing," Jay's voice crackled in her ear. Charles heard a quiet hissing as the moon's toxic atmosphere was pumped out and replaced with oxygen. Robin still hadn't moved from the window.

"Aaand…done."

Charles and Jay removed their helmets, placed them on an empty shelf, and unzipped the restrictive space suits. Robin finally pulled back from the window and took off her own helmet.

"Something up?" Charles asked.

"Turn your guns on," she said.

CHAPTER 7

JAY AND CHARLES GLANCED at each other. They grabbed for the small handguns tethered to their suits and pressed the power buttons.

"Should we open the door?" Jay asked as Robin hung up her suit. The older woman's creased face looked far more alert than Charles had ever seen it. Robin nodded, Jay re-plugged a cable, and the interior doors parted, letting them into the control station.

Charles did a double take. Part of the control panel had been smashed; the metal was dented inward, and its little buttons and light covers bugged out of their holes. The chair was overturned, and something dark was scuffed over the tile floor. Charles stepped in front of her team and raised her gun. The hallway beyond the control center was dark and empty, and the only thing she could hear was her companions' breaths.

"We need to search the building," Robin said, her voice a barely audible whisper. "We'll start with the sleeping quarters."

Charles nodded, led them through the open doorway into the hall, then turned left. Virtually every station was arranged in the same format: the kitchen and living areas were to the right, the work areas could be found through a hallway straight ahead, and turning left would take them to the sleeping quarters and bathroom.

Charles pressed the hall's light switch, but the ceiling lamps stayed dead. Either the power had cut out, or the lights were broken. As she heard plexiglass shards crunch under her boots, she assumed it was the latter.

Two dozen paces brought them to the bedroom door, which stood ajar. Charles nudged it open with her foot, slipped a hand inside, and pressed the light switch.

One of the lights spluttered, flickered, then died in a shower of sparks, but the second bulb turned on, casting strange shadows over the scene before them. Three walls each held a plain bed with a storage unit fixed above it. Two of the beds were made, but the third had its blankets mussed. A large object lay in the middle of the room.

Jay swore under his breath then gagged. Robin only paused for a second before pressing past Charles to approach the decomposing body.

It was a man—Charles thought it was anyway; the body was so bubbly and saggy, it was hard to be sure. He'd fallen on his back, his legs twisted awkwardly under him, arms flung out to the side. His remaining eye was milky white and bulged out of its socket, and his jaw hung open, almost as if it were dislocated, to display white teeth poking out of darkened gums. A pool of tar-black blood spread around his head like a toxic halo.

Charles stood frozen as Robin knelt beside the man. Her twelve weeks of active duty had shown her only two deaths, and both of those had been quick and low impact; they'd been followed by prompt funerals, a moment's silence at that night's dinner, then a return to regular work. She'd never once imagined what would have happened to the bodies if they hadn't been cremated, and the corpse in front of her was both horrifying and riveting.

"Oh—" Jay gagged again. "No—don't touch it!"

Robin pressed the tip of her gun to the side of the corpse's head, raising a flap of sagging skin. Behind it was a clear hole that went through the head.

"He was shot," she said. Charles was surprised to hear the older woman's voice was impassive. Robin lowered the gun and dipped its tip in the black stain around the man's head. The liquid stuck to the metal barrel, and when she pulled it back, long strands of the black substance dribbled from it.

"Is that blood?" Jay sounded nauseated.

"It must be. He's been dead for a while, probably since shortly after the distress signal." Robin rose and wiped the tip of her gun on the floor. "That bed isn't made. I'd guess he was attacked while he was sleeping."

"Jeez," Charles said, shaking free of her stupor.

"Don't let your guard down; we've still got to find the other two crew members." Robin approached the room's second door, which led to the bathroom. She twisted the handle, but the door didn't open.

"Want me to…?" Jay offered weakly, but Charles pushed past him, raised her right leg, and gave the door a hard kick. It burst open, hitting the wall and bouncing backward as Charles turned on the light.

A second body was propped against the sink. A blend of dried dark-red spots, white shards, and gray clumps was splattered across the shower's glass door, and the corpse's decaying hand clutched a gun.

Jay swore again.

"Two down," Charles said weakly. "One to go."

Charles had intended to lighten the atmosphere, but Robin glared at her. The older woman approached the corpse and gave it a superficial examination.

"What do you think happened?" Jay asked. He hadn't entered the bathroom but stood well back, pressing his thumbs into the bridge of his nose.

"This one went insane and shot his companions before finishing himself off," Robin said, backing out of the room. "It happens."

Charles rubbed her tongue over the inside of her mouth. It tasted acidic. "You've seen this before?"

"Once. Come on. We only need to confirm the third team

member's death, then we can get out of here and let Central send a purging crew."

Jay laughed weakly. "Purge? If it were me, I'd just write the whole station off."

"They can't. This station links the communication systems between Cyrus and Mandola. They'll need a new crew to maintain it."

"I doubt anyone will want to work here after *this*."

"They won't know," Robin sighed. "Central will move a new team in here and tell them the old crew was relocated. It happens all the time. There could have been a mass murder in your own station, and you wouldn't have a clue."

"Oh hell."

"Charles, stop gawking, or I'll lock you in with the body."

She waved to her leader, not taking her eyes off the wall. "No, hey, come back here. He left a message."

"What?"

Robin reentered the room, and Charles pointed. On the wall, written crudely in dark-brown blood, was the phrase *They take our skin*.

Charles rubbed at her arms. The temperature seemed to have dropped ten degrees.

"Don't try to read a deeper meaning into it," Robin said, apparently guessing what was going through Charles's mind. "He was crazy, so he wrote a love letter to his delusions before finishing himself. Come on. The quicker we go, the quicker we can get out of here."

Charles let Robin lead her out of the bathroom, past the corpse on the bedroom floor, and back into the hallway. Jay was waiting for them, his face a pasty pale gray. "Where next?"

"Living quarters," Robin said. They retraced their steps down the hallway, past the damaged control room, and then through the door at the opposite end of the hall. When Charles pressed the switch, none of the lights came on.

"Flare," Robin instructed, and Charles fumbled one out of her suit's satchels, pulled the tab, and held it above her head as it hissed and spat. The dingy red light threw writhing shadows around the overturned furniture, broken TV, and shattered glass bowls.

Jay nudged Robin and Charles then pointed to the wall behind them, where a dark liquid had sprayed across the gray-green paint. Robin nodded. "Spread out. There'll be a body here somewhere."

Charles went left, circling the overturned lounge chair, flare raised high in her left hand, gun in her right. Something had shredded the cushions, and their pale stuffing had spilt out like a puff of cotton candy. She'd just opened her mouth to point it out to Robin when a quiet snap from farther in the station startled her.

The three of them froze, turning toward the source of the sound. "Was that a door?" Jay hissed, panic clear in his voice.

Charles thought she could hear footsteps approaching them through the kitchen, whose closed door stood not far in front of her. A click to her left told her Robin had taken the safety off her gun.

Charles tossed the flare behind her so the light was at her back. The hairs on her arms stood on end, and her throat felt tight as she took a deep, stabilizing breath. She pulled the door open with a snap.

CHAPTER 8

A WOMAN WITH DISHEVELED hair and a face whiter than the tiles behind her stood on the other side of the door. Her large brown eyes squinted against the harsh light.

"You…came…" Her voice cracked, and suddenly, she was crying. Her body shook with heaving sobs.

Charles grimaced and glanced at her companions for help; Jay started forward, gun already pocketed, his arms spread to envelop the woman, but Robin grabbed his shoulder and tugged him back. She hadn't lowered her gun, and the shadows that caught in her creased face gave her an intense, manic look.

"Get back," she snapped as the new woman took a step toward them. "Back against the wall. Keep your hands where I can see them."

The woman obeyed. Her sobs quieted as she raised her hands over her head. "I'm sorry. I'm so sorry. I've just been waiting for so long, and when I heard you, I thought—" She broke off into a hiccup.

"Tell me your name," Robin barked.

Jay glared at his leader. "Hey, cut the lady some slack. Let's get her something to drink and a warm blanket before we start the inquisition, okay?"

"Unless you've forgotten," Robin spat through her teeth, "we have two bodies rotting away in the sleeping quarters. *Someone* killed them."

Charles tilted her head as she regarded the woman. She was small, with mousy brown hair worn long, and she was clearly terrified. "Do you really think she—"

"Maybe she did. Maybe she didn't. Either way, I do *not* want to have to face Central and explain how I got my team killed because I let my guard down. Now, I repeat: *What's your name?*"

"Ellan," the woman stuttered. Her hands were shaking as she held them above her head. "Ellan DeSouza. I was the station's scientist."

"That checks out," Jay said. "I read up on them on the trip here. She only finished her training four months ago, and this was her first assignment."

Ellan nodded eagerly, her limp hair fluttering around her face.

"Okay," Robin said, holding her gun steady. "Tell me what happened here."

"We were attacked," Ellan said, still blinking at tears as the flare hissed and fizzled behind them. "Our equipment said there was a large life-form that had come off an asteroid and was blocking part of our scanners. Jones and Mike went out to clear it while I stayed at the control panel. Then—then I heard screaming. And Mike was yelling at me to open the doors, so I did. They both came back in, but so did something *else*—" She broke off again and squeezed her eyes closed.

"It's okay," Jay cooed. "Take your time."

The woman rubbed the tear tracks off her cheeks as she took a few deep breaths. "I pressed the distress signal and ran. I don't know what happened, but I heard gunshots from the sleeping quarters, so I locked myself in the kitchen. I've been staying there ever since. There's something in the station; I can hear it walking around at night, looking for a way to get to me. When I heard you come in, I thought you were the monster, but then you started talking and—and—"

Again, Robin pulled Jay back to stop him from hugging the woman. He glared at her reproachfully.

"Your teammates are dead." Robin's voice was empty of emotion, and her gaze was guarded. "But I suppose you already knew that. So, you say there's a dangerous life-form in the station?"

Ellan nodded.

"You know what I think?" The girl shook her head, so Robin continued. "I think you're far too young to have been stationed here, and four months was enough to send you out of your mind. I think you killed your partners but lost the nerve to finish yourself off, so you placed the gun in your teammate's hand to make it look like he was responsible. I think you've spent this last week sinking into insanity and came up with this *monster* story so you could convince yourself you were innocent. What do you say to that?"

A flush of color had spread across Ellan's face. "I didn't... I'm not lying! Search the station yourself; you'll find it!"

"Yeah, we're going to do exactly that. You know what else we're going to do? Put you into quarantine on our ship. When we get back to base, Central will get to decide how much they believe your story."

"I'm not lying!"

"Jeez, Robin!" Jay snapped. "Give her a break already!" He turned back to the woman and lowered his voice, offering her the sweetest smile his face was capable of. "Hey, it's okay. I believe you."

"Monsters can't fire guns," Robin said bluntly. "Get up, DeSouza. I'll escort you to the ship. Charles, Jay, finish searching the station. I'll be genuinely amazed if you find anything, but regardless, it goes without saying that you should be cautious. Meet us back at the ship in no more than ten minutes."

"Sure," Charles said.

Jay crossed his arms and pouted as he watched Robin march the younger woman out of the room. "Remind me to never get on her bad side."

"You're already there." Charles grinned. "I agree she could use a brush up on her empathy skills, but she's only trying to keep us safe."

"You can't honestly believe that little dove is a killer."

"*Little dove?*" Charles punched Jay's arm. "Ha! You *like* her.

And for a moment there, I thought you were being a decent human being."

Jay pursed his lips but didn't retort. Instead, he marched into the kitchen, flicking the light on as he went.

It was the first undamaged room they'd found. The shelves, cupboards, and cooling unit were all neatly stacked. Charles skimmed the labels and snorted when she discovered they were arranged alphabetically.

"Damn perfectionists." She bumped one of the packets of liquefied fruit so that it no longer lined up with its companions. "I'll bet she spent the entire week rearranging the shelves in here to be *aesthetically pleasing*."

Without deigning to respond, Jay pointedly turned his back on Charles as he made a show of searching under the table. *Huh, he must really like her.*

The kitchen was empty, so Charles led the way through the door that divided the living quarters from the work area. The lights didn't work, so she lit another flare.

The room had been demolished: the workstations were broken and knocked against the walls, the lab equipment had been smashed, and the floor was littered with scraps of paper that had been torn out of their crumpled filing cabinets. It really did look as though a monster had been through it.

Charles hesitated by the door and watched as Jay paced through the destruction, crunching glass under his boots. He had his gun held to his eye, and sweat shimmered on his face in the flickering red light of the flare as he searched the room.

Something wasn't adding up. *Something about the bodies in the bedroom...* Her mind grappled with the memories, trying to discern what was disturbing her. Something clicked into place: Ellan had lied.

The scientist had said she'd locked herself in the kitchen to stay safe from the monster, but she couldn't have. Charles had opened both kitchen doors with an easy turn of their handles. She swore. "Jay, I think we should find Robin."

"What?" he stopped between a crushed shelf and a crumpled DNA extractor, glaring at her.

"I don't like leaving her alone with—"

Gunfire, harsh and loud, drowned out Charles's voice. She ducked instinctively then realized the noise was coming from deeper in the station.

Robin.

CHAPTER 9

"COMMANDER!" CHARLES YELLED AS she rushed down the hallway that led toward the air lock. She heard a crashing noise to her right. Jay's footsteps echoed behind her as he tried to keep pace.

Charles burst into the control station, panting, searching for her missing team member. The room looked exactly how it had when they'd arrived: crushed panel, overturned chair, and black smudges on the floor. No sign of Robin or Ellan. She squinted through the large plexiglass window, but the air lock was empty, and the door was still closed.

"Damn!" Charles shoved Jay aside as she ran back into the main hallway. She hesitated, trying to decide which direction to go. They'd just come from the passageway directly ahead. To the left was the corpse-infested bedroom, and to the right was the living area where they'd first met Ellan.

"Robin!" she yelled, praying the older woman would answer.

"I'm—ugh—here!"

Charles swung around to face the hallway that led to the bedrooms. Robin was doubled over, clutching a hand to her stomach. Ellan stood just behind her, arms around Robin's shoulders to support her. Drops of bright-red blood fell from Robin's hand as she straightened up.

Charles gasped. "You're hurt—"

"No, don't worry. It's not my blood." Robin wiped the back of her hand over her sweaty forehead, leaving a smear of pink gore in its wake. "The creature winded me. That's all."

"What—"

"DeSouza was telling the truth. There's a monster in this station. I was able to shoot and wound it, but it got away from us before I could finish it off."

Charles glanced at Ellan, whose eyes appeared even rounder than they had before, if that were possible. She was shaking but kept her hands on Robin's shoulders to steady her.

"Jeez," Jay hissed, hurrying up to them. "You're sure you're not hurt?"

"Yes, I'm fine." Robin was gradually collecting her composure. Her hands were trembling as she rubbed them clean on her suit, but her face had regained its serene mask. "We need to finish this thing off, though. We'll split into teams. Charles, you're with me. Jay, look after Ellan."

Jay didn't even try to hide the delight on his face. "Absolutely."

Robin hoisted her gun up and checked its ammunition level. "Charles and I will start in the work area. You two take the recreation room and kitchen. We'll meet up in the middle. Yell out if you see anything, okay?"

Jay fired off a mock salute then raised the gun in his right hand and placed his left on Ellan's shoulder. She gave him a shaky smile and leaned into the touch as he led her down the dark pathway toward the rec room. Charles waited until they were out of earshot before hissing, "Are you sure he's safe with her?"

"Oh, yes," Robin said, leading her down their path. "I trust her."

"Really?" Charles asked. She wrestled with that as they entered the destroyed workroom. "Just like that?"

"Search the back of the room," Robin said. "The creature is small and dark, so look carefully."

Charles sucked a deep breath in through her nose then raised her gun so she could look through the scope. Visibility was poor in the dimly lit room, so she moved carefully, her boots grinding on the broken glass and overturned specimen samples. The dancing shadows played tricks on her eyes, convincing her that she saw something small and menacing hiding in every dark crevice. Something nagged at the back of her mind, though, and she was only halfway across the room when she stopped and turned back to her leader.

"You said the blood on your suit wasn't yours. Whose is it?"

"The monster's." The older woman's eyes seemed very strange in the flare's dancing red light, and her mouth twisted into a wide smile. "It's *all* the monster's now."

That was when pieces of the puzzle fell into place.

Something about the two corpses in the bedroom had bothered her, but it had taken the sight of blood on Robin's suit to make her realize what was wrong. The corpse on the floor had gummy, black blood in a pool around its head. It had stuck to Robin's gun when she'd poked it. Charles had assumed that being exposed to the air for a week had turned it that way, but the blood from the body in the bathroom had been dark brown and dry—the way blood was supposed to look. *Natural.* Unlike the first body.

The words on the bathroom wall flashed back to her: *They take our skin.*

Charles stared at Robin, her mouth open but incapable of making a noise. Robin's face was splitting in half. A crack had started over her nose and spread up to her hairline and down to her neck. The crazed smile slid farther and farther around her cheeks as the center of her face opened like a book.

Inside was something unnatural. Something inky black, writhing and squirming to break free. Something *alive.*

Charles tried to scream, but her throat was frozen. She stumbled backward, tripped over a broken desk, and landed on a stack of papers with a loud thud. Robin's body was continuing to split, the two halves curling around behind her to free the dozens of thick black tendrils inside. They stretched out, poking at the air, tasting and testing, moving closer to Charles.

They take our skin.

Robin *had* encountered the monster. She hadn't been lying about that. She'd just neglected to mention where it was hiding—beneath her skin.

Charles's hand tightened around the gun. She raised it, aimed at the writhing black mess, and opened fire. The thick platinum rounds blasted holes through the place where Robin's head had been. The tendrils jerked and thrashed, and little bits of them flew about the room as the bullets separated them from their body. One of the largest arms shot toward Charles and snatched at her ankle. She kicked at it, scrambled backward, and closed her eyes as she emptied her clip into the beast looming over her.

Silence rushed in to fill the room as Charles's gun ran empty. Gasping, trying not to hyperventilate, she opened her eyes to see Robin's crumpled remains lying on the ground.

It was half-human, half-monster. What remained of Robin's body was limp, strangely deflated, inexplicably fused to the stilled black creature that had hidden inside her. The black tendrils lay in a tangle, many of them torn in half by the gunfire. A pool of dark blood inched out from the body, dyeing the scattered papers black.

Ellan was probably the first to be taken, Charles thought, dragging herself away from her superior's body, unable to avert her eyes. *I bet she didn't stay at the control panel like she said. They'd have needed their scientist to help identify the new life-form. And it got her and took over her body, but her companions wouldn't have known that, so they let her back into the station, and by the time they realized something was wrong, it was too late.*

A loud thump echoed through the building, and Charles gasped. "Jay!"

Robin had divided the teams carefully, she realized. She'd

kept Charles for herself and put Jay with Ellan. Jay had trusted the girl. Charles cursed and kicked herself to her feet, slipped on the scattered papers, caught herself on a bench, and ran through the door to the kitchen.

Food, stacked tidily, none of it eaten, no empty packets in the bin, Charles noticed as she tore through the room. *Of course. She wasn't alive, so she didn't need to eat.*

She skidded to a halt at the entrance to the recreation room, fumbling to fit a fresh clip of bullets into her gun. The nearly spent flare continued to splutter on the floor where she'd thrown it, tossing a red glow across the overturned furniture. Jay lay in the middle of the room, spread-eagle, his legs twitching feebly.

"Jay?" Charles hissed, approaching him. She didn't see Ellan. "Jay, can you hear me?"

His eyes were blank, staring at the ceiling, and his mouth lolled open. Charles pressed a hand to his chest. He felt cold. She gave him a gentle shake then pulled her hand back with a gasp as she felt his skin roil under her fingers. A tiny black tendril stretched over Jay's bottom lip, tasting the air for a second before retreating.

"No!" Charles gasped. She clamped a hand over her mouth, smothering the wail building inside her.

The body in the sleeping quarters. The body that leaked inky black blood. It must have been changing. The final team member had seen it changing, and he shot it then hid in the bathroom and killed himself because the alternative was too terrible to stand.

Charles pressed her palms against her eyelids as bile rose into her mouth. What she needed to do was clear, but the very idea made her want to be sick. She'd become fond of Jay, despite his merciless flirting and teasing.

It can't be real. He can't be infested. He can't be changing. He's Jay, for goodness sake; he's the ass who's impervious to harm.

Still, she could see the black things crawling around his mouth, poking at his gums, and rubbing over his large teeth. *Teeth like a horse's and a mouth like a gate to hell.*

How long had it taken Robin to change? It must have been fast; they'd found her within a couple of minutes of hearing the gunshots. And judging by the way Jay's fingers twitched, he wasn't going to stay still for long. There was no room for delay.

"I'm so sorry, Jay. You deserved better than this." Jay's head jerked at her voice, and his eyes rolled around in their sockets to fix on her. Something strange and cruel lurked there, and Charles knew she was no longer talking to her Jay. She raised the gun, aimed it at her partner's head, squeezed her eyes closed, and pulled the trigger.

The crack echoed through the rec room. Charles held still for a moment, tasting the gun's bitter propellant on her tongue, before opening her eyes. Jay was still. Her bullet had entered at his temple, and the hole was so small that she could almost pretend it wasn't there, except blood, inky black, oozed out from under his head.

Charles pulled herself up. Her legs felt unstable, but she couldn't stand being in the room with her dead partner for a moment more. She turned toward the hallway and started running, leaping over the toppled furniture and trying to make out a clear path in the dim light. She didn't know where Ellan was, and she didn't want to find out. She was the only member of her team left—and the only one who knew what had happened on Station 332.

Get to the ship. Get off the planet. Warn Central.

CHAPTER 10

CHARLES RAN AS QUIETLY as she could manage, not bothering to try any of the hallway lights. Her heartbeat throbbed in her head as she struggled to control her panic. The station felt different, in a strange, cold way, now that she was the last human within its metal walls. The air had become thicker and staler.

The air lock was empty at least. Charles shoved open the door, slid into the room, and scrambled to pull on her suit. She couldn't remember which cables Jay had used to close the doors and depressurize the chamber, but that didn't matter: all she needed to do was suit up, break the external door open, get through the sea of diamonds outside to the ship, and get off the damned planet.

She'd just wriggled her first foot into its boot when she heard the smooth *whoosh* of closing doors behind her. Charles jumped backward and swiveled in the same motion, knocking over one of the shelves.

Ellan stood against the opposite wall, having just reconnected the plug to lock the interior doors. She smiled at Charles. It wasn't a nice expression. "Hello, pretty."

Charles didn't hesitate to raise the gun and open fire. Five rounds hit Ellan squarely in the chest and face, but she didn't even flinch. Instead, her grin widened as the front of her suit split open. Black tendrils poured out, moving at an incredible speed. They picked up one of the tall metal shelves and hurled it at Charles. She ducked, but the shelf's corner grazed her shoulder, sending her tumbling to the ground with a gasp of pain.

Another black tendril darted toward her. Charles was too slow; a tendril snatched the gun out of her hand and flung it against the opposite wall with enough force to shatter it and leave a chip in the concrete.

"You shot my sisters," Ellan hissed.

Charles felt her breath freeze in her chest as she watched the bullet holes in the other woman knit together. Skin fused to skin, leaving Ellan's face smooth and blemish-free. "They were the firstborn of my colony, and you *shot them*."

Charles struggled to keep her face impassive as she crawled backward, placing as much distance as she could between herself and the inhuman woman. She'd been in a lot of stressful situations, including a couple of close calls during her short military service. Once, her teammate had fumbled and dropped a ticking grenade at her feet, and during another incident, her crew had forgotten about her and nearly left her on a remote planet with no oxygen. But for the first time, she was truly terrified. Not of what the monster was, but of what it could do to her.

It wants to steal my skin. Turn my body into its home, absorb my memories, mimic my mannerisms, use my face as a mask. Would it hurt? Would I feel it as its black tendrils wriggle through my flesh, melt into my organs, infiltrate my brain? How long would I be aware?

I'd rather die than find out.

Charles twisted to look over her shoulder, hoping to see something to defend herself with, but there were no guns within reach, just empty boxes and emergency oxygen units that had been scattered across the ground when the shelf hit her.

"I dealt with the others quickly," Ellan continued, gliding toward Charles. The black tendrils sprouted out of every gap in her suit, writhing around the woman's legs and carrying her across the room. "But now it's just you and me, my pretty. And we're going to have a little fun before I welcome you as my sister."

Charles lunged for the external door, grabbing an empty box in her left hand and an oxygen unit in the right. The emergency oxygen units were palm-sized and designed to fit inside a mouth. They were meant for evacuations, where the user needed only a couple minutes of oxygen to get to a safe location. Charles pushed the unit into her mouth and bit down on the plastic wings to break the seal, and clean air filled her throat as she reached for the door.

Ellan was fast. The beast's tendrils shot toward her, and Charles threw the empty box at them, praying that the surprise would buy her the precious seconds she needed to get outside.

If anything, it only enraged Ellan further. She growled—a deep, inhuman rumble—as she knocked the box aside and sent a cluster of tendrils at Charles.

Charles ducked as the black mass smashed into the door in front of her. The whine of twisting metal blended with Ellan's roar as the thick metal door burst out of its bracket and ejected onto the sand-like surface of the moon.

Okay, I'll take it. Charles bent double and barreled through the opening. The tendrils grazed her back as she slipped under them, then she was free, dashing through the drifts of diamonds. The ship waited for her just two dozen paces away, its black highlights contrasting beautifully against the sparkling ground.

A cold, black tendril wrapped around her ankle. Charles tried to hop out of it, but it tightened and tugged, sending her collapsing into the hard ground. The creature wrenched her backward and whipped her through the air. Her back hit the station's door with a thud that winded her so thoroughly that she thought she might never breathe again.

Ellan's face appeared in front of her. The woman's sweet, innocent visage had been twisted with malice and fury. The whites of her eyes had turned black, and her skin seemed to be cracking, showing tiny hints of the darkness that lived inside.

"Not so fast, my pretty." Her voice was barely human anymore. It was mixed with a grating, guttural growl that made her almost unintelligible.

Charles blinked her watering eyes, struggling to draw breath through the emergency oxygen unit in her mouth. She thought she must have cracked it when she'd been grabbed; the air wasn't flowing as freely as it should have. She could see something brightly colored out of the corner of her eye and twisted to look at it.

Dozens of cables snaked through the external door's access box, which Jay had never had the chance to close.

Feel free to heckle me into electrocuting myself...

It was a wild hope. She had no idea if Jay had been exaggerating about the electrocution, but it was her only chance. Charles stretched her arm out and grabbed a fistful of the cables, tugged them free of their sockets, and shoved their ends into Ellan's face.

Thank goodness for nonconductive suits, Charles found herself thinking, her mind numbed with shock as Ellan bucked, writhed, and began splitting apart.

The human skin broke into odd sections, fraying at the edges, peeling away as the monster inside tried to free itself. The wail was deafening, and the smell that crept around the edges of the breathing unit made Charles gag. The black tendrils pinning her bubbled, their moist surface blistering and popping, and then the creature dropped Charles.

She hit the ground hard and skittered backward, breathing as deeply as her aching ribs and damaged oxygen unit would let her. Ellan lay still on the sparkling diamonds, deformed so much that almost nothing human remained. Little puffs of dark steam rose from where the black flesh had burst.

She looked ridiculous. Ridiculous and repulsive and terrifying. An involuntary moan rose in Charles's throat, but she smothered it. If she was reading the light hiss correctly, her oxygen unit was leaking air, and she didn't have any breath to spare. There would be time enough to have a hysterical fit once she was inside a controlled environment.

Charles jogged toward the waiting spaceship, her boots sticking in the thick ground. Her oxygen unit ran out of air halfway there, so Charles held her breath. She was dizzy by the time she reached the door and pressed the button to open the air lock.

As she stood inside the tiny room, punching buttons to pressurize and filter the toxic air out, it was impossible not to remember how she'd stood there with her team members barely an hour before. Central had been desperately short on choices when it had cobbled them together, but Charles thought it had done a remarkable job, regardless. She wished she could have served with her partners for longer. She wished they'd met a kinder end.

A quiet beep announced that the air lock had pressurized. Charles spat out the empty oxygen unit and began gulping down the clean air before pressing another button to open the door leading to the main part of the ship.

The shuttle looked different now that it was empty, as though it were a room she remembered from a previous life, where she no longer belonged.

Robin had been their pilot, but Charles had also gone through the mandatory training for shuttle piloting. *I might not be as graceful in the takeoff,* she thought as she buckled herself into the pilot's seat and powered the ship on, *but I can do well enough to get off the hellish planet and back to Central.*

The ship rose off the moon in a flurry of the tiny, sparkling diamonds. Charles leaned toward the ship's window to watch the station disappear from view. She could still see Ellan's fried body just outside the station's door. Little wisps of black smoke rose from it like phantom tendrils stretching toward the sky.

Charles still had no idea what sort of creature had taken over her friends. It was clearly aggressive, intelligent, and extremely adept at mimicking its host. She hated to think about it, but it seemed increasingly likely that the problem wasn't isolated to Station 332. All of Central's more experienced teams had been dispatched on their own emergency response missions by the time she'd been drafted to visit Station 332. What were the odds they'd encountered their own aliens?

"I hope they fared better than we did," Charles muttered as she turned the ship toward the wormholes that would take her back to Central.

"Yes," Robin murmured in her ear, and Charles grabbed for the gun strapped to her suit even as she realized bullets would do nothing but slow the monsters down. "Let's hope."

PART 3

STATION 333

CHAPTER 11

"YOUR SHIFT FINISHED AN hour ago."

Kala jumped as the cool voice spoke in her ear. She turned to see Vivian standing just behind her. The tall woman's heavy-lidded eyes were fixed on the window in front of them.

"Uh, yeah, I figured I'd hang around for a while—"

"It's because his ship is late, isn't it?" Vivian's lip curled up as she spoke. Her long black hair was plaited so tightly that Kala couldn't see a single strand out of place, and her silver-and-steel-blue suit was immaculately ironed. Kala had heard that Vivian started her career in the military sector of Mendes Twelve, the communications hub near the center of the prestigious Mendes cluster of stations, where the standards were higher and the dress code was stricter. Vivian was so cool and precise in everything she said and did that it was sometimes hard to remember there was a live, feeling person inside.

"That's not your business." Kala crossed her arms and turned back the window overlooking the large metal hangar. "But yes, his ship should have been back this morning."

"He outranks you," Vivian observed.

Kala felt a flush of anger build inside of her. "What's that supposed to mean?"

Vivian finally moved her eyes, flicking them away from the window to glance at Kala's face. She let the silence stretch until Kala was squirming. "I was only saying he doesn't need a subordinate fretting about him. You're not being paid to wait at the door like a lovesick puppy."

The hot anger bloomed in her chest, rising across her cheeks and sticking in her throat. Vivian's implications were clear: she believed Kala had feelings for Stanos. She couldn't have been more wrong.

In the eight months she'd been staying at Station 333, Kala had spent a lot of time working with Stanos. Yes, he was handsome, and yes, he'd been kind and patient, even when she'd made mistakes. But Stanos was nothing but a good boss and an even better friend.

Kala opened her mouth to argue, but her tall, bone-thin companion had already turned and was halfway to the doors leading to the living quarters. Her long black braid swayed gently in her wake as she marched with a well-trained precision. Vivian paused in the doorway, one gloved hand hovering over the sensor to keep the door open, and glanced over her shoulder. "He also outranks you in combat training. He'll be fine."

"Thanks?" Kala said, but Vivian was already gone. The door slid back into place with a quiet *whoosh*.

Kala shook her head. She'd been living with Vivian for three months, ever since Vivian's previous roommate had requested a transfer to a different station. Kala would have thought that was enough time to get to know someone, but she seemed no closer to figuring out what went through the frosty woman's head than she had been on the first day.

Kala turned back to the window and leaned her forehead against it. The glass was pleasantly cold, and the business of the docking bays below made a good distraction. Stanos had been gone for just over a week, traveling to a part of the system where gamma rays made communication channels less than reliable and emergency assistance took days to arrive. She missed him, but more than that, she worried for him.

He and two teammates had been deployed in response to an emergency signal from a remote moon base. Without any information to go on—just a cry for help, broadcast into the vast emptiness of space—they had no way of knowing how serious the situation was. It could be as minor as one of the crew being injured and needing transport back to Central, or Stanos could have been walking into a death trap. They hadn't heard from him since his ship left easy communication range, and Kala knew that every hour he was late increased the likelihood that something had gone seriously wrong.

Worse, there had been a spate of similar distress signals—all coming from remote moons—during the week he'd been away.

Two distress signals a week was normal. Forty-five in ten days was alarming, and the gossip was that something was very wrong on the remote monitoring stations and that Central had deployed investigative crews equipped with full quarantine facilities, stunner guns, and the most advanced diagnostic tools available.

Vivian's right, though. Stanos and his team are well trained. That's why they were sent; they can cope with danger. They thrive on danger.

On the other hand, I thrive on security and knowing that my friends aren't dead, and there's an alarming shortage of that today.

She'd meant to stay no more than an hour after her shift, but even though time was crawling by and she was in danger of missing dinner if she lingered much longer, she couldn't summon the will to move. *Just a few more minutes. Just in case.*

A deep humming noise startled her back to attention, and she blinked furiously to wake herself up. The carrier doors were opening, then a familiar silver shuttle glided through the hatch and landed on the tarmac. The artificial gravity in the hangar was weaker than it was in the rest of the station, but the force was still enough to make the ship shudder as it hit ground. Kala waited until she could read the name emblazoned on the ship's side—*Delta Shock*—before she let a shaking, relieved smile spread over her face.

An enclosed walkway extended from the edge of the hangar until it touched the side of the ship. Kala was too far away to hear, but she'd been in enough spacecrafts to imagine the heavy hissing noise that meant the walkway was air-locked and it was safe to open the door.

Tinted windows lined the walkway, and Kala saw three figures walking behind them: two shorter, slimmer ones and one who was so tall his head nearly brushed the roof. Stanos and his two female crew members had all returned alive and with the correct number of limbs attached.

Only then did Kala realize how stupid she must look, hanging around the docking bay after her shift was finished. Vivian was right; Kala hadn't intended it that way, but she would look like a desperate puppy waiting for its master to return.

"Jeez, what were you thinking, Kal?" she muttered and quickly turned toward the living area's doors, hoping to slip out before Stanos saw her. She was a second too late.

"Holcroft!" a familiar voice called, and she turned back to the hangar doors that had just opened to admit the three returned travelers.

Stanos's long, sharp face was still damp with sweat from wearing his helmet, but he looked genuinely pleased to see her.

Kala returned his infectious smile. "Good to see you back, sir."

"You waited up for us? That's perfect, actually. I've got a small job I'm hoping you can help me with. You won't mind putting in a bit of overtime, will you, Holcroft?"

"No, of course not!"

His two crewmates, both middle-aged women Kala didn't recognize, swept past her and left through the door to the living quarters without saying a word. It was a bit cold, Kala thought, to leave their captain without saying goodbye. Maybe they'd had an argument on the trip back.

"Great." Stanos beckoned for Kala to follow him in the opposite direction, toward the labs. "It shouldn't take us too long if we work at it together."

CHAPTER 12

KALA HAD TO JOG to keep up with Stanos's long strides. She liked being asked to help; the station's recreational activities weren't especially stimulating, so she often found it more enjoyable to work late in the labs. She and Stanos had pulled a lot of long shifts together. They sometimes worked well into the early hours of the morning, both of them so absorbed in their jobs that they didn't realize how late it had become.

Kala was part of the science crew on Station 333. Her job was to examine, categorize, and document samples of life submitted from other, more remote stations. Their database held hundreds of thousands of samples, divided into twenty-nine rough categories, and it continued to billow out as humankind's long arm stretched farther and farther into the void of space.

At the bottom of the scale were life-forms that were little more than bloated bacteria. The list also included vegetative forms that couldn't think or move but still responded to stimuli. Then, less often, they found active life-forms—the equivalent of Earth's animals—that ranged from brainless to highly intelligent. While they hadn't yet found a creature with an intellect developed to a human's level, leading scientists predicted that they were out there, living beyond humanity's reach.

Whenever a new planet was colonized, an inevitable slurry of samples was sent to Station 333 and similar science crews on other central stations. Less frequently, established colonies sent in new samples when life-forms came in on asteroids or space rubble.

Kala followed Stanos into the empty lab. It was a large room filled with desks and cluttered by microscopes, test chambers, and DNA extractors. A double door to the right led into the containment area they used for larger samples—*anything bigger than your head goes in there*, Stanos had told her during her first day working there. Protective suits were kept at the back of the rooms, near the sinks and a door leading to the showers.

As they began pulling on their canary-yellow protective suits, Kala glanced at her boss. "What was the alarm about?"

"Hmm?" Stanos asked, apparently deep in thought.

Kala zipped up her suit and pulled a set of gloves out of the box hung beside the sinks. "The assistance request you just came back from. What was it for?"

"Oh, some minor drama with a life-form the station workers thought was dangerous. It was all resolved days before we got there, but they asked us to hang around for half a day to help repair their solar panels instead."

"Good," Kala said, then caught herself and laughed. "Well, not good for you if it was a wasted trip. But I'm glad there wasn't anything dangerous waiting for you."

"Me too," Stanos said, beaming at her as he tied off his gloves. "Ready?"

"Ready."

Kala followed her boss to the table they often shared. Stanos turned around to lean against its edge, ankles crossed, in the pose he always adopted when he needed to explain something to her. "Even though the initial threat wasn't a problem, I did find something I thought could be noteworthy while I was repairing the solar panels. I'd like you to take a look and tell me what you can about it. Okay?"

"Sure thing." It was odd that Stanos wasn't doing the study himself; he was both more qualified and more experienced than she was. *Maybe he already knows what it is and this is a test,* Kala thought, subconsciously straightening her back a little.

Stanos reached inside his suit and pulled out a small vial with a rubber stopper. Kala took it and squinted at the substance inside.

It was pitch-black, like ink, but clumped in a little ball. It seemed stuck to the side of the glass, but when she shook the vial, it came loose and bounced about.

"Is this the full creature or just a section of it?"

"Both," Stanos said. He was wearing a crooked grin, apparently enjoying her confusion. She had to raise her eyebrows at him before he explained. "If you cut a section off the parent life-form, it becomes an organism in its own right."

So he'd already examined it after all and wanted to see what she could find out about it. *Fair enough.* She decided to play along. She pressed the power button on the recording system installed at the back of the desk and began her usual spiel for cataloging new species.

"This is Kala Holcroft, examining a potential new life-form sourced from"—she glanced at Stanos, who mouthed the answer to her—"Station 691 on the eighteenth of March. Subject was submitted by Commander Julian Stanos, who will be assisting me with my examination."

Stanos gave her a slight nod to continue.

"Subject is round and approximately three centimeters wide." Kala turned the bottle to get a better look. "It appears black and smooth and currently lacks any other identifying features."

She pulled her face mask down to cover her mouth and nose then uncorked the bottle. Stanos made no move to cover his own face, so she assumed the creature didn't contain any spores and wasn't infectious. She tipped the black ball into one of the glass bowls they used to examine small samples then pulled her desk light forward to shine directly on it. "Subject has shown no sign of response to its environment. It appears either dormant or nonsentient. I'll begin exposing it to stimuli."

She picked her first choice out of the toolbar on her desk: a small metal rod, the heat pen, whose tip would gradually heat from room temperature to a little under a hundred degrees. Many life-forms, especially ones originating on planets close to their stars, went into hibernation at low temperatures, and the heat pen could activate them by simulating a warmer environment.

She pressed the tip of the pen against the ball and gasped. "Uh, okay, that was fast. Subject responded to the heat pen before a temperature was even set. Subject appears to have an appendage, which it's used to grab the pen."

To Kala, it looked a lot like an exceptionally ugly leech. The base of the ball had fixed itself to the glass bowl, and the bulk of its body had extended up in a long black tendril to grab her pen. When she pulled the metal rod out of reach, the tendril continued to swivel, probing at the air.

"Subject is definitely alive and active." Kala put the pen back in its holder and took up a pair of tweezers. She poked at the waving tendril, and it responded instantly, moving toward her and trying to wrap around the metal tool. "Subject shows interest in its surroundings and responds to my voice. It appears to have at least a rudimentary intelligence."

The next hour passed quickly as Kala introduced new factors to the creature one at a time, noting its reactions. Stanos continued to lean on the desk, not speaking or moving, merely watching her closely through dark eyes.

Most of the experiments resulted in the same sort of reaction: the creature grabbed at anything within its reach, except for when she raised the temperature of her heat pen, and it shied away from the burning metal. Then she offered the creature her pencil. It sucked the writing utensil toward its core, held it for a moment, turned it over twice, then spat it out. The creature seemed to be seeking something, and Kala could guess what it wanted.

"I'll offer it food," she said into the recorder as she swiveled her chair away from the desk to collect a sample from the chilled storage container. "It's the one thing that motivates every single life-form. What do you think we should try first, Stanos? Pipka?"

Stanos shrugged, though his smile widened slightly. "Your choice."

Kala grabbed one of the small green-gray creatures out of the cold storage and brought it back to her desk. Just about everything in the known system ate pipka. Not only were the small, rapidly reproducing plants useful for feeding to samples, but they responded quickly to medication, making them ideal for trial runs of new drugs. Every lab kept a small stock on hand.

The slug-sized plant made a moist, sticky noise as she dropped it next to the sample. The black tendril moved immediately, probing its new companion, then speared into the pipka's core. Kala talked quickly while she watched.

"Subject has pushed its protrusion inside the pipka, possibly to consume its insides or to inject a poison. Pipka is moving at a normal rate. The sample is…uh…dividing—"

The end of the sample's arm detached from its body and slid inside the pipka. The rest of the sample drew back into itself, returning to its plain spherical shape, apparently no longer interested in its prey. As she watched, the pipka began writhing, twisting around, and slapping its slimy ends against the glass bowl.

Kala watched in fascination as the pipka gradually slowed its movements, shivered, and fell still. She hadn't realized Stanos had moved to stand behind her until she heard his quiet voice in her ear, "What do you make of that?"

"I-I'm not sure. This could be one way the sample reproduces, by gestating itself inside a host. Or it could be eating the pipka from the inside out." She turned to look up at her supervisor. "What do you know about it?"

Stanos grinned at her. "Not much. That's why I brought it to you."

"But…"

That didn't make sense; Stanos had more experience and training. *Why does he need me to examine the strange black creature?*

Kala turned back to the pipka, raised her tweezers, and poked it. The moist slug-like plant moved, writhing as it normally did. The hole the black substance had entered through was no longer visible. If she hadn't watched it happen, she would have guessed the pipka hadn't been harmed at all.

No longer bothering to speak into the recorder—and Stanos didn't try to correct her—Kala picked up her scalpel and pressed its tip into the pipka's greenish flesh. It resisted for a moment, indenting, then the blade punctured the skin. A thick black liquid spewed out.

"Jeez!" Kala dropped the scalpel and pulled away from the table. "What—"

The pipka had changed. From the hole in its skin, a half dozen black tendrils stretched outward, probing at the air, swiveling about, searching for their attacker. One by one, they drew back inside the shell, and the cut Kala had made knitted itself together, resealing the skin so that it looked completely unblemished.

In the eight months she'd been at Station 333, Kala had assessed and categorized hundreds of new discoveries, and she'd never seen anything act like that before. She looked up at Stanos, expecting him to be just as shocked as she was, but his face was neutral as he continued to watch her.

"Do—did you—" she stuttered, trying to understand what had just happened. "You saw that, too, right?"

"Yes. What do you think happened?"

"It's—" She waved her arm at the pipka, which was lying still, looking no different from a fresh sample. "It took over the pipka. It somehow…replicated its body."

CHAPTER 13

KALA JOGGED TO THE crates at the back of the room, where samples from the previous day were kept. A rookie station guard had sent one in, convinced he'd discovered a new species, when in fact it was just a regular amettal that was missing its primary beak. The small, scaled, birdlike animal was common in the Meidoscycle system. Though not very intelligent, it was enough of a pest that they had to be regularly cleared from around stations. This particular specimen was destined for the euthanasia tank the next morning, but it would suit Kala's needs perfectly.

She grabbed the squawking, kicking creature, which was only a little larger than her fist, and returned to Stanos and the desk. The amettal tried to bite her hand, but its inner beak was small and too soft to do any damage.

The bowl holding the sample—*or, rather, samples,* Kala thought grimly—was too small for the amettal, so she grabbed a new bowl and dropped the hopping critter into it. She then used a pair of pliers to pick the pipka off where it had stuck to the glass, and placed it in the new container.

The amettal, seeing food, hopped toward the plant and began picking at its skin. Then it made a guttural noise of surprise. A hair-thin crack appeared in the slug's skin, and it quickly widened to let the tendrils poke out. They stretched forward, feeling toward the new addition to their environment, while the amettal hopped and squawked indignantly.

What happened next was almost too fast for Kala to see. One of the tendrils shot forward, but the amettal was too quick for it and managed to snip the tip off the stalk and swallowed it. For a second, the animal showed no signs of being affected, but then it suddenly twitched, jumped twice, began swaying, and fell onto its side.

"Jeez," Kala muttered, watching as the birdlike creature stilled. She pressed the button on the desk's stopwatch and waited.

Nearly three minutes had passed, and Kala was half-convinced the bird was dead, when the amettal finally leaped upright and began strutting around the bowl. It looked and behaved exactly as it had before—the only difference was that it paid no attention to the pipka, which had also fallen still. Kala watched with a mixture of fascination and revulsion; she wasn't prepared to cut open the bird, but she knew what she would find inside: an inky black mess filled with twitching, writhing tendrils.

Kala slammed a lid on the glass bowl to prevent the amettal from jumping out. She stared up at Stanos; he blinked back at her, unhelpfully silent as she grabbed her microscope.

"I'm kind of freaking out here," she said, aware that an edge of panic was creeping into her voice. "Now would be a great time to share whatever knowledge you have."

"Calm down, Holcroft. Just focus on your job and tell me what you can."

Kala drew a ragged breath and brought her tweezers and scalpel down on the original sample. The black ball began flailing its tendrils again as soon as she touched it, and Kala tried to slice off one of the tips. To her shock, the severed tendril immediately stretched back toward the main body and reconnected, making the ball whole again. "Self-healing…" she muttered and tried again.

It took her four attempts before she managed to separate a portion and get it out of the bowl without it reattaching. She dropped the tiny blob onto one of the slides and put it under the microscope.

"It's incredible." She watched the creature's mass shift and reform itself into different shapes. "It's almost infinitely adaptable. From what I can tell, it can take over living creatures, absorb their mass, and convert the body into a host. It can heal itself almost instantly and repair its host animal flawlessly. Even more alarming"—she paused to poke at the black blob, making it squirm and swirl—"it can mimic the host's behavior. You saw the amettal back there, right? It's been consumed by this…this… *thing*, but it's still behaving normally."

"Yes, I saw."

"You know what that means, right? It's absorbing and adapting to its host's characteristics and intelligence as well as its body."

She looked up from the microscope and rubbed the back of her glove over her sweating forehead. "This is big, Stanos. It could wheedle its way into any sort of animal colony without raising suspicion. Possibly even…even…"

"Even humans," he finished for her. "I've considered that already. Can you tell me what you think its weaknesses would be?"

"Weaknesses?" Kala laughed. She'd intended it to be a light noise, but it came out panicky. "We've already seen it deal with scalpels pretty well, so I'm going to guess knives and bullets might not do a lot. First thing I'd try is fire, based on how it shied away from the heat pen. Neurotoxins might also stand a chance against it, but with those aggressive healing properties, you'd have to hit it fast and hard."

"You'd consider it a fairly resilient creature, then?" Stanos pressed, his dark eyes watching her face eagerly.

"Yeah, that's the problem! It can reproduce nearly instantly, clone its host, heal injuries, disguise itself perfectly—we need to tell someone about this," she said, the realization hitting her. "This—it could already be spreading, taking over the native animals on moons and planets, and we'd have no way of knowing."

"Want to know what its biggest flaw is?" Stanos asked. He had his arms folded over his chest, and a spark of something fierce and exultant shone in his eyes.

Kala nodded.

"It can't learn on its own. It can absorb knowledge and memories perfectly and replicate its host, as you said, but it has no way of *using* that knowledge to increase its own intelligence. It can't *learn*; it can only *assimilate*."

"How could you possibly know that?" Kala asked. Then she saw the crack running down the length of Stanos's face. It was so fine that at first glance, it looked like an out-of-place hair, except that it was too precise. It ran between his eyes, down his nose, over his chin, and down his neck, dividing his face into two perfect halves. As he smiled at her, the line crossing his mouth widened a fraction, and Kala thought she saw something dark moving inside.

"We're reliant on having new knowledge passed on to us through our hosts. You've been very helpful tonight, Holcroft. Thank you."

CHAPTER 14

THE PLETHORA OF LITTLE clues Kala had overlooked came crashing in on her all at once. *He didn't help me at all. He knew about the creature but wanted me to examine it and give him my findings. He needed me to explain its weaknesses—*

The hairline crack in Stanos's face widened, peeling back his beautiful eyes and sweetly smiling mouth, exposing the twitching, reaching tendrils inside. Kala opened her mouth to scream, but no noise came out. She tried to step backward, but the desk blocked her escape. She felt a hot, sharp pain on one of her hands; she'd brushed the heat pen's holder and scalded herself.

Stanos would always chide me when I forgot to turn it off, she thought sluggishly as the thing that had once been her best friend split its suit in half. The skin was coiling around, releasing more and more of the black, glistening core, and tendrils as wide as her arm extending forward to snatch at her. *He'd chide, but in a kind way. He never got angry with me. Not once. Jeez, I'm going to miss him.*

She grabbed the heat pen's plastic base, which was hot enough to be uncomfortable but not quite hot enough to burn her. To her horror, the tendrils wrapped around her legs. They tightened until the pressure was painful, then began dragging her toward the remains of Stanos's body. She imagined being enveloped in the inky black mass, swallowed by it, and converted into it. Nausea rose inside her.

She was close enough to see the detail, to watch as the black flesh undulated and see Stanos's sagging skin hanging limply from the creature. Anger grew to drown out the horror, and Kala thrust her arm forward, sinking the heat pen into the place where Stanos's face had once been.

She'd guessed fire might be one of the creature's weaknesses. She hoped the scorching-hot heat pen was hot enough to wound the monster.

She was right. The slimy, black skin began convulsing and shriveling where the pen had touched it, and a terrible scream-ing, wailing noise rose from the beast. Stanos's arms, which had shifted to hang behind his back like malformed wings as the body opened up, began twitching. The tendrils around Kala's legs tightened and sent a shock of pain up her thighs. She pulled the heat pen back, stabbed it into one of the tendrils that clung to her leg, and felt the heat radiating through the slimy, twitching flesh. It tightened more, and Kala bit down against the pain. Then suddenly, the pressure was gone, and she was free.

Most of the heat had been sapped out of the pen—it was meant to be used on small specimens for short amounts of time—but she gave a final stab at the thrashing, wailing beast as she ran past it. That seemed to be the last straw for the creature. It expanded, black limbs shooting out in all directions, and the remaining parts of Stanos's body were shredded under the motion. The tendrils hit the cold storage, blowing the door off and scattering little plastic packets everywhere. Another arm hit the wall holding the protective suits, cutting through the thick yellow fabric and leaving a large dent in the wall.

So much for hoping my suit would protect me, Kala thought, ducking as she ran for the door.

Another of the tendrils launched at her. She *felt* it coming more than saw it and dove to one side. It grazed her shoulder, knocking her off balance and cutting a large hole in the suit before sailing past her and hitting the door with enough force to smash it off its hinges.

Without even pausing for breath, she kept running, ducking underneath the tendril, and racing through the open doorway. The thick suit made it hard to run, but she moved her legs as quickly as she could, leaning forward to use the momentum. She didn't stop to collect herself until her left foot got caught on her right pant leg and sent her crashing to the ground.

The creature was still in the lab; she could hear it thrashing, breaking their priceless equipment, and smashing through the glass windows that looked into the room for larger specimens.

I hope you cut yourself, she thought furiously, pressing her palms against her eyes. It was a stupid thing to hope for; even if the creature did cut itself, it would be repaired in a matter of seconds. She suspected that even the burns wouldn't bother it for long. Strangled laughter rose in her throat as she began to realize just how dire the situation was.

Get it together. You've got to tell someone. Got to warn them.

She stumbled to her feet, tugging off her gloves and throwing the face mask behind herself. She wasn't far from where she'd been standing earlier that evening, waiting so anxiously for Stanos to return. The door to the living quarters was only a few dozen paces ahead of her. She began to run for the door, knowing that it was only a matter of time before the creature behind her figured out how to get out of the labs. She couldn't risk it entering the main parts of the station.

Her thoughts were so focused on what was behind her that she didn't notice what was happening ahead until she swiped the door open. Screams filled her ears, followed by a staccato burst of gunfire. Kala stood in the doorway, shocked dumb, as she watched two guards race past her and disappear down one of the curved hallways leading to the bedrooms. One of the guards had a splash of something wet and red across his helmet.

Stanos came back with two copilots. A sick sensation boiled in Kala's stomach.

Gunfire from a passageway to her right drew Kala's attention. She wanted to scream "Bullets won't hurt them! You've got to use fire!" but she knew no one would hear her over the racket. A siren started far off in the building. More screaming—loud wails that rose then cut off in strange gurgles—came from immediately ahead of her.

Think! She pressed her palms against her temples. *What do you need to do?*

She could leave. The station had three hangars, and the entrance to one was just behind her. She wasn't a qualified pilot, but she'd watched her coworkers fly the ships often enough that she thought she could get one of the smaller ones off the ground and out the hatch.

Another scream and more gunfire rang out. The siren bored into her head, its somber *whoop whoop whoop whoop* uselessly warning the building's occupants that there was a problem, as though they didn't already know.

She could stay and try to fight the creatures, but she didn't have any combat training. *I'm a scientist. I'm not supposed to have to deal with these sorts of problems! My best weapon is my brain, and it's not like that's going to do much good against—*

Kala opened her eyes as a plan hit her. She might not be able to fight, but she had something that the people in the station desperately needed: knowledge of how to stop the creatures. *Fire.*

Half a dozen communication boxes were scattered around the station—they could broadcast her voice into every room. The closest one was in the recreation area to her right. She set out for it at a run.

A scientist burst out of one of the hallway's doors, screaming. Something dark red was sprayed across her chest and face, and her eyes were huge with panic. She dashed past Kala, senseless to her surroundings. Kala called after her, "Use fire!" But the woman showed no sign of having heard.

Kala swore and picked up her pace. She shoved open the recreation room's door and stopped short. The room had been painted with blood. Red sprays dribbled down the walls. Pools of it were spreading over the floor, changing the crystal-blue carpet into a dark, muddy purple, and even as Kala stood frozen, little drips fell down in front of her from the ceiling.

Bodies lay about the furniture, some whole, others torn in half. Others were mangled so badly that they looked like piles of dirty, wet rags with white bone shards poking out.

A hundred and fifty-nine people lived on the station. *How many of them died in this room?*

Kala turned toward the wall, only half-aware that she was hyperventilating. Her body was coated in slick, cold sweat, and she guessed that only the combination of shock and denial stopped her from mingling the contents of her stomach with the flesh littering the ground around her feet.

She reached for the communication unit, but something seemed different about it. She blinked through the haze of stress and fear. It had been smashed—broken, probably—by one of the thrashing tendrils or a body that had been thrown against it.

Well, that's it, her brain sang cheerfully. *You tried, but there's nothing to be done. Better get to one of the ships and hightail it out of here.*

Kala squinted her eyes nearly shut, fighting against her body's desire to collapse. The smell of blood and body fluids was thick, sticking in her throat and coating her tongue. *This isn't the only unit.*

She stumbled toward the door, averting her eyes from the carnage, half-afraid that it would burn onto her retinas, half-afraid that she would recognize one of the bodies. Her head felt foggy and light as she forced her legs to carry her to the door, out of the room, and down the hallway. As soon as her nose cleared of the visceral odor, she drew a deep, shaky breath and broke into a jog.

Where's the next closest system? The kitchen or the bedrooms or—

A tall figure burst out of one of the rooms in front of her. Kala had been so focused on watching her feet that she nearly ran into the tip of the gun.

"Get back! Get back!" a voice screamed at her. It was familiar, somehow.

Kala raised her eyes to stare at the woman looming over her. "Vivian?"

CHAPTER 15

KALA HAD NEVER SEEN the immaculate, precise scientist look so fierce…or so dirty. Vivian's long black braid was mussed, and patches of hair poked out at odd angles. Strands fell over her sweaty face, partially blocking one of her intensely wild eyes. Her neatly pressed suit was scuffed and stained with dark spots, and the hands gripping the gun had turned pale and veiny.

They stared at each other for a moment, the tip of Vivian's gun pointed at Kala's head, then Vivian let out a sigh and lowered her weapon. "Be more careful, Holcroft. Not everyone will give you the benefit of the doubt."

Kala rubbed a hand over her face. "There's, uh, alien body snatcher—"

"You noticed, did you?" Vivian barked. Her carefully cultivated aloofness was gone; in its place was cold fury. She kept turning her head, peering up and down the hallway. "There were only two of them to begin with, but they're taking over their victims' bodies. You can't trust anyone."

"Wait. Why are you trusting me?"

Vivian snorted. It sounded almost like suppressed laughter. "*They* don't stare at you stupidly when you point a gun at them."

"Ah." Kala glanced at the weapon and shook her head. "Bullets won't hurt them. They can repair damage at a phenomenal speed. You've got to burn them."

"What?"

"Burn them. You know, fire. I was trying to get to an announcement unit to—"

"But the one in the rec room's broken." Vivian grabbed Kala's arm and pulled her down the hallway. "Okay, we need to get to the weapons room. There are flamethrowers in there."

"What? Really? How did you know that?"

Vivian paused just long enough to give Kala an incredulous glare. "I'm ex-military. I never stay in a building if I don't know the exits, defenses, and emergency plans. Come on; we need to hurry."

"Okay, but the announcement box—"

Vivian's grip was too strong to fight as she dragged Kala around a corner and down the hallway leading to the military sector. "Stop being stupid. You won't be able to help anyone if you get killed halfway across the station."

It took Kala a second to latch on to the logic, but then she broke into a jog, following Vivian into the metal-lined passageways. Vivian stopped abruptly, and Kala nearly ran into her back.

A body in the middle of the hallway blocked their path. Kala recognized Denise, one of the senior researchers. Her bushy hair was thrown out in a halo around her head, and her open eyes stared sightlessly at the ceiling. Vivian swore under her breath and pointed her gun at the prone woman.

"What are you doing?" Kala hissed, snatching the tip of the gun and pushing it down to face the ground.

"She's changing," Vivian said simply. Her face had taken on a pale-gray tinge, but her eyes were hard. "I saw it in the rec room. The creatures can do one of two things to you: they can kill you, or they can take over your body. Trust me on this—the first option is the far greater mercy."

Denise's fingers were twitching. Kala thought of the amettal and the way it had twitched in the glass bowl before leaping to its feet like nothing had happened. She realized she did not, under any circumstance, want to see Denise get up again. Kala let go of Vivian's gun, feeling sick.

"It's the kindest thing I can do for her," Vivian said, her voice unusually soft. "Look away if it upsets you."

Kala turned to face the wall and squeezed her eyes shut as Vivian opened fire. The loud snapping sounds seemed to go on forever, and when the noise died off, Kala opened her eyes again. The hallway was filled with dust from the chipped concrete floor.

"Better safe than sorry." Vivian pulled Kala past Denise's now-still remains.

"They can't take over dead things," Kala said, trying to make sense of what had just happened.

"That's the logic I'm working off." Vivian led her around another corner at a fast jog. "They can infect you while you're alive, but a corpse is no good to them."

The door leading into the weapons room was hanging open. Kala and Vivian entered cautiously, but it was empty. Most of the guns had been taken, but the more unique weapons—grenades, knives, and the flamethrowers—were still on their racks.

"Good," Vivian said, a hiss of triumph in her voice as she dropped her gun and began gathering the half-dozen flamethrowers. "Carry these, Holcroft, and grab some grenades, as well."

"We're not going to leave some here?"

"No, we're going to take them and pass them out to anyone we see in the hallways." More gunfire came from deeper in the building, followed by the sound of something large being smashed. "Hurry, we don't have time."

Kala stuffed her pockets with grenades and fumbled to hold the five flamethrowers Vivian thrust into her arms. "Aren't you carrying any?"

"Just one." Vivian's eyes were severe as she pulled the straps of the backpack over her shoulders and hoisted the gun in her right hand. "Your job is to get to the comm box. My job is to keep you alive. Deal?"

"Deal," Kala said.

Then they were running again, down the same passageway, leaping over Denise's bloodied body, and heading back to the heart of the building.

Vivian hesitated, glancing up and down the hallways. "Nearest unit would be…"

"The kitchen," Kala suggested, but Vivian shook her head.

"I'd just come from there when I found you. The whole room's been decimated. I doubt the unit is intact."

"What about the meeting room?"

"Yes, that would work. Let's go."

They turned left, Vivian in the lead while Kala tried to keep pace without dropping her armful of flamethrowers. Down the hallway, frantic arguing came from one of the rooms. Vivian held up her hand to stop Kala then rapped on the door while yelling, "We're friends; don't shoot."

The voices inside fell silent. Then the door opened, and two guns were pointed at Vivian's face.

"How do we know you're not one of *them*?" a taller, thickset man barked.

Vivian glowered at him. "They don't exactly stop for pleasantries, do they?"

The tall man glanced at his younger companion, who nodded. "We're going to make a break for the ships. Want to join us?"

"Can't," Vivian said, "but we have something to help. Bullets won't stop them, but according to our scientist, fire will."

She inclined her head toward Kala, who unloaded two of the flamethrowers and a handful of grenades. "Spread the word."

Vivian didn't even give the men a chance to thank them before she returned to jogging down the hallway. The flamethrowers were heavy, and Kala struggled to keep up. Vivian quickly found another band of survivors, and they unloaded two of the remaining three flamethrowers.

A stitch was developing in Kala's side, but she managed to keep pace with her lanky companion as they approached the meeting room. Gunfire, loud and persistent, came from the inside. Vivian motioned for Kala to keep her head down, then she shoved through the doors.

At first, the scene in front of her didn't make any sense. She felt as though she'd stepped into a modern-art house, where everything was calculated to subtly disturb the viewer. Sculptures of familiar objects, changed to be not quite right, filled the space, and the music piped through the room was the steady *tat-tat-tat* of automatic fire.

She blinked, and reality filtered through to her.

The chairs, normally arranged in neat rows in the center of the room, had been tossed about like children's toys. They cluttered the floor like little land mines, and piles of them had collected at the edges of the room. To her right was the heavy wooden table their superiors had stood behind when making announcements to the station's crew. It was turned on its side, and three people huddled behind it; two had guns and were bobbing up and down, taking potshots at the thing on the other side of the room.

The inky creature, a dozen tendrils waving outward from its base, sent a shock of terror through Kala. It towered over her, and suspended from its top was the body of one of the middle-aged women who had returned with Stanos. The body hung limply, arms and legs swinging like a rag doll's as the creature moved.

Only her head seemed alive; it was held upright and was twitching from side to side, following the action of the room.

The creatures need our eyes to see, Kala realized. *That's why the monster inside Stanos wasn't able to follow me out of the lab—he'd destroyed Stanos's human body and couldn't see.*

The corpse's head rotated to look at them, the blank eyes wide and unblinking as the lips curled into a sneer.

CHAPTER 16

VIVIAN SWORE AS ONE of the tendrils shot toward them. It was fast, but Vivian's reflexes were faster. She'd already raised the nozzle of her flamethrower and pulled the trigger. Fire spurted from its tip, shooting fifteen feet forward before licking upward in a plume of black smoke. The tendril hit the flame, and a noxious odor and an ear-splitting shriek filled the room.

The limp body's mouth had opened wide to emit the wail. The partly human scream also held something very, very unnatural—deep, harsh, and gutturally horrible.

Kala felt her trance break. She dove toward the three people behind the table and pressed her remaining flamethrower into the closet one's hands. "Guns won't hurt it," she gasped, pulling grenades out of her pockets and passing them to the other two people. "Fire will."

Vivian was slowly advancing on the creature, swiveling her

flame to hit any tendrils that tried to reach her. The scream was increasing in volume and pitch as more and more of the arms were burned, and while the rest of the woman's body hung limp on its black master, the face was twisted into a snarl of pure fury. Kala couldn't understand why Vivian was trying to get closer to the beast until she saw the small white box attached to the wall behind it.

"Ah," she said, feeling dread and horror build in her as she stared at the communication unit. "Crap."

"What?" the woman beside her asked.

Kala thought her face was slightly familiar. Had they eaten breakfast together one morning? Wasn't her name Julie or Julia or something similar?

"I need to get to the comm box."

The woman glanced at where Kala indicated and nodded. She was pale, but she slung the flamethrower's backpack over her shoulders. "Right. Let's go."

She leaped out from the shelter of the table and moved to stand beside Vivian. Kala followed, feeling incredibly vulnerable with empty hands, and hung just behind the two women as they advanced on the creature.

Its arms moved with terrific speed, smashing chairs across the room and smacking indents into the walls. Kala ducked as the leg of a flying chair grazed her back. The two women in front of her kept moving forward, getting closer to the monster's body.

The creature began to retreat, and fear showed on the corpse's face as it drew away to one of the corners. Kala saw her chance and ran toward the communication unit. Vivian sidestepped to keep herself between Kala and the creature, while the other woman continued to march forward, anger marking deep lines on her sweaty face.

The stench was so foul that Kala felt like she was choking. She hit the wall next to the comm unit, pulled the microphone out of its holder, and pressed the button. An echo of the creature's wail filled the room as the noise was broadcast back to them.

"They're vulnerable to fire," Kala said, talking quickly, aware that she had seconds, at most, before the monster tried to stop her. "Bullets won't hurt them, but fire will. You can kill them with fire."

The creature roared, the unnaturally loud sound spewing out from its twisted human lips, and lunged toward Kala. Vivian raised her flamethrower, but the other woman leaped in first, directing her flame at the advancing body. Kala saw the black flesh bubble and blister under the heat, but the monster was too enraged be deterred again. A tendril shot forward, breaking through the woman's fire and spearing her through the chest.

Vivian took her finger off her trigger then turned and pushed Kala. They both hit the floor just in time to avoid two arms aimed at their heads. Kala rolled onto her back and began to scramble away from the monster. Julie or Julia, or whoever she had been, had managed to burn the corpse's face. The skin had melted and puckered, and both eyes had turned gray-white as they'd cooked inside her head. They swiveled uselessly in their sockets, but even as she tried to draw enough breath into her lungs to power her limbs, Kala saw the burnt flesh begin to repair itself.

"It's blind," she hissed to Vivian. "But it won't be for long. We need to get out of here."

"I'll cover your back."

Kala had nearly gained her feet when a deafening boom assaulted her eardrums. The floor buckled and shuddered, sending vibrations through her body and jarring her teeth.

A harsh bark of laughter came from Vivian. "Sounds like someone found the propane tanks! Hurry, Holcroft!"

She didn't hesitate. The propane tanks kept in the lower storage level were huge; if the whole stack had been lit, they could easily destroy most of the building. Kala clambered to her feet and started running toward the door. A burst of flame just behind her told her a tendril had tried to follow the sound of her feet.

The two other people who had been hiding behind the table were already gone. Another explosion rocked the building as Kala tried to get through the doorway, and she hit the wall and held on to it to steady herself, blinking through the smoke to see into the hallway. More screams mingled with people yelling for each other and the sounds of feet slapping on the concrete floors. A burst of warm light to her left told her the flamethrowers she'd given out were being put to good use.

She took off in the opposite direction, toward the hangars. The smoke choked her, so she bent down and held the sleeve of her suit over her nose.

Screams and calls for help echoed through the hall, and then a cluster of people raced out of a corridor behind Kala, catching her in their midst. Someone shoved her from behind, and she picked up her pace. Most of the people surrounding her were coated in splashes of blood; one was hysterical, and strange hiccups of laughter broke through her wails as she scratched at her face with bloodied hands. Another was yelling and pushing at his companions, telling them to split up and stop running in a group. A second later, Kala saw why: one of the creatures spilled out of the hallway behind them, dragging its bulk toward them, arms lashing out to grab at the stragglers, its own deflated human host swaying limply on its back.

Kala twisted around, trying to catch a glimpse of Vivian, hoping her companion wasn't trapped on the creature's other side. Someone shoved her, and she hit the floor hard, gasping as her lip split and blood flooded her mouth.

One of the black arms shot forward and speared through the chest of a man who had been directly in front of her. He screamed, and Kala shielded her face against the spray of his blood.

She couldn't think, or even *breathe*, but she scrambled in her pockets for a weapon. Her hand closed over a hard, cool, round object—her last grenade. She pulled it out, tugged the ring free, and hurled it at the black beast.

Kala didn't stop to watch where it landed but gained her feet awkwardly, ignoring the pain in her lip and the ache of her knees and palms where the concrete had sliced through her suit. Pressing both hands over her ears, she ran as fast as she could.

CHAPTER 17

THE EXPLOSION TRAVELED THROUGH her like a shock wave. The hollow inside of her chest vibrated, but she managed to keep her feet this time, squinting against the smoke and throwing the weight of her body forward to maintain momentum. The group that had swelled around her dispersed. Some veered off toward the living quarters, others toward the kitchen. She turned left, taking the detour that led to the hangar and the labs. Scorch marks marred the walls, and two bodies lay on the ground. She recognized them as the men she'd given two of the flamethrowers to.

They probably met Stanos while they were trying to escape.

The hallway overlooking the hangar was empty. As the door shut behind her, the sounds of fighting died into gentle background noise. Even an explosion didn't do much except shake the ground beneath her feet.

She could see the ship Stanos had arrived on, still connected to the extendable walkway. The fighting must have started before the hangar workers could refuel, clean, and settle the ship into its usual docking place. That was good news for her.

She counted the offshoots in the walkway until she found the one she remembered Stanos coming out of and followed it down toward the ship. The passageway was refreshingly clean and calm. Kala could almost believe the last hour had been a particularly traumatic movie, and she was now exiting the theatre and returning to the real world. *What a good show. The special effects were really something, weren't they?*

She stifled a hysterical laugh as she reached the end of the hall and punched the button to open the ship's door. It was compact but orderly inside. She thought about Stanos and his two copilots, navigating the ship home with borrowed memories, hiding their true, monstrous insides behind respectable human suits.

Kala glanced up the walkway toward the observation area. She could just barely see the doors leading to the living quarters, hiding unspeakable horrors. Vivian hadn't followed. She wanted to wait and watch the doors, hoping Vivian would come through them whole and unhurt, but Kala knew the odds were abysmal. Even with the flamethrowers, the fight had been a massacre. The station was as good as lost; Kala had done her best to give the occupants the knowledge of how to fight the monsters, but she needed to get out and warn the other stations. *How many mysterious calls for help had come in over the past ten days? Forty-five? Were all of those returning ships going to cause a repeat of Station 333?*

Kala locked the doors. Anger and grief tasted bitter on her tongue as she settled into the padded pilot's chair and began powering up the ship. *Focus. Get off the planet and send a signal to Central. People need to be told about this. Do your job.*

The Delta Shock hummed into life. Kala took two deep, stabilizing breaths, relishing the clean air of the cockpit, as she prepared to launch.

A flash of motion in the corner of her eye caught her attention. Kala looked up and felt a cold chill sweep over her body as she saw Vivian tearing along the viewing deck toward the walkway. Her right arm was blackened with soot, and drying blood painted the front of her suit. She unhooked and dropped the flamethrower as she ran.

Kala rose out of her chair, hope and fear battling inside her, as one of the beasts burst through the door behind Vivian.

"No," Kala muttered as she realized the impossible choice she had to make. *Is it Vivian? Or is it a monster wearing Vivian's body? If she wasn't being chased, I could keep her outside until I was sure…*

Vivian would reach the door in seconds, and only seconds after that, the creature would catch up.

You can't risk it. You need to alert Central. Her life is a small price to pay to get an early warning out. But Vivian saved you. Can you live with yourself if you don't open those doors?

Vivian was nearly at the end of the extendable walkway, fear painted across her face. Even though Kala couldn't hear her, she could easily read her lips: *Open the door!*

Kala made up her mind in a split second and slammed her hand onto the button. The door drew open, Vivian barreled through, and Kala pressed a second button, snapping the door closed and unsealing the walkway. The monster was moving quickly—too quickly to stop itself in time as the walkway retracted—and it tumbled from the edge. Its multitude of limbs flailed uselessly as it fell to splatter itself on the concrete hangar floor.

Kala didn't wait to see if the fall had killed the monster or if it was already repairing itself. Instead, she pushed on the ship's accelerator, directing it toward the open hatchway above them.

Neither woman spoke as the ship rose and exited the hangar. Kala gave the shuttle a burst of energy to escape the planet's weak atmosphere. Vivian took the copilot's seat, scratching at the flaky grime on her forearm. She smelled like smoke, blood, and sweat.

"You let me in," she said simply.

"Yeah."

"Are you an idiot? *I* wouldn't have let me in."

"Huh?"

Vivian scowled at her. The expression was comfortingly familiar. "I could be one of the monsters. What if I was just pretending to be chased to get you to open the doors?"

"You weren't." Kala gave her companion a weary smile. "Earlier, when we first bumped into each other, I was amazed at how...*determined* and *angry* you looked. Then, when you were running for my ship, you actually looked frightened. I've never seen either of those expressions on you before. That's how I knew you were human."

Vivian raised her eyebrow.

"Stanos—and the other monsters—mimicked their hosts to gain our trust. If you were one of them, you'd have worn an expression I was used to."

Vivian blinked at her then nodded slowly.

A noise, strangely muffled and deep, made them both jump. Kala turned back to the ship's screen and gasped. Station 333 was exploding. Billows of reds and yellows consumed the gray buildings, spewing black smoke.

"Looks like someone finally unlocked and lit the propane store," Vivian said.

They sat in silence, watching as their home burned. The fiery lights gradually died down, and the thick black smoke that rose into the planet's atmosphere dulled the glow.

"Will that be enough to kill them all?" Vivian asked.

"The creatures? It should get most of them, I guess."

The monsters weren't the only living beings to die, though. Kala couldn't stand watching the burning station. She turned off the screen so the cockpit was nearly black, illuminated only by the panel's display screens. She hoped it was too dark for Vivian to see the tear tracks on her face.

"You're not an idiot," Vivian said after a pause. "It was wrong of me to call you one."

Kala blinked in surprise. "Oh. Thanks." She cleared her throat. "And thanks for looking out for me back there. I don't know where I'd be without your help."

"You would be dead," Vivian said simply.

Kala felt a tired grin grow across her face. "Yeah, okay."

"Just like *I* would be dead without *you*." Vivian shot her an appraising glance out of the corner of her eyes. "I wouldn't have thought to use fire against them."

Kala nodded. She was trying very hard not to think about the lives that had been lost on her station. A hundred and fifty-nine people had been there just that morning. She wondered if any of them had managed to get to the hangars in time.

"You're terrible at this," Vivian interrupted, motioning toward the controls Kala was manipulating. "You're wasting fuel. Let me take over."

"Sure."

"If you want to do something, start sending alerts to all of the planets within easy communication distance. They need to know about what happened. And they need to know that they're at risk too."

"Yeah," Kala said, getting out of her seat so Vivian could scoot over. Her entire body was starting to ache from the last hour's exertion. She brushed her fingers over the tattered, dirty, blood-ied canary-yellow suit. It felt like months ago that she'd been following Stanos into the labs.

She settled into the copilot's seat and began pulling up the wavelengths she would need to use to contact other stations.

Vivian took over the controls, resetting some and altering others. "The ship's low on fuel," she noted, "but we have enough to set a course for an area we can be picked up in. I think you and I might actually make it out of this alive."

"And that's something," Kala said, smiling despite her aches, her fears, and the memories she knew she would never be able to erase. She typed the first code into her system and spoke into the microphone.

"This is Kala Holcroft and Vivian Magennie aboard the Delta Shock. Station 333 has been destroyed. Repeat, Station 333 has been destroyed. There is a new threat to our network that must be acted on immediately…"

PART 4

STATION 334

CHAPTER 18

MAREN LEANED ON THE wrench with her full weight, her teeth clenched, feet slipping on the tile floor. The dish-sized bolt designed to hold the station's interior hull together moved a fraction of an inch then froze again.

"Damn it," Maren hissed, easing off the wrench and stretching her aching arms. "Stop being so bleeding stubborn. Do you *want* me to call Saul on you?"

"Here's a tip." The cool voice came from the hallway behind Maren, making her jump. "Don't talk to the infrastructure. People will start thinking you're crazy."

The station's leader, Suriya, stood in the doorway that led to the work areas. She folded her arms across her chest and regarded Maren through heavy-lidded eyes for a second before flicking her gaze to the harshly lit metal hallway.

Maren grinned apologetically. "Sorry, it's just that I've

half drowned the damn thing in oil, and it still won't come loose—"

"There's an info package," Suriya said, cutting across Maren. The older woman continued to let her gaze flick over the hall, glancing at each door in turn. "Marked urgent."

"More cautions against sunbathing in a gamma flare, then?"

Suriya didn't laugh at the joke, but her eyes stopped roving the hallway to fix Maren with a cold stare. "The others are waiting in the comm room. Be quick."

Maren heaved a sigh as the echo of her superior's footsteps faded. She thought she'd done reasonably well at making friends with her coworkers during the eight months since she'd been assigned as the maintenance worker on Station 334…all except for Suriya. *To be fair, Suriya doesn't really have friends. Just some subordinates she likes more than others.* Maren pursed her lips at the stuck bolt, gave it a kick for good measure, and jogged after her leader.

Station 334, built on the second section of the semi-planet Cycern, was a vital link in the Mandola Communications System. On a busy day, they could process and redirect thousands of messages and assistance requests from planets up to thirty-five days' travel away. Currently, though, they were in their *hibernation* phase: Cycern's slow rotation had moved Station 334 to face the quietest section of their network, and the crew had been reduced accordingly. The other two stations on Cycern—488 and 491—had absorbed the surplus workers, who would pick up the slack on those stations.

Maren still wasn't used to how empty the station felt without its full crew. While in hibernation, the crew consisted of a minimum team of five. In a few weeks, when the planet had rotated another fifty degrees, 488 would be facing the void, and the full crew of eighty-six members would return. She was looking forward to it. The vast maze of hallways felt achingly lonely with just five people drifting through them.

She reached the communication room and eased through the door. Suriya had settled into a seat near the back of the room, her pale face creased into an expression Maren had come to associate with frustration. Saul, their defense technician, leaned against the wall, his scarred face impassive. And Mark, their scientist, sat beside Gin, who was Maren's favorite person in the entire universe.

Gin was their only remaining communications specialist. Normally, she would have been flanked by thirty of her peers, but while the station was in hibernation, she sat alone behind the dashboard that wrapped around half of the large room. She grinned as Maren entered. "…and that makes five of us. Shall we do a roll call, boss?"

"Just play the packet," Suriya sighed.

"Right-o." Gin swiveled in her seat and pressed a series of buttons with dizzying dexterity. Gin wasn't a small woman, but she was fast at her job. Her pink blouse and skirt looked horrifi-cally out of place in the dull-gray station, but she had a set of them and wore them like a uniform. Maren loved the woman for her subtle rebellion against the clinical environment.

The speakers buzzed into life, and Maren leaned forward to listen. A woman read the announcement, her voice clear, perfectly enunciated, and as nuanced as a robot.

"Tuesday, March 12. For immediate release. Central has become aware of a potential hazard to exoplanet stations and stations near the edge of our system. All stations are advised to exercise caution. Non-native life-forms are to be treated as biohazards and immediately terminated. Further updates to come."

The line crackled and went dead. Maren felt her eyebrows rise. Emergency announcement packets were uncommon—it had been months since the last one—and usually important. She was having a hard time figuring out what the packet was implying, though. "What was that about?"

Mark shrugged, scratching at his stubble. "Might be a new life-form they've found. Remember when a bunch of creeping Helen came off that meteor shower and they had to dispatch specialized teams to cull it?"

"Yeah." Maren perched against the edge of the dashboard. The other communications staff always yelled at her when she leaned on their equipment, but Gin never minded. "Except when that happened, they told everyone what the problem was. This time, we're just being given instructions to kill anything that lands on our planet. They said to treat it like a biohazard. Maybe there's a virus going around?"

"Doesn't really concern us anyway," Mark said. "We're not exo or fringe."

"We're facing fringe stations, though." Gin's bow-shaped mouth was pursed in concern. "I didn't say anything before because I thought it was just a really weird coincidence, but there have been a bunch of emergency help requests coming through lately. At least ten in the last week."

"Ten requests?" Maren asked, shocked. "But we're only getting messages from a hundred and fifty stations while we're in hibernation."

"I know. But it's not unheard of to get a spate of requests in one go, especially if there have been asteroids going through the area." Gin shrugged and rubbed a hand through her short, teal hair. "Like I said, I thought it was a coincidence."

Suriya stood and crossed the room to open the door. "Does anyone want to know what I think?"

"Yeah." Gin's face lit up.

"I think you should get back to your damn jobs." Suriya stalked out of the room, slamming the door as she left.

Undeterred, Gin called after her, "Copy that, boss!"

Mark shrugged, kicked out of his chair, and slouched through the exit as Gin turned back to her console. Saul also made for the door, and Maren, remembering the bolt that wouldn't come lose, hurried to intercept him.

"Hey, can I get a favor? I need to borrow your muscles."

Saul blinked at her but didn't answer. Maren was used to that; no reply was Saul's way of saying yes, so she led him out of the room and down the hallway toward the bolt. She quickened her pace to match the bearlike man's long strides. "So, being our defense technician, what's your reading on the info packet? Has it got you worried?"

"Hmm."

Maren peered up at her companion. It had taken her months to figure out what was going through his head, and still, most times, she wasn't sure whether she'd gotten it right. His strong face was emotionless...same as always. She didn't *think* he was too concerned.

"Bit weird that they'd send it to every station if it only applies to exo and fringe ones."

"Hmm."

"Maybe Mark's right, and there's a virus going around."

"Maybe."

They'd reached the bolt. Maren waved a hand toward it. "Damn thing won't unscrew for me. Would you mind?"

"This is why they won't promote you," Saul said. He was watching her out of the corner of his gray eyes.

Maren stared at him, trying to understand his meaning. "What? You think they're not promoting me because I'm weak?"

Saul gripped the wrench in one hand and gave it a shove. The stiff metal screeched as the huge bolt came loose. "No. It's because you're tiny." He turned and continued up the hallway, his boots thudding on the tile floor as he made for the recreation room.

Maren frowned at his back. "Huh. Okay. Thanks, I guess."

Saul's footsteps hadn't quite faded when the sirens started, announcing the approach of a gamma flare.

CHAPTER 19

THE VERY THING THAT made Cycern's stations ideal for communications centers also made them some of the most high-maintenance stations in the local system. They were skirting the edge of a cluster of wormholes, which they could use to receive, process, and send messages in a fraction of the time it would otherwise take. The closer planets could send recorded messages, while the more remote stations were able to send signals indicating that they needed new supplies, assessment, or emergency assistance.

The wormholes released bursts of gamma rays once or twice a day. The rays raised the temperature of the planet to over two hundred degrees and would roast any organism that wasn't shielded.

When she'd moved to Station 334, at least half of Maren's weeklong training had involved protocol for dealing with the gamma flares. The flares didn't follow any sort of schedule, but the station's early detection systems could predict when they were coming with a few hours' warning. A signal would be sent out, any crew outside the station returned immediately, and the hulking metal building would lock down for the two hours it took the flares to pass.

Cycern's stations had been carefully designed to withstand the incredible heat and damage the flares caused. The double-walled metal structures were expected to last for up to a century with proper maintenance, and they even did a good job of maintaining a steady temperature inside. Maren's job as the maintenance worker was to ensure that the building stayed in good condition and prevent disasters before they could occur.

She did most of her work on the outside of the station, where the gamma rays were most likely to wear down the shields, but her diagnostic tools had shown the insulation had deteriorated in part of the interior wall, so she'd spent most of that day trying to remove the steel plates to replace the packing inside.

"Damn, damn, damn," she groaned, struggling with another bolt stiff from a decade of neglect. When she worked on the outside of the station, she could use mechanical tools to undo and tighten the bolts, but the machines were too large to maneuver through the station's hallways. The wrench was leaving red bruises on her hands, but she didn't want to have to call Saul again.

She tried to shrug it off, but his words had stung. She'd never wanted to be in maintenance. In fact, she'd wanted, and had trained for, Saul's job: defense technician.

It was a fancy title, but the job description amounted to punching anything that threatened the station or the station's crew. As a defense technician, she would have patrolled the corridors, watched over the security systems, and led teams to remove life-forms that found their way onto the planet. During times of war or when significant threats arose, defense technicians were drafted into first-response teams.

Maren was qualified for the job, but her recruiting manager hadn't been able to find her a position. "There's a glut of defense technicians right now," she'd explained, folding her manicured fingers under her pointed chin as she offered Maren an insultingly sympathetic smile. "What stations are really looking for are maintenance workers. I could get you a position on a *very* prestigious station."

Maren had tried to hide the look of disgust that had spread across her face, but she didn't think she'd been very successful.

"Look," the recruiter had said, settling forward in her high-back leather chair. "I know it's not what you want, but it's the best I can do for you. Once you've got a job—especially on one of the bigger stations—it's easy to move between sections. Work as maintenance for six months then ask for a transfer to defense, and I can almost guarantee you'll get it."

It had sounded good at the time—better than being unemployed at least—but the promises had so far proven empty. Maren had applied for a promotion to defense at exactly six months after her employment on Station 334, but it had been rejected, just like the following three applications.

Maybe Saul has a point, Maren thought as she punched the bolt and hissed as she got a scraped knuckle for her trouble. She didn't look like defense; she was small, even for a woman, and her muscles refused to develop past toned, no matter how much she worked out.

She wasn't about to give up, though. Working in defense had been her dream since she was a child. A few weeks after her tenth birthday, her school had played a news segment on a rescue mission. Eight technicians fought and killed a mass of the aggressive plant crawling Helen that had trapped twenty workers inside their station. After the fight, they interviewed the team's leader. He'd been bruised, bloodied, and sweaty, but Maren had been captivated by the intense, fiery triumph in his eyes. She'd never seen someone look so *alive.*

The captain had become a minor hero after the battle, and news articles cropped up about him every few months. Maren had read them all. She'd developed something of a schoolgirl crush on the man and started taking classes that would ultimately let her join the ranks of his peers. When she graduated and failed to land a position as a defense technician, her recruiting officer had given her a list of stations that needed a maintenance worker. By pure luck—or fate, if she believed in such things—Maren recognized one of the stations as her childhood hero's post. She'd signed the transfer papers without hesitation.

When she'd finally met him, Saul was older and had a few new scars, but his gray eyes had been just as captivating as they had been in the video she'd watched more than a decade before.

"Damn it," Maren snapped, dropping the wrench off the stuck bolt. She didn't have a choice; the bolt was fused in place, and the only person on the station with any hope of moving it was Saul.

She stalked down the hallway, rubbing her oily hands on her discolored jumpsuit. The vast station had supposedly been designed for maximum efficiency, but to Maren, getting anywhere seemed to take an eternity.

Saul normally spent his days in the rec room, reading while he watched the security system he'd relocated out of the dark defense section. Maren had at first assumed it was his way of pretending to be busy without actually doing any work, but she'd quickly discovered nothing on the screens got past Saul.

"He's trained to be constantly aware of his surroundings," Gin, who had been working with Saul for years, explained when Maren asked her about it. "Just watching the screens would be our equivalent of staring at a blank wall. So he reads books to keep himself from going insane from boredom."

Maren pushed into the spacious recreation room. When the station was out of hibernation, the room was usually filled with clusters of off-duty workers watching movies, playing table tennis, and napping on the curved chairs. With their reduced crew, it felt unnaturally hollow.

The dozen surveillance screens in Saul's corner were turned on. Some showed key parts of the inside of the station, a couple showed the hangar, and still others monitored the outside of the station. But Saul's seat was empty. That usually meant he'd seen something and had gone to check it out.

Maren squinted at the screens and found what must have attracted the defense technician's attention. A buggy had pulled into their hangar.

"Huh," Maren said, smirking as she turned to jog down the hallway that took her to the other corner of the station, where the ships and vans docked. "Three guesses who *that* is."

The small screens fixed in the corner of every room were red, signaling the approach of a gamma flare, with a countdown of less than an hour. Maren had to admit, Holly had impeccable timing.

She paused just outside the hangar and leaned against the window to watch the sandy-haired woman fill out the paperwork to dock her buggy in the station. Saul stood beside her, arms crossed. He would be following protocol, Maren knew, to confirm the woman's identity and grant her clearance to be there, even though her presence wasn't a surprise to anyone.

Holly worked at the station on the first section of Cycern, 488. The drive between the stations was a two-hour haul across barren, red-dirt planes, and while it wasn't uncommon for teams to make the trip if they needed to redistribute supplies, pass on equipment, or exchange crew members when one of the stations went into hibernation, Holly easily accounted for the bulk of their visits.

"You're kidding me." Suriya was marching up the hallway, her nostrils flaring even as she maintained a calm, quiet voice. "She knows how I feel about this."

"What do you reckon her excuse is this time?" Maren asked,

grinning. "I bet she's here to check we got the information package. You know, because she's just so dedicated to station safety."

Suriya shot Maren a furious glare but didn't reply.

"I bet she wants to share some of the news that's come through her station," a bright voice behind Maren said, making her turn. "That's her favorite reason."

Gin and Mark had come out of one of the hallways. Gin had the look of delight she wore anytime drama visited the station, and Mark was clearly trying to hide a smile as he avoided Suriya's glare.

"Oh, good, we're all here," Suriya said, cold anger dripping from her voice. "Because mercy forbid any work gets done in this place."

"I'm on my break," Gin said.

"Looking for Saul," Maren supplied.

"Got to, uh, check the…kitchen…has enough food…" The guarded grin broke free across Mark's face as Gin laughed at him.

The doors slid open as Saul led Holly into the station. The young woman's eyes flicked toward Mark for a second before she diverted her attention to Suriya. "Great, you're here. There was a high-priority info packet earlier today, and I know communications can sometimes be dodgy in this place, so I wanted to check you got it."

Maren and Gin managed to keep their faces serious as they bumped their fists behind Suriya's back.

"If you need to check anything, send us a signal." Their leader's voice was barely above a whisper. Maren had learned early in her job that Suriya's volume was an indicator of how much trouble you were in: if she was talking normally, you were fine, but a quiet murmur meant you were seconds away from earning a month's cleaning duties. "There is literally no reason why you would need to drive over here."

Holly brushed her long hair out of her face, nodding and looking as serious as she could. "I understand, Commander. But all of the communication units were busy, and well, it's not *that* far to drive." She flashed a smile. "Sorry to bother you. I'll head back now."

"You very well know you can't." Suriya pinched the bridge of her nose. "Flare's coming."

"There's a flare? Oh, I didn't know! That's terrible timing. I'm sorry!"

Gin leaned close to Maren and whispered in her ear, "She's doing very well, isn't she? Girl should've been an actress."

"Do this again, and I swear I'll invent a reason to fire you both," Suriya snapped. "Now get out of my sight."

"I'll take her to a quiet part of the station, boss," Mark said, a little too eagerly.

Suriya's voice was so saturated with scorn that it was almost visible. "*Of course* you will. How very *helpful* of you." She turned on her heel and marched toward her office, leaving Mark to lead Holly in the opposite direction. They made it nearly to the end of the hallway before their hands found each other's and their fingers intertwined.

"Fourth time this month," Gin noted, grinning broadly since she was no longer in danger of incurring Suriya's wrath. "I really think they're going to get fired if they keep it up."

"There aren't any rules against romance." Maren shrugged. "Not technically, anyway. And it's not doing any harm. But talking about doing harm to stuff, I need some more help, Saul—"

She turned to face the defense technician, but the hallway behind her was deserted. "Jeez, he's gone already? How can someone so big be so quiet?"

"Find him later," Gin said as she threaded her arm through Maren's. "I've got something to show you."

CHAPTER 20

MAREN SETTLED INTO THE empty seat beside Gin. The control center, like the rest of the station, felt eerily quiet without its usual throng of workers. Gin's section of the board was lit up, but the rest of the eight-meter system lay dormant.

"So, you remember me telling you about that spate of emergency help requests we've had over the last week?" Gin asked as she pressed buttons and adjusted dials.

"Yeah."

"More came through this morning. A dozen more, mostly from the remote stations, but also a couple audio messages from the nearer ones."

"A dozen? Jeez."

"I showed them to Suriya, but she just told me to do my job and divert them to Central. But here's the thing…Central isn't responding to them. I'm getting the standard acknowledgment mark, but no notification of any response teams being sent out."

Maren frowned and rubbed the heel of her palm over her brow. Central was obsessive about protecting its system—when a station had trouble, Central usually dispatched a response team within the hour. "The audio messages. What are they saying?"

"That's what I wanted to show you. Listen." Gin pressed a red button and slid a volume adjuster upward.

"This is Commander Tarus on Station 509," a man said. He was speaking clearly, but his voice was tight. "My team found a life-form outside our station. We believe it's hostile. It's broken through the doors of our quarantine area, and while it's contained, we don't know how long we can keep it that way. Please respond immediately."

"And Central didn't send a team?" Maren asked, incredulous.

"That's right. Here's another one."

"Station 775." The speaker was a woman. "My team is dead. I repeat, my team is dead. Immediate assistance is needed."

"And this one."

"Station 318. My crew was attacked by an unidentified life-form." The man was clearly trying to stay professional, but his voice was edging into hysterical. "Donovon and myself made it back inside, but Kyle was killed. I saw him die." He paused, his breathing rough. "But now he's at the door. He's knocking to be let in. He died, and he wants to be let in."

Maren swore under her breath.

Gin was watching her carefully. "Want to hear the last one?"

"Yes."

Gin pressed another button on the dash, and a woman's voice filled the room.

"This is Karen Phelps." She sounded as though she were crying. "This message is for my parents, Lori and Pete. I want you to know I love you. I love you so much." Karen paused, and Maren thought she heard crashing noises and what sounded like tearing metal in the background. "I made a mistake. They said they were here to restock the station, and-and-and I knew they weren't due for another week, but I let them in. I'm so sorry." More tearing metal. The woman tried to say something else, but her voice broke down into sobs. Maren stared at the dash, horrified and captivated, until the woman got her voice under control and started to speak again. "I just need you to know that I love you, Mum, Dad. And I need you to be careful. You'll understand more soon, when it spreads, but for now, you need to get out of your house and go hide somewhere remote. Don't trust your neighbors. Don't trust anyone who offers to help you. Just...hide...and stay safe."

The wail of breaking metal, this one much closer than the others, was followed by a scream. It was one of the rawest sounds Maren had ever heard; it seemed to fill her and tremble in her bones until it ended abruptly. At first, she thought the recording had finished, but then she realized she could hear quiet thudding, dragging noises. *Like a body being pulled across the floor.*

Then someone ended the recording.

Gin was watching Maren, her normally bright face serious. "I'm not crazy, am I? This is pretty serious, right?"

"Yes."

The friends swiveled in their seats to see Saul leaning against the doorframe. His impassive face looked harder, as though it had developed more angles.

Maren stood up. "What should we do?"

"Exactly what we're doing now."

"What—but—"

"We do our jobs, wait for Central's instructions, and protect ourselves."

The big man glanced between the two friends as Maren struggled to get her thoughts focused. "We need to talk to Suriya about this. She'll listen to you, Saul."

"No." His gray eyes lingered on Maren for a second before he directed his gaze at the roof. "Be careful around Suriya. She's changed."

"Changed?" Gin had clasped her hands in her lap and was playing with the hem of her skirt. "I mean, she's more stressed nowadays than she used to be—"

"The station is empty. What's causing her stress?"

Gin stared at Saul for a moment then looked at Maren. "You… you think she's becoming unstable? Like, mentally?"

"I think you should be careful." Saul pushed off the doorframe and turned to the hallway. "Maren, I undid the bolt that was giving you trouble."

"Oh…right. Thanks."

Maren and Gin stared at each other, neither able to phrase the words they wanted to say, as Saul's footsteps faded down the hallway. A loud, prolonged beep signaled that the station was locking its doors and securing vents ahead of the gamma flare that was about to hit.

CHAPTER 21

DINNER THAT NIGHT STARTED as a quiet affair. While they were in lockdown for the flare, all nonessential systems powered down, including the main electricity grid. They ate reconstituted cereals and packets of lab-grown meats in the dim light provided by two backup globes.

Mark and Holly, both a little disheveled, had come in late and pulled their chairs so close together that their elbows kept bumping as they ate. They inclined their heads toward each other, exchanging whispers followed by giggles, as Suriya glared at them from the other end of the table.

Saul had spoken more in those brief minutes in the communications room than he did in most full days, and he made up for it by maintaining a stiff silence. Maren and Holly both toyed with their food, too disturbed by what they'd heard to have much interest in eating.

"You're a jolly bunch tonight," Mark said when they'd nearly finished. His energy, which Maren normally found infectious, was making her skin crawl. "What? Did everyone's favorite pet die on the same day?"

Saul didn't look up from his plate. Suriya scowled at the couple but remained silent. Maren and Gin exchanged a glance, and Maren knew that, as little as Mark was in the mood to hear it, he should know about the messages. "Gin's been getting a lot of assistance requests lately."

"Yeah," Mark said around a mouthful of thick, gray paste. "She told us this morning."

"Well, there're even more now. And some audio messages. There are…things attacking the stations. People are dying. Central isn't sending any help."

Maren watched Suriya out of the corner of her eyes, but their leader gave no indication of having heard her.

Mark wrapped his arm around Holly's shoulders and pecked her cheek. She giggled and gave him a playful shove in response.

"Well," he said as he detangled himself, "it's only a problem for the exo and fringe stations, right? Stop stressing about it. Central will figure something out."

Hot anger ran through Maren's veins. She tightened her grip on the fork, turning her knuckles white. "Are you kidding me? You seriously can't be this self-centered. People are dying!"

Mark scowled at her, his good mood dissipated.

Holly scraped her chair a few inches away from him.

"Yeah, and what do you want me to do about it?" he asked.

"It's not my problem if some clowns on another station can't follow proper procedure—"

Maren's palm made a beautiful cracking noise as it hit Mark's cheek. His eyes bugged in shock as he lurched back in his chair, almost tipping it. A second of silence passed as they stared at each other, Mark holding a palm against the hurt cheek and glaring daggers. Maren leaned halfway across the table, panting, hand still held in midair in case she decided Mark needed another dose.

Then Holly split the quiet with a shriek. "How dare you! *How dare you!*"

She threw herself toward Maren, but before either woman could land a blow, Saul forced himself between them.

"Sit," he said pointedly, shoving Maren back into her chair. "Cool it," he instructed Holly, pushing her in the opposite direction.

"You're going to fire her for that, right?" Holly yelled, turning her anger toward Suriya. "She assaulted him!"

Suriya didn't seem to be completely aware of what had just happened. Her back was as straight as a poker, and she was examining her hands, which were folded on the table in front of her. She'd eaten even less of her dinner than Maren had.

"Well?" Holly's voice rose in pitch and volume. "You seemed pretty damn happy to throw threats around earlier, so how about acting on them?"

The older woman turned her hands over then licked her lips before looking up. "Holly, get out of my station."

"What?" Holly and Mark said together.

"You've outstayed your welcome. The lockdown will be lifting in a few minutes. I expect you to be in your buggy, ready to drive out those doors, as soon as they unlock. Understood?"

Holly was pale. She was trembling with fury, but she knew better than to argue with a superior. "Fine."

"Saul, make sure she leaves. I don't want to ever see her again. Not today. Not ever."

When Saul tried to nudge Holly's shoulder, she shrugged his hand off and stalked out of the kitchen's door, head held high, long, sandy hair swinging behind her.

"Bye!" Mark called, but she didn't respond.

Suriya scraped her chair back, turned, and left through the opposite door without another word. Maren and Holly exchanged a glance as Mark stared at his plate.

Maren knew she was lucky. It was well within Suriya's rights to fire, or at least parole, her workers for striking another team member. She was grateful that, as little as Suriya liked Maren's company, she at least hated Holly more.

The footsteps in the hallways faded until the only thing Maren could hear was the distant creaking metal of the station's outer layer, which was relaxing now that the gamma flare had passed. Then there was a quiet beep, and the small screen in the corner of the room, which had been red, turned green, signifying the lockdown was over.

"I hope you're happy." Mark pushed his chair out and left through the same door Suriya had taken. The station's regular white lights turned on with a quiet hum, and Maren blinked against the sudden brightness.

"I'm really not, that's the whole point," she said, but she doubted Mark heard her as he slammed the door.

She sighed, shoved aside her uneaten meal, and dropped her forehead onto the cool table. "I screwed up," she said, her voice muffled by the table. "He's going to hate me forever now, isn't he?"

Gin sighed as she patted Maren's shoulder. "Eh, he'd probably forgive you for hitting him. He *was* being kind of a jerk. But yeah, getting Holly sent away is going to be tough to recover from."

"Well." Maren sat up, gave her friend's hand a squeeze, and pushed back from the table. "I've caused enough damage today. Better go see what the flare managed to do."

CHAPTER 22

THE AFTERNOON SEEMED TO drag on. Maren managed to get the steel panel off the wall and replace the insulation inside. It was worse than her diagnostic tools had shown; she would need to request a proper maintenance team to help her go through the whole building and check for faults. Because of the station's precarious position near the wormholes, it had to be maintained impeccably. If part of the wall buckled or split from the heat, anyone within searing distance would be cooked where they stood.

Maren had just finished fixing the plate back into place when she noticed a shadow over her tools. She turned to face the bear-like man standing half a dozen paces behind her. "Saul! How long have you been there?"

A hint of a smile flickered over his mouth before it settled back into neutral. "There's a meeting in the communications room. Urgent."

"Right." Maren dropped the welder she'd been using to fix a tear in the metal sheet and jogged to catch up with Saul. He slowed his pace slightly so she could keep up with him.

Maren wished he were easier to read. Being a defense technician, he would understand better than any of them how bad the situation might be. Central prided itself on its fast response time to threats, but if the other communication stations across the network had received as many assistance requests as Station 334 had, Central's resources would be thin. If there was a shortage of emergency response teams, then defense technicians like Saul would be the first to get called up for service. She wasn't sure she liked that idea. Saul was the quietest out of them, and he easily blended into the background, but Maren hated the idea of seeing him leave. The station wouldn't feel right without the tall, patient man standing in the shadows. *Unless...*

I could go with him.

Saul pushed open the door to the communications center. Gin was kneeling on the ground beside her chair, hands fluttering over cables she'd pulled out of the belly of her communication system, her eyes huge and frightened. "I'm sorry. I'm sorry. I don't know what's wrong."

"Jeez," Maren hissed, running to her friend. She dropped to her knees and wrapped her arms around Gin's shoulders. She could feel the woman shaking. "Gin, what's wrong? Are you okay?"

"The system's down," a voice said.

Maren looked up to see Suriya pacing the length of the room, pinching the bridge of her nose.

"The whole damn system. And our *communications specialist* can't fix it."

Gin glanced between the two women and swallowed. Sweat stood out on her forehead, and a red dampness rimmed her eyes as she started talking so quickly it was almost unintelligible. "I—I've tried everything. I thought it was just a black spot— you know how the system doesn't always come on immediately after a flare?—so I waited for an hour, but it didn't pick up the signal. I've rebooted it and checked the connections. It should be working. *It should—*"

"I don't care if it *should*. I only care if it *is!*" Suriya slammed a fist onto the desk, sending a mug of pens flying and making Gin flinch. "Every minute this system is down, we're losing messages! I need you to find out what's wrong, and I need it fixed. *Now.*"

"Don't yell at her," Maren snapped, aware that she was skating on thin ice but unable to stop herself. "Can't you see she's trying? She's smart. Give her some space, and she'll work it out."

"It—it could be an external fault," Gin said, glancing between the two women. "The receivers could be damaged, or—"

"Ah." Suriya stepped closer to Maren. The harsh lights made the lines on her face seem deeper than normal, turning them into heavy crevices in her pale skin. Her eyes were wide and demented, and in that second, Maren realized that Saul had been right to warn her to be careful around their leader. "So it's maintenance's fault, then?"

"I didn't say that!" Gin protested, but Suriya ignored her.

"Forgot to check the external systems, maybe? Or couldn't be bothered to fix a fault you found?"

Maren bristled. Maintenance might not have been her first choice of career—or even her twentieth—but she worked hard and had not once in her eight months of duty neglected her job. She struggled to keep her voice calm and even as she replied, "Flares can have unpredictable effects. Even the best-maintained system isn't immune to issues. You know that."

"The systems haven't failed in the last eight years!" Suriya screamed, her voice cracking from the strain. "Someone is responsible for this! And it's you, Maren. I knew from the moment I saw your weaselly little face that you would be a failure, and now you've broken the whole damn system. I swear—"

"*Enough.*"

Everyone jumped as the bellow cut through Suriya's screams. Saul stepped closer to his commander, his gray eyes fixed on her. Maren had never seen the defense technician angry before, and it was a terrifying sight. Saul, who usually leaned against walls or lounged in a chair, had straightened his back and broadened his shoulders. His hands hung by his side, their backs facing outward in a subtle sign of aggression. His lips were pale, and there was pure animalistic ferocity in his eyes. His voice was a hard and deep rumble as he addressed Suriya. "Systems break. No one in this room is to blame. I will *not* let you abuse your team like this."

Suriya took a step back and licked her lips as she stared at her defense technician. He seemed huge, so much larger than he looked normally, as though he'd grown to take up at least half of the room. *He's like a lion*, Maren thought dumbly as she held the trembling Gin in her arms. *A lion that can pass itself off as a lap cat.*

"Stand down," Suriya managed. Her eyes were bulging in her skull, but she'd reduced her voice to a whisper. "That's an order."

"No."

Their leader inhaled sharply, but she didn't dare yell while Saul seemed so dangerous. "This is insubordination. I could have you paroled."

"No." Saul had fixed her with an unblinking gaze. He took a half step closer, looming over her. "As defense technician, I have the right to detain you if I believe you are a danger to yourself or others. And I am *seconds* away from acting on that right."

They stared at each other for what felt like an eternity. A vein in Suriya's throat twitched, then she broke the silence. "Perhaps I was out of line." She glanced at Maren and Gin, who were still kneeling on the floor, then turned and left the room at a walk that was just a fraction too slow to be classified as a run. Saul exhaled, letting his shoulders lower, and he seemed to deflate to his normal size. He crouched beside the two friends and patted Gin's back. "Okay?"

"Yeah," she said, drawing a stuttering breath. "Yeah, I'm fine."

Saul placed a massive hand on Maren's shoulder and gave it a brief and surprisingly gentle squeeze. "We'll worry about Suriya later. Let's fix the system first."

CHAPTER 23

"RIGHT, YEAH." GIN CLAMBERED to her feet, brushing dirt off her pink skirt. "I think it must be an external fault. I've checked all the equipment in here, but there aren't any errors."

"I'll go out and see if I can repair it," Maren said, getting to her feet as well. "Saul, will you stay with Gin?"

"No," he said simply. Maren sighed.

"I know you're normally supposed to accompany any excursions, but I don't want to leave Gin alone…"

With Suriya, she finished internally. Saul crossed his arms and blinked at her. Normally, she took his silence as agreement, but she was pretty sure he was digging his heels in this time.

"I'll get Mark to hang out with me," Gin said quickly. Her fingers still trembled on the dashboard, but at least her smile was back. "He doesn't have any work to do today anyway."

"Okay," Maren said reluctantly. "The intercom still works, right?"

"Yeah, there's no problem with short-range stuff. We just can't pick up anything more than a hundred meters away."

"Great, stay on the system while we're out there. I might need you for troubleshooting help anyway." She turned to Saul. "Ready?"

His silence was definitely a yes, and he led her into the hallway and through the first door on the left, which took them into the air lock.

Trips outside the station, onto the dusty red surface of their semi-planet, were scheduled regularly. Maren's maintenance duty had her out at least twice a week to check and repair infrastructure, and Saul journeyed outside an extra time each week to check for and clear off any life-forms that meteors or space junk had deposited on the planet. Mostly, the life-forms were harmless and no more intelligent than a plant, but they could cause structural damage if they clogged up vents or equipment, and a couple of them could be a hazard to the buggies that frequently traveled over two hundred kilometers an hour when crew members journeyed between stations.

Maren pulled her white suit over her uniform, zipped it up, then locked the gloves and boots into place. Saul was checking his equipment, which included an array of knives and a gun armed with neurotoxins for any aggressive life-forms they might meet.

"Is it too late to apologize?"

Maren, who had been strapping her right boot to the suit, rose and turned slowly. Suriya stood in the doorway. She looked as if she had just finished being sick; her face was sallow, and dark circles were developing around her eyes. She looked between Saul and Maren and tried to smile. "That was crazy back there. And I'm really, really sorry."

"Yeah," Maren said slowly. "Crazy."

"I know it doesn't excuse my behavior, but last week, I received a notification that there was an investigation into my job performance and that I might be removed to a smaller station." She paused, took a deep breath, and continued in a calmer voice. "It's had me under a lot of pressure to make everything perfect, and when the system went down…well…" She waved her hand then let it drop limply to her side.

Maren turned to Saul. He was watching their leader, his expression unreadable.

"I'd like to come and help, if you'll have me," Suriya said. "I have some experience with the communication rigs on this station."

Again, Maren looked to Saul. He gave a small nod then picked up one of the suits from the shelf and tossed it to their leader. She caught it, flashed him a thin smile, and began pulling the pants over her legs.

She'd almost completely suited up when a loud mechanical *whoop* came from the corner of the room. Maren glanced in its direction and saw the screen had turned red and was counting down from seventy minutes. She swore. "Another flare? Already? Today does *not* want to be nice to us, does it?"

Suriya was looking at Saul. "What do you think? Do we have time to get out there?"

"Protocol," he said simply.

Flare safety protocol, which was drilled into them at least once a month, was excessively clear on what should happen when the system detected an incoming flare. When the siren sounded, any crew outside the station was to return immediately. The only excuse for leaving the building during a flare countdown was the unlikely situation that a crewmate had become stranded and needed help.

"I know, I know," Suriya hissed. She ran her fingers through her hair, and stress lines were creeping back into her face. "We've lost our entire system, though. If it's a simple fault, we could have it fixed in under ten minutes." She looked back at Saul and shrugged. "You know how important this is, and you know how dangerous it is too. I'll let you make the call."

Saul glanced at the window set in the external door then looked to Maren.

She shrugged. "I'm game if you are."

"Okay," he said. "But we're coming back when the countdown reaches forty minutes, whether it's fixed or not."

Suriya nodded, looking relieved. "That's fair. But we'd better move fast." She grabbed her helmet off the rack and pulled it over her head. Maren followed, twisting her heavy helmet onto the neck of the suit until she heard the whirr of the connection being fixed and saw the green light on her sleeve panel.

"Hey, Gin, can you hear me?"

"Absolutely can." Gin's voice crackled through the helmet's speakers, sounding tinny. "I'm seeing signals for three suits. Is that right?"

"Yeah, Suriya's here. She's coming out with us."

Suriya's voice piped through the speaker as her suit came online. "Gin, please allow me to give you a brief apology now, and the promise of a more complete, in-person apology when we get back."

There was silence for a second, then Gin, sounding as though nothing had happened, said, "Don't worry about it, boss. Now, I don't want to be a wet blanket or anything, but there's a little red screen here warning me about the imminent annihilation of anything squishy and humanish that isn't inside the station."

"Yes, thank you. Saul thinks we have enough time to attempt the repairs before the flare gets too close. Isn't that right, Saul?"

Silence.

"Well, he does. We'll be back before the countdown hits forty minutes at the most."

"'Kay. You'll need to be fast. That only gives you twenty-five minutes."

"Yeah," Maren said, lining up beside her leader and Saul at the air lock's external doors. "It's a bit of a short warning this time."

"A side effect of the broken system. We're not getting signals from the satellites. Okay, let me know when you're ready."

"Ready now," Suriya said as she tied her tool pack to the back of her suit.

"Ditto."

"Hmm."

"Right," Gin said, and Maren could hear the quiet beeps coming from the control panel. "I'm checking system statuses...

confirming suits are functioning correctly...depressurizing the air lock...and doors are opening in three, two, *one*."

The air lock's external door slid to one side with a quiet *whoosh*, and a billow of red dust engulfed the three teammates. Even after eight months of twice-a-week trips outside, Maren impulsively squinted against the grit, despite the protective helmet.

"Clock's ticking," Suriya said. "Let's move."

CHAPTER 24

THEY WALKED IN SINGLE file, Saul leading the team, with Maren in the rear. The planet, a flat expanse of red dust, was stuck in a perpetual state of twilight, and ribbons of flaming reds and yellows stretched across the cloudless horizon. Sometimes, when they received a crate of beer with their supplies or if she was feeling especially homesick for her native planet, Maren would sit by the windows and admire the glowing sunset. Mark liked to tease her for being sappy, but unknown to the scientist, Maren wasn't the worst offender. Gin, perpetual romantic, had entire notebooks dedicated to poetry about the view.

The communications receivers were fixed to the roof of the station, surrounded by retractable metal guards that would automatically cover the sensitive equipment during a flare. Saul led them around the side of the station, where red sand had created a drift against its wall.

The external gravity was slightly lower outside than it was inside the station, allowing Maren to skip along the surface, but it was still a hard slog up the unstable slope. The sand shifted continuously under her boots, sliding her back down the incline, and she was panting by the time she reached the top. She let Saul haul her over the lip and onto the roof.

"Just to let you guys know, you've got sixty minutes until incineration," Gin said. "You might want to pick up the pace... or grab some marshmallows. Whatever."

Maren laughed and joined her companions in a jog across the roof. The metal was mostly even, though she could see the outer plating lifting in some areas. She would need to do some heavy maintenance soon.

Before long, they reached the first step—a section where the roof increased in height, leaving them facing a wall that reached just above their helmets. They could have walked along the wall until they reached the ladder, but it was faster to travel in a straight line. Saul grabbed the back of Suriya's suit and tossed her on top of the step then did the same for Maren. She enjoyed the sensation of flying for a second before hitting the roof and rolling, mercifully protected by the uniform's thick padding. She turned back to offer Saul a hand up, but he was already vaulting onto the higher level. He landed with the grace of a huge cat then sprung forward into a brisk jog.

Maren couldn't help but remember his words as they continued racing toward the second step. "*This is why they won't promote you...because you're tiny.*"

If he can do it, so can I, Maren decided, and as they got closer to the second step, she sped up instead of waiting to be tossed over. When she was two paces away, she jumped, intending to use her momentum and the lower gravity to leap over the ledge. But she misjudged the force needed and smacked into the wall.

"Ow," she grumbled, falling onto her back. The impact had thrown her head forward and bumped her nose against the helmet's glass, and she squinted against the sting.

A deep, barking noise came through her helmet's speakers, and Maren raised her eyebrows. *Is that Saul laughing? Well, I'll be damned. I honestly thought I'd meet a unicorn before I heard that.*

He knelt beside her, trying to smother his mirth as he offered her his gloved hand. "You okay?"

"Yeah, yeah," she groused.

"What's happening?" Gin asked from the communications room. "What's 'ow'?"

"Maren ran into a wall," Suriya said, also sounding amused.

"It looked much more majestic in my head," Maren said, and Saul, after pulling her upright, grabbed her shoulders in both hands and threw her over the ledge.

She rolled and got to her feet as Suriya was thrown up beside her. The communications system was only a dozen paces ahead. Its multitude of sensors, dishes, and plates poked out of the roof like a demented cityscape.

"Start looking for issues," Suriya instructed as Saul leaped over the ledge and landed next to them. "Maren, work on the left section. Saul, you take the right. I'll begin in the middle. Look for obvious stuff first. Gin, how long do we have?"

"Countdown reads just under fifty minutes."

"That's okay. It's faster to get down than it is to get up. Let's go."

Maren jogged into the heart of her section and started pacing through it, looking for anything out of place. She didn't see anything obviously wrong, such as a broken dish or large life-forms covering the sensors, but the system was bulky and complicated. If the fault was in a small section—if one of the smaller connections had been severed or a chip had come loose—it could take them hours to find it. Luckily, the problem ended up being easy to identify. She was on her second walk-through of the equipment when she saw that one of the large tubes carrying a bundle of cables from the main part of the system into the station had been severed.

"Hey, hey, there's a cut cable here." She knelt beside it as her companions ran to her side. "Damn, what a pain. This has to be one of the main cable groups."

"No," Saul said, crouching beside her as Suriya picked up one end of the tube and examined it. "This is *the* main cable group. And it's not an accident."

"What?"

"He's right," Suriya said. She sounded angry. "Someone cut this. *Deliberately.*"

"Shoot," Gin whispered.

Maren picked up the end that Suriya wasn't holding and looked into it. The outer tube, which was about as thick as her arm, held a bundle of twenty multicolored wires. The ends had been sliced through cleanly. "Jeez. Who?"

"Isn't it obvious?" Suriya said. "Holly."

"She wouldn't!" a male voice barked through their headsets. Maren had forgotten Gin's promise to stay with Mark while they were out of the station. "She's not that sort of person!"

"Quiet," Suriya snapped. "We'll deal with your friend later. Gin, how long do we have to get this fixed?"

"Countdown is at forty-eight minutes. I don't think you'll have time."

"We've got to." Suriya had turned to look at Saul. Her helmet's glass was too dark for her face to be visible, but Maren could hear the desperation in her voice. "The bare wires won't survive a flare, even with the shields over them. And that could irreparably fry the entire system."

Saul's sigh was slow and deep. "Work fast," he said. "I won't let my team stay out here for a second beyond what I feel is safe."

Suriya had already disconnected her tool pack from the back of her suit and unzipped it. "Maren, start stripping the wires' ends. I'll bind them together."

"Right." Maren grabbed the strippers from the pack and fitted its end over the first wire, a brown one. She squeezed the handle so that the specialized scissors cut through the wire's plastic sheath, leaving the copper cord inside intact, then she stripped off the last half-inch of plastic. She quickly found the matching brown wire on the other half of the cable bundle and mimicked the motion. Suriya swooped in, pulling both cables out of the sheath, and coiled the internal copper cords together before binding them tightly with stretching plastic tape.

They worked feverishly, Suriya binding the cables as quickly as Maren could strip them, while Saul stood above the women and surveyed the surrounding area. Maren glanced up between stripping cables and saw the red-tinted sky was lightening as the flare approached, washing the vivid colors on the horizon into oranges and pale yellows.

"Forty minutes," Gin said far sooner than Maren had expected. "How're you guys doing?"

"Getting there." Suriya didn't pause in her work; her fingers were moving deftly despite the thick gloves as she tied and bound wires together.

Maren counted quickly; they'd done fourteen wires and had six left.

"We need to go," Saul said, his voice as gentle and patient as ever.

"Give us a few more minutes!" Suriya begged.

Saul turned back to the horizon. Maren found herself wondering if he enjoyed the view as much as she did, but she pushed the idea from her mind so that she could focus on her task. The wires were hard to grab through the thick gloves, and it was taking all of her attention to strip them efficiently.

"Thirty-eight minutes," Gin said, and it seemed almost as if no time had passed before she said, "Thirty-five minutes."

"Suriya," Saul said.

"We're on the last wire." Stress was bleeding through Suriya's voice so clearly that it made Maren's heart ache. "I can't stop now. You go ahead while I finish."

Maren knew Saul too well to think he would even contemplate doing that. The large man crossed his arms, watching them intently as Maren stripped the last bit of plastic off and Suriya knitted the copper together.

"We've just got to reconnect the sheath," she said, sounding breathless. "Then we'll run for the air lock, and we'll be inside with plenty of time to spare. This is fine."

Saul exhaled deeply, and Maren knew he didn't like how close they were cutting it. Yes, there was still time to get inside comfortably, but all it would take was one minor disaster—a sprained ankle, or a blockage in front of the air lock doors—and they could be in serious trouble.

Maren held the two halves of the sheath together while Suriya sprayed a foam sealant around the divide then bound it in thick tape for good measure. "Okay," she said, sounding almost manic in her relief. "It's done. Try restarting the system, Gin."

There was a second of silence, then Gin, sounding ecstatic, said, "Yes! We're online!"

"Great, okay, good." Suriya laughed. "Nice work, team. Let's get out of here." She buckled her toolkit onto her suit then let Saul lead them back toward the first step.

The sky's purple hue had turned light lilac. Maren had never actually seen a flare—the station's windows were all covered during the lockdown—but she'd been told the sky would turn entirely white during its peak.

Saul reached the edge of the first step, but instead of jumping, he skidded to a halt and pulled his gun out of its holster.

"What's up?" Maren asked, slowing down as she approached him. "Is it a life-form?"

Saul didn't reply but held out a hand to wave her back. Maren ignored the signal and stepped around him to look over the ledge.

On the expanse of roof below them, as still as a statue, stood a suited figure. Maren couldn't see who it was through the tinted helmet, but its head was tilted upward to watch them.

"Holly?" Suriya barked as she caught up. "I'm surprised you've stayed for so long."

The figure didn't speak or move. If they hadn't dashed across it barely twenty minutes before, Maren might have thought someone had left an insane modern art statue on the roof to remind them of their transient nature or something equally pretentious.

Mark was chattering in her ear. "Holly's there? Is she okay? I can't hear her. Why isn't she on our system?"

"Gin, please shut the idiot up," Suriya snapped. "And bring Holly online. We can't hear her."

"Hang on, hang on." Gin was still bright, but stress had edged into her voice. "The system's only coming back one section at a time. The radar is still down, so I can't see or hear anyone who isn't directly connected to the short-range radios."

The figure was unnerving Maren. It hadn't moved an inch in the time they'd been watching it. Saul seemed to be sharing her uneasiness; he kept his gun up, aimed at the other's helmet.

Maren tilted her head to one side and felt a thrill run up her spine. The figure had mimicked her motion, letting its head loll sideways. *Huh, so you're alive after all.*

"Jeez," Suriya hissed. "What's her problem? First cutting the cable. Now this. Does she think it's going to intimidate us?"

"Oh," Maren said suddenly, clutching at Saul's arm. She'd realized something, and the idea made her sick to her stomach. "It's too tall."

CHAPTER 25

"WHAT?" SURIYA ASKED.

"It's too tall to be Holly. *Way* too tall."

Suriya's helmet swiveled to look at Maren then turned back to the figure waiting below them. She swore.

Holly was a little shorter than Maren, who stood a petite five feet four inches. The suit below them had to belong to someone edging up on six feet.

Did Saul realize? Is that why he hasn't lowered his gun?

Maren turned to glance at him again, and Saul swiveled suddenly, spinning in a semicircle to see behind them. Maren followed his motion, and the sick sensation increased. Half a dozen suited figures stood behind them, just in front of the communication system. Maren blinked at them, shocked, then looked back at the first figure and found it was flanked by four new companions.

"Gin?" Suriya said, her voice thin. "What can you tell us?"

"The scanner's just booting up now…hang on…hang on… *what the hell?*"

"How many are there?" Suriya asked. She and her teammates had subconsciously drawn together, back-to-back. Maren saw more figures out of the corner of her eye, walking toward them across the red desert.

"At least fifty," Gin said, and Mark swore. "Who are they? Where the hell did they come from?"

Something nudged Maren's shoulder. Suriya had taken a half step back, bumping into her, and Maren glanced over her shoulder to see what had startled her leader.

The first figure, the one they'd assumed was Holly, had raised its hands to its helmet. It was twisting it, unlocking it.

What does he think he's doing? The air isn't breathable.

Time slowed down. Maren could hear her heartbeat echoing in the suit, punctuated by short, sharp breaths. The speakers in her helmet had fallen quiet as the others waited, equally silent, equally tense. The other being's helmet unlocked, and he lifted it off his head in a smooth motion, exposing his face.

Maren recognized him. She didn't think she'd ever spoken to him—if she had, it must have been a brief hello as they passed in the hallways—but he was definitely familiar. Curly, sandy brown hair framed a wide face with a light, short beard. He'd been part of the crew working in Station 334 before it had gone into hibernation. That meant he'd come from Station 488, their sister station on the first third of the planet, where their surplus crew had been spending the past month.

"Greg?" Suriya sounded incredulous. Maren wondered if she, too, felt as though she were dreaming.

Then Greg smiled, showing two rows of beautiful white teeth, before opening his mouth completely, as though he intended to show them his tongue. Maren's nausea returned in a rush as long black tendrils poked out of his mouth. They stretched toward the three-person crew above him, as thick as fingers, wet, and inky black. Saul opened fire.

Maren flinched and threw her hands up to block her ears, even though her helmet was in the way, as Saul's gun fired round after round into Greg. Two hit his head, and three hit his torso. The tall man stumbled backward, arms pinwheeling. The horde of suited strangers all turned their helmets, watching their leader, as Greg regained his balance.

The left half of his head was gone. Squinting, Maren glanced at the hole, prepared to turn away if there was too much gore for her to stomach. To her shock, though, there was no gore at all. No blood, no skull fragments, no gelatinous brain pulp...just black.

Living black. It was the same substance that had come out of his mouth, and it was writhing, bubbling, and expanding to fill the hole. Where it touched the edges of his tattered skin, it fused and changed color to match Greg's complexion then grew inward, knitting his head back together. An eyelid appeared, then an eyeball popped into the space behind it. Hair grew. Flesh sealed together. When the squirming skin finally stilled, Greg looked as if he'd never been shot at all. His mouth spread wider into a huge grin, and he laughed—a dead *ha, ha, ha, ha* so void of humanity that hearing it come from a human mouth felt surreal.

Maren's ears were full of a ringing sound. Her body felt weightless, as though she could lift her feet off the ground and float in midair. Her brain was so sluggish that, for a second, she considered doing just that. A voice was trying to press through the ringing, but she couldn't make out the words. But when Saul's glove squeezed her arm, hard enough for her to feel it through the thick suit, she realized he was talking to her.

"Get into the station," he barked. "Get into the station and lock the doors. Bring Suriya if you can, but don't slow down for her if she won't run."

The ringing sound suddenly made sense: it was Suriya's screams.

Saul shoved something into Maren's hand. She looked down and saw it was a spare gun. Something clicked inside of her, and she tightened her fingers around it. "Understood."

Saul raised his own weapon and leaped over the step, firing toward the man below him as he fell. Maren grabbed Suriya's arm, vaguely relieved to hear the scream choke off—*she must have run out of breath*—and pulled them both over the ledge in Saul's wake.

Her knees jarred as she hit the metal roof, but she didn't dare stop moving. Suriya didn't seem to understand what was happening, so Maren linked her arm through the other woman's and began dragging her.

The figures around them exploded. Their suits shredded, and their helmets burst off as the inky black tendrils spilled out.

Maren caught glimpses of the remains of human bodies as she ran past them. A couple of the creatures still had half of their faces attached. Others had shreds of flesh sticking to the black substance. One had an arm, flopping limply, as though it were waving to them.

I wonder if Holly is here somewhere?

The tendrils were moving impossibly quickly. They lashed toward the running crew, snagging at ankles and bashing into suits. One hit Maren's back, and she stumbled. Cracking gunfire came from Saul's gun as he shot the tendril that had attacked her.

"Don't slow down!" he snarled as he leaped over a tendril that tried to trip him.

Suriya was whining, making a high-pitched sound, like a dog that had lost its owner. Maren tightened her grip on the older woman's arm as she tried to keep her moving. A black tendril caught her ankle and tried to pull her down. She aimed her gun and fired three rounds. They cut through the black substance and sent it thrashing back toward its owner.

"Guys?" Gin's voice came through the whining and the bursts of gunfire. "There's a problem here."

"No kidding," Maren screamed. They'd reached the second step, mostly thanks to Saul's well-aimed fire, and she could see a group of suits waiting for them below. Even as she was trying to count them, they burst apart. More blackness spilled out. Tendrils waved through the air, reaching toward her.

"Eight minutes!" Gin squeaked, then her line went quiet again.

Saul leaped over the ledge, launching himself into the mass of beings below. He held his gun in his right hand and swung a long, serrated knife in his left. They cut through the tendrils, sending twitching tips pattering to the roof, but every arm he severed seemed to be replaced by another two.

Maren pulled her partner up to the edge of the step and tried to push her over, but Suriya started pulling backward.

"No, no, no, no, *no, no, no!*"

"C'mon," Maren grunted, but the other woman was shaking her head so violently that Maren wouldn't have been surprised if she gave herself whiplash.

"Keep running, Maren!" Saul yelled.

"Gah!" Maren managed to get herself behind the other woman and physically pushed her over the edge. "Jump, idiot!"

Suriya shrieked as she fell toward the reaching arms. Maren leaped after her, firing her gun at the arms that were trying to engulf her leader. She landed poorly, jarring her legs again, and dragged Suriya up. The tendrils coiled around her like gigantic, ugly leeches. They were digging into the crevices and rubbing around her helmet's seal, searching for an opening. Maren struggled to pull free, but a being from the ledge above landed on her, knocking her to the ground and winding her.

For a moment, she saw only black—writhing, twitching, coiling black covered her helmet. She was drowning in them. Then a spear of light broke through as Saul's knife hacked the arms out of the way. She stretched her hand toward him and tightened her other fist on Suriya's suit as Saul dragged them both free.

"You guys doing okay?" Gin called into her helmet. She sounded panicked, as though she were seconds from hyperventilating.

"Could be better, honestly," Maren called back as Saul helped her haul Suriya toward the edge of the roof. The red sand stretched ahead of them; above it, the gorgeous sunset had washed almost completely into pastel pinks and yellows, and the glare coming from the sky made it hard to see.

"Three minutes!"

Saul grunted and fell as one of the beings latched onto his legs and dragged him back. The black body, round and with more than a dozen arms extending from its surface, seemed to tremble with excitement as it pulled its prey into itself.

"Don't stop," Saul barked when Maren hesitated. "Get inside. I'll follow!"

Suriya had stopped fighting and hung like a limp doll at Maren's side. Maren wrapped her arms around the other woman's torso and pulled her toward the ledge. It was the highest drop-off, and her position was far from optimal for landing well, but there was no time to hesitate. She threw them both over and did her best to aim her legs at the ground so she could roll when she hit it.

Pain shot up her back as she misjudged the distance, and for a second, there was nothing but dizzying motion and tumbling limbs mixing with the red dirt and near-white sky. Then they rolled to a stop.

Maren drew in a pained gasp. Her ribs ached, and fire ran up her left arm from where she'd landed on it. The door was close, though, just a dozen paces to her right. She grabbed Suriya, who seemed to be unconscious—*please, please don't let her be dead*— and threw the woman over her shoulder before hauling them both up.

The lower gravity was her saving grace, but it still took all of her effort to stand with Suriya on her back. Maren stumbled toward the door to the hangar, panting into her headset, "Maren and Suriya entering air lock, Saul to follow."

"Roger. Two minutes," Gin squeaked.

Even with its bright lights, the air lock seemed shadowy compared to the oversaturated outside world. Maren let out her breath in a heave as she crossed the threshold and dropped Suriya onto the floor, then she turned back to the entrance, expecting to see Saul just behind her.

He wasn't. He was on the dirt, just past where they'd dropped off the roof, struggling with four of the monsters. The gun lay out of his reach, but he still had the knife, and he was slashing at the creatures that had him pinned.

"Saul?"

"Lock the door!"

"One minute," Gin whispered.

Maren heard a crack, and Saul screamed. *His leg,* Maren thought with a rising wave of nausea as she saw one of the tendrils twisting his foot. *They broke his leg.*

She swore. There was no time. She grabbed at the equipment on the shelf, and her hand fixed on a grenade. She pulled the pin as she dashed out of the air lock and toward her defense technician.

"Fifty seconds."

Twenty paces separated them, then fifteen. At ten paces, Maren threw the grenade toward the writhing mass of blackness.

The suits are built to withstand equipment explosions. That should be enough to keep him safe, right?

She was blown onto her back as the grenade exploded in a ball of red-and-black fire. Saul and his attackers disappeared from view, and when the fire cleared, Saul lay alone in a patch of smoking, tar-black lumps.

"Thirty seconds."

The man's off-white suit was blackened, and he wasn't moving. Maren couldn't remember ever running so fast. Her body ached, her heart felt about to burst, and she was drenched in sweat inside her suit. But when she skidded to her knees beside Saul and his helmet turned in her direction, she thought she might cry from relief.

"Get up." She grabbed his arm and pulled. "We've got to get inside."

"Damn you, Maren." He rolled to his knees and hissed with pain. "I can't stand."

"Lean on me."

She wrapped his arm over her suit's shoulders and pulled him up with her. Adrenaline was lending her strength as she got them both to their feet, unsteady and stumbling.

"*Ten seconds, Maren!*"

Saul couldn't put any weight on his broken leg and let it drag across the ground as Maren pulled him toward the hangar. She could hear his pained gasps and feel his arm shaking even through the suits, but he managed to match her speed. They were close.

"*Five seconds! Get in!*" Gin screamed.

Maren closed the distance with three steps then threw them both over the threshold of the hangar. She felt the door skim her boot as it dropped behind her. Then there was a crash, and the door shook. One of the beasts had hit the locked barrier; she could see it through the window, a shred of its human face still attached to the hideous body, one blank eye rolling comically. Then the second reinforcement door slid past the glass, blocking the monster from view.

CHAPTER 26

MAREN LET HER BODY go limp as she lay on the air lock's concrete floor, Saul on her right and Suriya on her left. Her chest was so tight from fear that breathing was nearly impossible.

"Maren?" Gin whispered. "Maren, I swear, you'd better be inside."

"I am." She grinned. "We all are."

Gin released a string of swear words, half of which Maren had never heard before, and finished with, "So help me, I'll kill you myself if you ever scare me like that again. Air lock pressurizing."

Maren felt the gravity return to normal as the station's systems kicked in. She twisted her helmet loose, pulled it off her sweaty face, and inhaled deeply. Suriya still hadn't moved, but Saul had pushed himself into a sitting position and was taking off his own helmet.

"You okay?" she asked.

"That was stupid." He threw the helmet aside. His face was blanched pale from pain, and he had a smear of blood on his jaw from where his lip had been cut, but his expression wasn't angry. It wasn't happy either, and Maren squinted at him, trying to figure out what he was thinking.

"What, you think I can't look after my team?"

"No." His lips twitched slightly, and Maren thought he might actually be trying to smile. "If you'd left me, you'd have automatically become Station 334's defense technician. Saving me was a bad career move."

Maren blinked at him then burst out into laughter. Once she'd started, she couldn't stop and had to wrap her arms around her torso to stabilize her aching ribs. "Damn it, Saul! Reckon there's still time to open a window and toss you back out?"

This time, he did smile—a proper, deep smile that showed his teeth—and Maren found she liked it quite a lot.

The internal door behind them slid open, and Mark pressed inside, his face as white as a sheet. "What can I do? Oh, hell, you guys have gone hysterical, haven't you?" His eyebrows descended in a distrustful frown. "I'm not good with emotional stuff."

Maren glanced at the external door, where she'd last seen the black creature, and sobered. "I'm okay, but Saul's leg is broken. Can you help me carry him?"

"Yeah, sure." Mark sounded relieved. "I can do that."

Maren shimmied out of her suit while Mark cut Saul free from his. The tough, reinforced fabric had suffered serious damage at the hands of the creatures and Maren's grenade. It had tears through many of its layers, and the front of it was charred black, but Maren still needed a pair of wire clippers to slice it open.

"Jeez, that looks nasty," Maren said as she cut Saul's uniform off his broken leg. Large, dark-red bruises were forming along the shin. "How badly does it hurt?"

"Yes" was all he said.

"Well, we can put a splint on now and give you some painkillers, but we'll need to wait for Suriya to treat it properly."

Maren glanced at the older woman, the only one out of them with comprehensive medical training, and once again felt a flutter of fear in her chest as she wondered if their leader was in a fit state to do *anything*. She hadn't moved at all since they'd gotten inside. Maren imagined pulling the helmet off her leader's head and seeing a ghost-white face underneath, twisted into a death grimace, and pushed the image out of her mind with a shudder.

She pulled the first-aid kit off the wall then grabbed two straight, smooth brackets from the shelves and held them on either side of Saul's leg while she bound them tightly with a bandage. "Sorry," she said as he squinted against the pain. "Mark, can you get him two of those tablets?"

"No," Saul said through gritted teeth.

"Come on; they'll help the pain."

"Dull my senses," he managed. "Can't afford it."

Maren sighed and tied off the bandage. "Okay. Well, we'll get you somewhere you can rest at least. Mark, help me get him up."

They each hooked an arm under one of Saul's shoulders and lifted him. Maren's legs felt weak as the adrenaline leaked out of her system, but Saul was able to carry almost all of his weight as he lifted his injured leg high and hopped between them.

"Where to?" Mark asked as they exited the air lock and turned down the hallway.

"Let's get to the communications room," Maren said. "We'll get Saul onto the bench, go back for Suriya, then see what Gin can tell us about the those…things…whatever attacked us."

"Maren."

She'd been so busy watching their feet, Maren hadn't realized Gin was standing in the hallway ahead of them. She had her arms wrapped around her body, and tears were leaking down her cheeks as she shook.

"Hey, hey, it's okay," Maren said quickly. "We're here. We're all right."

"No, it's…it's…Holly."

"What?" Mark nearly dropped Saul, and Maren had to tighten her grip on the bear-sized man to stop them from tumbling over.

"Hey," Maren barked. "Get him into the room first."

Gin stepped out of the way so they could move into the communications room. Maren used her spare hand to swipe a bundle of paperwork off the bench that ran along the back then they eased Saul into the clear space. He leaned back with a sigh.

Maren turned to Gin and gripped her shoulders. "Okay. What about Holly?"

"She's outside." Fresh tears were leaking down Holly's cheeks as she pointed to the screen suspended above her desk. "She's dying."

CHAPTER 27

MAREN, HORRIFIED, MOVED TOWARD the screen. It was tuned to the camera above the air lock's external door, which they'd barely gotten through moments before. A woman stood outside, wearing her full suit, beating her gloved fists against the door. The camera had been calibrated to look through the tinted helmet glass, and Holly's delicate face, wide eyed and drenched with sweat, pleaded with them.

"No!" Mark screamed, shoving past Maren and pressing his hands to the screen as though he could help her through the camera. "Holly!"

"How?" Maren asked, dumbfounded. "The flare's already started—"

"It hasn't fully hit yet," Saul said from the back of the room. He had his arms crossed over his chest as he watched the screen. "And she's in the shaded part of the station. She's got one, maybe two minutes."

Mark turned on Gin and seized the front of her blouse. "Open the doors!"

"I can't!" she yelled back, fresh tears running down her face. "We're in lockdown, remember? I'm not able to override the system. No way in; no way out!"

Mark swore, staggered away from Gin, and grabbed Maren's suit. His hands, clammy and shaking, clasped at her collar. "Please, there's got to be something we can do. You can't let her die out there. *You can't.*"

Maren looked back at the screen. Holly was suffering; she gasped in thin, pained breaths as she continued to beat against the door, but it was clear she didn't have long.

"There's no way out during a lockdown. The whole station is airtight. You'd need to override the system's settings, and to do that, you'd need the commander's authorization chip, and I don't even know where to start looking for that—"

"And even if you did, I wouldn't give it to you." Suriya stood in the doorway. One bony hand was clamped tightly on a chip attached to a chain hung around her neck. Maren had seen it before but never assigned any significance to it.

Suriya was swaying slightly, her eyes fixed on the screen above the communication desk. A very strange smile spread over her face. "No. We'll watch her *burn.*"

She's lost it. Maren gaped at their supervisor. *She was already on the edge, and those monsters out there pushed her over it.*

Holly, outside the door, lost her balance and fell to her knees. She was still knocking at the door, but the motion was weak and erratic. Her eyes had glazed, and her mouth was open as she drew slow, pained breaths.

"You monster!" Mark lunged for their leader, snatching at the chip hung around her neck, but Suriya saw him coming and sidestepped.

"*I'm* not the monster," she hissed, her demeanor turning cold and angry. "*She's* a monster. She's one of them. Oh, yes, she wears a pretty face, but inside, she's just *black, black, black.*"

"Are you insane?" Mark screamed. "She's nothing like those-those things. Something must have happened at her station, so she came back to us for shelter! Let her in!"

"She may be one of the creatures." Saul watched the screen intently, his brow creased as he examined the woman's face. "But I can't tell…and I don't want to lose one of our own. We should quarantine her in the air lock."

"Yes," Maren gasped, stretching a hand toward Suriya, begging her for the chip. "We'll do that. Don't let her die out there, Suriya. Please."

"I'd rather see every single one of you die than let one of those beasts into my station," Suriya snarled, drawing away.

Mark launched himself at his commander again, and this time, Suriya didn't see him in time. His fist connected with her jaw, sending her crashing to the ground. In her shock, she let go of the chip around her neck. Mark grabbed it, snapping the chain with a ferocious tug that made Suriya gasp.

"Here," he barked, shoving it at Gin. "Open the damn door!"

She took the chip but hesitated. Her eyes found Maren's, silently asking if it was okay.

"I said open the door!" Mark drew his gun and pointed it at Gin's face.

She flinched and raised her hands.

"Hey!" Maren yelled, but Mark had the gun on her before she could take more than a step forward.

"No one move! I swear I'll shoot! Gin, open the doors—both of them. Now!"

Gin swallowed, turned to her control board, and slotted the chip into the authorization connection. The light above it switched to green.

Maren glanced at the screen. Holly lay on the ground, immobile. The heat made the red dirt behind her seem to glow.

Gin's fingers were moving over the control board in a blur as she muttered. "Confirming authority. Accessing lockdown system. Overriding lockdown protocol. Opening air lock internal door. Opening air lock external door."

Mark whirled and ran through the door. Maren listened to his footsteps fading down the hallway then turned back to the screen as Gin changed the camera to the one that looked inside the air lock. Mark appeared, dropping his gun, and wrenched up the external door. There was a blast of light, and the entrance seemed to shimmer from the blistering heat coming through it, but Mark barely hesitated before reaching out, grabbing the suited figure on the threshold, and dragging her inside the air lock. He slammed the external door then began working Holly's helmet off.

"Lock the doors," Saul said, his voice quiet.

Gin nodded and pressed a series of buttons to reseal both air lock doors. Then she withdrew the chip from the authorization connection.

"Do you, uh, want this back?" Meekly, she offered the chip to Suriya.

The tall woman had gathered herself to her feet and was hovering in the corner of the room, the back of her hand pressed to her bleeding lip. She glared murderously at Gin as she took a half step forward and snatched the chip to her chest. After glancing at each of them in turn, she swiveled toward the door and left at a run.

"Jeez," Maren muttered. She'd covered mental health briefly during her training for maintenance and much more extensively during her defense technician training. "Breakdowns are much more common than you might expect," the instructors had all said. "Keep a close eye on your coworkers for any warning signs." Humans were beautifully resilient but also incredibly fragile... and something about the solitude and restrictions of space could tap on a person's fragile parts, quietly and gently, until that person broke.

Many larger stations—including 334, when it wasn't in hibernation—had full-time psychologists to identify and treat problems before they could take root. Crew members who showed signs of fracturing were quickly reassigned to less stressful, more Earth-like planets. Maren couldn't help but wonder if Suriya's letter, suggesting her relocation to a different station, had been a result of a mental health assessment.

Maren turned her attention back to the screen looking into the air lock. Mark had gotten Holly's helmet off and was cradling her body, caressing her face with more tenderness than Maren had ever seen him express. Gin leaned forward on her desk, hands clasped under her chin. Maren placed an arm around her shoulder, felt her friend tremble, and squeezed.

Inside the air lock, the young woman twitched then stirred, and her eyes opened.

"Oh, thank goodness," Gin whispered, slumping over her desk.

Maren let her breath out with a whoosh, but she didn't dare look away. She couldn't see him, but she suspected Saul was watching the screen just as intently as she was.

Mark pulled Holly into a semi-sitting pose, still cradling her head. Holly smiled and raised a hand to stroke Mark's face. She was speaking to him, but the screen didn't relay sound. Mark's shoulders shook, and Holly covered the back of his hand with hers. Maren could lip-read what the woman was saying: "Thank you."

She leaned up as Mark leaned down, and they kissed. Maren, realizing she was intruding on a very personal moment, cleared her throat and turned away. "You doing okay, Saul?"

"Hmm."

"Want some of those pain tablets now?"

His eyebrows lowered, and his mouth narrowed. "Look."

Maren turned back to the screen.

The couple was still kissing, but something wasn't right. Mark seemed to be struggling to tug his head backward. He let go of Holly, but she stayed pressed against him, her hands on either side of his head as she held him still. He started twitching.

CHAPTER 28

GIN SMOTHERED A SHRIEK, and her hands began fluttering over the control panel. "The chip—I don't have the chip to open the doors."

"I doubt we could help him anyway," Saul said.

Mark was actively fighting her, batting his hands against Holly's chest. As he pulled to one side and their angle changed, Maren was able to see Holly's face. It had split down its center, from the hairline to the chin, and terrible, squirming black tendrils were stretching out to stick against Mark's face. His body was convulsing horribly, but he couldn't escape the blackness.

Gin scrambled out of her chair, both hands covering her mouth. She looked nauseated as she watched the screen. Maren, whose stomach had been unsteady for most of the afternoon and was threatening to upend itself again, couldn't tear her eyes away from the repulsive spectacle.

The monster that had been Holly pushed Mark onto his back. He'd stopped fighting, and his arms were limp by his side, though he was still twitching. Holly finally pulled back, the tendrils lazily retreating into her face. The skin pulled back over them, knitting together seamlessly, until there was no sign of the creature anymore. It was just Holly, leaning over her lover, smiling down at him with such sweetness that it was hard for Maren to imagine the woman didn't adore him.

"Oh hell." Gin turned and was sick in the wastebasket.

The corners of Saul's mouth drew down, but his voice maintained its usual softness as he said, "That's how they reproduce."

"What?" Gin gasped, appearing over the lid of the bin.

Saul didn't reply, so Maren explained as she shakily poured a glass of water for Gin out of the pitcher in the corner. "Saul thinks—he thinks they don't have babies—but they spread through infection, like a virus."

There was more motion on the screen. Mark was sitting up. He swayed for a moment, then Holly helped him gain his feet. They stood facing each other for half a minute, eyes locked, then they both turned toward the door. Mark's movements had none of his usual swagger; they were mechanical, perfunctory. He and Holly stood side by side, stock-still, their blank faces fixed on the door.

"I don't want to watch," Gin said, tears in her voice. "I want to turn the camera off."

Saul sighed. "We need to ensure they don't try to escape." He paused, taking his eyes off the screen to glance at the women. "Look away if it bothers you."

Gin slumped into her chair, holding her half-consumed glass of water loosely, as she stared at the dials. Mark and Holly showed no signs of movement, and Maren, with mental health so prominently in her mind, scrambled to find a distraction that would keep her friend's mind off the monsters in the next room.

"The system's back up at least, right?"

"Yeah." Gin took a gulp of water. "Good job on fixing it, I guess."

Saul's eyes were still alert, but he had leaned back against the wall. "There's a light on your dash, Gin."

"Huh?"

"The urgent-info-package signal."

Gin laughed, and the sound scared Maren. It wasn't Gin's normal bubbly, infectious chuckle, but a dead and cold sound. "Yeah, I wonder if there's anything dangerous out there they need to warn us about."

"Saul's right." Maren patted Gin's shoulder. "We need to listen to it. It might have something to help us."

Gin looked at her, then at Saul. Her eyes fell very briefly on the screen before she turned back to the communication desk. "Yeah, sure. Okay."

Maren breathed a little easier as she watched Gin's fingers dance over the control panel. Her friend's face was returning to the serene state she usually adopted when working.

"Okay, so, with the system back up, we've been receiving

a swarm of messages. Looks like this thing is spreading—and quickly."

"Yeah," Maren sighed, glancing back at the screen where Mark and Holly stood next to each other, as still as mannequins. "I imagine it would."

She thought of the crew of Station 488 and how they'd surrounded Maren's small team. She'd known a lot of them from before the hibernation. Kelly, Chai, Devon, Petros, Mag…the extent of the loss hit her, and suddenly she was having trouble breathing. She would never get another chance to watch Kravos dance on the dining room tables when he got too drunk. Ella would never finish her mural. Jules would never again laugh at Maren when she had a bad hair day, and she wouldn't hear Ignus tell her to shut up. Pete had talked incessantly about his wife and child waiting for him on Mandola, and he would never get to see them again—or get to kiss his toddler's cheek or embrace his wife. *No chance to say goodbye. All gone. All dead.*

Maren wrapped her arms around her stomach, trying to squash the ache blooming inside. *Don't cry, idiot. Save your own mental breakdown for when Gin and Saul are safe.*

She looked at them, and the tightness in her chest eased. At least Gin, her favorite person in the universe, was safe; and at least Saul, who had unknowingly been her inspiration and idol, was still alive. She realized that those two people were more important than just friends; they were as good as family. And as long as her family was with her and safe, she could survive anything.

Maren stepped behind Gin and wrapped her arms around the other woman's torso, giving her a fierce hug.

Gin peered up, and her face dimpled into a familiar smile. "Hey, I'm okay. I'm better now."

"Good."

"Ready for the info package?"

Once again, Maren glanced at the two people in the air lock and nodded. "Go for it."

Gin pressed two more buttons, and crackling filled the speakers. Usually, the info packets started with an announcement of the speaker and the location, which was almost always Central, spoken by a crisp, cool woman or man. This one, though, was different: for nearly half a minute, the only sound was low, ragged breathing, punctuated by thick gulps.

"This is..." A woman's voice spoke at last then hesitated before continuing. "This is communications manager Cody from Station 651. I am currently at Central, which I evacuated to after the death of both of my coworkers. My superiors do not think I should be sharing this information with you, but I have barricaded myself in the communications room with the intention of warning you and preparing you to the best of my abilities. I suspect I will only have a few minutes until they realize I'm here.

"You may be aware of the emergency information package sent earlier today. It is, I'm afraid, inexcusably negligent. To clear up some rumors: Yes, we are under attack. Yes, Central is aware. Yes, Central is hopelessly underprepared for this threat. And yes,

Central intended to keep the vast majority of our network in the dark while they attempted to protect the sections they thought were savable. They didn't want anyone to *panic*."

The woman's laugh was filled with bitterness and grief, but a frenzied banging sound interrupted her. Maren guessed Central's security had discovered the barricaded door.

"I have never before seen anything like the being that is currently threatening to overwhelm our society. In one form, it looks like a black, slimy creature with many long, flexible arms. In another form, it looks like your roommate, your best friend, or even your child. It is a parasite; it doesn't kill its hosts—not completely at least—but it *absorbs* them and *becomes* them. It can mimic their face, their speech, their expressions and mannerisms. It even takes their memories. There could be one standing beside you this minute, and you wouldn't know except if you cut them. Humans *bleed*. The aliens *don't*."

The beating on the door was becoming louder, more frantic. It sounded as though someone had found a makeshift ram.

"I'm calling them Cymic Parasites in honor of my mentor, Doctor Cymic, who sacrificed himself to ensure I could escape. He was able to identify what they were and what they could do. The parasite lives inside its host, using the human face to gain trust, but it can roll up its disguise at any moment and attack. You cannot kill them with knives or guns. I've only found one thing effective against them: fire. If you cook them, you kill them. Grenades, flamethrowers, incinerators—use whatever you can get your hands on to defend yourself. Bullets and knives can only ever slow them down."

There was a splintering sound in the background; the door was breaking.

"This is spreading quickly, and it's spreading violently. Hundreds of stations have already fallen or are in the process of falling. Do your best to get to one of the safe sections of the network—I believe Central, certain parts of Bargove, and the Eastern quadrant of Eulectics System are being turned into safe havens, and they have makeshift testing facilities at their ports to guard against the Cymic Parasites."

The shouting voices became clear, followed by more splintering. Cody chuckled. "Looks like my time is up. I've done as much as I can. The rest is up to you. Good luck."

CHAPTER 29

THE COMMUNICATION ENDED WITH a quiet click. Maren, her arms still around Gin, felt her friend shudder. She gave her another squeeze then pulled away to pace through the room.

A glance at the screen showed Mark and Holly hadn't moved. They might as well have been hibernating. Saul had his arms crossed, and his half-closed eyes stared at the floor. None of them spoke for a long time; Maren couldn't find the right words, and her companions seemed deep in thought.

Gin broke it at last with a surprisingly resigned tone. "This is the end, isn't it?"

"What?" Maren stopped pacing.

"How can you fight a monster when you can't tell them apart from your friends?" Gin was looking at the screen, and her voice was choking up. "That woman spoke about safe places, but really, all it will take is one tiny mistake—an act of mercy or one of the staff letting their family through without testing—and the whole planet could be wiped out in a day."

"People are going to learn how to fight these things," Maren said. "They'll develop scanners and protective suits and special guns. Yes, it's nearly impossible to tell a Cymic Parasite apart from a human at the moment, but that won't be the case for long. We'll find efficient ways of identifying and killing them."

"Fast enough, though?" Gin asked. Her eyes were rimmed red, but at least she'd lost the earlier listlessness that had scared Maren so badly. "Look how fast they're spreading! Look how many stations are still sending through requests for help!"

"Hey." Maren gripped Gin's shoulders and gave her a gentle shake. "We're getting through this. All three of us. We're going to be safe here. We've got food and water to last us for months. Sooner or later, someone will rescue us, then we'll get to one of the safe planets. It's going to be fine."

Gin was crying again. *Damn it,* Maren thought. *She's gone into shock.*

She went back to the water pitcher and refilled Gin's glass. There was a quiet beep above her, and the red light in the corner turned green, signaling the end of the lockdown. She heard quiet rumbling noises from through the station as the external-facing doors' reinforcements were reset. "I'm going to get some blankets, okay?" she said as she pressed the glass into Gin's hand. "I'll be back in a minute."

"Maren," Saul said, his voice low.

She shot him a grin. "You want a blanket, too?"

"No. We need to go."

Maren followed his gaze to the screen, and her heart sank. Holly and Mark had moved; she saw a flutter of Holly's light-brown hair as she disappeared below the camera's line of sight. *Toward the door.*

"What are they…?"

A loud thud from down the hallway answered her question. They were trying to break through the door, to get into the station. *Of course—the air lock doors are double-sealed during lockdown. Holly and Mark hadn't gone into hibernation; they'd been waiting.*

Maren squeezed her eyes closed, trying to think of somewhere they could hide. The weapons room was her first choice; it was double reinforced and had enough ammunition to supply a full station, but it lacked food and water. They would be forced to leave it in less than a day. The kitchen had more than enough supplies, only its doors were made of thin metal. *But…*

"We need to get to the rec room," she said, striding toward Saul as the beating coming from the hallway became louder. "It backs onto the pantry, plus Saul's monitors will be invaluable."

"Good," Saul said, easing himself off the bench. Maren placed herself on his right and wrapped his arm around her shoulder so she would be taking most of his weight, and Gin quickly took his left side. Together, they moved out of the communications room, pausing briefly to check the door to the air lock, which had developed a bulge. Then they turned right, toward the rec room.

Saul was moving quickly, but Maren could tell the leg was hurting him. His face, which had regained its color after the rest in the communications room, had turned white again, and the hand on her shoulder gripped her so firmly that it was almost painful. She placed her hand over his, squeezing back, trying to convey that it would be okay. Saul glanced at her, and she thought she saw his mouth twitch into a gentle smile before his gaze returned to the hallway ahead.

Not for the first time that day, the size of the station frustrated Maren. She knew a lot of stations—especially the rural ones—were much smaller and only intended to house a staff of three. The crews there often complained of feeling trapped, claiming the restrictive space was enough to send them crazy, but Maren thought there were definite benefits to being able to cross a station in under a minute.

They took a left, then a right, and followed another long hallway before reaching the entrance to the rec room. Just as they eased Saul inside, a loud screeching, metallic noise came from deeper in the station.

They're out, Maren thought, and Saul's quick intake of breath confirmed her suspicions.

Saul released her and leaned against the wall instead. "Go. I'll lock this door. You get the others."

Maren sprinted right, toward the second entrance to the rec room, while Gin ran in the opposite direction.

The rec room had been designed as an emergency containment room. It was large enough to hold the station's entire eighty-six staff, and the double-reinforced and insulated doors could be manually locked in case the lockdown equipment malfunctioned or the station's outer hull was breached. Maren skidded to a halt beside the second set of doors and slammed her fist against the red button below the communication unit. The door slid down, blocking the corridor outside. An identical communication unit just outside the doors would let other station members open them. She would need to lock the doors manually with an access code that couldn't be overridden.

"Saul?" Maren called.

"Five-one-one-six-eight-two-seven," he called back.

Maren entered his code then selected the "door lock" option. The light turned green.

Every member of the station had a unique access code, but some held more weight than others. Maren, being a maintenance worker, had one of the lowest code ranks, which almost every other station member could override. On the other hand, only the station commander could supersede the defense technician's code.

"Locked," she called, already running toward the final door. A second later, Gin echoed her with another, "Locked!"

Maren paused in front of the fourth door, her hand hovering over the access pad, and glanced down the hallway, which led into the pantry. *We need water. If Mark and Holly tried to follow us through the main passageway, this could be our best chance to grab some supplies.*

"Maren!" Saul called, but she ignored him and dashed through the doorway, her boots echoing on the concrete floor.

The pantry, a rectangular concrete room the size of a small warehouse, held enough long-life food and bottled water to last a full station for over a month. The shelves closest to her door were filled with powdered nutrients and vitamins, but she jogged past them, trying to remember where the water was stored.

A quiet, grating sound made her pause. She listened, trying to figure out where it was coming from. *The dining room? The bathrooms beyond that?*

She quieted her steps as much as possible as she continued to creep through the warehouse. The shelves, laid out in neat rows on either side of her, were filled with every edible supply the station might need, including baby formula and food devoid of every possible allergen.

The scraping sound seemed to be getting closer. Maren barely dared to breathe as she lowered herself into a crouch. She needed to get back to the rec room as quickly as possible, but if rescue took more than a day—and she strongly suspected it would—they would need as much water as she could carry.

Finally, right at the opposite end of the storage room, Maren found the water. There was a large silo set into the wall with a tap at its base, and the shelves surrounding it were filled with plastic jugs and bottles filled with the precious liquid. Maren grabbed two jugs, which were all she was capable of carrying, and began slinking back the way she'd come. The scraping sound had fallen silent, but somehow that frightened her more than the noise had.

The jugs of water were heavy, and Maren's injured knee and back began to ache before she'd taken a dozen paces. She paused to adjust her grip, and when she looked up, Mark blocked her path.

CHAPTER 30

A SMOOTH SMILE SPREAD over Mark's face. It was a very familiar look; one he'd given her hundreds of times before, whenever he was trying to charm her into helping with his chores. "Hello, Maren." His voice was happy, friendly, and just a little bit mischievous. "How've you been?"

Maren swore as she froze. She could feel sweat beading over her body and a metallic taste enter her mouth as the adrenaline kicked in, lending her energy as she assessed her predicament. Mark was blocking the most direct passage back to the rec room, and Maren was both weaponless and weighted down with the water.

"I'm not angry at you for getting Holly sent out of our station earlier, you know," Mark said, hands in his pockets, rolling on the balls of his feet. His every expression, every motion, was so characteristically *Mark* that if Maren hadn't seen the slack-faced zombie facing the air lock doors as he waited for the security to be dropped, trusting him would have been all too easy.

"It worked out for the best, anyway." He tilted his head and winked. "We can be together now. Forever. And not just Holly and me, but you, and Gin, and Suriya, and Saul. We'll all join together, like a big family. You'll be my sister. Doesn't that sound nice?"

I could drop the water and make a run for it, but he'd catch me easily. Holly must be somewhere nearby too.

Mark took a step forward, and Maren echoed him by stepping backward. Her arms were aching from holding the jugs, but she didn't dare drop them.

The monster wearing her friend's skin chuckled, and his smile widened until it looked painful. "Don't worry. This will only take a minute." His smile widened again, splitting open his face, and writhing black tendrils filled the gap where his teeth should have been. Maren felt rooted to the spot, and she opened her mouth to scream, but the noise died in her throat.

A loud crack made her flinch, and the spot that had been Mark's deformed head seemed to explode. A shower of black flesh flew across the room, one lump hitting Maren's face. It squirmed, still very much alive, and Maren gagged as it wriggled into her open mouth. It tasted vile, like a mixture of rotting meat and metal.

"Don't swallow," Saul yelled, and Maren doubled over, trying to spit out the foreign creature. It stuck to her tongue, so she dropped one of the water bottles and shoved her fingers in her mouth. She grabbed the slimy shape, tore it out, and threw it aside with a gasp of disgust.

Mark stood before her, swaying drunkenly. His head was completely gone, and the neckline of his uniform had been blasted away from the heat of the bullet. Already, though, the black substance was growing out of where his neck ended, twisting around itself to form the shape of a head, the ragged edges of the skin blooming upward.

Beyond Mark was the hallway, and at the end of the hallway, pointing a gun at Mark's remains, was Saul. "Run!"

Maren did. She skidded past Mark and raced toward the hallway, toward safety, the remaining jug of water clutched to her chest. Mark seemed to sense her motion, and one hand lashed out, grabbing at her, but she ducked under it.

A scraping sound gave her warning, and Maren leaped to one side as a shelf toppled over. Its contents crashed to the ground she'd been standing on a second before. Maren caught a blur of motion out of the corner of her eyes, then suddenly, Holly blocked her path. The woman's face was split in multiple places, letting the pulsing black out to taste the air, and what remained of it looked furious. One of the tendrils shot out toward her, blindingly fast. Maren threw herself to one side and felt the black arm graze her suit.

Another loud crack from Saul's gun left half of Holly's torso burst open, leaving the head dangling by a few strands of black. Maren pushed herself forward, into the hallway, ducking as Saul fired more rounds past her. The cracks were deafening in the concrete passageway, and Maren squeezed her eyes closed as she skidded through the opening and into the rec room.

"Now," Saul snarled, and Gin, who had been standing with her hand over the red emergency button below the control panel, pressed it. The door dropped, and there were two loud thuds as the creatures hit the other side.

"Five-one-one-six-eight-two-seven," Saul said, his voice quiet again, his gun still trained on the closed door. Gin entered the access code, sealing out the monsters. As soon as he heard the quiet beep of the door locking, Saul dropped his gun to the ground and leaned against the wall. He'd been putting weight on the broken leg, Maren saw, and his face was ghost white as he held out a hand to her. "Come here."

Leaving the water carton on the ground, Maren stepped toward the defense technician. He gripped her shoulder then raised the hand to press against her neck, his large fingers seeking her pulse. When he found it, he let out a sigh and closed his eyes. "You okay?"

"Yeah." She took a shuddering breath and smiled at him. "Thanks."

"It's my job."

He let go of her, and Maren realized how unwell he was. His eyelids fluttered as he slid down the wall, his broken leg at an odd angle. "Gin," Maren said, quickly grabbing Saul's arm and pulling him up. Gin hurried to his other side, and they managed to drag him to one of the maroon four-seater couches and lay him down. Being as careful as they could, they lifted his broken leg.

Maren hurried to one of the tables and grabbed a bowl of potpourri, which had been left there by one of the station's old staff. She tipped the dried flowers out, dusted it clean with her sleeve, and filled it with water from the jug.

"Here," she said, kneeling beside Saul and pressing the bowl to his lips.

He drank then laid his head back and closed his eyes. His breathing was still ragged but at least a little less raspy. With an overwhelming sense of helplessness, Maren stayed kneeling beside him, watching his chest rise and fall.

Gin sat beside Maren, her large green eyes filled with a mixture of awe and fear. "You sure you're okay?"

"I think so." Maren wiped her sleeve over the sweat on her forehead. Her heart was still beating hard, and her legs felt weak, but at least she wasn't hurt. "Sorry about that. I put you guys in danger."

"Got us some water, though," Gin said, a little of the usual optimism creeping back into her voice. "So that's pretty cool, I guess."

Maren glanced at the jug of water she'd left by the table. It held eight liters. That should last the three of them...*a little over three days*. She grimaced. "Central better get its rescue teams organized pretty damn quickly."

Gin squeezed her hand, and Maren squeezed it back. Then she clambered to her feet, the aches, bruises, and strains suddenly returning with a vengeance as the adrenaline wore off. She stumbled to one of the cupboards that held bundles of throw blankets and spare supplies. She grabbed three of the blankets and the first-aid kit that was stored on the top shelf. She gave one of the blankets to Gin then spread the other two over Saul's unconscious form.

Then, very carefully, she unwrapped the bandages from Saul's leg. The bruising had spread and turned an angry red. Maren frowned, wishing she'd joined the optional emergency medical care course offered during her training. She repositioned the crooked braces and strapped the leg back up. Saul shivered but didn't wake fully.

"That's the best I can do." Maren sighed and closed the first-aid kit.

A pounding noise on the door behind them made Maren jump. One of the creatures had circled around to try the other doors, she guessed. Gin grimaced then got up and crossed the room to where Saul had set up his security video equipment. She unplugged it, pushed its gurney across the room until it stood in front of Saul's lounge, and replugged it into the nearest wall. Images from the cameras positioned about the station filled the screens.

"Here." Gin grabbed a bundle of pillows from the nearby couches and threw half of them at Maren. "We may as well get comfortable. We might be here for a while."

CHAPTER 31

THE HOURS TICKED BY slowly. Both Maren and Gin watched the screens, trying to keep track of Holly and Mark, who had split up to rove through the station. Every now and then, they would return to one of the rec room's four doors and try to open it, first by pressing on the handle then by entering their access codes, but Maren and Gin had no intention of opening any of the passageways if they could help it.

Saul stirred a few times before falling into what Maren hoped was a natural sleep. When she pressed her hand to his forehead, she found it hot and feverish, so she'd used a small amount of their precious water to wet a cloth and dab it over his face. Gin took stock of what was kept in the rec room's fridge and found a few cans of fruit juice, some packets of chips, gummy candy, and a bag of dehydrated fruit slices.

They ate some of the food to replenish their energy and drank enough water to keep themselves hydrated. Maren ran the calculations through her head a half dozen times: if they drank just enough to stay healthy, they would have enough fluids for three days. They would either need to be rescued or have to take their chances in the pantry again.

Saul's leg would need to be set, and soon, before the bones started fusing. Neither she nor Gin knew enough to do it themselves. Suriya had doubled as their medical officer during the hibernation.

Mark and Holly stalked the hallways of the station for nearly four hours before settling down in the pantry, hidden behind the rows of shelves. Nearly an hour passed before Maren saw more motion on the screen.

"Hey," she said, nudging Gin, who'd fallen asleep on her shoulder. "Look."

Suriya shambled down the central hallway. She moved slowly and erratically, pausing frequently, her head swiveling to watch the passageways around her. Her right hand gripped a long, sharp serrated knife; Maren could see the fluorescent light glinting off its edge.

Gin shivered and rubbed at her face. "Jeez, I'd forgotten she was still here. You don't think…"

"She's still human," Maren said, watching in fascination as the older woman bent forward to look down one of the side passageways. "That's why Mark and Holly were going through the station; they were searching for Suriya, but she must have managed to hide somewhere they didn't think to look."

"Jeez," Gin muttered. "Should we let her in?"

Suriya turned to glance behind herself, and for a moment, Maren was able to see her face. The commander's eyes bugged, her lips were drawn tight, and there was an edge of ferocity to her that Maren hadn't seen before. Suriya swung the knife slowly as she turned forward again, and Maren realized what was so disquieting about the way she was behaving. She wasn't hiding; she was stalking. Instead of trying to reach a safe part of the station, she was searching for prey.

"Nope," Maren said, wrapping her arms around herself. "I don't think that would help *anyone*."

"Good call," Saul said, and both women swiveled to look at him. His eyes were open, and his face had regained some of its color.

Maren felt a rush of relief. "Hey, you doing okay?" she asked, getting to her knees. "Want some water?"

"Not just yet." Saul was watching the screens, and Maren had the impression he'd been awake for some time without them knowing.

Suriya continued down the hallways, searched in the communications and dining rooms—barely twenty feet away from where Holly and Mark lurked in the pantry—and finally tried the rec room. Maren heard the door behind her rattle a second before she saw Suriya shake the handle on the screen. Their leader then turned, seemed to think for a moment, and continued down the hallway that led to her office. She slipped inside, closed the door, and was lost from their view.

"What do you think Holly and Mark are doing?" Gin asked. "Do you think they're tired?"

"I'd guess they're waiting." Maren stretched, arching her back. Everything felt sore. "I don't know if they need to eat, but they know *we* need to, and that we'll be forced out of here when we run out of water."

Gin sighed and rubbed her palm over her face again.

She looks exhausted, Maren thought with a pang of pity.

"So we're just going to cross our fingers and hope help comes before then?"

"That's the plan, yeah. At least we're a pretty important station."

"Not quite important enough." Gin chuckled, but it was a hollowed sound. "Remember, Central probably dispatched just about all of their emergency response teams to the early requests, back when no one knew there was a problem. How many of those teams would have made it back? Alive, I mean. Central won't care about having a highly connected communications system. They'll care about fortifying and protecting the planets they can still save. We're unnecessary."

Maren sighed. She hadn't thought about it that way, but Gin was right. There was no point in saving a communications station that received signals from remote planets if you were preparing to let those planets fall.

"What are we going to do?" she asked.

Gin shrugged, still watching the screens. "Survive as long as we can, I guess. We've got a gun with enough bullets to…you know…if we don't want to be absorbed by whatever got Holly and Mark."

"Jeez," Maren said.

Gin leaned her head on Maren's shoulder, a small act of comfort in the face of certain death.

"Do you have any regrets?" Gin asked.

"Huh?"

"Like, things you wished you could have done."

Maren thought it over briefly. There were a lot of things she'd be sad to never have the chance to do, she realized. "I never got that promotion to defense technician. And I was sort of looking forward to my leave coming up next year. I miss my home planet. I want to see trees again. Lots of trees and rain and snow and real dirt. Everything's so dead here." She could feel her throat choking up, so she cleared it quickly. "How about you?"

Gin was quiet for a moment before answering. "I really wanted children."

"Yeah?"

"Yeah. Find a nice guy, settle down on a civilian planet, have a couple of kids. Maybe four or five."

Maren laughed. "Four or five? I'd go crazy."

"Shut up. Children are adorable." Gin poked Maren's arm. "You can dress them up in really cute clothes and tiny shoes and hats and cook them pancakes in the shape of smiley faces and take them to the park on Sundays…yeah, I guess I really wanted some of my own." A mischievous smile spread over her face. "I guess we have the opposite problem. I spent too much time on my career, you didn't spend enough."

Maren laughed then tilted her head back to look at Saul upside down. "What about you? Did you want kids?"

He raised his eyebrows.

"Okay, okay. Anything you regret?"

"No," he said, leaving Maren with the distinct impression that he was lying. They sat in silence for another minute before Saul spoke again. "I can't get you back to your home planet, but I can give you something else."

"Hmm?"

"As of now, I'm officially resigned from the defense technician post. As the only other qualified crew member on the station, that role now belongs to you. Congratulations."

Maren stared at him then felt a huge grin spread over her face. It was a meaningless position now that they were trapped, but the thoughtfulness touched her deeply, and she blinked back tears. "Wow. Thanks, Saul."

"Hmm." He closed his eyes again, but she thought she saw the corners of his mouth twitch up.

They sat in silence for a long time, sharing a bag of gummy candy and water. After an hour of the silence, Gin got up and started pacing the room while Saul slept and Maren watched the screens. It was mind-numbingly dull, and Maren had started to drift off when a siren made her jump. The screen in the corner of the room had turned red and was counting down from two hours and fifteen minutes.

Maren clambered to her feet and stretched. Her muscles had become stiff, but at least the aches were easing.

"Wish there was a way to let the rays into the station," Gin said from where she was perched on the billiard table near the back of the room. "I bet it would fry them up real good."

"Yeah." Maren flashed a smile at her friend, who returned it wearily.

Gin's eyes were rimmed with red, and her cheeks were missing their healthy pink flush. Maren tried to remember the last time Gin had slept properly. It must have been at least a day—Gin's shift had been nearing its end when the communications system had broken, and she'd had nothing but stress since then. "Hey, grab a blanket, find a quiet corner, and get some sleep."

"No, I'm good," Gin said, making her smile a little larger to demonstrate.

"Really, you need sleep. We've got to watch the screens in shifts, anyway, so you may as well rest while I'm awake."

Gin nodded, kicked off the billiard table, and fetched some throw blankets from the cupboard. Then she retreated to one of the couches in a shadowy corner of the room.

Maren paced through the recreation room a few times to wake herself up before returning to Saul and the screens. There wasn't anything to see; Holly and Mark continued to camp in the supplies room, carefully hidden from sight, and Suriya hadn't ventured out of the office. Maren couldn't help wondering what their commander was doing—sleeping, maybe, like Gin, or awake, sitting in the wicker chair nestled in the corner, watching the door, that vicious kitchen knife swinging like a pendulum in her bony hand.

The red screen in the corner of the room counted down to the next flare: two hours, then one hour forty-five, then one hour thirty. Maren felt as though it were echoing the countdown on her life. She had four days, with luck, before thirst forced her into the supplies room or compelled her to face Saul's gun. *Four days isn't long. There's so much I wanted to do. So many things I'd planned for.*

You got one of them at least, she reminded herself, glancing at Saul's sleeping face. *You get to play defense technician for a handful of hours. Tick that one off the bucket list.*

Motion on the screens caught her eye, and Maren leaned forward. Suriya was hurrying down the hallway, apparently not trying to be quiet anymore. Maren glanced at the screen monitoring the storage room entrance, expecting Mark or Holly to come out, but they didn't seem to have heard.

"What's she doing?" Maren hissed, watching as Suriya went into the communications room. The older woman pulled the small chip off the chain she'd retied around her neck and fitted it into the communications panel. Maren felt a rush of horror as she realized what was about to happen.

CHAPTER 32

"GIN?" MAREN REACHED BEHIND herself to shake Saul. "Gin, this is bad!"

"I'm awake," Saul muttered when Maren didn't stop shaking him. "And yes, I've been watching."

"Is there anything we can do?" Maren wasn't able to keep the panic out of her voice. The metallic taste of fear had returned to her mouth, making her feel queasy.

Saul's silence was an answer in itself.

"What?" Gin asked, kneeling on the cushion pile next to Maren. "What's happened?"

Maren pointed at the screen, where Suriya was typing on the panel. "She's used her chip. She's going to override the lockdown, I'll bet. She'll open the doors and let the gamma rays fry the Cymics."

"Well...that's good, isn't it?" Gin asked, looking between

Maren and Saul. "This is an emergency lockdown room. It's safe against the rays, even if they contaminate the rest of the station. The Cymics will die, and we'll be safe."

"Yeah," Maren said, right as Suriya turned away from the panel and looked directly at the camera. A sickening smile stretched over the woman's face. "That would work great if Suriya hadn't gone—what's a polite way to put this? Nuts. Bonkers. Psycho. She's going to kill us all."

Gin blanched. "She wouldn't do that."

"You think? She doesn't know whether we're still human or if we've been taken over. And by this point, I don't think she cares. Remember what she said earlier? *I'd rather see all of you die than let one of those beasts into my station.* She's going to make good on that threat."

"Oh hell," Gin said.

Suriya's whole body started shaking. For a brief, hopeful second, Maren thought she might be having a fit, but then she realized the commander was *laughing*.

Maren squeezed her eyes closed, trying to think. "If we stay here and do nothing, we'll cook. We go out to try and stop her, and the Cymics will hear and come after us."

"And even if we do stop her, all it does is buy us a couple extra days." Gin slumped back, her face drawn, as she pulled a gray tasseled pillow to her chest. "We're not going to get rescued. We're not making it off this station."

"We've...we've got to try." Maren shook her head. "There's still a chance someone will come."

Gin pressed her forehead into the pillow. "Don't, Maren. The odds are far too slim." She sighed, the sound muffled by her cushion. "If it was just a choice between death and death, I'd say yeah, let's try for those three extra days. But, Maren, I'm scared. I don't want to become…like Mark. Or Holly. I don't want them stealing my body."

Maren swallowed. "I don't either."

Suriya finished typing then swiveled away from the bench with a happy clap. Maren remembered how Mark had moved when Holly had infected him. He'd twitched, jerked, and finally fallen still, only to stand up again, his body no longer his own. The idea of having her skin taken by one of the Cymic Parasites was unbearable.

"What do we do, then?" Maren asked. "Wait for the gamma rays?"

"It's the lesser of two evils for me." Gin raised her head. Fresh tear tracks sparkled on her cheeks, but she looked surprisingly calm. "If I have to go some way, I could do a lot worse than a quick, hot death."

Maren nodded slowly then turned to the man behind her. "Saul?"

"I agree with Gin," he said. "But what about you?"

She thought on it for a moment, chewing the problem over but unable to find a solution that didn't result in death. It felt insane to watch and do nothing as her boss put a timer on her life, but Gin was right; the horror of being consumed in a gamma ray was less terrible than the horror of becoming a Cymic or dying of dehydration.

"Okay," she said. "We stay."

The red screen above them clicked from one hour twelve to one hour eleven. Gin's hand found Maren's shoulders and squeezed, then Gin stood up. "If it's okay with you guys, I think I'd like to be by myself for a bit."

"That's fine," Maren said. She and Gin shared a smile, then Gin returned to the couch in the corner of the room, where she laid down, wrapped the throw blankets around herself, and stared at the ceiling.

"You want some time to yourself, too?" Maren asked Saul, but he shook his head. "Good. I don't really want to be alone right now."

Saul had never been much of a talker, and while Maren was usually more than happy to carry the conversation for both of them, she felt drained. There was so much she wanted to say and do, but all of her time was gone. She watched the clock count down her minutes and tried to keep her hands from shaking. She couldn't stop herself from glancing at the screens every few seconds. Suriya was sitting in one of the chairs in the communication room, her legs pulled up under her chin as she waited for her chance to shut off the lockdown and open every door in the station.

"I'm sorry," Saul said.

Maren twisted around to frown at him. "What for?"

"For not being able to keep you safe." Saul's eyes were fixed on the screens, but Maren didn't think he saw them. "That's the only thing I regret."

"Not your fault," Maren said thickly.

"You deserve better than this."

Maren was shocked to see the emotion etched across Saul's face. He was always so stable, so reliable. His brow creased above his soulful gray eyes as he refused to look at Maren, and the sight of his vulnerability filled her with desperate recklessness. She checked the countdown. Fifty-nine minutes.

"Would you let me tick something else off my wish list?" she asked.

Saul finally met her eyes, raising his brows in a silent question. Maren leaned closer and kissed him.

Saul froze underneath her. Maren, embarrassment rising through her in a hot rush, made to pull back, but then Saul answered the kiss before she could move away. His lips parted under hers, tasting her, as his weathered hand came up to caress the side of her face and tangle in her hair. Electricity ran through her; every hair on her body rose as her world shrunk to the kind, quiet man who was pouring a lifetime of passion into that one kiss. She pressed her hand to his chest and felt his heartbeat as his lips moved with hers, firm yet pliant, exploring and questioning while setting her body on fire.

When she drew back, she was breathless and flushed. Saul's hand lingered just below her jaw, his thumb caressing her cheek, his eyes filled with the fire that Maren found irresistible.

"Sorry," she whispered, trying to smother a smile.

"Don't be." His voice was deep and hungry. "I've wanted to do that for a long time."

His hand gently nudged the back of her neck in a soft request that Maren had no desire to deny, and she returned to him for another kiss as Saul's other hand came up to caress her back.

A crackle of sound came from the speakers, and they pulled apart again, shocked out of their moment of intimacy.

"This is Captain Matthews on board *Gypsy Flight*," the voice said, tinny but loud enough to hear. "We're evacuating to Central and collecting as many passengers from stations in our path as possible. Do you need rescue or assistance?"

Maren and Saul stared at each other.

"Rescue," Maren hissed, and hope bloomed through her like a hot flame.

Gin appeared at their sides. She stared for a moment at Saul's hand, which was still held against the small of Maren's back, then shook her head. "They must be overriding our intercom system," she said, dragging her fingers through her short hair. "We'd need to get to the communications room to send word back."

Maren looked at the screens. Suriya must have left the room while Maren was distracted, and she didn't appear in any of the video feeds. Mark and Holly had reappeared at the entrance to the storage area. They stood side-by-side, staring at the hallway ahead, then glanced at each other. If they were talking, their lips weren't moving.

"I repeat. This is Captain Matthews. We're rescuing as many stranded crews as possible on our evacuation to Central. If you require transport or assistance, please reply immediately."

"We can't let them leave without us," Maren said, feeling sweat break out on her body. "We've got to get word to them."

"Yeah." Gin bounced on the balls of her feet, rubbing her hands over her skirt, her previous calm replaced with frantic stress. "Okay. You and me, Maren."

Maren scanned the screens again. Mark and Holly had disappeared. "No, I'll go alone. You and Saul stay locked in here. I'll get in touch with the ship, and they can help us all get out." She grabbed Saul's gun from where they'd left it on the ground and checked its charge. "Do you have any more of these, Saul?"

"Look under the screens."

"No," Gin said, arms crossed over her chest, as Maren rummaged through the equipment tray under the trolley. "I've got to come. You don't know how to use the systems. We need to scan and identify the correct wavelength to reply to that ship. It's a very precise process."

Maren glanced at the countdown. They had only forty-eight minutes left—forty-eight minutes to get word to the ship, get Saul out of the recreation room, unlock the station's doors, and evacuate to the craft…all while trying to avoid Holly and Mark. "Fine, fine, jeez." She pulled the spare gun out of the trolley and handed it to Saul. "Keep this with you, just in case." *Just in case we die out there and you need a painless way to end your own life.*

He gripped her hand before she could pull back, and his intense gray eyes bore into her. "Be safe, Maren."

She found it hard to look away, so instead, she bent and kissed him quickly, savoring the electric sensation for half a second before pulling back. She brushed his stubbled cheek with her thumb then turned toward the door that opened onto the most direct route to the communications station. She could feel his gaze following her as she jogged to the control panel beside the door, and she didn't think it was her imagination that his voice carried intense undertones as he repeated his code for her to open the doors.

CHAPTER 33

MAREN SET THE DOORS to lock again after she'd left then peered into the hallway beyond before leading Gin outside.

"So," Gin said, a coy note to her voice as the reinforced barrier pulled closed behind them, "any exciting news you want to share with your best friend?"

Maren felt her face turn red as she smothered a grin. "Later. Once we're no longer in imminent danger of death."

"Fair enough."

The station's hallways felt even emptier than they had before. Maren led Gin toward the communications room, her gun turned on and clasped in both hands. She tried to guess where the station's other three occupants might be: Suriya had left the communications room, seemingly as a result of the announcement. Did she hope to get to the ship and make it off the station alive? If so, she would probably be suiting up in the air lock.

Mark and Holly had also left their camp. She had a horrible premonition that they were intending to intercept her on the way to the communications room. If she'd been able to afford a couple more minutes, she would have taken a less direct route, using the back ways and circling through the maintenance sections to stay off the main path, but by the sound of it, that ship wasn't going to hang around for long.

Her plan was simple to the point of stupidity: run as fast as she could, shoot anything that moved, and hope they got to the control room in one piece and before their only hope of getting off the station left.

She ran quickly but quietly, rolling her feet with each step to muffle the sound. Gin, who had never trained for combat and wasn't used to running, wasn't so good at being stealthy. Her footsteps echoed through the empty hallways like a beating drum.

No point worrying about it, Maren reminded herself. *They knew you were coming as soon as you opened the door.*

She rounded a corner and stopped, holding out one hand to keep Gin behind herself. She'd caught a flash of dark motion coming from a doorway ahead of them. Maren glanced past the door; the communications room was at the end of the hallway, tantalizingly close.

"Jeez," she hissed. Every nerve of her body felt alive as she tried to figure out what to do. They could make a dash for it and hope for the best or turn around and take a different route—

"This is Captain Matthews," the voice said through the

speakers. "My crew and I are preparing to leave. If there is anyone alive on this station, please signal immediately."

No time. Gotta risk it.

"Run as fast as you can," Maren hissed to Gin, giving her a shove to bring her abreast. Maren ran beside her, keeping herself between the doorway and her friend, her gun trained on the dark opening. As they drew closer, not trying to mask their footsteps anymore, Maren saw motion inside the shadowy room, but by then, it was too late to stop. They were nearly at the door then abreast of it, and all of a sudden, they were on the other side without the monster having a chance to attack.

Maren had just drawn a relieved gasp when the door on the opposite side of the hallway burst open, and one of the monsters launched itself at Gin.

A trap, Maren thought numbly as the black tendrils hit Gin, slamming her into the floor. Maren turned her gun on the monster but was a fraction of a second too slow; one of the tendrils hit her shoulder, knocking the gun out of her hand and making her stumble.

"Run, Gin!" Maren yelled as the second monster came out of the room behind them, but Gin was sitting on the ground, her face blanched white as she stared at the creatures.

Maren stumbled forward to put herself in front of Gin. Her heart faltered as she saw the beasts properly. While the monsters outside the station had shredded their human shells, Mark and Holly had preserved theirs as their true forms had slid outside. Each black monster, taller than and four times as wide as a human, had at least a dozen tendrils extending from its core, waving and twitching in the air. But suspended from the front of the mass were the remains of their human hosts; the bodies were limp like deflated balloons, swaying loosely. Boneless legs and shriveled fingers swung each time the monster moved.

Only their heads were intact; they lolled on the top of the empty bodies. Their eyes followed Maren and Gin, and their mouths twisted into delighted smiles.

They need the heads to see, Maren realized as she hesitated a fraction of a second too long. One of Mark's tendrils hit her side, smashing her into the wall, forcing the air out of her lungs. She gasped, trying not to be sick, as she collapsed to the floor.

Holly turned her attention to the stricken Gin as Mark cornered Maren, the smile on his face growing to unnatural widths as he advanced on her. Maren, breathless and unable to get to her feet, turned her face away from the specter in front of her. She didn't want to see Mark like that. And she certainly didn't want to watch his face crack into that maniacal grin as he ended her human existence.

Her eyes landed on the red countdown screen. Twenty-eight minutes. *Gin was right; it really would have been much nicer to wait for the flare. Much more…palatable.*

She also saw the small black shell below the screen. While every room in the station had the flare warning system, only a dozen had those black shells. They held the cameras that monitored the main sections of the station.

Saul will be watching, Maren realized, dread flowing into her core and making her dizzy. *I can't let him see this. Can't can't can't can't can't.*

Mark leaned over her, and his tendrils, slimy and cold, latched on to and restrained her arms. Maren had no room to pull away, so she did the opposite and kicked against the wall, shoving her body into Mark's as hard as she could.

His black flesh felt disgusting and cold, like a horribly mutated slug. Maren's right arm pressed into the empty skin, and the sensation of human flesh with nothing behind it was almost enough to make her scream.

Mark hadn't been expecting the attack, and the effort was just enough to bowl them both over. They tumbled to the floor, the multitude of tendrils loosening a fraction, and Maren was able to wrench her arms free. She hit the floor and rolled, trying to put as much distance as possible between herself and the repulsive creature. In front of her, just out of arm's reach, lay the gun.

A high, terrified sound filled the hallway. It took Maren a heartbeat to realize it was Gin, screaming as she thrashed and kicked in Holly's grip.

Maren lunged forward and snagged the gun at the same moment Mark's tendrils latched on to her ankle. She let him pull her back into himself as she rolled onto her back and aimed at Holly.

The crack sounded unusually loud as it bounced off the steel walls. A large section of the black creature was blasted open, and black smoke rose from the scorched flesh as Holly writhed and squirmed. A second scream joined Gin's, and Maren grinned viciously as Holly wailed in pain and rage.

Gotcha.

She turned back to her own assailant. Mark's smile was gone. Instead, he looked furious. His human face was bubbling, the skin distorting horrifically. He tried to snatch the gun out of her hand, but Maren slipped her hand under his grasping tendril and shot a round directly into his human face before lowering the gun and sending another round into the black core.

His tendril twitched as each round hit him, squeezing her leg so hard that it brought tears to her eyes. For a second, she thought she might join Saul in the Broken Leg Brigade, but then the tendril loosened enough for her to kick free.

She'd barely turned over when Holly hit her. Bright light exploded across her eyes as she was tossed down the hallway like a rag doll, her aching limbs screaming in protest. A headache started up in the back of her head. She'd managed to keep a hold on the gun, though, and she fired a blind shot in the direction she thought the attack had come from. She heard the hot sizzle and pop of heated metal and knew she'd hit the wall instead.

"Left!" Gin screamed from somewhere behind her.

Thank goodness you're okay, Maren thought as she raised the gun and fired another blind shot. This time, she was rewarded with a bestial scream.

Her vision started to clear as she scrambled to her feet. She caught a glimpse of pink—Gin—and ran in its direction. Something large hit the wall just behind her, and she knew she'd narrowly avoided another attack. She was disoriented, but Gin grabbed the front of her suit and dragged her through a doorway before slamming it behind them. One of the beasts hit in her wake, rattling the metal structure and cracking the small window. Maren, dizzy and sick, let herself slide to the floor.

"Hey, hey, talk to me." Gin slapped Maren's cheek.

Maren grimaced. "Ow, stop that. I'm fine. Jeez."

She felt far from fine—her stomach was threatening to upend itself, everything hurt, and her vision was taking its sweet time normalizing itself—but Gin had hit the same cheek Holly had slapped, and Maren really wished she'd stop.

"Okay, okay. We're okay," Gin said.

The other woman was on the verge of hyperventilating, but as the double images that swam through Maren's vision coalesced into one, she saw there was a flush of delight over Gin's face too. Maren looked around and saw why. They'd made it into the communications room.

CHAPTER 34

"THE SHIP," MAREN GASPED, shoving Gin toward the panel. "Go, go, go!"

The door at her back shuddered again, sending shock waves through her sore ribs, as Mark and Holly tried to break in. Maren wished she could stay on the ground—it was easier than trying to balance on wobbly legs—but she remembered the sound of screeching metal in the distress message Gin had received the day before, and she had a sinking feeling the protection wouldn't last for long. She got to her feet and braced herself against the wall as she trained her gun at the door. The small, cracked windows showed snapshots of the black things outside as they pressed against the glass. Then Holly's face suddenly filled the space, mouth open in a wild grimace, half of her forehead missing from where Maren's shot had hit her, the eyes rolling wildly before fixing on Maren.

"How long?" Maren asked, torn between her need to hold focus on the door and her desire to look away.

"One minute." Gin, spared the sight of Holly's deformed face, was typing on her panel faster than Maren had ever seen her fingers move before. "I'm looking for the frequency they used when they contacted us so I can get us on the same wavelength and broadcast—"

"Okay, I have no idea what you're saying, but it sounds important," Maren said, trying to keep her voice light as Holly's face disappeared from the window. "How about this: you do your job while I do mine. Deal?"

The creatures slammed the door. A large dent appeared in the metal, and part of the door separated from the frame.

"I think I've found it," Gin said, delight filling her voice.

With a second slam, the door buckled inward even farther. One of the black tendrils slipped through the gap, and Maren lunged forward to stomp it back out. It squirmed under her boot and reluctantly retreated. "Great. You gonna call them?"

Gin was already pulling her headset on with one hand while her other fingers adjusted dials and pressed buttons.

"Captain Matthews? This is Ginevieve Mull from Station 334. We need assistance. Repeat, we need assistance. Please confirm."

The creatures outside the door roared and slammed into it. The gap widened, and the top bolt started to pull loose. Maren pressed her back against the door, hoping her weight would be enough to keep it in place.

Gin was frozen over her communications station, fingers

hovering a fraction of a centimeter above the panel, head quirked to one side as she waited for an answer. "Captain Matthews, I repeat: there are people on this station in urgent need of assistance. Please confirm."

The radio was silent except for bursts of static. A horrible dead weight settled in Maren's stomach as Gin turned to look at her, distress painted over her face. *We were too late. They left.*

Then a voice flooded the room, breathless, as though its owner had been running. "This is Captain Matthews," he said. "Ginevieve, I've received your message. How many on your station need assistance?"

"Three," Gin said then moved the mic away from her mouth so she could let out a string of curses as she slumped over the panel, shaking with relief.

"Copy. We have plenty of space. We've just come from your sister Station 491, but it's already been overrun."

The beasts hit the door behind Maren. She tried to brace herself, but the force threw her forward and jarred her neck.

"I'll be honest," Gin said. "We've got a couple of problems here too. Do you have any defense technicians that can help?"

"Yes, several. Stay put. We'll come to you. Twenty minutes."

"Twenty minutes?" Maren called, hoping Matthews would hear her from across the room. "Can you get here faster?"

"Negative. When you didn't reply to my earlier communications, we prepared to leave your planet. We're almost at the atmosphere, and I'm just now diverting the ship to land."

Maren looked at the red screen in the corner of the room:

it read twenty-four minutes. That would be enough time—just barely enough—for her and Gin to leave the station and get on board the ship before the flare hit, but there would be no time for Matthews's defense technicians to rescue Saul. *And Saul's getting on that ship. That's not negotiable.*

"Okay," Maren said as the beasts hit the door. The metal screeched, and Maren thought it might break. She shoved her back against it, and, mercifully, it held…barely. "We'll make it work. Meet you outside ASAP."

"Confirmed," Captain Matthews said, and the line cut off.

Gin pulled the headphones off and swiveled toward Maren, her face full of bright exaltation that died as soon as she saw the door. "Oh, shoot. Damn."

Tendrils were creeping around the bulging doorframe and trying to grab Maren. She stomped on any that came near her feet and ducked to keep her head clear of the ones above her. "Get back," she called to Gin over the wailing noise the monsters were emitting. "I'll shoot through them, then we'll make a run for it."

The motion behind her stilled. Maren took a deep breath then leaped away from the door, twisting and aiming her gun in the same motion. She fired twice, and the first shot blasted through the warped metal. The second hit the metal wall halfway down the hallway, which was empty.

"Wha…"

They heard you say you were going to shoot, so they got out of the way. They've tasted those guns enough times to be wary of them. But they won't be giving up, not this easily. They know you need to get to Saul, so they're going to wait and let you *come to* them.

Maren bobbed her head, trying to see down the hallway. The fight had broken most of the lights, and the single remaining fluorescent was flickering. She could see the doors lining each side of the path. Some closed, some open, any one of them potentially hid their attackers.

Gin was sheet white as she placed a hand on Maren's arm. "We're going to run?"

"No," Maren murmured, as an idea started to form in the back of her mind. "No, I don't think we'd be lucky enough to get past them again. Watch the hallway a moment."

Maren pushed her friend to stand in the place she'd been occupying and pressed the gun into her hands. Then she pulled a small switchblade out of the utility set she kept in her pocket and jumped onto the control panel. Above the panel, set high in the wall and painted a matching gray to discreetly blend in to the room, was the grill that covered the ventilation system.

Most members of the station overlooked the vents. Maren herself had never really noticed ducts before she'd been put in charge of maintaining them. Since being stationed in 334, though, she'd spent countless hours crawling through the vents to reach inconvenient parts of the station that had suffered heat damage. She knew the passageways so intimately that, even without the map she usually brought, she was confident she could find her way to the rec room.

The transmission from earlier in the day had said the Cymic

Parasites absorbed their host's memories. Maren was banking on the idea that neither Mark nor Holly had been consciously aware of the ventilation systems, and so the monsters wouldn't be either.

Maren dug the edge of the blade under where base of the cover was pressed against the wall. She gave it a tug, pulling the vent free so it swung on its top hinges.

"Here, quickly," she hissed to Gin as she pocketed the blade.

Gin was fairly lax about letting her friend lean against the board, but Maren would never forget the look of horror that crossed Gin's face when she saw Maren's boots digging into the knobs and dials of her much-loved control panel.

"It doesn't matter!" Maren grabbed Gin's arm and tugged her onto the panel as well. "Jeez, you communication clowns get so uptight about your precious equipment."

"Only because you maintenance morons keep stuffing it up!" Gin huffed back but handed back the gun before letting Maren haul her into the vent.

"Crawl forward as quietly as you can," Maren said. "It connects with another vent after about a dozen feet. Go into that side passageway so I can pass you."

Maren waited until Gin's shoes were in danger of disappearing from sight, then with a final glance at the door to make sure it was empty, she hoisted herself into the vent.

It was a narrow space, barely large enough to let her crawl on her hands and knees, and it took a fair bit of squirming to turn herself around so that she was facing the entrance. She hooked her fingers through the grill and pulled it down until it locked back into place. It wouldn't stop the Cymics from following her if they realized where she and Gin had hidden, but at least it wouldn't look astray if—rather, when—they became impatient enough to enter the room.

And that didn't take long. Maren had barely managed to get herself facing forward again before a terrifying wail flooded her ears. Maren held her breath as she listened to the shuffling, scraping sounds coming from the creature as it searched the room. A loud bang, followed by a sizzle, told her the control panel had been destroyed. It was quickly followed by another wail and the screech of metal being torn apart.

"Go, go," she whispered to Gin, who had come to a halt in front of her. With their noise masked by the creature's furious destruction of the communications room, they crawled down the narrow steel passageway as quickly as they could.

The noise gradually faded behind them and then eventually ceased as the creature gave up on its rampage. Gin reached the offshoot and wormed into it so Maren could pass her.

"How long do we have?" Maren asked, careful to keep her voice quiet. Any sound they made would be muffled by the wall's insulation, but she didn't want to take any chances.

Gin had a far better head for time than Maren did. "Not more than nineteen minutes."

"Damn." The vents were safer than the passageways, but that came at the cost of time; if they'd been running, they would have been back at the rec room already. "Can you go any faster, Gin?"

"I'll try."

The vents were almost pitch-dark, save for the slivers of light that speared through the grills placed every twenty feet, so Maren closed her eyes while she crawled, calling up the mental image of the ventilation system's pathways. She led them past the meeting room and around the storage section then skirted the edge of the second-quadrant sleeping quarters. The only sounds she could make out were the shuffle of her hands and suit pants over the cold metal as well as Gin's labored breathing as she tried to match Maren's pace.

Then two loud bangs shocked her so badly that she jumped, hitting her head on the vent's ceiling. Her headache flared as her mind scrambled to figure out what was happening. *Gunfire. Whose?*

It couldn't be Holly or Mark. They'd shown no interest in finding a conventional weapon when they'd been roving through the station. *Does that mean it was Suriya?* She'd been sporting that viciously sharp knife last time Maren had seen her, but it wasn't impossible that she'd found a gun in the interim.

The noise sounded as though it had come from ahead and a little to the left of them. *Which would put it in...*

"The rec room!" she gasped. "Saul!"

CHAPTER 35

THREE MORE SHOTS ECHOED around her. Maren began moving again, ignoring her weary, aching muscles as she pushed herself through the vents as quickly as the cramped confines would let her. *If Saul's using his gun, that means they've gotten to him. Instead of hunting us, they've gone directly to our destination, broken through the doors, somehow, and he can't even run—*

Terror lent her strength. She rounded the final corner and saw the slivers of light belonging to the recreation room's vent ahead of her. As she drew close to it, she wormed one hand behind her, pulled the gun out of her belt's holster, and clamped it between her teeth. Then she kicked the vent open and threw herself into the room below feet first.

Saul was sitting propped upright in the lounge, the blankets Maren had placed over him discarded to the floor. He had his gun clasped in both hands, and his eyes narrowed as he aimed.

Even from her position across the room, Maren could see the harsh lines of concentration crinkling his brow.

On the opposite side of the room, advancing on him with slow, careful paces that reminded Maren of a stalking panther, was Suriya. The knife swung idly by her side as she slunk closer to Saul, and the crazed delight on her face set Maren's blood to ice.

Of course, she opened the rec room's door. She's the only person in the station with a higher permission than the defense technician.

Saul fired another two rounds. He wasn't shooting to kill, or even to injure, but was aiming at the floor just in front of Suriya's feet. The first shot made her hesitate, and the second caused her to take a half step backward, but then she stepped around the smoldering black holes the bullets had left in the carpet and moved even closer.

"Suriya!" Maren yelled, aiming her own gun at the older woman's face. "Get back!"

"She's past reason," Saul said. He sounded resigned. "She won't talk."

Suriya opened her mouth in a twisted grimace and laughed until her body convulsed from the effort. She let the knife swing like a pendulum, the light shining off its long, tapered blade. Her face seemed to have transformed in the time since Maren had last seen her; deranged intent had replaced the normal cool restraint.

Maren knew Saul was right, but she couldn't stop herself from trying. "Suriya, relax. We can get off the station. A ship's coming to pick us up. Just put the knife down, and we can talk about it."

Maren thought their leader was contemplating the idea, but

then Suriya lunged forward, knife aimed at Maren's face. Her finger was poised over the trigger. She knew she had to pull it—the blade was a second away from slicing into her, but she hesitated. *It's still Suriya. Damaged, deranged, but still the same person inside. Can I live with myself if I kill her?*

There was a loud crack, then Suriya stumbled to a halt, so close to Maren that she could feel the other woman's breath on her face. Suriya's eyes, bloodshot and wild, met hers, then Maren scrambled backward, putting space between them.

A glitter of silver to her right caught Maren's attention. The knife, its blade dented, lay on the carpet. Maren glanced to her left and saw smoke coming from Saul's gun.

Saul finally raised his gun to point at Suriya's face, his eyes hard and unforgiving, his voice dangerously low. "Move so much as a step closer to her, and I *will* kill you."

Suriya's eyes darted from Saul to Maren to the knife. Sweat stood out clearly on her face, plastering her hair to her forehead and neck as she chewed the inside of her cheek. Then the red screen in the corner of the room emitted a beep—a final warning in advance of the lockdown ten minutes away—and Suriya turned in a flurry of motion, snatched her knife off the ground, and ran for the door she'd come through.

Saul waited until she'd disappeared from sight and the door slid back into place before lowering his gun with a heavy sigh. "Come here." He held one hand out to Maren. She went to him gladly and gripped the offered hand, acutely aware of how grateful she was that he hadn't been hurt.

"You came through the vents?" he asked, and she nodded. "Clever girl." A smile spread over his face. It was a genuine toothy grin that crinkled his eyes, and it made Maren feel like her heart might be melting through her ribs. "Well done, Maren."

She reached out to brush his hair off his forehead then pressed her cheek to his in a gentle nuzzle. "I'm glad you're okay," she said.

"Same to you." He kissed her neck then pulled back, his gray eyes concerned. "Where's Gin?"

"Jeez!" Maren had completely forgotten about the friend she'd left in the vent. She turned toward the hole in the wall and saw Gin's blue eyes, round as saucers, peeking out of a white face. "Gin! Are you okay?"

"Yeah, course," Gin said, the rest of her face coming into view. "There was just a lot of gunfire and yelling, so I thought it might be smart to stay hidden. I was going to come out when it went quiet, but, well, you two seemed to be having a moment, so..."

Maren, feeling heat grow over her face and ears, jogged to the vent to help Gin down. "Come on, we don't have time to waste. Saul, we were able to get in touch with the ship. They'll be touching down in a few minutes, and we've got to get to them before the flare."

Saul glanced at the screen in the corner—eight minutes left— and his frown deepened.

Maren knew what he was thinking. "Yeah, it'll be close. We won't have time to go back through the vents."

"Take the path through the North Quarter." Maren raised her

eyebrows at him, and Saul nodded toward the screens. "That's the way Suriya took, and nothing stopped her."

"Okay then. You up for some running, Saul?"

"Hmm."

Maren thought that meant yes, so she tucked the gun back into her belt and hooked Saul's hand over her shoulders while Gin came up on his other side. They lifted him to his feet then started toward the doors.

"You'd be faster without me," Saul started, but Maren gave him a quick jab in his ribs.

"Don't even think about playing the hero. If you stay, I'm staying with you."

He sighed but was wise enough to not protest any further.

They were only a few paces from the door when it slid open. Maren snatched for her gun and, holding Saul up with her left hand, aimed with her right—but the hallway was empty. She glanced behind herself and saw the rest of the room's doors had opened too.

"Suriya," Maren muttered, scowling. "But the monsters destroyed the panel. How'd she—"

"She set it on a timer, I'll bet," Gin said. "Scheduled to cancel the lockdown when it was too late for us to do anything about it."

"You can do that?"

"If you're a little clever with it, yeah."

"Okay." Maren pulled the three of them through the door and set off down the hallway. "We need to go fast, then. No time to suit up. We'll have to take temporary oxygen units."

She turned right, as Saul had advised, taking the slightly longer path through the northern section of their station. Her heart, strained by all of the activity that day, fluttered hard against her ribs as she carried the bulk of Saul's weight. She kept her breathing light so she could listen, but she couldn't hear or see anything unnatural. They were near the end of the hallway that led to the air lock when Saul pulled her up with a hard tug. She looked at him, but he shook his head to indicate she should be quiet.

"What's—" Gin started, but Saul clamped a hand over her mouth.

That was when Maren became aware of the faint shifting noise coming from just around the corner ahead of them. Saul carefully pulled the gun from Maren's hand. Then, leaning on her to keep himself steady, he tugged a knife from his back pocket. He threw it toward the end of the hallway so that it skittered to a halt just before the corner.

Mark's monstrous form took up most of the hallway while his limp human skin swayed from where it was suspended. He lunged toward the sound, and two of his tendrils slammed into the floor and walls, leaving large dents in their wake.

Saul's gun cracked three times, blasting holes in the rippling black creature as its human opened its mouth to release a deep bellow.

"Go," Saul said, urging them forward, as Mark collapsed to the ground in a mess of smoking, writhing flesh. "Quick, before the other one comes."

They ran for the safety of the air lock ahead, clambering over the twitching tendrils that littered the floor. Maren sensed more than saw Mark beginning to rebuild his form behind them, but they barreled through the open air lock door and slammed it closed before the creature could collect itself.

"Here," Maren said, letting Gin take Saul's weight as she eased out from under his arm and began searching for the temporary breathing units.

Temps, as the crew called them, were small round devices that fit into the mouth. They held enough oxygen to last for ten minutes and could be quickly handed out and activated in case of an emergency evacuation.

Maren rattled through the collection of equipment boxes and spare parts until she found the crate holding the small forest-green pucks. She took three and passed them out.

"They're here." Gin pointed to the external door's window with her free hand.

A large white shape was descending toward the planet's surface, its engines kicking up plumes of red dust that glittered in the eternal sunset. The light, normally red, had turned bright yellow from the approaching flare.

Maren stuck the Temp in her mouth and bit through the plastic seal to activate the oxygen flow. Gin gave her a thumbs-up, and Saul nodded, so she pressed the button to open the external door.

CHAPTER 36

HEAT WASHED OVER THEM. Maren had forgotten how warm the planet was without the suits; though, she supposed, the gamma flare wasn't helping matters. She put herself back under Saul's arm, and the three of them left the air lock at a brisk walk, squinting against the clouds of dust blowing against their faces.

That was easy, Maren thought as the aircraft settled into the dirt ahead of them and its landing gear dug into the ground. *Incredibly easy, actually. Almost ridiculously easy compared to everything else that's happened today…*

The doors opened as they reached the ship, allowing them into the small round room that acted as the craft's air lock. Shelves nestled against the walls were filled with suits and any equipment the crew might need when exploring a strange planet. A tall, broad-shouldered man stood inside the room, the lower half of his face covered by an oxygen mask. He held out a hand to pull them in.

"Ginevieve and companions?" he asked. "I'm glad you were able to make it out okay. I thought you said there were only three of you, though."

Maren hesitated. *There are only three of us, aren't there...?*

Saul reacted first. He pulled Maren and Gin to the side, slamming them into one of the shelves. A knife grazed Maren's shoulder, stinging where it cut through the suit and into her arm. It was closely followed by Suriya.

How did she get here so fast? Maren ducked sideways, catching a glimpse of the madness in the other woman's eyes as the momentum carried her past. *Unless...she was in the air lock with us and followed us out when we left. We wouldn't have been able to hear her over the noise of the landing ship, and we were so focused on moving quickly, we didn't think to look behind ourselves.*

Suriya stumbled, caught off balance after her target had moved. Captain Matthews moved forward and attempted to wrestle the knife out of her hands, yelling, "Claire! Jan!"

They tumbled against the wall. Suriya kicked and shrieked while Matthews attempted to hold her still. Their motion knocked equipment off the shelves. Saul had his left hand pushing Maren back, shielding her as much as he could in the cramped conditions, while his right hand trained the gun on the struggling pair.

Then Matthews shoved Suriya against the external doors, and Suriya's elbow hit the button beside the panel when she tried to thrash free. The doors slid open, dropping Matthews and Suriya into the desert outside. They hit the red dirt with a hard thud, rolled apart, then came together to grapple once again.

Maren was immensely grateful she hadn't had a chance to spit out the Temp. The planet's air was technically breathable for short stretches of time, but more than a few minutes' exposure was toxic. Matthews's mask had come off in the squabble, and Suriya hadn't had one to begin with.

The door behind Maren opened, and two masked women pushed into the room. The taller one jumped through the open external doors to assist Matthews while the shorter one hesitated in the opening, waiting to see if she was needed. She waved for Maren and her companions to move back, out of harm's way.

Suriya was screaming in fury, her vocal cords tearing in the toxic air, as she fought the captain and his companion. "Monsters. *Monsters!* I'll see you dead!"

Matthews yelled back, "Calm down. Stop! We're here to help!" He had Suriya pinned on her stomach with both hands behind her back, but she still hadn't released the blade. She was hissing and screaming. Sand blew into her mouth and stuck to her sweaty face. Matthews removed one hand to reach for a cord in his belt, and Suriya took the opportunity. She swiveled around, pulling the knife-bearing hand under herself, and plunged it into Matthews' stomach.

Maren grimaced and heard Gin gasp beside her. The woman who'd remained with them went stiff as she watched her leader reel backward, hands clutched around the wound. His face had blanched, and his eyes were large with shock. Suriya scrambled away from him, panting, her face twisted into triumph. Matthews grabbed the knife's handle and pulled it out of his stomach.

Maren felt her blood run cold as she saw the blade was coated with something black.

Then Saul's hand disappeared from where it had been pressing her against the wall. The woman in the hatchway was turning toward them, the façade of concern disappeared as a black crack ran down her face, rapidly widening. Saul slammed both hands into her, shoving her out of the hatchway.

Maren also leaped forward. Saul was unstable on just one leg, and she grabbed his suit's sleeve and pulled him back against herself to keep him inside the air lock. The falling woman's face was pulling apart, and when she hit the ground in a plume of red dust, one of the tendrils launched itself toward them. Maren had already pressed the door's button, though, and the tendril hit the glass with a loud smack.

Saul sagged back, and Maren grabbed him, keeping him upright as they gazed at the horrific scene outside.

The first woman, the tall one, had leaned over Suriya's prone form. Without the knife, and her strength sapped by the poisonous air, Suriya was unable to fight as the tendrils forced themselves down her throat. The tall woman pulled back, smirking, then stood to join her companions as Suriya started to twitch.

Maren, horrified and mesmerized, was only vaguely aware of Gin pressing buttons on the control panel to her right. By the time Gin spat out her Temp and said, "Air lock stabilized," Suriya had stopped moving. Maren, both hands occupied keeping Saul upright, spat the plastic puck onto the floor. A second clatter told her Saul had done the same.

"We need to get out of here," Saul said, his voice thick from pain again.

"Okay." Maren carefully swiveled the large man toward the internal doors then hesitated. "Uh. Please tell me one of you knows how to pilot a ship."

"I do," Saul said. "Get me to the cockpit."

Gin pressed more buttons on the panel to open the internal doors, letting them into the ship. Maren spared a glance over her shoulder as she helped Saul in and shuddered to see the area outside the ship was empty, save for a small splatter of black and the discarded knife.

The ship was large, and Maren recognized the layout as belonging to an emergency supplies unit. All stations were restocked every six weeks, but if there was a disaster or the station was going to run out of essential supplies before the restocking, an emergency supplies unit was sent to them. The three-person crews typically lived on their ships for months or even years at a time, bouncing between whichever planets needed their help. *That means we'll have plenty of food and water, at least,* Maren thought as she led Saul left, through a set of heavy doors, past a lounge area, and toward the front of the ship. *They might actually be large enough to be carrying more than a basic range of medical supplies. I'd give just about anything for one of those intelligent metal casts for Saul's leg.*

The living areas were smaller than the ones on Station 334, but it was comfortable and decorated in attractive muted colors. Maren found the cockpit and helped Saul into the large leather seat in front of the dashboard. As soon as he sat down, the creases on his face smoothed out, and he started working on the dash, preparing the ship to take off.

"We're going to be safe in here, right?" Gin asked, sitting on Saul's other side. She eyed the dash with envy; Maren wouldn't be surprised if she managed to coax Saul into teaching her how to pilot the ship. "From the gamma flare, I mean."

"Yes," Saul said. The engines started with a heavy rumble that reverberated through the seats. Saul pulled the harness over his shoulders, connected it, pulled the straps tight, then stared at Maren and Gin until they hastily followed his example. He started to press the throttle forward, but just as the ship started to move, it stalled.

"What…" Gin asked.

Saul's lips had narrowed into a thin line. He typed quickly, bringing up the cameras that monitored the outside of the ship. Maren gasped—a black beast gripped the rear of the ship, covering the thrusters and storage units. It was unlike any of the Cymic Parasites Maren had seen before; it was massive, easily large enough to cover the ship's rear quarter and drag it to a halt.

CHAPTER 37

HOW DID IT GET that big? Maren wondered in sick fascination. Then, as the creature moved, she understood. It wasn't one beast. It was hundreds. They stuck together, rippling over each other, flowing into new shapes. They were simultaneously many and one, liquid and solid.

A glitter of silver behind the station explained where they'd come from. Forty buggies, most likely from Station 491, were parked just out of view. *That means we've lost both of our sister stations. Damn it.*

Saul pressed on the throttle again, and the ship dragged forward painfully slowly before pulling to a standstill. He hissed in frustration.

"They're too heavy," Maren said, hands pressed over her mouth as she watched the monsters swarm the rear of the ship. "But the flare will be here in a moment. If we just wait—"

Saul's frown wasn't comforting. He was pressing more buttons, charging something up.

"They're trying to pull the ship apart," Gin said. She'd drawn her knees up under her chin and had both hands gripping her short, teal hair. Her face looked ghostly pale in the light reflected from the dashboard.

Sure enough, the mass was constricting, squeezing the craft's back end. A metallic wail came from deep in the ship, and Maren felt her heart flutter. "If they compromise the hull, we'll be cooked."

"Hold on," Saul said.

Maren glanced at the dashboard and saw he was drawing all of the ship's power to the rear thrusters, and she suddenly understood what he had planned. "Wait. If they're holding us back, the ship will—"

"I know," he said. "Gotta try." He pressed the button to activate the thrusters, and a high, painful whine rose from the ship's hull as it was stressed to its limit.

Maren watched the screen. The Cymic had enveloped the rear of the ship. While the monster had been clever enough to avoid the main engines, its bulk was covering the giant grill that served as the rear thrusters, used only for a fierce burst of speed. As the thrusters activated, they shot a stream of intense fire straight into the creature's core.

The scene was one of the most gratifying things Maren had ever seen. The Cymic froze and shivered, then the flames broke through its body, digging a hole through its center and shooting clouds of black smoke and soot at least forty meters behind the ship. The remainder of the creature coiled up, peeling off the craft as it tried to protect what was left of its body.

That's when the ship moved. The thrusters were only supposed to be used to get the ship out of a planet's atmosphere or to accelerate in space. Using them on a grounded ship was disastrous. The ship lurched, pressing Maren back into her chair, then the seat's harness dug into her chest as the ship, filled with far too much momentum, caught on the dunes and flipped.

The world swam in the large curved window in front of Maren. One second, she was looking at the ground, which had turned from its usual dirty red to a near-glowing pink, and the next, she was staring at the sky, which had tinges of color in one direction and was pure white in the other. Saul had shut off the thrusters, but the momentum spun the ship twice, three times, four times—then it landed hard enough to jar Maren's teeth.

The ship skidded across the surface of the planet, digging up clouds of dust and shaking its occupants as it caught on dunes and rocks before finally grinding to a halt. After a moment, Maren realized the ship had landed upright, then she finally let herself breathe and released her white-knuckle grip on the chair.

"You both okay?" Saul asked. He'd also blanched white, but his hand found Maren's and squeezed.

"Yeah," Gin squeaked, "but I'm not sure the ship is."

The screen showing the rear of the ship was like something out of a monster movie. The back section was crumpled, dented, and torn in so many sections that there was no question about the hull remaining strong enough to withstand the flare. Even though Saul had air-locked all of the sections to protect them from the poisonous outside air, without the reinforced outer hull to shield them, the flare would melt through the inside of the ship like a flamethrower through butter.

The horizon's glow was so bright, it was almost painful to look at. Rolls of blue-white gamma rushed over the surface of the planet behind them, burning up the writhing remains of the Cymic. She looked at Saul, who met her gaze, his eyes wide and helpless.

"Drive," she said, realizing what they needed to do to survive. "Go, quickly. Outrun it."

Gin was hyperventilating as she watched the flare. "We can't outrun it! It's faster than this ship!"

"No, we can," Maren said, suddenly aware of how hot it was in the cabin. Sweat was building over her body, and she was finding it hard to breathe. "We just need to get to the dark side of the planet. Go, Saul, quickly!"

But Saul had started directing power to the thrusters the first time Maren had told him to, and the ship was shuddering and groaning as it tried to move its damaged bulk. The rear thrusters had been nearly destroyed, but they still managed to spit fire as two out of the four units spluttered to life.

The ship jerked forward over on the dunes, but this time, Saul had more control over their course as he eased their speed up notch by notch. Maren glanced to her right and saw the hills and rocks of their planet blurring past the window; not far behind was the blue-tinted rolling wave that consumed everything in its path.

Being on the quiet side of the planet meant the gamma rays only skimmed their station, rather than hitting it head-on. That didn't reduce their potency, but it was buying them precious seconds. The ship stopped shuddering as it rose from the surface, and Saul applied all of the ship's energy to the thrusters. Maren was gasping; the air was so hot that every breath she took felt like as though it might suffocate her. Her throat and nose were dry, and the sweat her body produced evaporated before it could cool her. Maren could see the flare in the screen's rear; the back of the ship was turning pink from the heat as the crackling blue hues spilled closer. Ahead, in the far distance, were faint hints of pinks and yellows. Everything else outside the ship was white.

Then the repressive heat seemed to ease slightly. Maren drew a breath, and though it still burned her lungs, it wasn't as intolerable as it had been before. The glow faded, and Maren could make out the shapes below them. Saul was keeping the ship low, only a dozen meters above the dunes. Maren looked upward through the window in the ship's ceiling and felt her heart skip a beat. The gamma flares drifted above them, flowing through the sky like a flashlight's beam through a dark room. The flare painted the heavens white with electric flecks of blue swirling through it. She'd always thought her planet's eternal sunset was one of the prettiest things she'd ever seen, but the deadly vision that wove across the sky took her breath away.

Saul flew the ship for another four kilometers while Maren

and Gin admired the lights. When the temperature returned to endurable levels and the white glow was distant enough to no longer pose a threat, he lowered the ship onto a clear patch of desert. The craft shuddered and groaned as it hit the planet's surface, warning that the hull likely wouldn't withstand much more abuse. Maren patted the armrests, silently thanking it for holding together for as long as it had.

"Jeez," Gin said after a moment's pause. "I can't believe we're actually alive."

Maren glanced at Saul. He'd collapsed back in his seat and closed his eyes as he drew deep, long breaths through his nose. Now that the temperature had returned to a pleasantly toasty level, sweat developed over his face. "Nice work, Saul," Maren said.

Though he didn't open his eyes, his mouth twitched upward at the corners.

Maren undid her harness and stumbled through the cabin, the shock and adrenaline making her legs unsteady. She went to the storage cupboards at the back of the room and dug through them. Then she returned to her seat with three bottles of water and passed them out. "Drink up. I'm betting we're all pretty dehydrated right now."

"Are we going to be safe here?" Gin broke the seal on her bottle's lid and took a long drink. "The flare can't leak around the planet?"

"Nah. It's like light. It can only travel in a straight line." The water had been stored in its plastic bottle for months, and Maren knew it should taste terrible, but at that moment, it was one of the sweetest things she'd ever drunk. She consumed half of her bottle in one go then sat back and inhaled deeply. The pilot room was gradually cooling to just a little warmer than average room temperature. Her throat still felt raw, but she seemed otherwise fine.

"I can't believe those guys were Cymics," Gin said, curling up in her chair. She'd kicked her shoes off and shed her pink jacket. "They seemed so...normal."

"They were probably planning to keep up the façade for a few hours," Maren said. "They'd get us in the ship, make us feel safe, and tell us they were taking us back to Central. They wouldn't make a move until we were off guard, without our guns, and separated in different parts of the ship. Hell, they might have even meant to play it extra safe and attack while we were sleeping."

"Thank goodness for Suriya," Gin said. She and Maren shared a glance. "She might have been off her rocker, but she made the right call about Captain Matthews." Gin sighed. "I know she tried to stab you and everything, Maren, but I wish she hadn't died...*like that*."

"Me neither. She didn't deserve it. I don't think we could find a single person in the galaxy who deserves it."

They were silent while they sipped their water. Gin finished hers first and stretched out of her seat. "I'm getting another bottle. You guys want one?"

"Hmm."

"Yeah, that would be good, thanks."

As Gin rummaged through the cupboards at the back of the room, Maren felt something brush the back of her hand. She glanced down and saw Saul's hand had drifted near hers. A smile crept over her face as she responded by entwining her fingers with his, feeling a pleased tingle spread through her chest at the way his calloused fingers melded against hers perfectly.

Gin slammed the cupboard door closed. "There aren't any bottles here, so I'll get some from the lounge area. It should be far enough forward in the ship to be safe."

"'Kay."

Maren waited until Gin had left the room before looking at Saul. He'd been watching her, and she felt her breath catch in her throat. He might not speak much, but his eyes were capable of communicating novels' worth of emotions. She felt as if she could melt into them as they spoke to her about his affection for her and asked a gentle question.

"Yes," she answered him, feeling a thrill run up her spine at the idea. "Yes, whatever happens, we'll stay together."

Saul's smile crinkled his beautiful eyes. It was a heartfelt expression, and Maren thought it must be capable of heating her heart more than any flare could. He inclined his head toward her, and she rose to meet him.

Their lips touched. Saul's hands found their way up to tangle in her hair and caress her back as she half crawled out of her chair to press against him, her own fingers exploring the muscles over his shoulders and the crook of his neck. His lips were gentle as he explored her mouth, and Maren felt herself melting into his embrace, her body on fire, her mind shorting out as her hands began seeking more of his body to touch.

Then the door behind them slammed, and they pulled apart, both breathing heavily and wide eyed as they glanced back at Gin. She was examining the handful of bottles, packets of food, and blankets she'd scavenged from the lounge area, and Maren couldn't tell how much she'd seen.

"I took a look at the system reports while I was back there." Gin sank into her chair and tossed the bottles of water to her companions. "It's pretty nasty. The rear landing gear, especially, was damaged."

Maren cleared her throat, aware of how red she'd turned.

Saul had relaxed back into his chair, but he was smirking as he watched her out of the corner of his eyes. "Is that so?"

"Yeah, don't worry, though." Gin was in high spirits as she pulled open a bag of dried fruit. "I've got a plan. When we're ready to land, just attach me to the back of the ship where the rear landing gear used to be." She paused, her eyes merry as her companions blinked at her in confusion. "*Because I'm a third wheel.* Get it? A third wheel?"

Maren stared at her for a moment then broke out into laughter. Once she'd started, she couldn't stop, and she doubled over, laughing hysterically as Saul patted her back.

"Yeah, I thought it was pretty good." Gin grinned smugly as she leaned back in her chair, then a frown flickered over her face. "I wasn't kidding about the damage, though." She popped a slice of dried apple into her mouth then offered the bag to Saul, who passed it on to Maren. "From what the system was saying, the cockpit, lounge area, bedrooms, equipment rooms, and forward thrusters are mostly fine, but the supplies hangar is cracked open, the fuel reservoirs are leaking, and the rear thrusters are pretty much shot."

"We can still fly with the front thrusters, as long as we're economical with our fuel," Saul said. He'd leaned forward and was working over the control board.

"How bad is the supplies hangar?" Maren asked. The glow from Saul's touch was fading, and she stretched then grunted as the aches in her body reasserted themselves.

"Most of the stuff should still be secured in place, albeit a little toasty," Gin said, "but the hull is open. We won't be able to get in there without breathing equipment."

"That shouldn't be a problem," Maren said. "They'll have plenty of breathing equipment, and we'll still be able to get in there with space suits once we're in flight. Insulating the insides of the ship might be a problem, but I bet we can work something out."

Saul sat back from examining the dozens of flashing warning lights on the panel. "We should be able to get to Central with what we have."

"That's where we're headed, then? Central?"

"Or another, safer planet," Saul said. "We'll see what the communication channels are saying once we're out of the atmosphere."

"'Kay," Gin said, relaxing a little as she ate more of the fruit. "Will we be hanging around here for long?"

Maren and Saul glanced at each other. "I'd prefer to leave

quickly," Maren said, and Saul nodded. "As soon as the gamma flare's over. We're alone now, but we don't know what's still living in the other stations."

Gin whistled. "Good point. I'd be happy to never see another of those things for as long as I live."

Not that that's likely to happen, Maren thought but kept it to herself. Gin was finally relaxed, and Maren didn't want to spoil her friend's mood. *Besides, we're at least a couple of weeks away from any planet we'd want to land on. A lot can change in a couple of weeks. Humanity will probably have found ways to fight back by then. Effective ways. Safe ways.*

As trained defense technicians, both Saul and Maren would be drafted into whatever fight humanity was capable of mustering— whether it was a highly organized military assault or a desperate last stand against impossible odds. Gin was in the lucky position of not having military training while still being valuable; her experience with communications would probably secure her a position as a priority civilian, and she would be relocated to a safe area where she would work on efficiently redirecting messages between secure planets.

Maren felt herself relax as the three friends sat in silence, watching the gamma flare paint the sky white and blue. Gin would be safe doing what she loved, and Maren would finally get a chance to exercise her talents as a defense technician. The Cymic Parasites weren't to be taken lightly, but in that moment, she felt as though she could handle anything, as long as she and Saul were together.

As if he could hear her thoughts, Saul enveloped her hand with his, and they twined their fingers together. She looked at him and smiled, and he smiled back, warm and reliable, and he squeezed her hand as they both turned back to watch the lights dance through the sky.

PART 5

STATION 335

CHAPTER 38

MITZI LAY ON HER side, swiping her long fingers over the remote that controlled her television. Faces and scenes flashed across the wall, their voices blending into a pleasant drone as the screen's light washed over her.

"There were more delays on the Cendle Expressway today…"

"…speculating about Pattel's relationship with the deceased…"

"…said that the cleanup is already underway…"

"…in other news, Olympic Champion Tarvis Prey…"

More than a hundred news stations, and not a single one reporting on the greatest catastrophe humankind has ever experienced. Mitzi, disgusted, turned off the television with a quick flick and rolled onto her back. The ceiling, an ugly brownish gray, had a clock fixed to it. It read just after ten in the morning, though the windowless room was so dark that she wouldn't have known morning had arrived. The clock was the only decoration in her tiny cube of a room.

She'd only meant to stay there for a few weeks, after all. But the weeks had turned into months, and four years after she'd signed a temporary contract for the Pennan Heights accommodation, Mitzi still couldn't bring herself to personalize her room beyond the simple narrow bed and the clothes she hung in the closet. If she bought nicer furniture, wall hangings, and beautiful bed throws, that would mean she'd accepted the eight-feet-by-eight-feet box was her home. And she couldn't stand the thought.

The cheap, distasteful accommodation had only one thing going for it: close proximity to a number of her old work colleagues. They were aging, like Mitzi. Most of them had earned promotions into management roles, and one, the oldest, had already retired.

"The day I retire is the day I hug a moving train," Mitzi had once said. She'd loved her job in defense, and the dishonorable discharge had hurt her more than she dared to admit to herself.

She didn't work with them anymore, but her old work friends still invited Mitzi whenever they went for drinks or a meal. Sitting around the table with the four people she'd once fought alongside, slinging jokes and discussing work, was the happiest part of her week. Mitzi absorbed the defense workers' gossip like a sponge. She knew who was getting promotions and who was retiring. She'd heard about the Helio-Korre merger before the media even had. And thanks to their meetings, she was also being kept abreast of the Cymic Parasite massacre.

Bolin had told her they were no longer receiving communications from any of the fringe stations, and recently, even some of the larger sectors had started going dark. Estimates had put the total loss of lives in the billions.

Despite that, the situation had only made it on the news when Central issued an official press release. "The news sites are being leaned on," Marcus had said the night before as he swirled his beer and tried to avoid Mitzi's accusing glare. "Central doesn't want people to panic."

"I dunno. This strikes me as the sort of thing that *deserves* a little panic."

Pen laughed. She was lounging back in her seat, bordering on drunk, her half-eaten piece of lab-grown steak hanging limply from the fork she was brandishing. Her steel-gray hair fell over her face, but she couldn't be bothered to push it back. "Oh, yeah, definitely. Except that panicking won't help anything. If you tell people what's really happening and why they haven't heard from dear Uncle Harold in the last week, then what do you think will happen?"

"People will be prepared?" Mitzi hazarded, wishing it were true but already knowing the real answer.

"People will turn *vigilante*," Pen said, jabbing the steak in Mitzi's direction. "It'll be the Salem Witch Trials all over again. Friends will be accused, families will become estranged, and neighbors will be shot for no reason except someone had a gun and got jumpy. Central thinks it has better chances of fighting the Cymics if people stay ignorant, compared to, you know, constant rioting and murdering."

Mitzi had grudgingly agreed. Even with the media suppression, rumors were flying through the community, and regular services that she'd taken for granted were breaking down. She'd been twenty minutes late to the dinner that night because some morons had staged a protest that had turned violent and interrupted the shuttle system.

Still, Mitzi was frustrated that she had to rely on her friends so heavily to remain in the loop. It was even more frustrating that the rest of the planet knew even less than she did. At the rate the Cymics were spreading, they could wipe out half of humanity within a week if Central didn't do something drastic.

Mitzi reached above her head and picked up the communications block she'd discarded there. *Zero new messages.* She tossed it back with a frustrated groan.

As distressing as the Cymic massacre was, it had offered Mitzi a small spark of hope. On their first drink night after the threat had become known, Pen, intoxicated, had let slip that Central was panicking because it suspected it had lost most of its best fighters. It had been sending them to the thousands of assistance requests that had been flooding in, and Central was becoming increasingly concerned that the help requests were traps. Very few of the dispatched ships had actually returned.

They'll call me, Mitzi had told herself a hundred times during the following week. *I may have been dishonorably discharged, but I didn't receive a criminal conviction. They're desperate. They'll call me.*

But two weeks after the first reports of the Cymic Parasites had started filtering through, she still hadn't received a summons. Bolin worked in human resources, and he'd cautiously admitted that they were drafting increasingly inexperienced people to work in the defense. "Our ranks are seriously depleted, and we need help more than ever before. Central's taking just about anyone with two legs and a brain."

So why haven't they called? I spent twenty years in defense. I led twelve highly successful missions. I'm not as young as I was, but I'm fit and healthy. They need me!

Mitzi groaned and rolled onto her other side, facing the bare brown-gray wall. Four years working any menial job she could get had been soul crushing, but it was nothing compared to knowing she could be useful…if only Central would swallow its pride and overlook what had led to her being discharged.

Someone banged on the door, and a feeble, cracking voice called in, "Mitz, you still alive?"

Mitzi sighed as she recognized the voice of her neighbor, Cali. Mitzi wanted to ignore her but knew that would only cause trouble. "Probably."

"Come down and have dinner with us, honey. You've been locked in that room for days."

"Hmm."

"You can have some of my famous meatball soup."

Mitzi shuddered. "Thanks. I'll, uh, think about it."

"See you soon," Cali croaked, and Mitzi listened to the footsteps disappear down the hallway.

She means well, Mitzi coached herself as she bit down on the frustration. *She doesn't realize you want to be left alone. Or how disgusting her meatball soup is.*

Mitzi relaxed, breathing deeply, trying to shake the built-up tension out of her chest. It was hard to keep track of time in the dimly lit room, and she was on the edge of drifting off when a quiet beep above her head sent her heart into her throat.

She twisted, kicking the blankets off the bed as she snatched up her communication block. There was one new message, marked as urgent and with an official seal.

Her hands were shaking almost too badly to press the buttons to confirm her identity and open the message. She scanned the contents quickly, a fever of excitement building in her stomach and making her want to scream as she saw the words *summoned*, *mission*, and *immediate*.

Finally.

Mitzi read the message again, this time more carefully, as she pulled her boots out from under her bed and strapped them on. Central was calling her back into service for an urgent mission scheduled to leave that afternoon from the fourth port. The craft was scheduled for takeoff at two. Mitzi glanced up at the clock on the ceiling and felt her heart falter when she saw it was nearly noon. She would be able to make it, but without much time to spare.

Why'd they give me such late notice? They're not hoping I'll miss the flight, are they?

Boots tied, Mitzi jumped out of bed and grabbed the coat she'd hung in her near-empty cupboard. She shoved her identification card and wallet into her pocket then left the room without even a look back. She didn't waste time locking the door—she didn't have anything worth stealing—and bolted down the flights of stairs, too impatient to wait for the elevator.

She lived on the eighth floor of the twenty-four-story accommodation block. For most of the occupants, it was little more than a cheap hotel; the rooms had only just enough space for a bed, and each floor shared a communal bathroom, kitchen, and living area. Mitzi passed groups of people on the stairs. A few called out greetings, which she returned absentmindedly. When she reached the foyer, she veered right into the cramped reception office.

The building's owner sat behind the desk, his greasy hair slicked back on his distorted skull. Mitzi had heard rumors that he had once been in defense, too, until a mission had gone wrong and damaged his skull and spine. She had no idea if it was true or not, but it would explained his bitter attitude.

"Just wanted to let you know I'm leaving," she said, breathless, as she swiped her card over the desk's scanners to pay for her remaining rent.

His black eyebrows descended as he glared at her. "For how long?"

"No idea. Probably forever."

Mitzi dashed from his office before he could stop her and ran into the outside city.

It wasn't quite midday, and her sector's biosphere cast a strange dull light. The city had been built for efficiency. The buildings were all between twenty and twenty-nine stories high, and the streets were stacked on top of each other, each new level held up by steel and concrete pillars. Mitzi had gone to the ground floor of the city, which was where the shuttles were located. Shuttles were the fastest form of transport available, and a shuttle was the only thing that would guarantee she would get to the station on time.

Mitzi ran, weaving through pedestrians, counting the seconds as she dashed the eight blocks to the nearest shuttle station. She hadn't had time to read the attachment that would detail exactly what the job was, but she already guessed it would be dangerous. That didn't matter. As a commander in the defense sector, her favorite missions had been the ones she hadn't expected to come out of alive.

Mitzi reached the tunnel that led into the shuttle station and, murmuring apologies she didn't mean, pressed through the tightly packed lunchtime crowd while bobbing to try to read the signs flashing across the roof.

"To Donokan…to Maybury…to Jovat Two…"

Then she caught sight of the sign she'd been looking for: to Port Four, Shuttle Twenty-Nine. She pushed down the green-tiled side passageway, groaning at how congested it was, and squeezed through the crowd as vigorously as she could without being unforgivably rude. She heard a whistle at the end of the passageway and made a final desperate lunge, shoving between a couple who had been holding hands, just in time to see her shuttle disappear down the tunnel.

Mitzi swore, earning herself dirty looks from a knot of elderly women. Heart in her throat, she looked at the timetable. The next shuttle to Port Four wouldn't come for another forty minutes.

The ship was set to launch in less than two hours, and if she wasn't there on time, it would leave without her.

She'd guessed she must still have some enemies in Central who hadn't been able to forgive her for what she'd done to Captain Jones—and this tight schedule confirmed it. Captain Jones had been well liked, and Mitzi wouldn't have been surprised if someone, or possibly a few someones, were subtly sabotaging her chance to reenter the defense sector. Bumping her name to the bottom of the list when selecting captains would have been easy, or they could send her summons out a few hours too late so there was a good chance she wouldn't make it on time.

Central didn't give second chances very often. If she missed that ship, she would be blacklisted. If she were ever summoned again, it would be when the war was all but lost.

She couldn't miss the ship.

Mitzi ran back up the hallway she'd just come from, pushing against the flow of traffic. If she took the shuttle to Redding, she could change to a service taking her to one of the suburbs that clustered around the ports then get a direct line to Port Four.

Desperation made her ruder than she normally would have been, and by the time she was boarding the shuttle to Redding, she thought she must have shoved ahead of at least half of the commuters.

She settled into one of the cylindrical shuttle's padded seats just as it pulled away from the station, and she pulled the harness on, panting, a stitch developing in her side.

Damn, Mitz, you've let yourself go these last four years.

The man in the seat to her left shot her a dour look before returning to his novel. Mitzi closed her eyes and took a moment to enjoy the sensation of the shuttle rocketing along its tracks, then pulled her communication block out of her pocket and opened the attachment that had come with her summons.

"Oh, good," she murmured, a wolfish grin spreading over her face as she read through the mission description. "This is going to be even crazier than I'd hoped."

CHAPTER 39

THE CHANGE AT REDDING went without a hitch; the crowds were thinner there, and she was able to run the eighteen stations and leap through her shuttle's doors just as they were closing. She collapsed into her seat in the nearly empty carriage, panting and grinning to herself. Her grin didn't die until the shuttle ground to a halt six minutes later.

This is a direct service. It shouldn't stop for another twenty minutes.

Mitzi hesitated for a second then unbuckled her harness and scooted over to a window. The shuttle had stopped in one of the downtown shopping sections. Brightly colored signs coated the metal-plated buildings on either side of the street. Strangely, there were no pedestrians in sight.

Mitzi turned her head so her cheek was pressed to the cool glass, and she looked toward the front of the shuttle. A flickering yellow glow in the distance caught her eye, and she thought she could hear quiet, periodic booms. *Drums.*

"We have experienced an unexpected delay," a cool woman's voice said over the speaker system. "Please remain in your seats."

"Like hell," Mitzi growled. If the shuttle had stopped because of a protest—and the beating drums made her increasingly certain that was the cause—she could be stuck for hours.

She slipped out of the aisle seating and tried the doors. They were sealed shut and wouldn't open until the shuttle was docked at the station. A swearword slipped out as Mitzi turned and dashed down the length of the shuttle, toward the emergency exit near its front. The chanting was rapidly growing closer. By the time she'd reached the emergency doors, Mitzi could see the glow of harsh flashlights—used to blind anyone who tried to break up the protest—and hear wild whoops and shrill calls.

The Cymic situation had started the riots, but there was no guarantee that was what the protest focused on. An air of hysteria was gradually overwhelming the city; more often than not, the riots had no real purpose except for the marginalized, and those who felt they were marginalized, to unleash their frustration.

Mitzi pressed the button to unlock the emergency exit door and wrenched it open. The protesters had gained on her shuttle faster than she'd expected. As soon as she opened the door, hands grabbed her arms and pulled her into the swell of bodies.

"I completely agree with whatever you guys want," Mitzi yelled then squirmed out of the hands that had a grip on her and began worming through the riot.

It was a colorful, chaotic mess. Many in the crowd had splashed themselves with neon paint or dyes that made their clothes shine in the erratic flashlight beams. The militia was already descending on them, pouring out of side streets to clash with the protesters. The last thing she needed was to be mistaken for a protester and stunned, so Mitzi shied away from them and began pushing through the screaming, aggressive rioters, moving against the flow to stay away from where the two groups were meeting. She heard several quiet snaps as the militia started firing tranquilizer rounds into the crowd. The clash of metal on plexiglass followed as the civilians beat their homemade weapons against the militia's shields.

You made the right choice. Mitzi had reached the edge of the crowd, where the older and less aggressive protesters were watching the action. She glanced back at the riot, which had spilled onto the tracks. *That shuttle would have been stuck for ages.*

On the other hand, she no longer had transport. As Mitzi jogged through the streets, relieved to leave the enraged yells and tranquilizer snaps behind her, she tried to calculate how much time she had left. Not enough to find another station—besides, with one shuttle delayed, there was no guarantee that the rest of the network was running on schedule. Taxis were expensive, but that was her only chance of getting to Port Four.

Mitzi ran until she reached one of the main roads and was able to signal for a taxi. The sleek gray self-driving car pulled up to the curb, and Mitzi jumped into the passenger seat.

The taxis were small, with just enough room for two passengers and a case of luggage, though they had a minibar between the seats and a clear screen installed into the front windowpane, where a map flickered into view.

"Where would you like to go today?" a bright AI voice asked.

"Port Four, Central," Mitzi replied, pulling her card out of her back pocket and swiping it over the screen to authorize payment. She put on her belt and leaned back into the padded leather seat as the car re-joined the flow of traffic. "Fast as possible, please."

"I will maintain a safe and legal speed," the AI said, and Mitzi groaned.

Traffic was heavy, and Mitzi started tapping her fingers on the dash as she watched the suburbs pass at a crawl. "You seem anxious," the AI said after a moment, injecting a note of fake concern into its voice. "Would you like me to pick some music to match your mood?"

"No, absolutely not," Mitzi said. "Just divert all of your energy into driving as fast as possible, okay?"

"My technology does not work in that way," the AI said, sounding so happy that Mitzi was tempted to punch the car. "However, I would be delighted to engage you in a discussion. I have many preset topics of conversation, and my news database has only a two-minute lag from real time."

Mitzi pursed her lips. "Okay, sure. What can you tell me about the Cymic Parasites?"

"Allow me to read the latest media statement," the car said, seeming overjoyed at the prospect. "For immediate release: Central wishes to advise—"

"Okay, yeah, I've already heard that one. 'The threat is serious but not insurmountable. Stay in your homes after dark. Follow all commands a public official gives you. Don't panic.' *Et cetera.* It's about as useful as a dead mule."

"Dead mules can be used for many purposes," the AI said. "For food, provided it has died within a safe timeframe and was not carrying any harmful bacteria or viruses. Its bones can be fashioned into tools—"

"Shut up," Mitzi grunted, sinking lower in her seat. The car was speeding up as it made its way out of the city center. Mitzi's stomach had developed a gnawing, empty feeling that told her she'd forgotten to eat both breakfast and lunch, and she grudgingly swiped her card over the minibar's scanner. The lid popped up, offering a range of drinks and foods. They were all horrifically overpriced, but her money wouldn't be much use to her once she was off the planet, so she took one of the apple juices and a sandwich.

"My scanners show that you're low on magnesium," the AI said, so painfully enthusiastic that it made Mitzi's teeth hurt, "which can be a valuable supplement to help you cope in times of stress. May I recommend a nutrient-rich vitamin slice?"

"What are you, my mother?" Mitzi snapped, but she took the recommended cube of gray chalk and washed it down with the apple juice.

Both Mitzi and the AI were silent for the following fifteen minutes, as the car carried her through the industrial part of the city, past another housing sector, around the outskirts of a pristine public park, and toward the more business-focused suburbs around Central's ports.

"I've just been alerted to a potential hazard on our path," the AI said, startling Mitzi out of her reverie. "I'll be adjusting our route."

"What?" Mitzi glanced at the clock on the dashboard; she had only ten minutes until the ship's launch. "Will that take long?"

"Expected time to destination: twelve minutes."

Mitzi swore. "You've got to get me there faster! I've got a ship to catch!"

"I will take you there in the fastest legal and safe manner," the AI replied. "Please enjoy your trip!"

Mitzi hunched over, pressing her palms against her closed eyelids. Next to the shuttles, the taxis were the fastest form of transport. She had no option but to grit her teeth and hope the car's time estimate wasn't accurate. "What caused the hazard?" she asked, trying to keep her voice calm and level. "Is it another riot?"

"That's correct. Good guess!" the car chirped. "In fact, there are multiple riots in our pathway."

"Terrific," Mitzi groaned. *I can't wait to get off this stupid planet.*

She kept flicking her eyes from the clock to the streets every few seconds for the rest of the trip. She could see plumes of smoke in the distance, and once, they passed a street that had been looted. Windows had been smashed, and broken bricks and discarded goods filled the street.

It's getting worse. People are panicking because they know

284

something's wrong, but they don't know what it is or how they can help. If Central just explained the situation properly, we might stand a chance of banding together.

"How long now?" she asked when the clock read two minutes to two.

"Four minutes to destination. We're right on schedule!"

"No, we're not." Mitzi scratched at her scalp. Fear of losing the ship and losing her last chance to get back on the defense force made her want to lash out. She watched as the clock ticked past 2:00, then 2:01, and finally 2:02.

"You have arrived at your destination," the AI said, all bubbles and rainbows. "I hope you've enjoyed your trip!"

"And I hope you die in a fire," Mitzi spat back, tugging on her seat belt until the car came to a stop and allowed Mitzi to unlock it.

She was at the front gates for Port Four. The building, all gray stones and metal accents, rose like a mammoth wall in front of her. Mitzi ran for the front doors, hoping desperately that something had delayed her ship but knowing the ports ran to a precise timetable that was almost never disturbed.

The inside of the port's foyer was large, airy, and almost disturbingly white. Screens lined the walls, each flashing different departure and arrival times for the hundreds of docking areas. Terminals—some advertising available seats on commercial flights, others for checking in—filled most of the vast room. Mitzi ran to the nearest information desk, which was mercifully free.

"*Teal Riot*, Ship 81157," she said, speaking so quickly that it was a miracle the manicured woman in front of her could understand her. "Has it left yet?"

The assistant gave her a quick, vaguely sympathetic smile as she typed the digits into her computer. "Not yet, but you won't reach it in time. It's on the runway—"

"Which one?"

The woman chuckled, shaking her head. "It's about to take off. You won't reach it."

"Tell me which one, damn it!"

"Platform twelve, third floor," the assistant said, her eyes widening slightly as she pointed to her left.

Mitzi yelled a quick "Thank you!" over her shoulder as she started running again. She'd lucked out that she only needed to get to the third floor, and she lucked out again when one of the lift doors opened just as she reached them. She squeezed herself into the compartment, breathing hard, and tried not to look too manic as the doors drew closed and the box started ascending.

She'd loved the ports during her time as an active defense technician. They carried such a wide variety of people, all who had such diverse skills and job descriptions, that she'd spent a lot of her time watching the strangers around her, trying to guess their jobs and personalities. She'd gotten quite good at it.

To her left were two emergency response personnel. That was an easy enough guess; their black uniforms were slightly thicker than normal and clearly made in a government facility. Both had short, slicked-back hair, which was normal for someone used to wearing an emergency response protective helmet. They were young, though, probably barely out of the academy, and judging by the way the woman's mouth was twitching, they weren't looking forward to the job they'd been given.

To her right was a maintenance worker dressed in dirty overalls and carrying a crate of tools. Behind him was, she guessed, a merchant and a couple of tourists, one who held a young baby to her chest. The tourists were clutching their tickets so firmly that they seemed frightened they might be taken away.

Not tourists, then…civilians fleeing a planet that was becoming too dangerous for their young family.

The lift pinged as it reached the third floor, and Mitzi squeezed out between the doors while they were still opening. Near-empty gray hallways spread to her left and right. She turned left and counted the dock numbers on the signs she ran past. When she reached twelve, she speared off into the side passageway. Long glass windows let her see into the interior dock, where a large craft—*her* craft—had started its engines.

CHAPTER 40

"STOP!" MITZI SCREAMED, BEATING on the windows as she ran past them, aware that no one in the ship would be able to hear her. Someone yelled from the hallway she'd just come down, and without turning around, Mitzi knew she'd attracted the attention of the security guards.

The door that opened into the ship's boarding room was at the end of the hallway, and Mitzi skidded to a halt in front of it, banging frantically. "I'm here! I made it, damn you!"

Someone wrenched open the door, and a familiar man exhaled at the sight of her. "Hell, Mitz, get in here."

Mitzi jumped through the doorway, and her companion slammed the door closed in the security guard's face then beamed at her. "Do you have any idea how close you cut that? I was just leaving."

"Nic," Mitzi gasped, pressing at the aching stitch in her side and feeling happier to see the pilot than she'd ever been in her life. She wanted to hug him but settled for punching his arm as hard as she could.

"Quick, we'd better take off before they decide to cancel the flight altogether." Nic ushered her into the cockpit and slid into the leather pilot's seat while Mitzi took the passenger seat. The ship had already been prepped for takeoff, and Nic quickly unlocked the passageway that connected the ship to the station before he pushed down on the lever to urge the engines into action. Their ship shuddered then ground forward, toward the air lock.

Mitzi didn't dare speak as they eased the ship into the dark room then waited as the doors closed behind them and the air was pumped out. The gates ahead of them opened, letting them outside the city's biosphere and giving the ship a clear run toward the atmosphere. Nic kicked the engines into action and sent the ship soaring toward the sky, and Mitzi could finally breathe properly.

"I didn't think I was going to make it." She massaged her temple, where a headache had flared.

"I knew you would." Nic's cocky grin stretched across his face. "As soon as I saw your name on the mission's list, I knew you'd get here come hell or high water. It's good to have you back, Captain."

Mitzi laughed, realizing that she was, really and truly, back. *You made it, girl. You're in the defense force again...even if it is for just one trip.*

"You won't believe how hard I had to delay, though," Nic said, grinning wolfishly as their ship rose above the planet.

Mitzi gazed out the windows at the little bubbles below, each bubble holding a city, all interconnected by tunnels. "Yeah?"

"Yeah. I made two trips to the bathroom, and even pretended I'd dropped my keys in the waiting area. The staff was furious, but I didn't want to leave without you."

Mitzi reached across the seats to give Nic's shoulder a tight squeeze, then she punched his arm again to stop him from getting any ideas that she'd gone soft.

Nic was much younger than Mitzi, but they'd been on several missions together. She was glad to have him as her pilot. He had a level head and just enough of a sense of adventure to agree to her plans.

"Buckle up," Nic said, indicating the lightening sky. "We're nearly at the atmosphere. After that, it's just a short trip to the wormholes and three hours to touchdown at your location. You ready for it?"

"I'm so ready," Mitzi said, pulling the harness over her shoulders and locking it into place. "Your little mind isn't even able to comprehend how ready I am."

"Good."

The ship started to rattle as it reached the atmosphere, where bright light enveloped them.

Nic pressed a button to close the windows, and with the ship on autopilot, he settled back into his seat. "You might want to share some of that readiness around. Your new crew isn't looking so hot."

In the excitement of getting to the station, Mitzi had completely forgotten that she was supposed to have a team under her command. "Oh yeah? What're they like?"

"I didn't get to talk to them, but I watched them board from my window. You've got six. I'd be surprised if half of them have been off the planet before. They all look terrified."

"Hmm. Terrified is better than cocky. I thought I was supposed to have a full set, though."

A full set meant a team of eleven under a commander.

"Yeah, you were, but only six showed up. It's not unusual. In the chaos, Central's records are going to hell, and they have no manpower to chase down people who skirt their duties. It's the easiest thing in the world to just *not show up* for your summons."

"People aren't worried Central will catch up to them after this whole mess is sorted?"

"Sure, but what's the worst Central's going to do? Fine them? Most people are quite happy to take their chances with a slap on the wrist instead of, you know, taking a job that will dice their life expectancy in half."

The ship stopped shaking as it left the atmosphere, and Nic recalled the blinds. Space, vast and terrifying, stretched out ahead of them, full of possibilities. Shivers ran down Mitzi's spine and into her toes as she surveyed the countless stars, each one a shepherd of its planets, its planets' moons, and its own collection of asteroids.

Humans, the dominant life-form in the known parts of

space, had set up more than two thousand stations on a range of planets and moons stretching for forty square light-years. But the farther humanity probed into the inky blackness, the more clear it became that they'd only touched the smallest fragment of sand in the universe's beach. The Cymic Parasites were proof of that; after hundreds of years of space exploration, most people had come to believe they were reasonably secure. Then, in the space of a few weeks, up to a third of those two thousand stations had been consumed by an enemy humans still didn't fully understand.

The red light above the dashboard turned green as her ship finally left the system of wormholes. Mitzi sighed, relieved to be free of the bone-shuddering turbulence, and unclipped her harness. "Right. Where'd my team get put?"

"In the storage room," Nic said. He was bent over his control panel, his forehead creased as he carefully adjusted dials. "The door on the right after the lounge area. You've got just under three hours till touchdown."

"Thanks." Mitzi clapped him on the back before passing through the door at the back of the room.

Teal Riot, their ship, looked as though it had originally been a privately owned shuttle. Mitzi guessed Central must have claimed it after losing too many of their own ships. The rooms had been stripped of everything nonessential in an attempt to lighten it and increase its speed, but there were still enough touches of elegance—mahogany paneling, plush seats, and large clear windows—to make it feel like a vacation cruiser. Mitzi crossed through what had once been the ship's lounge area but was currently storing seven cloth-covered shapes, and paused outside the door to the storage room, where her six-person crew was waiting for her.

CHAPTER 41

NORMALLY, CENTRAL ARRANGED FOR teams to spend some time together—usually undergoing a week or more of training in each other's company—before a team was dispatched on a mission, but there had simply been no time before their mission. With the Cymics moving so quickly, every hour counted.

Mitzi knew she'd have to make a strong first impression if she was going to get any respect from them. She ran her hands through her short bob of black hair to smooth it back then shoved the door open. Quiet chatter abruptly fell silent, and four out of the six people inside unbuckled and stood.

Mitzi paused in the doorway for half a minute, glancing at each occupant before stepping into the dingy, cramped room. It had probably been the kitchen before the conversion, judging by the tiled walls and exposed pipes. Its equipment had been stripped and replaced with twelve crash seats, six against opposite walls. There was just enough of a walkway between them for Mitzi to pace comfortably, so that's what she did.

Look confident. Speak loudly. Command respect.

"I'm Mitzi, and I'll be your tour guide on this delightful field trip. Quickly now, tell me your names."

She stopped in front of the first man on the left. He was the oldest out of all of them, probably older than Mitzi herself, but the thin, reedy man looked completely uncomfortable in his new silver-and-blue suit. His eyes bugged a little when Mitzi focused her attention on him, but he swallowed and answered quickly, "Franc, ma'am."

"Captain," Mitzi corrected. She squinted at the man, trying to figure out his occupation. It clearly had nothing to do with defense. "Let me guess; you were in banking before Central volunteered you for this mission. No? Some job involving money?"

"Accounting, ma—Captain."

Mitzi gave him a tight smile. "I hear accountancy schools have terrific combat training."

It had been a joke, but Franc only frowned at her, perplexed. Mitzi grimaced and turned to the woman beside Franc, one of the two people who'd remained seated. She was young, probably still a teenager, and her long, dark hair framed her face.

"Name?" Mitzi asked.

The girl pursed her lips as she looked Mitzi over. As her sullen eyes met Mitzi's, she said with a careless shrug, "Mir."

Oh good, this one's going to be trouble.

"First thing, Mir, in future you'll reply to me immediately when I ask you a question. Secondly, are you missing half your brain? It's insanity to have long, loose hair in combat. It'll get in your face and blind you anytime you try to turn quickly—which is exactly the time when you want your vision clear."

The girl had turned sheet white, and her lips were clenched. She no longer tried to meet Mitzi's eyes but stared at the floor with such intense hatred that Mitzi wouldn't have been surprised if it had crushed the kid's parents.

"Use this." Mitzi plucked a hair tie out of her pocket and flicked it at Mir. It hit the girl's chest and bounced onto the seat beside her, where Mir pointedly ignored it.

Fine. Be that way.

Mitzi turned to the third person on the left hand side of the room—another girl, a couple of years older but still too young to be much use on the battlefield. Her strawberry-blond hair was cut in a short crop, and her delicate, graceful face didn't instill Mitzi with much confidence. *The pretty ones always expect to be looked after.*

"Skye," the girl said in a clear, loud voice before Mitzi had even opened her mouth. "It's an honor to serve on your crew, Captain."

Mitzi raised an eyebrow. *Huh. Maybe I was wrong.*

"You looking forward to killing some Cymics, Skye?"

The girl hesitated for half a second. "Not especially, Captain, but I'm prepared."

Mitzi nodded slowly, feeling half a smile creep over her face. "Good answer. Welcome to the crew, Skye."

She pivoted on her boots to face the other side of the room. A man, a grin plastered over his angular face, was waiting for her. "Unlike my delightful companion, I am very much looking forward to blasting some Cymics. The bastards have a lot to answer for."

Terrific. Mitzi massaged the bridge of her nose. The man in front of her was in his early twenties and probably had some sort of training, which, judging by his posture, was basic at best. "You forgot your name, genius."

"Adam, Cap. And don't worry. I've been through some pretty comprehensive combat training." He flashed her a wink. "You can rely on me."

"Yeah, no, I'm completely certain I can't. Though I'm glad at least someone on this team has some training. All eight minutes of it."

Adam opened his mouth as Mitzi turned away, and she held up a hand to silence him. "Don't talk unless I talk to you. Understood, hotshot?"

His charismatic smile had turned into a scowl. "Yes, *Captain.*"

If she'd had more time, Mitzi would have reprimanded him for the scorn he'd enveloped her title in, but they had less than three hours until they reached their destination and a lot of ground to cover. Besides, this job was basically a punishment in its own right. *Five minutes on a Cymic-controlled planet should deflate his ego pretty quick.*

The fourth member of her team, another girl, was standing to attention, her eyes focused on a point of the wall somewhere above Mitzi's head. She was shaking like a leaf. "Ellen."

Mitzi squinted at her. She looked different, somehow, than she had when Mitzi had entered the room. It took her a minute to pin down what it was; the girl's long white-blond hair had been tied up into a tight knot at the top of her head.

"What happened to your hair?"

The girl swallowed, and her eyes flicked to Mitzi before she turned them back to the wall. "Loose hair has no place on the battlefield, Captain."

Mitzi chuckled, nodding slowly. "Good. You're almost certainly going to die, but at least you won't look like a moron when you do."

The final passenger was the only other member, apart from Mir, who had remained seated. His face was unhealthily thin and angular, and his bony hands gripped a small paperback book, which he seemed to be reading furiously.

"Name?" Mitzi asked, folding her arms as she leaned over him.

The boy swallowed but didn't speak.

"It's Eoin, Captain," the girl to his right whispered. She looked terrified to be speaking out of turn.

"Is it, now?" Mitzi purred, turning back to her. "Do you want to tell me why he's reading a book during a debriefing that could keep him from becoming Cymic food?"

Mitzi had kept her voice low, but the girl flinched as though she'd been yelled at. "I'm sorry. I don't know."

"Uh-huh." Mitzi glanced at Eoin again, but he was focused on his book. "That better be a damn good story, kid."

Mitzi returned to the head of the room, taking languid steps, then swiveled neatly to face her team. "I'd heard Central had lost almost all of its best fighters, but I didn't realize they'd lost the mediocre ones too. I'm not going to lie; none of you are giving me much confidence. It's abundantly clear you don't have any experience, except for Captain Hotshot over there, who's probably going to trip and shoot himself the first chance he gets. You're all screwed."

She darted her eyes around the room, searching for the spark of defiance, the look of *I'll show you* that almost inevitably followed her harsh words. There was none. Adam had lost the cocky smirk and looked bitter and frustrated. Mir, still seated and pale, had her eyes fixed on the floor, seemingly deflated. Franc and Skye both looked anxious. Eoin hadn't turned the page on his novel since she'd entered the room. His eyes were fixed on the same spot, and sweat coated his forehead. Ellen, the girl beside him, had her head bowed deeply and turned away.

Cripes, is she actually crying?

Mitzi felt a knot of guilt build in her stomach as she realized her tactics had been completely backward. She'd used the shtick she employed against trained fighters who would buck her if she gave them any leeway. But these people weren't fighters; they were kids—and one middle-aged accountant—who'd been coerced into a war they didn't want to fight. And they were terrified.

She hadn't needed to give them a wake up to reality. They'd been staring reality in the face since being summoned that morning. Mitzi had simply confirmed what none of them had wanted to say: they had very, very bad odds of completing the mission and even worse odds of making it off the planet alive. They didn't need shaking up. They needed their hands held.

"Jeez," Mitzi hissed. *I'm rubbish at hand-holding.*

She stormed into the lounge area, grabbed one of the folding seats, then brought it back into the equipment room. She flicked it open, slammed it on the ground at the head of the two rows of seats, and collapsed into it with a sigh. "Okay, you four, sit down already. Someone get Ellen a tissue. Eoin, I'm sure it's riveting, but would you please put your book down for half a minute?"

For a second, she thought he wasn't going to comply, but then Eoin closed the paperback and tucked it into his suit's pocket. His sunken eyes were red rimmed.

"I want to make a deal with you." Mitzi tried to moderate her voice to be slower and calmer as she gazed at her new team. "Yes, this mission sucks. Yes, your life expectancy took a nosedive the moment you were signed up for it. But it's not impossible, and it's not a death sentence." Skye and Adam risked looking at her. Mitzi took that as a good sign. "Here's the deal: I'm going to do my absolute best to get every single one of you out of there alive. But in return, I need you to trust me."

"Okay," Skye said at once.

Mitzi flashed her a tight smile.

"Good. Now, I know a tiny bit about all of you. It's your turn to learn about me. As you know, I'm Mitzi DeLacanto. I was a recon team leader for twelve years until my retirement."

"I heard it wasn't a retirement," Adam said. His voice had a smug, accusatory edge, and Mitzi had to fight the urge to slap the smug disdain off his face. "I heard you were discharged."

"Yep." Mitzi's voice was full of forced brightness. "Dishonorable discharge at that. Do you know why?"

He smirked. "Yeah. You shot your commander."

CHAPTER 42

MITZI CLOSED HER EYES. She could still see him, just as clear as if he were in the room with her, his chiseled face creased in concern as he raised his hands in a placating motion. She shook her head to clear the image and hoped her new team wouldn't notice how abruptly she was changing the subject. "Okay. How much do you guys know about the Cymics?"

Murmurs came back to her:

"Not much."

"I know they're dangerous."

"They're a plant, aren't they?"

"Right." Mitzi sucked on her teeth. Even with the media being suppressed so heavily, she would have thought Central would have provided at least a basic overview for the civilians it had called into service. "Let's start there, then. To the best of my knowledge, the first Cymic attacks began eight weeks ago with the corruption of a fringe station near the extremes of our network. The crew put in an emergency help request, but they had been *turned* by the time rescue arrived a week later. The crew that had been sent to them were also turned, and they began stopping off at other stations as they made their way back through the system. The Cymics are sort of like a virus; they spread, and spread quickly. Those other stations sent out their own ships, and the ones without ships put in assistance requests to lure humans to them. The threat became—to keep with the virus analogy—an epidemic."

The ship rumbled and shuddered as it went through a patch of space dust, but no one in the storage room seemed to notice. They were riveted; Mitzi guessed this was possibly the first honest, complete explanation of the parasites they'd heard.

"Central realized something was wrong about two weeks ago, when things started coming to a crux. One of the larger research stations was completely destroyed during a fight. Survivors— station crews who had either been lucky enough or innovative enough to escape the Cymics—began sending warnings to Central. At that time, Central still had no idea what it was up against. It had received thousands of emergency help requests, many times the normal, and had people sending it warnings about a black monster that can replicate human faces. Everything was chaos. Central couldn't get a straight story or figure out what the threat was or how dangerous it might be. It sent a very general warning for all stations to be wary of life-forms they encountered. Of course, that was next to useless."

"I remember that," Ellen said, her eyes as large as saucers. "Didn't they send a second, more complete message the next day?"

"You're from a station, are you?" Mitzi asked, and Ellen nodded. "You're mostly right. A survivor had managed to get back to Central. She was frustrated and terrified by Central's silence, and barricaded herself in their communications room, where she sent a message to as many stations as she could, explaining as much as she could. Her knowledge was incomplete, but she was able to disseminate enough information to allow many stations to fight back. Some people say she's responsible for humanity still being alive today."

"So, how do you fight them?" Adam asked. "I heard they can be killed with fire."

"Hold on. I'm getting to that." Mitzi raised her hands, begging for silence. "Right, so, since that message, a lot of stations learned how to fight the monsters, and more and more survivors were able to make it back to Central and share their knowledge. And, as of last week, Central, that behemoth of bureaucracy, finally started putting up a fight. They worked out systems to detect Cymics and installed them at the ports of as many major stations as they could. They set up artillery points to shoot down any crafts that tried to bypass their checks. They started disseminating basic survival information and sending weapons to the stations they could afford to. This gets me onto my next point: what a Cymic actually is."

"They can change their appearance to replicate any person,

can't they?" Franc was fidgeting with the neckline of his suit, looking incredibly uncomfortable in it.

"Not quite. Cymic Parasites are, as the name implies, parasites. In their native form, they're black, slimy creatures that have no eyes, ears, or nose, but a multitude of tendrils they can use to attack their prey. They don't eat, but they spread themselves by finding hosts. If a Cymic found a human, for instance, they would force their way into the body, either through the person's mouth or by stabbing through the flesh, and infest their new host. Conversion only takes a couple of minutes. The insides of the human are liquefied and absorbed, and the parasite spreads through its new container, consuming nearly everything.

"This is the bit that really sucks: it keeps the human skin. Well, it's not really human by then—it's the Cymic replicating human skin—but it looks and feels for all the world like proper flesh. The Cymic merges with human DNA and learns how to imitate its host's appearance perfectly. Every hair, every scar, everything. Not only that, but it absorbs its host's memories and knowledge. So it not only looks like it's human, but sounds and acts like it too. You see how it could spread so quickly?"

Mitzi's team all nodded, except for Mir, who bowed her head.

"Yeah. There's almost no way to tell a Cymic apart from a regular human. Your twin brother could be turned, and, provided he kept up the human appearance, you could go weeks without noticing. It's the perfect disguise."

"So how *can* you tell?" Adam asked.

"Blood." Mitzi raised her right hand, pulled a penknife out of her pocket, and pressed the tip of the blade to her palm, putting a tiny nick into the flesh. A drop of blood beaded at the cut then ran down toward her wrist. "Cymics keep our skin, but they don't keep anything else—not our skeletons, our organs, or our blood. If you cut a Cymic, all you'd see inside is black stuff."

Satisfied that her demonstration had impressed her new crew, Mitzi replaced her blade. She plucked a cloth out of her back pocket and clenched in her fist to cover the cut. "Many stations without Central's detection software are using that very crude blood test to know which visitors they can trust. They'll let the crew of a strange ship into their air lock and ask each of them to cut a finger or a palm, to check that they bleed. If the visitors refuse, the station cooks them."

Adam opened his mouth, and Mitzi nodded before he could speak. "Yes, you were right; they can be killed with fire. Also by extreme heat, electricity, and high doses of neurotoxins. Things that don't work on them are guns, knives, crushing, pulverizing, freezing, starving…or basically anything else that would kill a human. Because the Cymics absorb their host's DNA, they can repair any damage, no matter how severe, within a few minutes. You can literally turn one into paste, and he'll piece himself back together in front of your eyes. Fire, neurotoxins, and electricity are really the only things that work against them."

"Are they hard to kill?"

The question was so quiet that Mitzi thought it might have come from inside her head; then she saw Ellen shooting her tentative, anxious glances. Mitzi opened her mouth but hesitated.

They're your team. They deserve the truth. "Yes."

Ellen nodded, as though that was the answer she'd expected.

"The Cymics have three forms," Mitzi continued. "There's the native form, where they're a large, slimy, black monster. In their native form, they're incredibly fast and strong. The main upside is that they can't see, smell, or hear you, though they can feel vibrations in the air and through the ground. The second form is the human form. That's where they're wearing their host's skin and look exactly like your neighbor or your sister or your best friend. They're the most dangerous when they're in their native form, but they're hardest to kill in their human form." Mitzi paused and offered her team a tight smile. "Have any of you ever shot another human at point-blank range?"

They all shook their heads.

"Yeah, thought so. It's tough. I'll bet none of you picture yourselves as cold-blooded killers, but you're going to have to come to peace with that before we touch down. The Cymics in human form will look like whoever their host is—whether it's a disabled person, a pregnant woman, or even a child. They might beg. They might cry. But you can't show them so much as a second of mercy. As soon as they have the upper hand, they'll kill you without a second's hesitation."

Ellen was blanched white and shivering. Mitzi felt pity tug at her. If there was any one person not suited to this expedition, it was the girl hugging her chest and blinking back tears. Mitzi wondered how angry Central would be if she left Ellen behind on the ship. *Probably very. Screw them, though.*

"You said there was a third form?" Franc asked after a moment. He had his long, knobbly fingers clasped.

"Yeah, we call it merged. It's where the parasite comes halfway out of its skin. You've got the deadliness of the native form, but the perception and shock value of the human form. Being merged makes the Cymic slower and more clumsy than if it was completely native, but it lets it use its human skin to see and hear you, and even talk to you. I wasn't able to find any photos of what that looked like, but I hear it's not a pretty sight."

The storage room fell silent again. Most of Mitzi's crew had their eyes focused on the ground, processing the new information, though Eoin had surreptitiously pulled his book out of his pocket. Mitzi opened her mouth to tell him to put it away but decided it wouldn't do any good. She was aware of how quickly time was getting away on her. They would be touching down soon, and she still hadn't told them a quarter of what she needed to. They appeared disheartened again, though, and she cast around for something positive.

"Here's a bit of good news at least," Mitzi said, injecting enthusiasm into her voice. "The Cymics can only get you while you're alive. As soon as a person dies, they're useless to the monsters. They can't convert anything that's dead."

"Yay," Adam said bleakly.

"On top of that, if someone's in the process of being turned—that is, they're infected, but the parasite hasn't yet taken them over completely—they can still be killed by destroying the human brain."

"Excuse me, Captain," Skye said, and Mitzi nodded for her to continue. "What are we actually going to be doing?"

"Oh, for the love of—" Mitzi pressed her face into her palms. "Central didn't tell you what the mission was?"

They all shook their heads.

"I asked everyone I could find." Skye twisted her hands together. "They all told me it would be explained on the trip."

"Lovely." Mitzi's tone was bitter, but as she looked up at her six-person crew, she found herself surprised. "So, wait—you all agreed to a job you're phenomenally underqualified for, where there's a very high chance of death, and you didn't even know what it is?"

Skye shrugged. "We all have our reasons. We were talking about that before you came in. I've been trying to get into a defense technician training course for years. They kept rejecting me, but now they need fighters, and, well, here I am."

Mitzi looked the woman up and down. She could guess why the girl had been rejected. With her short crop of strawberry-blond hair, smooth skin, and delicate features, Skye looked far too pretty to be considered a fighter. Regardless, Mitzi was a little impressed.

"What about you?" She turned to Franc.

He shrugged. "They've been saying it's fight or die. That they need people to take a stand if there's any hope for humanity to live." He looked uncomfortable saying it, but Mitzi thought it was a genuine sentiment. "I want my grandchildren to know that I stood up for what's important, what's right, even if it's difficult. Hell…I just want there to be a world for my grand-children, whether they remember me or not. We've all got to make sacrifices."

"Wow, okay." Mitzi glanced at the other side of the room and smirked. "Adam, I can guess why you're here. So you can be an awesome hero and save the world and have all the ladies begging for your attention."

"You know it." He flashed her a devil-may-care grin.

"But you, Ellen. You clearly don't want to be here."

Ellen sniffed. Her hands were clenched so tightly that her knuckles had turned white. "I dunno. Same reason as Franc. I just want to make a difference."

"Yeah." Mitzi sighed. "I'm calling bull on that. What's the real reason?"

Ellen shook her head vigorously.

"Ellen," Mitzi said, letting a low note of warning slip into her tone. "Don't lie to your captain."

"My name's not Ellen," she blurted. "I'm Taurun. Ellen's my older sister. She got the summons. But…she's been trying to get into medical school. She'd die if she had to fight."

Mitzi raised her eyebrows. "And you think you'd fare better than her?"

Ellen no longer tried to stop the tears leaking down her cheeks. "No. But better me than her. She's really smart. She's into politics and humanitarian causes, and-and I've never really known what I wanted to do with my life. She could do so much good—"

"Oh my goodness," Mitzi groaned. "Someone give the damn martyr a hug. Dibs not me."

No one moved for a moment, then Eoin slowly raised a hand and awkwardly patted Ellen's shoulder twice.

"Great, thanks, Eoin," Mitzi muttered as Ellen put her head in her hands. "Don't suppose you want to share your reason for coming here today?"

He shrugged. "It seemed like a good idea at the time."

His voice surprised Mitzi. It was low, nasally, and as nuanced as a robot's.

"Still think it's a good idea?" she asked.

"No." He turned back to his still-open book.

"Okay, good. And that leaves…Mir. Why'd you come?"

The surly teenager on the left bench was twirling Mitzi's hair tie between her fingers. She fixed Mitzi with a cold stare. "No reason."

Yep. You're definitely going to be a problem.

"Well, I guess there's no time like now to tell you what we're doing. Central has been putting up defensive measures for the last week, but they all focus on keeping Cymics *out of* our safe planets. Any station that was infiltrated was dropped like a hot potato. Until now. This is the very first *offensive* mission." She gazed around the room, meeting every set of eyes. "That means we're going to Station 335, which is on a semi-planet that was recently attacked by Cymics. We're going to rescue any humans who may still be alive and throw this little thing"—she pulled a small, square, black box out of her pocket—"into the reactor. The planet was a fuel planet. They harvested and refined gasoline on it. There are pipes running all over it. And this box is a detonator. If we can get it into the main reactor, get back on the ship, and get a safe distance away, then we'd be able to detonate it and, theoretically, set the entire planet on fire."

"Cleanse it." Franc leaned forward, pressing his fingertips over his mouth.

"Exactly. The fire would burn for a couple of days until the fuel ran out. Then the planet should be completely, entirely clean."

"Is it important?" Adam asked. He had his arms crossed again. "I mean, yeah, it would be nice to kill them, but—"

"Don't worry your vainglorious little head," Mitzi said. "It's plenty important. At the moment, communications between Central and the Meidoscycle system are delayed by up to two days. All of the communication stations between the two systems have been turned, which means we have to use long-wave transmissions, which take forever to reach their destination. As you can imagine, it's causing chaos. Things are changing so quickly, and there's no way to share our knowledge and plans. But if we can clean one of the planets between the two systems, we'd be able to parse shortwave transmissions by bouncing them through the intermediate planet. All of a sudden, communication time is dropped from two days to just three hours. The two systems could actually collaborate again."

"Right," Skye said, looking excited. "And we're going with this planet because…"

"Because it's an easy target, yeah. We set it on fire, it's guaranteed to be clean. As soon as we confirm the attack, Central will send a construction ship to build a communications station as quickly as possible. By the time their ship arrives, the fire should be all but over."

"One final question," Franc said. "Why do we have to do it on foot? Couldn't we just shoot a missile at some of the pipes?"

"'Fraid not. Central's already gone through the plans. The planet was designed to be impervious to that sort of attack. It used to house over twelve hundred workers and cost quite a few hundred billion to build. Central didn't want the whole thing gone in a freak accident or a terrorist attack. It's got all sorts of measures built in to protect it. If one section of the station does somehow get set on fire, the rest will go into lockdown to contain the damage. Even if you were lucky to get past the anti-missile defenses, all you'd do is burn a few hundred square meters of the thing, and the Cymics would reclaim the land as soon as the flames were gone. On the other hand, if we get the detonator into the reactor, the flames will, theoretically, override the lockdown system and spread too quickly for the backup segmentation to contain."

"Theoretically?" Mir had finally looked up from under her dark bangs. "Whoa, careful there. Don't be too certain."

"Thanks for the attitude. It's really helping things," Mitzi snapped back. "Look, Central's run the calculations. They say it will work. Will it? I have no clue. All I have to do is get in there and do my job."

"So that's all?" Adam asked. "The ship will drop us off outside this reactor room or whatever, we throw the detonator in, and get out? No fighting the Cymics?"

"Don't worry. You'll have plenty of chances to fight. The reactor is kept well underground in a secure, locked area. We've got about a kilometer to travel by foot before we get there. And we're supposed to look for surviving humans, too, and get them out if at all possible." She glanced at her watch and swore. "Okay, we're miles behind schedule. Follow me. It's time to suit up."

CHAPTER 43

MITZI STOOD, KICKING THE folding chair to one side, and pushed the door open. Back in the lounge area, she stopped in front of one of the seven cloth-covered objects. "There's one of these for each of us. They're not quite custom-made, but Central at least tried to give you one close to your body proportions. Find the one with your name pinned to it and say hello to your new best friend."

She swept her cloth off and stepped back to admire the object under it. She'd seen illustrations, but this was her first time inspecting the ADE in person. It was a full-body suit, painted a deep scarlet with silver highlights. The outside was composed of metal plates, and the inside held several layers of padding.

"This is ADE." She patted the shining metal chest plates, hoping she didn't look as inexperienced as she felt. "Armed Defensive Exoskeleton. It's designed specifically to combat the

Cymics. And congratulations. You're not only on the first-ever offensive mission, but you're the first to test ADE in the field!"

Mir, who had been admiring the plated hands on her suit, dropped them quickly. "Wait. These haven't been tested before?"

"Eh." Mitzi tried to think of a way to make it sound better than it actually was, but she came up with nothing. "They've been sort of tested. In the laboratory. They all work. Technically. But yeah, there might be a few kinks that need ironing out."

"I'm not wearing that." Mir crossed her arms and stepped away from her suit. "What if it suddenly decides to contract me into a pretzel?"

"I'm told it only does pretzel reshaping on Tuesdays," Mitzi growled. "And if you want to have any chance of getting through this mission in one piece, you'll wear the damn suit."

Franc was looking his over carefully, feeling around the armored legs and feet. "Could you explain how they'll help us?"

"Oh, yeah, sure. Well, it's plated with a titanium-lexic blend, which makes it very strong and very light. Theoretically, you should be able to survive being smacked across the room."

"There you go using that word again," Mir grumbled.

Mitzi's patience was wearing thin. She pursed her lips. "Look, I'm sorry, but right now all of this *is* theory. It *should* work flawlessly. Will it? Probably not. But there's literally no time to spend on testing it. If we can't get the upper hand on the Cymics, you might not have a home to return to next week. And the best chance of getting an upper hand, right now, is to get that shortwave link set up between Central and Meidoscycle. Every hour we waste tips the tables against humanity even further."

Mir glared at the floor. For a moment, Mitzi considered leaving her on the ship too. *Surely she'd be more harm than good during the actual attack.* But she needed as many hands with her as possible, so she closed her eyes and counted to ten before continuing. "Okay, so aside from the armor, you've also got some weapons. See that pack on the suit's back? That's a built-in flamethrower. The nozzle's holstered in the suit's thigh, right here. Squeeze the trigger to activate it. You should get about forty minutes of high-intensity flame."

"What about these?" Skye asked. She was holding up one of a series of six round, palm-sized gray objects hung around the suit's waist.

"Those are grenades. Pull them off the suit to activate them. Make sure to throw them as far as you can. I can't promise the suit will protect you from the blast." Mitzi pointed to a pouch hung just below the row of grenades. "In here, you've got knives, a screwdriver, and a flashlight. All useless against the Cymics, but they're still handy things to have. And here"—she held up the right glove—"is filled with electrical outputs. Press the button on your neck to activate it. If a parasite has you pinned, put your glove anywhere on its flesh and give it a shock to make it let you go. I'm told the battery should give us each around five shocks."

"And this?" Skye pointed to a second gun strapped to the suit's left thigh.

"That holds neurotoxin darts," Mitzi said. "They're the third thing that can kill the Cymics. Fire, electricity, neurotoxins. One dart should do it, but you can use two to be doubly sure. They're great for stealth kills, but they'll take a few minutes to work, so if you're grappling with one of the monsters, you're better off using the more immediately effective flamethrower."

"These must have been expensive," Franc muttered, feeling between two of the plates.

"Oh, yeah, absolutely. But Central's manufacturing them as quickly as it can. These seven are from the first completed line." Mitzi checked her watch again. "Okay, there's about thirty minutes before we touch down. Suit up, ducklings."

Mir sighed and crossed her arms.

Skye felt around the plates on the suit's chest, a frown creasing her delicate face. "Um, Captain, how do they open?"

Mitzi's smile was frozen as she gave her suit a quick once-over. "To be honest, I'm not exactly sure. Maybe one of the buttons does something…"

The seven of them started searching their suits, trying to find an opening. Mitzi was feeling around the neck when a shriek and a flash of yellow light made her jump. She swiveled around to see Ellen stumbling away from the suit's hand, which was spewing fire.

"Jeez." Mitzi jogged toward the flame and quickly pressed the button to turn it off. "You okay, Ellen?"

"Taurun," the girl corrected, looking mortified. "I'm fine."

"Yeah, I'm calling you Ellen." Mitzi sighed and took the girl's elbow to pull her away from the rest of the crew, who had returned to looking for the suit's opening mechanism. "Listen, you're going to be fine. I'm leaving you on the ship. You can go and sit with the pilot, Nic. He's a nice guy. He'll look after you."

Ellen's eyes widened then squeezed shut. "No. I said I was going to fight the Cymics."

"Well, you're not. I'd prefer knowing you're safe here."

"I made a promise," Ellen stuttered. Her eyes opened, and tears began leaking down her cheeks again. "I can do this. I can *help*."

Mitzi examined the girl's face. Her lips trembled, but her eyes didn't invite objection. Mitzi raised her eyebrows. "Well, okay then."

There was a quiet whirring noise behind them, then Skye yelled, "Captain! I found how the suits open. It's a button near the palm!"

Mitzi gave Ellen's forearm a quick squeeze then turned back to the suits. As promised, Skye's opened. The chest, leg, and arm plates split outward, showing the padded insides, with a perfect human-shaped hollow for its commander to fit into. "Terrific! Show me where."

Skye pointed to the small button on the right inner wrist, and Mitzi quickly found it on her own suit. "Okay, be careful with that one. It's right behind the electrocution button. The last thing I want is my crew fried before we even leave the ship."

For a moment, whirring sounds filled the lounge area as the suits opened up, then Mitzi led her team by stepping into the hollow inside.

The intercom above her head crackled, then Nic's voice came through the speakers. "Just wanted to let you guys know we'll be touching down in ten minutes."

Mitzi cursed. She'd been hoping to give her crew at least an hour of practice inside the suits before they had to use them on the battlefield. "Okay, we've still got a couple of minutes. How do we close these damn things?"

She glanced at her team, all standing inside the open suits like exposed mummies in their sarcophagi, all watching her expectantly. *Think, Mitzi: if the suit seals around you, you can't move your hand...*

Mitzi's fingers found a button in her suit's palm, and she pressed it. The suit whirred again, and the plates started folding around her. She fought against a spike of panic as the sensation of being trapped began to overwhelm her. She'd never been good with enclosed spaces. The plates gradually covered her, moving slowly and gently, so they didn't pinch anything, until the faceplates covered her eyes, blocking out all light.

Her panic spiked as the inside of the suit stayed dark. *Isn't there supposed to be a visual dash? Cameras? I can't see a thing. Is it broken?* She tried to take a step forward, but the suit's heavy legs were resistant. Mitzi struggled to control her breathing as sweat broke out over her. Then Skye's voice, muffled, called, "Press the button again to turn it on!"

Mitzi's shaking fingers found the small knob near her palm and pressed it. The plates surrounding her tightened as they locked into place, and the inside of her helmet flickered to life.

"Okay." Mitzi sighed, feeling the panic in her chest subside. "Let's see what we've got here."

The screen wrapped around her face like a long, narrow TV. She could see the ship's hull, strikingly bright and saturated. *Night vision.* Mitzi squinted against the light, but then the screen automatically dimmed to a kinder level.

Several signals ran along the base of the screen. She could see six numbers, with a list of details below them.

1. Active, intact
2. Active, intact
3. Offline

Only when number three's status changed to *Active, intact* did Mitzi realize they were statuses for her crew members.

She tried to take a step forward and was delighted when the suit responded to her movement. It was clearly designed to support and mimic its owner's actions, to reduce fatigue, and increase speed, but it hadn't been calibrated properly. Mitzi had only intended to take a small step, but the suit sent her reeling forward. She tried to pull up short and nearly overbalanced.

A man's voice cursed in her ear, coming through the headset, and she turned to see one of the suits had fallen to the ground—Adam's, judging by the voice. The others were having just as much trouble as she was. They staggered around the room like drunk robots, bumping into the walls and each other.

"I hate this," a voice shrieked.

"Mir?"

"Let me out! I want to get out!"

"Calm down," Mitzi said, trying, and failing, to keep her voice patient. She turned to face the girl, and her suit compromised by spinning her an extra fifteen degrees. She bit down on her own frustration with great difficulty. "This is new, and difficult, but give yourself a few minutes to adjust, and you'll be fine."

"Hey." Nic's voice came through the headset, sounding simultaneously amused and anxious. "Talking about minutes, you have two left."

"*Two?* Circle around," Mitzi barked. "We need some time to get used to this."

"We're already within a hundred meters of the planet's surface. Central's orders: if the ship wakes the Cymics up, they might try to bring us down. I'm supposed to drop you and return to a safer height to wait for the pickup."

Panicky breathing was grating on Mitzi's nerves. She wondered if she could silence certain suits. "Ellen, please stop hyperventilating," she said, her voice tight with barely contained stress.

"It's not me," the soft voice murmured back.

Mitzi frowned. "Mir?"

"I want to get out," the girl whined.

Mitzi groaned. "Bit late for that, sweetheart."

"One minute," Nic said.

Mitzi swore. "Okay, everyone to the doors. Yes, Mir, *everyone.* Come on, quickly."

As they staggered forward, their suits overcompensated and

sent them reeling into the closed boarding doors in the side of the ship.

"Line up," Mitzi said, trying to mask the stress in her voice. Someone, she wasn't sure who, was muttering a prayer. Ragged breathing filled her ears. She could feel her own muscles tense, preparing for whatever waited for them on the other side of the doors.

"I can't touch down," Nic said, talking quickly. "There's no clear area large enough for the ship. I'll take you as low as I can, but you'll have to jump."

Mitzi licked her dry lips. "The suits should handle that. We'll only have seconds to get off the ship, so everyone needs to go on Nic's signal. Okay?"

A muffled beep echoed around them as the doors drew apart, and Mitzi leaned forward, eager for her first glimpse of the planet. There wasn't much to see; the ship was kicking up plumes of dust and obscuring their view, but broken bricks and twisted metal jutted up from the ground in all directions.

"Go now," Nic said. "This is as close as I can get."

They were hovering nearly ten meters off the ground, and for the first time, Mitzi felt truly frightened. If the suits failed to protect her as well as they advertised, the leap would be suicidal.

She inhaled sharply then turned to her crew. Six helmets were looking in her direction, waiting for her signal. "You heard him," she said. "Jump!"

Two suits leaped, plummeting into the swirling dust—Skye

and Adam. After a second of hesitation, Franc jumped, followed by Eoin.

"Quickly," Nic urged, his voice quiet but insistent.

Mir was backing away from the opening, shaking her head. "Oh no you don't," Mitzi snarled, stepping behind her. She placed both hands on the girl's shoulder and shoved. The suit's energy easily pushed Mir through the opening. Her shriek was only slightly gratifying.

Ellen was frozen on the edge. Even through the suit, Mitzi could see her trembling.

"Want me to…?"

Ellen gave a very small nod, and Mitzi pushed her too. Whether from a bravery she hadn't shown before, or because she was simply too terrified to make a noise, Ellen fell silently.

With clenched fists and squinted eyes, Mitzi followed her team, leaping from the safety of the ship and into the hostile world.

CHAPTER 44

HER STOMACH LURCHED AS she fell. Instincts made her flail her limbs, grasping for something to stop her fall, but she managed to hit the ground feetfirst then rolled to disperse the worst of the impact.

The suit worked perfectly. Mitzi felt shudders run through her bones as the metal-plated exoskeleton absorbed the shock and protected her limbs from being snapped by the impact. She staggered to her feet and quickly counted the shapes around her. She had six companions: four standing, two still sitting on the ground.

"Everyone okay?"

A chorus of *yes* came back to her, plus one "I hate you" from Mir. Mitzi offered a hand to the nearest sitting figure, Eoin, and pulled him to his feet, the exoskeleton's assistance sending them both stumbling backward.

"Good luck, team," Nic said. "I'll be offering whatever assistance I can from a distance."

The engines whirred as the *Teal Riot* lifted away from them, rising toward the atmosphere, its rounded steel hull shining in the sun's weak light. It was quickly enveloped by the dust that seemed to saturate the area, and Mitzi reflexively raised a hand to shield her eyes from the grit, only to smack her suit's face instead.

Franc, Skye, and Adam had already unhooked their guns and were turning in slow circles, scanning the area. There wasn't any motion, but that didn't mean they were alone.

Nic had set them down in a relatively clear hollow among the destruction. Wildly twisted metal beams and the skeletons of buildings surrounded them on all sides. The heavy dust of demolished bricks covered every surface, and she could see more than a few structures that had been scorched with fire.

"They must have put up a hell of a fight," Mitzi muttered. She turned toward a pile of bricks that had once been a wall and climbed it as well as she could in the too-eager suit, stumbling and staggering. When she reached its top, she turned in a quick circle, surveying the area. The dust was taking its time to settle, obscuring nearly everything.

"The suits have infrared," Nic said. Mitzi could no longer see the ship, but his voice sounded close and comforting. "I can activate it, if you like."

"That would be terrific."

There was a click, then the screen in front of Mitzi's eyes turned blue. It took her a second to adjust, but then she was able to make out the dull ruins, plus six hot spots waiting for her at the foot of the rubble pile. "I can't see anything except my team members. Is that good?"

"Eh," Nic said and turned the infrared off. "Not especially. The Cymics don't carry any heat in their native form, so they won't show up. The only time you'll see heat signals is when they change into the human or merged forms—or if there's an actual human waiting for rescue in this place."

"What're the chances of that?"

"Not great. I'm scanning the planet for heat signals now, and so far, it's not finding anything."

"Right." Mitzi had turned in two complete circles, examining everything within eyesight. She'd scrutinized the map of their intended path during the brief shuttle ride to the port, but once she was on the ground, nothing looked familiar. "Can you tell me which way I'm supposed to go?"

"Sure. Do you see a large dark tower to your right?"

Mitzi squinted. "I see the *remains* of what I assume was once a large dark tower."

"You're looking for the entrance to a subterranean stairwell near the base of the tower. We're going two floors underground to get to the reactor room."

Mitzi scrambled down from her perch. As long as Nic's ship hadn't woken them—and it looked as though it hadn't—the Cymics would be in a sort of hibernation, where they slept while they waited for noise or movement. Normally, Mitzi would have treated it as a stealth mission and snuck through the passageways, but her team was too untrained to know how to be stealthy. That meant their best chance probably lay in moving as quickly as they could and completing the job in the shortest space of time. If they were fast, it might be possible to get off the planet before many of the parasites even knew they were there.

"Everyone stay close. Adam, you keep up front with me, so I can keep an eye on you. Skye, Franc, stay at the rear and cover our backs. I need you guys to stay alert. If you see or hear anything move, let me know immediately. And remember, if something comes toward you, you're going to want to shoot first and ask questions later."

"It's emptier than I expected it to be," Adam said as he jogged forward to stand beside his leader. "Almost...*too* empty."

"Cut the dramatics." Mitzi waited for her ducklings to line up in the correct formation; the three riskiest members—Mir, Eoin, and Ellen—would be shielded between the more reliable. It wasn't ideal, but it was the best she could do. "From what my colleagues have told me, the Cymics prefer to be in their native forms when they're not trying to infiltrate stations...and their native forms like to be underground, where it's dark and quiet." She walked briskly, leading them through the easiest path among the rubble, trying to pick out the streets as she headed for the large black ex-tower.

"And water," Nic added.

"Wait, I thought they could survive without drinking?"

"Yeah, this is new. I just heard about it this morning. They can live without water for...well, the scientists reckon a really, really long time, but given the choice, they seem to prefer to congregate around damp areas."

"Good to know." A bank of rubble blocked their path, extending too far to either side to walk around, so she started to climb over it. It had once been a garage; there were buggies, all of them damaged, buried under the bricks. One vehicle's nose poked out of the debris like an iceberg bobbing in the ocean, and as she stepped around it, she felt her blood run cold as she saw it had been torn in half.

"Stay close," she repeated, even though her team was huddled so tightly they would bump into her if she stopped walking.

They went down the other side of the collapsed garage, using the metal supports and exposed pipes to keep their balance. Mitzi found the suit increasingly easy to walk in. Her body was slowly becoming used to its movements being exaggerated, and she was learning how much energy it needed to use to get the response she wanted. It had been disquieting at first, but the suit's boosts were saving her a lot of energy. On the ground, Mitzi quickened her pace into a light jog and was delighted to see that her team was able to keep up with her.

Then a splash of color on the ground caught her attention, and she pulled up, causing Adam and Ellen to bump into her, sending her reeling. A body lay in the ruins ahead of them, its limbs twisted into strange shapes. The bacteria on the planet were slowly consuming the corpse, causing its skin to sag. Its eyes seemed to bulge as the lids shrank back around the eyeballs, and the mouth was pulled unnaturally wide, showing its teeth in a gruesome smile. It looked like a wax figure that had been put in a hot oven.

Adam swore, and Ellen gasped. Mitzi turned to the right and tried to usher her team away from the body, but they gathered around it, captivated by the macabre spectacle.

"Did a Cymic kill it?" Mir asked. Her voice was low and anxious, but it had lost the panicky tone she'd had in the ship.

Mitzi shook her head. "They'll always convert their victims if they can. They see death as a waste. Most likely, she was killed by accident—either friendly fire or a building collapsed on her. Let's keep moving."

The team hesitated, riveted by the sight in front of them, and Mitzi sighed. *Be patient. You're used to this sort of stuff, but death is new to most of them.* "Come on. I doubt this will be the last body we find."

She was right. Barely twenty paces on, they found another corpse lying over a collapsed signpost, strangely bubbled. The eyes had disappeared entirely, and in their places were pools of thick black goop. Dark froth had dribbled from the open mouth and dried on the brickwork below. A small black hole in his temple, also filled with black, was the only other mark on the dead man's face. Mitzi poked at him with her gun, and his head lolled. "This was one killed during conversion."

"You mean—"

"Yeah. Look at that black stuff. A parasite had gotten him, so one of his colleagues shot him before he could turn completely. Trust me, it was a merciful thing to do."

Again, the crew seemed to want to linger, but Mitzi set off at a brisk walk, forcing them to jog to catch up to her. She didn't want them spending any more time in the area than they had to.

"The stairwell's about twenty paces ahead of you," Nic said. "It'll take you on the most direct route to the reactor."

Mitzi wasn't looking forward to leaving the surface of the planet. Its sickly gray light and the broken remains of the buildings weren't welcoming in any sense, but they were at least safer than what lurked in the darkness below her feet.

Her team seemed to feel the same way. They huddled more closely together as Mitzi led them through the hollowed-out shell of a tower. When they came out the other side, she saw the stairs they'd been aiming for.

CHAPTER 45

THE STRUCTURE OPENED OUT of the ground like a yawning mouth, several meters wide and with a concrete roof that had mostly survived the attack. A dirty sign tacked to the lip of its roof read *West Fifth Quadrant*. There were still lights fixed to its walls and ceiling, but without power, the stairs disappeared into the darkness after the fifth step.

Mitzi stood in the doorway for a moment, her eyes searching for movement in the darkness. Then, with a deep breath, she stepped over the threshold and into the gloom. The night vision turned on with a quiet click, and the stairs and walls suddenly stood out in a sickly green glow.

Something had damaged the inside of the stone stairwell. Holes had been gouged into the walls, and several steps had their ends chipped off. Some dark liquid had dried on the walls, and Mitzi moved past it quickly.

The steps seemed to go on forever. When they finally reached what Mitzi had taken for the end, it turned out to be only a landing, and the stairs continued to their right.

"Jeez," Mitzi muttered, grateful that her suit was putting in most of the effort for her. "You'd have to be fit if you lived here."

"They had elevators for the lazy people," Nic said. She could hear faint typing through the headset and wondered if he was still looking for heat spots. "But they wouldn't work anymore, of course."

There was more dried liquid on the ground, painting a dark streak down the steps. Something large had been dragged that direction. Mitzi kept close to the edge of the stairs to avoid stepping on it and sped up, eager to reach the end of the climb. "We must be more than a level down by now."

"Pretty much. Most surface buildings had basements, and below the basements were the pipes."

"The oil pipes?" Skye asked, her voice filled with wonder.

"That's right. Carrying crude and refined oil to different sections. It'll all burn with enough heat, of course. But you're going below that, past the first underground floor and into the second underground floor. That's where the reactor is. If you can make a clear run of it, you should be able to set the detonator and make it back to the surface in less than ten minutes."

"I like the sound of that." The stairwell ended, and Mitzi hesitated. Ahead of her stretched a long hallway with multiple offshoots and several doors. Every light had been broken, and shards of glass littered the ground. One door several meters on had been torn off its hinges.

"Turn left," Nic instructed. "There's another stairwell to take you down to the second underground floor."

Mitzi turned then hesitated. She could see the opening to the second flight of stairs, strangely shaped in the harsh green light, but her instincts were screaming at her to back away.

"Nic?" She was whispering, even though she knew sound couldn't easily escape the suit. "I think I can hear something. Is there any way to enhance the external audio?"

"Sure thing, doll. Hold on a second."

Mitzi felt her team shift uneasily behind her. There was a quiet click, then the sounds of the hallway were played into her helmet, magnified twofold, and the noise that had disturbed her was suddenly much clearer: dripping water. It was infrequent and distant, but the way it echoed from the lightless tunnel set Mitzi's teeth on edge. "Is there another stairwell?"

"Not one for more than a kilometer. Is there a problem?"

"Let's find out." Mitzi beckoned for her team to follow her.

They inched their way down, taking much more care than before, breathing shallowly so they wouldn't obscure any sounds. After ten steps, Mitzi held out her arm, drawing her small team to a halt. "Silence," she hissed.

A new sound, quiet and indistinct, was mixing with the dripping. It reminded Mitzi of fingers rubbing over stone.

"What's that?" Mir hissed, grabbing Mitzi's arm and pointing. Mitzi followed the finger and saw a large shadowy spot in the corner of the landing. She squinted at it, trying to make out what it was, but the glowing-green night vision obscured any identifying features.

Mitzi signaled for her team to retreat, then she remembered they wouldn't understand her hand motions. "Move back, all of you."

The shape shifted, seeming to turn toward her, rising to shoulder height. It was large, black, and sluggish after days of hibernation, but it seemed to shiver when Mitzi stepped closer.

So this is what a Cymic looks like, huh?

Mitzi unhooked her flamethrower's gun, and the monster twitched in response to the noise. She'd heard they could respond to vibrations in the air, but she hadn't expected them to be quite so attuned. She raised the nozzle at the Cymic, aiming carefully. *Don't want to stuff up the first shot.*

Then she abruptly found herself on her back, gasping from surprise, her companions' shocked cries filling her helmet. The alien had moved with lightning speed, shooting out thick tendrils to smack her off her feet. Only the suit had saved her from broken ribs and ruptured organs, but she was still winded.

The Cymic was on top of her, and her vision was filled with its multitude of flailing limbs, which poked at her suit, tugged at her, and tried to worm their way between the plates. Mitzi struggled against it, trying to wriggle away, but the monster was at least three times as large as she was, and it had her pinned.

A roar came through her helmet's speakers, making her wince. She tilted her head back and saw Adam was charging toward the monster, head down and flamethrower nozzle held ahead of him like a lance. He hadn't pulled the trigger, though, and the black metal nozzle remained cold. Mitzi grimaced. *What the hell does he think he's doing? He's not...Oh, jeez, he is. He's going to try to use his flamethrower like a sword, isn't he?*

Motion to her right caught her attention. "Watch out!" she yelled, a second too late as a thick tendril smashed into Adam. It threw him off his feet and slammed him into the wall, and he tumbled to the ground, chips of broken stone raining down on him. Mitzi felt her blood run cold at the sound, and she could only pray his suit had protected him from the worst of the damage.

The monster was tugging at her, trying to peel her suit away, and to Mitzi's horror, she heard the squeal of bending metal. *Please, please let that be something nonvital.* She pressed her left hand against the monster and felt around her neck for the button that would activate the electricity pads in her suit's palm. One of the tendrils lay across her neck, keeping her head down, and she couldn't get her hand under it.

Voices filtered through her helmet, but she couldn't spare enough energy to listen to what they were saying. She twisted, desperate to get to the button, but the monster wouldn't let her move even an inch. More squealing metal accompanied increased pressure on her right leg, and Mitzi knew it would only be a matter of seconds before the creature broke through her suit.

Then fire, bright and harsh, burst across her vision, sending her screen white as it overwhelmed the night vision. Skye's voice came through the cacophony of sound in her audio: "Forward!"

Thank sweet mercy for Skye.

The night vision, unable to cope with the brightness of the

fire above her head, switched off. For a second, Mitzi saw the Cymic as it actually was. Huge, black, and glistening, it looked like a hideous mutated slug with a dozen probing tendrils. Then the flames drew closer, and the beast shrank away from the heat, still reluctant to let go of its prey.

"Forward!" Skye yelled again. The flames connected with the monster, and a terrific, overwhelming scream rose from the beast, filling Mitzi's ears and making her gasp.

"Volume down! Volume down!" she yelled, unable to cope with the noise. The flames above her flickered away from their target as her team cowed under the deafening, excruciating bellow. Then Nic adjusted something on his end, and the noise was reduced to a low rumble.

Gasping, Mitzi looked up. The creature still refused to let her go, but it had retreated to the lower half of her body. Its black skin had bubbled and burst where the flames had touched it, and plumes of black smoke rose from the holes. Mitzi, disgusted, pressed her left hand against the flesh and jabbed at the button on her neck. The suit bucked as it sent a shock of electricity through the glove, and the Cymic jerked, twitched, then burst open. The skin split in multiple places, its black liquid insides being forced out of the cracks. Then it sagged as though it had been deflated, and Mitzi was finally able to drag herself out from under it.

Hands gripped her under her arms and pulled her to her feet. Mitzi turned to see Skye, the anxiety on her face easy to see even through the cloudy helmet. Behind Skye stood Mir, Ellen, and

Eoin, each holding nozzles with faint wisps of smoke rising from their tips. Franc had left his on and turned it to a low setting to provide them with light.

"Thanks," Mitzi said, giving Skye's shoulder a quick pat, then turned to Adam. He still lay on the ground where the parasite had thrown him, but he was stirring. Mitzi dropped to her knees in front of him and quickly looked over the damage to his suit.

There were dents across the chest plates where the tendril had hit him. Mitzi prayed that the suit hadn't been crushed badly enough to break any of his ribs. It had knocked the wind out of him at the very least. He was gasping, pulling in deep breaths as his legs kicked against the ground.

"Hey," Mitzi said as gently as she could, gripping Adam's shoulders to hold him still. "Can you hear me?"

"Gnn," he murmured, and his head lolled to one side. Mitzi's heart skipped a beat when she saw the dent in back of his helmet. She pressed her hand to the indent, and Adam flinched.

Crap.

Skye and Ellen had knelt by Mitzi's side. Even through the suit, Mitzi could see Ellen was trembling.

"Should we take the helmet off?" Skye asked, her voice reduced to a whisper, as though talking too loudly could hurt Adam. Mitzi supposed it might.

"Yes," Mitzi said, feeling chills crawl up the back of her neck, "but not now. We need to get out of this stairwell."

"What's wrong?" Franc asked. He kept his flamethrower spitting a lick of fire to light the hallway, and he was watching the oozing black lump on the floor. Puffs of toxic, dark smoke rose from its corpse, and bubbles appeared occasionally then burst on the liquefied parts of its flesh.

Mitzi was listening as hard as she could. Farther down the hallway, she could still hear the echoing drip, but other sounds had joined: shifting, dragging sounds of large creatures recently awakened from their sleep. "There're more coming. We need to get out of here." She turned back to Adam. "Can you stand?"

"*Ghh.*"

Mitzi swallowed, flicking her eyes toward the dark stairwell behind her. She spoke as quickly as she could. "Mir, take his right side. Ellen, his left. Move fast, but try not to jostle his head. Skye, lead the group."

Skye squared her shoulders and raised her flamethrower nozzle. "Where to?"

"Up the stairs and into the hallway we passed. Find a room we can barricade ourselves inside. Stay alert."

CHAPTER 46

THE SHIFTING NOISES WERE growing closer. Mitzi got to her feet, raising her flamethrower's gun and pointing it toward the darkness. "Eoin, stay behind Skye. Franc, with me."

She waited until Ellen had pulled Adam to his feet and Mir had reluctantly put his arm around her shoulders, then she began edging backward, keeping herself between the darkness and her team. Shapes materialized at the edge of the shadows. Mitzi twisted the band on the gun's handle to increase the flamethrower's reach.

Adam moaned as his companions began pulling him upward, and Mitzi's stomach lurched. After twenty years in the force, she'd never been able to tolerate seeing her team injured. She'd once been denied a promotion because she "couldn't make necessary sacrifices." The phrasing had enraged her so much that she'd thrown her phone across the room. She'd never understood how

Central could expect her to serve with and nurture a team for months or years then just abandon them if they were injured during their duty.

The batch with her was even worse. They were too inexperienced to be on a battlefield, but Central had still asked them to fight and die if necessary. Mitzi felt personally responsible for them, that she was failing by letting them be hurt.

The shadowy shapes at the edges of her vision drew closer, teasing their way into the flickering golden light, stretching toward their fallen sibling. Mitzi poised her finger over the gun's trigger. "Ready, Franc?"

He made a vague noise far back in his throat. His hands were shaking, but he had kept even with Mitzi, refusing to retreat any faster than she did.

Mitzi pulled the trigger and was delighted by the burst of flame that shot forward, sending harsh light down the landing and painting the roof black with smoke. Her flame hit the nearest Cymic, and it coiled away from her. The terrible screeching, screaming noise filled her helmet again, but the sound was thankfully tolerable since the volume had been turned down.

The light had shown her the back of the landing and the turn of the stairs, and Mitzi suddenly found it difficult to breathe. The space was writhing black, filled with at least ten of the Cymics. Their tendrils searched along the floor and the walls, edging toward her cautiously.

They won't be cautious for long, though.

The creatures were pressing forward more insistently,

stretching their tendrils farther. Mitzi pulled her trigger again, forcing the creatures back a second time. As soon as she took her finger off the trigger, they burst forward, spilling up the stairwell with a dizzying speed, shooting their limbs toward Mitzi and Franc.

Dual streams of flame met them, stopping the bulk of the attack, but the monsters weren't easily deterred. They sent smaller, thinner tendrils under the heat of the flames to worm up the stairs and snatch at their attacker's feet. One aimed for Franc, and Mitzi lowered her flame to cook it, but the second of distraction meant she didn't see the tendrils coming for her own boots. They wrapped around her legs, tightening quickly, and tugged her down. She hit the stone steps with a loud crack, silently thanked the suit that had stopped her head from being broken open like a raw egg, and sat up. The tendrils pulled her downward, toward Franc's flame, and he turned the nozzle away to avoid burning her. That was a mistake. Without the fire to deter them, the creatures surged forward again, threatening to envelop Mitzi. She pulled her gun's trigger and felt the heat through her suit as the fire hit the creatures in front of her and rolled back. The screeching increased in pitch and intensity, but as soon as a monster released her to pull back, another took its place.

They're too fast and too strong. We're not going to win with just fire.

"Franc, run!" she barked, jockeying her gun to hold it in one arm and reaching her spare hand down to grab at the white grenades strapped to her belt. She glanced behind herself and saw

Franc was hesitating, reluctant to leave her to fight the Cymics alone. Mingling gratitude and frustration made her snap more harshly than she'd intended, "Don't you dare disobey me. Run, idiot. I'm right behind you!"

He dropped his gun and ran up the stairwell, the suit allowing him to take the steps three at a time. Mitzi pulled the grenade off the belt and tossed it as high and as far as possible, then she rolled over, shielding her head with both arms as the parasites rushed over her and began picking at the gaps between her suit's plates.

She'd been told the grenades were strong enough to blow a hole through a stone wall. That wasn't a lie; if anything, the manufacturers had underestimated their creation's power. It blew through two walls—and the ceiling to boot. The explosion was close to deafening, and the rumble of collapsing infrastructure jarred through the padding of her suit and rattled at her bones. Mitzi felt weight press onto her as the ceiling crumbled, but she didn't dare wait until the shudders subsided. The heat from the grenade would have killed many of the Cymics, but not all of them. She wriggled, fighting to get free from the rubble, and felt a spike of panic when she wasn't able to escape from a section of the wall that had fallen on top of her.

Keep calm. You can get out of this.

She squirmed, and her heart jumped as one of the Cymics trapped under the rubble with her began writhing, pulling itself up her body.

Then the weight was suddenly removed. The wall was being lifted up—not enough to be thrown free, but enough to reduce the pressure and let Mitzi pull herself out. In a quick motion, she pressed her hand to the hideous creature that was clinging to her and jabbed at the button on her neck. Mitzi squinted against the scream and explosion of oozing black flesh as the electricity tore through the Cymic.

"Hurry," Franc gasped. "I can't hold this for long."

Mitzi kicked herself free of the Cymic's corpse and scrambled backward until she was out from under the broken wall. Franc dropped it, letting it land on the dead creature with a horrible sticking, squishing noise.

Mitzi grimaced as a black substance oozed out from under the crumbling edges of the stonework. "I thought I told you to run."

"Sorry," Franc muttered, sounding a little sheepish.

"I'm kind of glad you didn't." Mitzi clambered to her feet and glanced at the section of the stairwell she'd destroyed. There didn't seem to be any movement in the weak light of Franc's simmering flamethrower. The walls and roof had been demolished, exposing sections of the rooms beyond them, and the stairs had been completely blocked with rubble. That meant there was no getting to the lower floor. "Damn it."

"What do we do?"

"Catch up with the others and regroup." Mitzi turned, clapping Franc on the back, and began jogging up the stairs. Her muscles were shaking from stress, and her coordination was poor, but she didn't slow down. "Skye and co, how are you doing?"

"Sort of okay?" Skye's voice sounded faint and reedy, and her words were mingled with a hacking, hysterical laugh from Ellen.

"Two Cymics were waiting at the top of the stairs, but we killed them."

"Good girl," Mitzi said. "How's Adam?"

"Nonresponsive. I think he passed out. The others are carrying him."

Mitzi swore under her breath and quickened her pace, leaping up the steps three at a time, occasionally sparing a glance behind herself to make sure Franc was still with her and nothing was creeping up behind them.

They reached the top of the stairs, where it opened into the passageway. To her right was the stairwell that would take them to the surface, but Mitzi ignored it and went left, where she could see the flickering flame coming from Skye's flamethrower. The hallway seemed to stretch on forever; passageways periodically branched off each side, and doors, some open, studded the walls, all offering access to dark rooms. Mitzi ignored the closed doors—better not to tempt fate—but stopped beside each open doorway, poking her nozzle inside to check the contents.

"Look for an empty room," Mitzi said as she came abreast of Skye. "Somewhere we can barricade ourselves inside while we check on Adam." She looked into the open doorway they were passing and grimaced. Three corpses lay in the corner, each holding a gun. Trickles of dried blood accompanied small holes in their temples. *They preferred to be dead than a Cymic. Can't say I blame them.*

"Here's a rec room," Skye said, holding a door open.

Mitzi paused in the entrance, searching for motion, then cautiously stepped inside.

Station recreation rooms often doubled as secure areas in case of emergency. That meant their doors could be locked with reinforced bolts, and there were emergency systems in place for in case the power went down. Mitzi stalked through the room, checking behind the couches and the TV that had been smashed to the floor, then made sure the door was still intact before beckoning her team in with a grin. "This is perfect. Get in here, you lot. Mir, Eoin, Skye—put Adam down on that couch. Careful of his head. Skye, lock the door."

CHAPTER 47

MITZI PULLED HALF A dozen glow sticks out of her pouch, snapped them, and tossed them around to light the room in subdued blues and greens. Then she knelt beside Adam, who was no longer moving.

"Nic, you still with us?"

"Always and forever, doll."

"Tell me how to unlock a suit."

"I can do that from my end. Which one?"

"Adam's."

Nic was silent for a moment as Mitzi listened to him type. Then Adam's suit clicked, and the plates relaxed their grip. "That's unlocked. You can pull it open now."

Mitzi tried, but her gloves were too thick to get under the plates. Grumbling, she stood up and pressed the switch inside her glove to deactivate her own suit. It whirred as it unlocked and split open, and Mitzi stepped out with a sigh of relief. Being without her suit felt strange, as though gravity were heavier than it was supposed to be, and every movement took more energy than it should have. The cool air felt good against her sweaty skin, though.

She returned to Adam and pried his suit open, starting with his helmet. "Help me lift him out if this," she said to the team standing around her, and she waited while they deactivated and stepped out of their own suits.

Between the six of them, they were able to carefully lift the man's body while Franc pulled the damaged suit out from under him then laid him back on the couch. Mitzi went to his head first. A sinking feeling grew in her chest when she saw the trickle of blood that ran from the back of his skull and down his neck. She checked for a pulse and smiled when she found it. *Weak, but that's better than not having one at all.*

"There should be some bottled water in the fridge or one of the storage cupboards," she said. "And a first-aid kit. Someone get me those and some cloths."

Skye, Franc, and Ellen, apparently relieved to have something to do, spread out at once and started pulling open cupboard doors. Mir retreated to a dark corner, where she huddled in one of the chairs, and Eoin, after staring at Adam's still face for a moment, sat in the chair opposite and pulled the book out of a pocket.

"Seriously?" Mitzi asked, incredulous, as he opened it to a dog-eared page. She shook her head. "You know what? I'm not even mad. Stick to your principles."

Franc appeared at Mitzi's side with a bottle of water and a small bundle of washcloths. Mitzi cracked the bottle's lid off, wet one of the cloths, and began dabbing at the back of Adam's head. A moment later, Skye returned with the first-aid kit.

"Cut his shirt off," Mitzi said, feeling her stomach flip over at how quickly the washcloth turned pink. "See if he has any broken ribs."

The room was silent as Skye pulled a pair of scissors out of the kit and started cutting. Mitzi threw aside the first washcloth and wet a second one, which she used to blot at Adam's face. He stirred, murmuring deep in his throat.

"I don't think anything's broken," Skye said. "There might be fractures, though. He's bruised pretty badly."

Mitzi glanced at Adam's chest and nodded. Dark discoloration was growing across the skin, but there were no indents or plumes of red that could indicate broken ribs. "Could be worse. I'm going to say we're not leaving this room for a bit. See if you can find more water and some food, and rest up as much as you can."

Skye stayed beside Mitzi, but Franc and Ellen moved off to fetch supplies from the cupboards. Someone said something that was too faint for Mitzi to hear, and she craned her neck to see Mir in the corner of the room, curled up so that her knees were resting under her chin as her dark eyes glared at the back of Adam's chair.

"What was that?"

"Why?" Mir repeated, a little more loudly. "Why are we wasting time with him?"

Mitzi, thinking she must have misheard the girl, stared at her.

Seemingly uncomfortable with the silence, Mir spoke again. "It's going to be nearly impossible to get him off the planet, even if we don't go to the reactor room. And you said it yourself, every hour counts in this war. We should leave him. Complete the mission as soon as possible."

"Leave him?" Mitzi echoed, dropping the cloth and standing up.

Mir shrugged. "He's an acceptable loss."

Mitzi stalked toward the girl, who shrank back in her chair, even as she glared her defiance. "When I was sworn in as a commander, my vows included a pledge to protect my team above my own life. I've *never* reneged on that promise, and I'm not about to start now."

"Really?" Mir asked, a cruel bite in her tone. "I was under the impression that Captain Jones would disagree."

Mitzi felt as if she'd been punched. Her vision blacked out, and for a moment, she was back in that office, gun in her shaking hand as she faced Jones. He quirked her a lopsided smile. "What're you doing, Mitz?"

Then he turned toward her, raising his hand toward her face. Mitzi felt the trigger, resistant under the pressure of her finger, then heard the crack as the gun kicked back in her hand. She smelled the smoke and the blood…

Her vision cleared, and she was once again staring at Mir. The girl's lips spread into a nasty smile as she appreciated the effect of her words. Mitzi slapped her.

She regretted it almost as soon as the echoes died out. Mir

raised a hand to her red cheek, looking livid, and Mitzi fought to get her anger under control.

"I promised you lot I'd do everything in my power to get you off this planet alive," she said, her voice low and shaky. "Even idiots like Adam. Even spoiled, sheltered brats like you. And I swear, I would rather hug a Cymic than abandon a single one of you here to die. Shame on you for thinking otherwise."

They stared at each other, Mitzi furious, Mir defiant. Then the younger girl squeezed her eyes closed, and her shoulders started to shake.

"Oh, jeez," Mitzi said, feeling her anger ebb out of her. "Okay, hey, stop that. Don't cry. C'mon."

Mir pulled her legs up and buried her face in them as she dug her fingers into her hair. "Leave me alone."

Mitzi stared at her, feeling helpless, unsure whether she should hug the girl or kick her in the shins. Then Skye appeared at her side, her pretty blue eyes flicking between her commander and her peer.

"Mir?" she said quietly. "Who did you lose?"

After a silent moment, Mir raised her head. Her face was blotchy, but her eyes were still hard and angry. "I don't know what you mean."

"Was it a friend? A boyfriend? Your parents?"

At the last word, the color drained from Mir's face, and Mitzi finally understood. She sighed and dropped to the ground beside Mir, sitting cross-legged. "So that's your reason for coming on the mission, huh? You wanted revenge?"

The fight seemed to leave Mir, and she slumped forward, looking unexpectedly vulnerable as she let her long hair fall down like screens in front of her face. "I didn't think it would be like this."

"No," Mitzi said, remembering the pressure of the creatures as they'd tried to pull her suit apart. "Me neither. What happened to your parents?"

For a minute, Mitzi thought the girl wasn't going to answer, but then she said, "They were on one of the exostations. It was one of the earlier ones to go quiet, before anyone knew what the problem was. Their messages just stopped coming one day, and no one could tell me why or what had happened—only that a rescue ship had been sent. When the whole Cymic thing was announced...I kept hoping maybe they'd be one of the lucky ones. That they'd escaped in time."

She wasn't crying, but her voice was raw. Mitzi respectfully kept quiet while Skye leaned on the edge of the seat.

"I have dreams about them sometimes, that they've come back. They hug me a-and tell me they missed me—but of course, it's not them. It's the monsters. And that's the worst thing of all." Her voice was a whisper, so full of pain, longing, and revulsion that Mitzi's heart ached for her. "They're probably still out there, looking and talking and acting exactly like my mum and dad, except they're *not*."

"That sucks. I'm sorry." Mitzi didn't know what else to say.

Mir glanced at her and shrugged. "Lots of people are going through the same thing. I got invited to a support group. I couldn't imagine anything more horrible."

Skye chuckled. "Oh, yeah, I got an invite to a group too." At Mitzi's questioning look, she wet her lips and shrugged. "Two of my best friends. They were on Station 333—you know, the one that exploded. I don't know if they actually got turned before… well. They're dead either way." She waved a hand around the room. "I'll bet everyone here has lost someone. Maybe not a close family member or dear friend, but at least someone they know. What are the estimates, one in three humans are gone?"

Mitzi raised her eyebrows. "You've been keeping your ear to the ground, I see."

"Yeah. A couple of my friends got accepted to be defense technicians, even though I wasn't. They've been keeping me as up-to-date as they can."

Mitzi thought of her own friends, their weekly meals together, and how they'd passed on as much information as they could. She might never see them again, she realized; there was a very real chance that she might not make it off the station…

She swallowed and squeezed her eyes closed. "Want to know why I was discharged?"

Skye was silent, but Mir said, "Yeah?"

"I killed my commanding officer, Captain Jones." She exhaled and forced her voice to stay steady. "I'd suspected he was stealing intelligence for a civilian rebellion started by his cousin, but I couldn't get anyone to believe me. He was really well liked. Charismatic, funny, friendly to everyone he met. Hell, even I liked him. When I figured out what he was doing, I was devastated. I cornered him in his office one night after the building had closed and confronted him about it. I'd brought a gun. Turns out, so had he."

She squeezed her lids shut. Again, there was the lopsided grin, the voice saying, "What're you doing, Mitz?" and the flash of silver as he raised his hand toward her.

"I shot first." It was hard to speak, and she had to pause to wet her lips. "He would have killed me if I hadn't. I went to court on murder charges."

"You didn't get a conviction, though," Skye said.

"No. My lawyer told me to claim it was an accident. He said there wasn't enough evidence that Captain Jones was colluding with the rebellion, and if I tried to claim I'd killed him in self-defense, I'd receive the death penalty. So I pleaded guilty to manslaughter. I didn't know what else to do. The court accepted it, and I received a dishonorable discharge from my job."

Mitzi opened her eyes and focused on the ceiling tiles. "I was right, though. Six months after my case finished, it was proven that Captain Jones had been leaking classified documents to the rebellion for years. Because I'd pleaded guilty, though, I couldn't appeal my case. So the manslaughter charge stayed, and with it died any chance of getting my job back."

"That sucks," Skye said, echoing Mitzi's own words back at her.

Mitzi chuckled. "Sure does."

Mir didn't say anything, but she pulled something out of her pocket. Mitzi glanced at it and raised her eyebrows when she saw it was the hair band she'd given the girl on the ship. Mir pulled her hair up and tied it back tightly, still refusing to meet Mitzi's eyes.

Across the room, Franc cleared his throat. "Excuse me, Captain?"

"Yeah?" Mitzi bounced to her feet, shaking off the stupor the conversation had cast over her. "Is it Adam?"

"No, no, it's the suit—I think Nic is trying to talk to us."

Mitzi jogged to her suit, which stood open, waiting for her to step back into it. "Nic?" she called into the helmet and heard his voice come back faint and tinny.

"Just thought you should know. I've been scanning the planet for heat signals, and I've just now gotten a response."

"There's someone alive here?"

"Uh, no, I wouldn't say that exactly. The heat signals appeared out of nowhere. You know what that means, right?"

"Yeah." Mitzi turned back to the room, surveying her team. Skye was still sitting with Mir. Ellen had joined Eoin on the lounge chair opposite Adam's unconscious form, and Franc stood off to one side, a half-drunk bottle of water in one hand. "The Cymics are changing into their human forms."

CHAPTER 48

MITZI SQUEEZED HER EYES shut and inhaled. "How many?"

"I wish I could give you an accurate number, but the place is lighting up like a Christmas tree. There must be hundreds... possibly thousands of them."

Right as Nic finished speaking, a series of deep, metallic clangs came from the door to their right. Three distinct knocks followed.

The atmosphere inside the room was so thick, Mitzi could have cut it with a knife. The team held their breath, watching the door and waiting. There was silence for half a minute, then a voice called, "Hello?"

It was a woman, and she sounded young and unsure of herself. Mitzi shook her head at her companions, indicating that they should remain quiet.

"Hello, is someone in there? My name's Sun. I need rescue, and my friend is hurt. Please, let me in."

Mitzi had been warned about how convincingly the Cymics could imitate their hosts, but it was still painfully challenging to imagine the pleading voice as anything except human.

"Please, please, open the door! I think I can hear them coming!" Raw panic filled the voice. "You have to help me—I don't want them to catch me." She sobbed, fearful and breathless. "I don't want to...to become... Please, they're coming up the stairwell. Help me!"

Mir's eyes were wide. *What if?* she mouthed, and even Mitzi found herself filled with doubt.

"Nic?" she hissed, low enough that whatever was on the other side of the door wouldn't hear her. "Are you certain? There's no way a human could have gotten to us?"

Nic's voice was fond and a little sad. "Doll, no chance in hell. They're gathered so thickly outside that door that I can't count the individual dots. Don't be fooled."

The voice rose into a terrified scream. Mitzi had heard that noise before, several times during her active duty. It was the sound a person made right after realizing death was inevitable. She crossed her hands over her chest and hunched her shoulders against it, fighting against the part of her that wanted to wrench open the doors and save the person on the other side.

The scream broke off, and silence filled its place. Mitzi finally let herself breathe again, and she was surprised to find sweat covered her torso.

"What was that?" a voice mumbled, and Mitzi almost smiled. She hurried to the couch where Adam was blinking, disoriented, at the strange shadows the glow sticks were throwing about the room. "Ugh…my head hurts."

"Yeah, it'll do that for a bit," Mitzi murmured, picking up the cloth and dabbing it over his face. "Try to be quiet. We've got Cymics outside the door."

Mitzi took a quick assessment of her team. Mir was leaning back in her chair, eyes on the ceiling. Skye was still watching the door, her face white. Franc had sat down and held his head in trembling hands. Ellen had sought comfort by leaning against her new friend, Eoin, and Eoin…was still reading his book.

"Mitz?" Nic's voice was faint, and Mitzi got up to stand next to the suit again. "Still there?"

"Yeah, we're fine."

"I don't want to alarm you, but you might want to get a move on. The station's heating up. More and more lights are coming on. I guess they're sending messengers to alert their buddies. You might want to make your move before they find a way into your room."

Mitzi rubbed a hand over her face. "Right. What's the fastest way to the reactor, assuming we can't get down the first stairwell anymore?"

"Well, you could follow the hallway for a kilometer to get to the next stairwell…"

Mitzi heard typing noises then a frustrated sigh from Nic. "It's not pretty out there, doll. They're blocking the door, plus every passageway you could take. I don't know what to suggest."

"Go through the roof."

The voice was so quiet and unfamiliar that it made Mitzi jump. She turned to see Eoin, eyes fixed on his book. He shot her a glance before returning his gaze to the pages in front of him. "This is a load-bearing level. There's a crawlspace above the ceiling where they put the support beams to prop up the buildings on the planet's surface."

Mitzi blinked at him. "How do you know that?"

"I read it."

"Really?" Mitzi grinned as she crossed the room, feeling a little surge of pride for her black horse. "So that's what the book is about! You've been reading up this station to prepare yourself! Clever, Eoin."

She plucked the book out of the boy's hands and glanced at the title, expecting it to be an instruction manual for station maintenance or possibly an architectural guide. She frowned at the book's actual name. "*Prominent English Monasteries of the Eighteenth Century*. What the hell, Eoin?"

He shrugged, reaching for the book. "I already read about stations. Years ago. Now I'm learning about monks."

"He reads a lot," Ellen said, offering Mitzi a small smile, as though that explained her friend's behavior. Mitzi dropped the book back into Eoin's hands with a sigh.

"Well. Regardless. You're sure we can get into the roof?"

"Yes."

Mitzi sucked on her teeth as she worked through the plan. If they could use the crawlspace to get out of the room then drop back into the hallway beside the stairs, they might just stand a chance of getting to the reactor before the Cymics noticed they were missing.

"Okay," she said, waving Skye and Mir closer so she could explain the plan in whispers. "We're going through the roof, then. Adam is in no fit state to fight, so he'll need to rest here."

"No, I want to fight!" Adam said, trying to push himself up from the lounge.

Skye placed a hand on his shoulder and shoved him back down.

"Perfect, because you're going to be fighting that concussion until we can get you to a medical team. Now, can I get a volunteer to stay with him?"

Mitzi stared pointedly at Ellen, who only hesitated for a moment before raising her hand.

"Great, that's settled. Stay with hotshot here, and don't let him move around too much. I don't think the Cymics will try to break in. We need food and water, but they have all the time in the world and are probably content to wait for us to come out. That said, keep as quiet as possible once we're gone. Eventually, the Cymics will realize we got out, and it's in everyone's best interests if they think *all* of us have escaped. They should remove, or at least reduce, the number of guards around the door, which will make it easier to bust you out once we've set the detonator. Everyone clear on that?"

Mitzi waited until her entire team nodded before she stood up. "There's no time like the present. Let's get moving now while at least some of the Cymics are still asleep."

She stopped in front of her suit to give it a quick examination before she stepped inside it. The fire had tarnished its beautiful shiny plates, and the right leg, which the parasites had tried to break into, looked horribly mangled. There were dents and nicks over the back where she'd been thrown to the ground, and parts of the paint had been scraped off. It wasn't as pretty as it had been when she'd first seen it, but it had lived up to Central's claims of durability.

Mitzi climbed inside and pressed the button to close and lock the suit around herself. The screen flickered to life in front of her eyes, and she checked the little icons along the bottom, waiting until four of them registered as being active. She took an experimental step forward and once again felt the reeling sensation of too much power, but it was less disorienting than it had been the first time.

"Eoin, can you tell me the best way to get into the ceiling?"

His suit turned, examining the support pillars and the protrusions in the walls that indicated braces, then stepped to a spot near the right-hand side and pointed at the ceiling tile.

"Right-o, then." Mitzi grabbed a coffee table, dragged it to the space under the ceiling tile, then climbed onto the wooden surface. It groaned under the weight of the suit but held, and Mitzi pulled the poly-zincrom tile out of its holder.

Eoin had been right. There was a space between the ceiling and the floor above. It wasn't quite high enough to stand, but they would be able to run at a crouch. Mitzi hauled herself into the gap, using the metal beams to carry her weight, and held a hand down for her team.

"Quietly," she murmured as she pulled Skye then Franc up. "Don't let them guess what we're doing."

Eoin let Mitzi pull him into the crawlspace, but Mir hesitated.

"You want to stay?" Mitzi asked, hand extended.

Mir glanced at her then at the door separating her from the Cymics before gripping the offered palm.

Mitzi grinned. "Good girl."

CHAPTER 49

MITZI PULLED MIR INTO the ceiling space and waved to Adam and Ellen, who were still out of their suits. Adam looked sulky and jealous, but Ellen seemed relieved to have a job she could cope with.

Mitzi turned back to the crawlspace. It was a mess of pillars and metal brackets coming through the floor in odd formations and often at strange angles. Metal cables thicker than Mitzi's arm speared through the area.

"Go straight ahead," Nic instructed. "I'll tell you when to get back into the hallway."

Mitzi, bent double, began slinking through the jumble of supports, weaving under cables and around metal pipes. She'd always enjoyed stealth missions; the pressure to move both quickly and quietly combined with the danger of discovery made her feel alive like little else could. Mitzi didn't try to stop the grin that grew across her face.

She didn't think her team was enjoying it as much as she was, though. The breathing coming through her headset sounded ragged and stressed, and they were having trouble keeping up with her pace. Mitzi slowed down so they wouldn't be separated.

"You're doing good," Nic said. "All of the heat signals are converging on the rec room. I can't promise there won't be Cymics when you get back into the hallway, but at least they won't be human. Bear left a little."

Mitzi altered her direction, dropping to her knees to get under a series of cables that had been bolted to the ceiling. The surface changed from poly-zincrom interspaced with metal bars to metal sheets, and she had to slow to a snail's pace to keep the noise down. Every time her suit touched the metal, it set up a dull, echoing clang.

"Tell me we're close," she said through gritted teeth, inching forward.

"You're still a little way from the stairwell, but feel free to drop down anytime. You're right above a hallway."

"Thank goodness." Mitzi halted, unzipped her utility bag, and grabbed the screwdriver inside, then she felt around until she found the edges of one of the metal sheets and unscrewed the bolts holding it down.

She pulled it aside. The hallway below glowed green in the night vision, but she couldn't see any suspicious shapes. Mitzi eased her legs over the edge while Skye held her hands and lowered her to the ground as quietly as possible. She then reached up and helped her four teammates down.

The hallway was completely still and dark. Open doors and empty passageways created pockets of darkness every ten feet, and the hair on the back of Mitzi's neck prickled as she beckoned for her team to follow her.

It was an absolute maze, Mitzi realized as Nic directed them when to turn. There were small plaques at each corner, giving the name and compass direction of their pathways. If the section went for as far as it seemed to, Mitzi might have spent the entire day meandering through it and still missed large areas.

"Take the next right, and you should see the stairwell," Nic said.

Mitzi squinted around the corner and, to her relief, saw the indistinct ridges that marked the stairwell leading upward. Inky black filled the passageway down. She approached the opening and hesitated on the top step, holding her breath to listen. A dull drip echoed off the concrete walls.

"Brilliant."

The Cymics must be getting halfway down the stairs, between floors, and breaking through the walls to get to the water pipes. If we're lucky, the ones that used to live here will have gone to wait outside the rec room.

Mitzi began moving down the stairs, every nerve in her body alert for signs of movement in the grainy green below. Their suits made dull thuds on the worn concrete stairs, but she hoped the parasites were too far away to hear or see.

"Nic?" she whispered as they reached the landing. "No sign of them?"

"No heat spots, at least."

"Good." Mitzi turned the corner and hesitated. The dripping sound was louder, but the walls were intact, and she couldn't see any exposed pipes.

Then a drop of water hit her helmet and rolled down the glass screen, and a surge of dread rose in Mitzi's chest. She raised her head toward the shadowed stairwell ceiling four feet above her head and felt her blood run cold at the sight of a tendril reaching toward Franc.

"Run!" Mitzi swung her flamethrower nozzle up and pulled the trigger in one motion. The bright fire overwhelmed her night vision, blinding her, but she focused on the place the monster had been as her companions stumbled past her. Then the night vision clicked off. There wasn't just one Cymic; there were dozens, all clinging to the ceiling where they'd been absorbing water from the broken pipes that ran between the floors. Three of the creatures had reached around the flame, so close that their sticky black flesh nearly grazed her helmet. Mitzi threw herself backward to avoid them, letting the motion of her body turn the nozzle upward. Fire connected with the tendrils, and screeching, wailing screams filled her ears.

She rolled out from under the monsters then kicked herself to her feet. "Get moving!" she yelled, sprinting toward her team, who had hesitated up the hallway. "Go, go!"

Sounds followed her as she ran, and Mitzi glanced behind herself, but the passageway seemed empty. She paused, unzipped her pouch, and pulled out the flashlight, trusting proper light more than the grainy night vision. The narrow beam of golden light flickered over the stone walls and ceiling as Mitzi scanned every shadowy corner until she was certain she was alone with her team.

"They didn't follow us," she said, backing away from the stairwell, where she thought she could still see the dark shapes hovering on the ceiling, reluctant to move. "Why not?"

"Mitzi," Franc said, his voice very quiet and filled with dread.

She turned to see what had caught his attention, and her breath seized in her throat.

Franc had his own flashlight pointed down the hallway, in the direction they needed to travel to get to the reactor. Eoin and Mir were frozen, but Skye had drawn her flamethrower and was pointing it at the creature caught in Franc's shaking light.

A child of no more than ten or eleven, judging by her height, stood facing away from them. Her waist-length auburn hair shimmered in the golden light, and her dress, a pretty white thing dotted with pink flowers, seemed to shift in a nonexistent breeze.

Mitzi swallowed, drawing her own flamethrower. *Don't hesitate. It's not human. It's not a child. Don't let it fool you.*

And yet, even as she raised the gun and aimed it at the girl, she hesitated to pull the trigger. The child was missing a shoe; her left foot still wore a little black boot, but the right one was only covered by a dirty white sock, frayed from walking through the building.

Her mother wouldn't like seeing her like that, Mitzi thought then mentally slapped herself. *She doesn't have a mother. Not anymore.*

"Captain?" Skye whispered. Mitzi had drawn even with her and could see Skye's eyes through the helmet, wide and frightened. She was waiting for Mitzi to make the first move, but for all of the certainty she'd felt in the *Teal Riot* when she'd instructed her crew to never hesitate, she wasn't sure she could pull the trigger. Her hands were shaking too much to hold the gun steady.

Then the doors along the hallway opened, and the girl became the least of Mitzi's worries.

People filed into the hallway. There were all ages, from children to the elderly. Some towered above Mitzi, while others looked as though an overenthusiastic hug could have broken them. Dark skin mingled among pale skin, and long hair with short crops. And yet, somehow, they all looked incredibly similar.

It took Mitzi a second to work out why. They all wore identical expressions: bland, with a faint smile tugging at the corners of their lips. It was uncanny enough to make the hairs across the back of Mitzi's arms rise.

"Mitzi? Doll, answer me!" The voice in her headset finally made its way into her brain. Nic had been talking for at least half a minute, Mitzi realized, but she hadn't caught anything he'd said. "Mitz, there are red spots everywhere. Can you hear me? They're *everywhere*."

"Yeah, I see them," Mitzi murmured. It felt surreal, as if she'd slipped into a disturbed dream and was just waiting for it to get bizarre enough to wake her up.

The girl finally turned, rotating slowly to show Mitzi her dark, unblinking eyes. Her face held the same bland, faintly smug expression as the others. The front of her dress was stained with dried blood; it bloomed across her chest, and Mitzi knew the girl must have collapsed facedown for it to have pooled like that.

Mitzi had let the flamethrower droop during her stupor, but she raised it again and replaced her finger over the trigger.

The girl's face was changing. She was grinning, her smile unnaturally wide and stretching her face in ways it was never supposed to bend. The girl's smile held none of the sweetness Mitzi would have expected to see in a child's; hers held only dark, deep maliciousness. Then her face started splitting. A crack ran from her hairline down the center of her nose and across that maniacally grinning mouth then disappeared below the neckline of her dress. The skin peeled apart like a banana, and inside was the horrific black substance that writhed and stretched outward, grasping for her.

Mitzi pulled the trigger, even as she realized it was too late. The flames engulfed the girl as her friends around her changed, rushing forward and reaching past the pluming flame.

"Back, back!" Mitzi yelled, staggering backward herself as three streams of flame joined her own.

"They're behind us," Mir shrieked, and Mitzi risked a glanced over her shoulder. The Cymics from the stairwell had crawled out of their shelter to block the team's retreat.

Mitzi swore, her brain racing to find a way out. "Backs together. Keep the flames going."

Her team obediently crowded around her, Franc facing the same direction as Mitzi, the other three turned toward the stairwell. Their five streams of fire weren't able to completely surround them, but it was enough to deter most of the parasites.

We can't keep this up. Mitzi panned her flame from side to side, covering as much of the hallway as she could. *How long until the fuel runs out? Six minutes? Five?*

The Cymics were writhing just beyond the flame, changing shapes in the flickering light. As they shed their human skins, the living darkness inside spilled out. Mitzi glanced to her right, where Franc was waving his gun's nozzle too quickly, making the flame ineffective. Beyond him, edging forward in search of an opening, was a merged Cymic.

CHAPTER 50

MITZI'S MOUTH FILLED WITH a metallic tang as she bit the inside of her cheek. The creature, inky black and covered in the twisting tendrils, towered almost to the ceiling. Its human skin hung from its front, the toes hovering a foot above the floor. The stubbled face of a young man was full and looked natural, but the body hung limply, like a deflated balloon. The pale flesh contrasted with the black monster behind it as the limbs swung, boneless and shriveled, whenever its host moved.

The Cymic's grinning human head was incongruous with the empty body below it, as its eyes followed Mitzi. She turned toward it, passing her stream of fire over Franc's, and felt a small spark of satisfaction as the flame hit the human face, twisting its sardonic grin into a shriek of horror.

"Watch out!" Franc yelled, twisting to shoot his flame at a monster that had tried to take advantage of the gap in Mitzi's guard. She turned back to help him, and her heart faltered as she saw more of the Cymics had become merged, showcasing their deflated human forms like desecrated trophies.

There's too many of them. They know our fuel will run out eventually, so they're not giving us the chance to move forward or escape to the stairwell. And we can't use the grenades, or the building is likely to collapse...

Though, she thought as she took a half step forward to dissuade a Cymic that had skirted too close, *is that such a bad thing?*

"Hold on to your boots!" Mitzi yelled, dropping her flamethrower. She pulled four grenades off her belt and threw two into the mass of parasites ahead of them. After flipping the other two behind them, she snatched the final two off her belt and tossed them to either side. "Brace yourselves and get ready to run!"

Her team dropped their nozzles and hunkered down beside her. For a second, the Cymics surged into the opening, then everything went white as the explosions shook the building.

Mitzi forced herself to keep her eyes open. White dust burst from the decimated hallway's stone floor, and bricks and chips of rock sprayed out, showering the huddled team. Then fire, lagging a second behind the dust, rolled outward, enveloping both the parasites and her suit. She only became aware of the heat when it had passed over her, and by then, the grenades she'd thrown to either side had detonated.

She'd already damaged the structure of the hallway, and the two new grenades destroyed it completely. Mitzi rose a few inches into the air as the concrete floor buckled under her boots, then her stomach flipped as they dropped through the space that had once been the floor.

The impact ran through Mitzi's body like a miniature shock wave. Judging by the grunts and gasps that came through her helmet, she wasn't the only one who had been shaken. She tumbled backward, unable to find footing on the rubble, and bumped into two of her teammates, though she couldn't tell who through the thick, cloistering white dust. The three of them ended up on the floor, struggling to regain their feet as the pile of rubble shifted under them.

"Up," Mitzi gasped, getting to her knees. The bricks in front of her bulged as something *alive* tried to escape, and she recoiled. "Not all of them are dead. Up, quickly!"

A human hand, missing three fingers, its skin hanging in shreds, shot out of the rubble and grabbed blindly for Mitzi's leg. She kicked it, crushing it, then leaped over the twitching appendage. As soon as she had solid footing in the hallway, she turned around to ensure all of her team had made it out. They were clearly shaken as they staggered away from the shifting pile. Skye was closest, so Mitzi grabbed a grenade from the woman's belt and threw it toward where she could see Cymics trying to worm their way out of the rubble.

That should slow them down, at least.

"Can we get into the reactor from this level, Nic?"

"'Fraid not, doll. You can admire how big and pretty it is through the surveillance windows, but the only access comes from the floor above. Follow this passageway for a while, and you'll get back to the first stairwell. We'll cross our fingers you didn't damage the lower portions *too* much."

Mitzi had learned to hate Station 335's long hallways with their empty offshoots and closed doors. She started running, taking advantage of the exoskeleton's boost to carry her as quickly as she dared down the long passageways. Nic occasionally gave instructions on which way to turn, but for the most part, the suits were quiet except for her teammates' heavy breathing.

Then there was a flicker of motion at the bottom of her helmet's screen. Mitzi frowned at the symbols and numbers. It took her a moment to recognize what had changed: all six suits were online.

"Adam?" she asked, feeling frustration rise into her chest. "You better not answer me, you moron."

There was a familiar chuckle. "Sorry, Cap, I'm tired of waiting. The Cymics have left outside the door, so I can sneak out, no problems."

"Damn it, Adam, you stay in that room." Mitzi cast around for a reason that might keep the boy stationary. "I need you to make sure Ellen's safe."

"Taurun," a quiet voice corrected.

"Yeah, okay, sure. You need to keep her safe."

Adam chuckled again. He sounded smug, like a child who had gotten away with stealing from the candy jar. "Hey, don't worry about it, Cap. I'll keep her with me."

"No!" Mitzi barked. She was struggling to argue coherently

while running and listening to Nic's commands. "You've got a concussion, for crying out loud! Stay in the room. We'll pick you up on the way back through. If you just start running through the station, goodness knows what—"

"Central summoned me to fight," Adam said, his voice colder. He sounded offended. "And I don't plan on napping while everyone else does all the work. I'm disconnecting you now."

"Hey, wait. What—"

But there was a quiet click, and a small symbol representing silence appeared next to the glowing suit on Mitzi's screen. She swore, banking sharply to make a turn as Nic instructed. "You can do that? You can disconnect communications?"

"Yeah," Nic said. "Looks like Adam had a chance to figure out the settings while he was waiting for you. The suits can do a lot if you know how."

Mitzi grimaced. "Okay, so we've got Captain Brainless and Ellen running around the station somewhere, and we can't go back to meet them without passing the Cymics again…this is a disaster. Nic, do what you can to keep them safe."

"Sure thing. Turn right."

"Nic?" Skye asked, breathless. "Are we being followed?"

"Good question," Nic said. The *takka-takka-takka* of his keyboard seemed strangely comforting. "They've all turned back to their native forms, so I've lost the heat signals, but…no, wait, there's one. And there's another. Jeez. They're alternating between their native forms and their merged forms, probably to track you more easily. And they're catching up. Fast."

"How close?" Mitzi asked. Her lungs burned, and her mouth was dry. *Even if we make it to the stairwell first…*

"Really close." Nic sounded stressed. "Half a minute away. Less."

Franc, who was abreast of Mitzi, glanced at her. "I have an idea. But you'll need to trust me."

"We don't have much of a choice, do we?" They'd reached a T-intersection, and Mitzi turned left.

Franc was panting, but his eyes were narrow with determination. "Get into one of the rooms, get close to the floor, and stay quiet."

"What?"

"Quickly, before they get close enough to see us!"

Mitzi swore. She darted into an open doorway just ahead. *If Franc thinks we can just hide from the Cymics, he's seriously underestimated them. They won't stop searching until they find us.*

"Crouch down and stay completely quiet," Franc said. A window in the room faced out to the hallway, and Mitzi knelt under it, pulling Eoin and Mir down with her. They pressed their backs against the wall so that anything passing the window wouldn't see them.

Strangely, though, the echo of footsteps in Mitzi's headset hadn't completely stopped. She glanced at her companions. Mir was on her left, with Eoin and Skye on her right, but Franc was nowhere to be seen.

CHAPTER 51

"FRANC, WHAT THE HELL?" Mitzi hissed.

"I'll lead them away," he replied through the headset, his voice tight but exhilarated. "It'll give you all the time you need to get to the reactor."

He was deliberately making noise, Mitzi realized, running as loudly as he could, slapping his hands on the walls as he passed them and kicking any rubble that got in his way. Mitzi's blood ran cold. "They'll catch you."

"Don't worry about me. We can keep in touch through the headsets. I'll find a way to lose these guys, and I'll meet up with you before we leave."

Mitzi didn't dare reply. She could hear the Cymics rolling through the hallways, gaining on her hiding place. She held her breath, her gloves tightening on Eoin's and Mir's arms as though that could keep them safe.

It was a terrible sound: scratching and slithering, like a lizard slinking across leaves. She tried to guess what form they'd taken to make noises like that. *Probably merged.* She could picture them, their human skin limp and disregarded, desecrated in the worst way, reduced to a flap of useless flesh hanging off the creatures' true bodies.

The monsters were right outside the window. She could hear their slinking, scratching motion, punctuated by the wet sticking sounds as their black flesh touched the walls. Something heavy hit the window above her head, and it took all of Mitzi's self-control not to gasp. Mir's arm twitched under Mitzi's hand, but her companions maintained their silence.

Mitzi's body ached from the tension as her trembling muscles screamed to be shaken out. She was terrified that one of the creatures might pause, push open the door, or even press its hideous, corrupted human head against the glass to see inside. She and her three team members were sitting ducks, trapped in close confines, where the grenades were just as likely to hurt them as help them, and the flamethrowers could only hold their attackers back for so long before the fuel ran out.

Then the noises started to fade, and Mitzi realized the ghastly parade had passed them. Her lungs were burning, and she allowed herself to take a thick, shaking breath.

She glanced to her sides. Mir was shaking, doubled over, her helmet-covered head cradled in her hands. To her other side, Skye was pressed against the wall so tightly that Mitzi wouldn't have been surprised if she'd fused to it. And Eoin…had his book out again.

"Really?" Mitzi said, incredulous, then shook her head.

The helmet turned to her a fraction. "It's hard to read without proper light. I'd really prefer to go back home."

It was such a simple statement—and yet so accurate of how Mitzi felt—that she found herself laughing, the weak chuckles too quiet to attract the Cymics' attention, as relief warmed her core. She shook her limbs, freeing the cramps, and rolled onto her haunches. "Yeah, I'd really prefer to go home too. Let's do that."

She approached the door and glanced into the hallway. It was clear. "Franc, how are you doing?"

"Good so far." She could still hear him running. He was probably in a completely different section of the station by then. "Keeping ahead of them so far, thanks to the suit. They must be in their merged forms to be slowed down like this."

"Nic," Mitzi said, "keep an eye on Franc too. Make sure he doesn't turn into a dead end or run into another batch of Cymics."

"Will do, doll."

Mitzi glanced up and down the hallway a final time then turned back to the remaining three members of her team, who were still huddled against the wall. "C'mon, kids. Let's go."

They turned left out of the door, following the Cymics' trail. Mitzi kept them moving at a quick pace, aware that every minute they spent in the dark hallways gave their inhuman companions another opportunity to turn the tables. The stress of the incessant dark doorways and the waning adrenaline made Mitzi feel clammy, making her crave a hot shower.

"Stairs are ahead of you," Nic said just as Mitzi saw them. "Go up one level, and you won't be far from the reactor."

Mitzi paused at the stair's landing and glanced at the steps leading to the lower levels. "How deep does this place go?"

For the first time, her question was answered with silence. Frowning, Mitzi beckoned to her team to follow her up the stairs, toward the second floor. "Nic?"

After another few seconds of silence, Nic came online, sounding hassled. "Sorry, I'm trying to keep tabs on the other half of your team, and they're not making it easy. Station 335 has eighteen levels at its deepest point, and ten levels where you are right now."

Mitzi whistled. "Large place."

"Oh, absolutely. With a massive population to match."

As the suit propelled her up the stairs two at a time, Mitzi remembered the child she'd been unable to shoot and felt her mouth twist in disgust. A huge population—not just workers, but the workers' families too—they had all been consumed before Central even realized there was a problem.

She tried to imagine what it must have been like, living on the station as the Cymics spread through it, hearing screams in the distance but not knowing what caused them. She imagined the pounding of running feet and saw the fear in the faces that passed. They would have hesitated, unsure what the danger was, trying to decide whether to follow the crowds or seek safety in their home, taking mental stock of where their families were. Then they must have seen the giant black monsters chasing on the heels of the slowest runners, snagging their human prey easily, coming too close to escape…

Mitzi put her hand against the wall to steady herself; it had been stained with a splash of blood. She pulled the glove back, acutely aware that people, many of them, had died in that very stairwell, trying to flee or to hide. She wished she could spit the dirty taste from her mouth.

"Is that—" Skye asked, and Mitzi pulled up short, turning back to the stairs, angry at herself for losing focus. There was a dark shape ahead, and she pulled her flamethrower nozzle out of the holder, feeling the tenseness return to her muscles.

The shape wasn't moving, though, and Mitzi crept forward, prepared to pull the trigger at the slightest motion. She sighed when she got close enough to see what it was: boulders, slabs of cement, and crushed bricks piled up, blocking their path.

Damn, our demolition experiment earlier came farther down the stairwell than I expected.

Mitzi replaced her flamethrower nozzle and began poking around the edge of the pile, looking for a way through. She hated the idea of having to return to the passageways, especially when they were so close to their destination, but the rubble was heaped nearly to the roof. She swore.

"Can we climb over it?" Skye asked.

"I can't see a space wide enough."

"Get out of my way, damn it," Mir said, shoving through them. "What's the point of having super suits if we don't use them?"

She clambered up the pile, slipped as part of it shifted under her, then regained her balance. Mitzi realized what she was going to do and, with a final glance at the passageway behind them, beckoned for Skye and Eoin to follow.

Mir had her hands planted on one of the top slabs of concrete, and Mitzi came up beside her, mimicking the pose. The remaining two team members quickly joined her. Together, they put their heads down and strained against the massive weight. The rubble underneath Mitzi's feet shifted, but she pushed forward, leaning her weight into the task, praying that the suits would be strong enough.

With a grating, grinding noise, the slab shifted under their hands, raining dirt and dust down on them. They moved forward, not giving it any slack to roll backward, pressing it up the stairwell, until they had created a gap wide enough to fit through.

"Go, go!" Mitzi said, and her team scurried through the opening. As Mitzi followed them, the slab started moving again, unable to resist gravity as it slid back into place. Mitzi squeezed through the gap as it closed, then stepped back, staring at the wall of rubble.

They were back on solid ground at the top of the stairwell. To her left was the hallway that would take them to the reactor. To the right was the destruction that had once been the stairwell to the first floor.

"Franc?" Mitzi asked. "We're on the right level, but the stairwell's blocked again."

"Don't worry about me." He sounded breathless, and she

could still hear the steady rhythm of his feet. "I'm miles from that stairwell anyway. Nic can direct me up a different one."

"Good luck," Mitzi said, then she turned to the hallway ahead of them. "Okay, Nic, where to?"

"Straight ahead for twenty-five meters, and you should see glass doors to your right. Go through those."

"Gotcha." Not far ahead was a set of doors set into the dark concrete wall. They were white and modern, with clear plexiglass windows. The doors were shockingly, achingly different from the surrounding hallways. There was no handle, but a keypad next to them. "Do we need a code?"

"Yeah, hold on a moment." There was a rustle of papers, then a pause, and Nic yelled, "Not that way, Franc. Go right! Right!"

There was a moment of quiet, then a yell extended into a shriek, and Mitzi held her breath and clenched her fists as terror for her missing team member sent her stomach roiling. She could hear the sounds of a scuffle then the roar of the flamethrower followed by silence.

"Franc?" she whispered. He didn't answer. She looked at the symbols at the bottom of her screen. Franc's icon was flashing red, and the little note beside it read *Damaged*.

Then suddenly, Franc's voice came through her headset, breathless and weak but Franc nonetheless. "I'm okay. It's okay."

Mitzi closed her eyes in relief. "You sure?"

"Yeah. One of them jumped me from behind a door. I killed it, but jeez, it messed up the suit pretty badly."

"And you're not hurt?"

"Winded, definitely. I'll probably have some lovely bruises tomorrow. But the inside padding seems to be reinforced, and they couldn't get through it."

"Thank goodness for that," Mitzi sighed. "Get Nic to direct you somewhere safe."

"But first," Nic said, "let's get you through that door. The code is five-five-eight-two-zero-six-zero-nine. Got that, doll?"

Mitzi punched the numbers into the keypad. Her gloved fingers were too thick to hit them properly, but she managed, and the doors drew apart with a quiet *whoosh*. Harsh white light washed over them, and Mitzi had to squint against it until the night vision turned off.

"Follow the passageway straight for a while. You'll need a personnel code to get through a few other doors, so use nine-two-five-seven. That's the commanding officer code. It should get you through everything. Let me know when you get to the big reception-looking area."

His line went quiet then, and Mitzi knew he'd silenced their connection so he could give instructions to Franc. She led her team forward, into the new section of the building.

It was like stepping into another world. White tile and white paneling had replaced the concrete. The fluorescent lights were still on, probably thanks to a backup generator that protected the most delicate and valuable part of the station.

There was something unnatural about it; the space was clinical and strangely hostile in a way that Mitzi doubted it would have felt before the parasites' arrival. Large glass windows were set into the wall to their right. Mitzi could see labs beyond, where white chairs sat behind white tables covered in glass vials and petri dishes. A machine was moving in the background, rotating a glass tube, its light blinking red in a request for assistance that would never be answered.

A white lab coat lay draped casually over the back of a chair. A half-full mug sat on a desk near the window. Mold grew across the top of the coffee. Ten steps away, a spray of dark brown obscured her view through the glass. The tables beyond weren't as orderly or clean. Vials had been overturned and smashed on the ground. Equipment had been broken. One table had been broken in half, showing the dark gray of the interior carbon. Beside it was a body, sprawled at a bad angle, bloating as it decayed. Mitzi spared it only a glance before continuing past the windows. Mir swore quietly, but her team was silent.

They reached another set of doors. A dark stain smeared outward from it, as though a painter had dragged a giant brush along the hallway. Mitzi took a deep breath. "Brace yourselves. I don't think we're going to like what's behind the door."

CHAPTER 52

MITZI HEARD MIR AND Skye raise their flamethrower nozzles as she typed the pass code into the access panel. The doors slid open, and the large circular room beyond looked completely different from the immaculate hallway.

Mitzi stifled a moan. Only two of the eight ceiling lights were still intact. A third blinked fitfully, its cover broken and a wire hanging loose. The white tile walls were marred with cracks, black smears, and bloody sprays. The round reception desk in the middle of the room was missing one side, and the counter had been torn away and thrown against the opposite wall with enough force to break the tiles.

In the middle of the room, corpses were piled higher than the reception desk. Mitzi thought there must be at least forty of them. The exposed faces were contorted into bloated grimaces. Some were missing limbs. All wore the same silver uniform that Mitzi knew belonged to the science workers.

"Did the Cymics put them there?" Mir asked. Her voice was thin, bordering on panic.

Mitzi put out a hand to pat her shoulder. "I think so. Probably to clear the walkways. It must get inconvenient to climb over bodies all the time. They probably did the same through the rest of the station, which is why we only saw bodies on the surface."

Mitzi's voice was calm, but her insides felt so hot that she wanted to scream. Sitting at home during those two weeks before her summons, she'd absorbed every trace of information about the Cymics that she could. She knew the destruction they left in their wake—entire stations of thousands wiped out, without regard for gender or age and without mercy. Seeing it so fully and completely that she understood it in her soul, not just her mind, was a very different matter. It made her light-headed. It made her *furious*.

"C'mon," she said, still keeping her voice light for the sake of her team. "Not far now."

Not far until we can roast these monsters like they deserve.

Dried blood had seeped from the corpse pile, spreading over the tiled floor. Mitzi led her team in a wide circle, skirting the blood even though it meant climbing over the reception desk. She couldn't stop watching the pile out of the corner of her eyes. She knew her companions probably were too. The bodies, as limp as rag dolls, had been thrown there without care. Limbs poked out at odd angles. Some were so mangled that it was hard to guess what body part she was looking at. And the faces, frozen in the grimace they'd worn during the final seconds of life...

Mitzi's heart was thundering. Her hands felt hot and sweaty, and she felt dizzy.

Focus. You're a captain. A leader. Your team needs you to be functioning at your best. Compartmentalize it. Bottle it up. Save it for when you need courage, because you will *need it before this day is over.*

She squeezed her eyes shut, locking up the emotions, slowing her heart. When she opened her lids again, her head was clear. She saw the three doors leading out from the back of the room and remembered she was supposed to contact her pilot.

"Yo, Nic, we're in the reception-looking place."

There was a short silence, and Mitzi waited, knowing that he was probably busy helping Franc or Adam. She hated having her team split up. It made her feel helpless when she couldn't see them, couldn't make sure they were safe…

"Okay, doll. You'll want to take the door closest to the left. You've got another long passage, then you'll be in the reactor-monitoring sector. And you know what's beyond that?"

"The reactor," Mitzi said, feeling a shaky grin grow across her face.

"Bingo. Use your code, and keep me posted if you need help."

The four-number code activated the door, and she climbed through, into another long hallway with doors leading off each side. The lights were dimmer, allowing shadows to encroach on the edge of the passageway and barely showing the dark stains across the wall and floor.

"Keep your eyes open," Mitzi said to her team as she quickened her pace to a brisk jog. "Remember, the bodies in the reception room were only the scientists who died during the fight. There'll be plenty more who were turned."

Halfway down the hall, the doors to the right gave way to more windows overlooking some sort of control room. Green and red lights glittered in the low light. The area seemed to stretch on for a long way, and Mitzi guessed the hallway would open into it.

They reached the doors at the end, and once again, Mitzi typed in her code and stepped back, waiting for the doors to open. They didn't. Instead, the panel turned red and gave a long, deep beep. Mitzi frowned and tried a second time, with exactly the same results.

"Nic? Can you give me the code again?"

"Nine-two-five-seven."

"That's what I typed. It won't open." Mitzi tried it again, just to be sure, but the panel only flashed the red light and beeped angrily.

She could hear Nic shifting papers. "That's a top-clearance number. It should get you in to just about everywhere."

"Sorry, it's not. Do you have another number I can try?"

"Yeah, hang on... Don't go that way. There's red lights every-where! Jeez, turn back!"

"Who's that?" Mitzi asked, feeling her anxiety rise. "Franc or Adam?"

"Adam," Nic said. "I didn't want to tell you before, but I've lost contact with Franc. I don't know if his suit malfunctioned or..."

He let the implication dangle, and Mitzi grimaced. She hoped, desperately, that it had only been a malfunction. Though even if it was, that meant there was no easy way to connect them for their escape or to warn Franc if he was walking into danger.

She didn't want to think about her little team growing smaller.

"I have another number to try, though," Nic said. "Six-six-one-eight. That's from one of the specialists with clearance to the reactor."

Mitzi tried it. The light turned red and beeped. She swore.

"Didn't work?"

"Nope."

"Okay..." Nic sounded stressed. "It looks like someone put the room into lockdown during the invasion. That means—*Left, left, take the left! What the hell, Adam?*—Sorry, Mitz. That means it can only be opened with a commanding officer key card, not just a code."

Feeling sick, Mitzi raised a hand to rub at the bridge of her nose but only managed to bang the front of the helmet. "Okay. Where do we find one of those key cards?"

"Uh..."

"Nic?"

"They're normally worn around the necks of the commanding officers."

Mitzi turned, very slowly, to look back up the hallway they'd come from. She could picture the pile of bodies, limbs askew, faces distorted, and bathed in their dried blood. She saw herself climbing the pile, pulling aside bodies, digging through the rotting flesh, searching for the small piece of plastic that was her ticket into the next room.

It was too much. Her limbs were shaking again. She tried to breathe deeply, but her throat was tight and raw. She could only draw a thin gasp. She glanced at her companions. They were watching her, waiting for her instructions, concerned frowns barely visible under the helmets. *I can't ask them to do this. They're barely more than children, and they've already seen far too much today. It's got to be me. What did Franc say, way back in the ship? "We've all got to make sacrifices." This will be my sacrifice.*

Mitzi took a faltering step down the passageway. A drop of sweat ran down her forehead and onto her cheek.

"Captain?" Skye asked, and Mitzi gave her a tight smile.

"Stay here while I look for a key card."

She took another step forward as her three-person team bunched back into the corner of the hallway. She could feel their stares on her back. Her feet felt as if they were made of lead, but she forced herself to take a third step.

Then a loud bang made Mitzi jump. The suit overcompensated, sending her reeling into the wall, and she twisted quickly to face the figure behind her.

CHAPTER 53

FRANC, SUITLESS AND PANTING, stood inside the control room. He'd beat his fist against the window to attract their attention.

"What the hell?" Mitzi approached him, but he'd already turned and jogged around the corner, to where the doors hid him from view. There was silence for a second then a beep, and the doors drew apart.

"Franc!" Mitzi cried. She went to hug him, remembered the suit would crush the reedy man, and settled for patting his shoulder instead. "What happened to you?"

He looked delighted with himself; his face flushed with success as he grinned at them in turn. "I was jumped by a Cymic. I think you heard that part. I was able to kill it, but it damaged the suit too badly to function, and I had to get out of it. I couldn't even bring any of the weapons. It's been pretty hairy. I kept thinking I could hear things just around the corner. I had no idea which direction to go or how to find you, but then I stumbled through a hole in the wall into this room, and I knew it must be close to the reactor."

"And you opened the doors—"

"I tried to get through them first, but they were locked. There's a body behind the big control panel back there, and he had a card around his neck." Franc raised the white plastic square and shrugged. "It worked, I guess."

"Ha!" Mitzi slapped his shoulder again, sending him reeling. "It's good to have you back, Franc. All right, gather up, ducklings. We're on the home stretch now. Since Franc lost his armor, he's vulnerable. Skye, Mir, bring up the rear of our party and keep your weapons at the ready. Eoin, stick by me. Franc, hang in the middle and try not to die."

Once they'd lined up in formation, Mitzi led them through the door and into the control panel beyond. Hundreds of desks were spaced throughout the vast room, most of them facing a wall with a dead projection screen, but some were clumped together as though their owners had been working on joint projects. A raised platform at the back of the room held five chairs and a long silver desk. Mitzi guessed it must be for the commanding officers, so they could watch over the work. A hand was draped over the edge of the desk: the officer Franc had gotten the card from.

Mitzi slowed her pace. There didn't seem to be any parasites in the science section, at least none that had woken up, but the multitude of desks provided almost infinite hiding places, and the emergency fluorescent lights weren't much help at dispersing the shadows.

On almost every desk, something caught Mitzi's eye that gave a sliver of insight into its owner. There were the neat ones, with papers categorized and stacked perfectly, and messy ones, with papers and litter coating every nonessential surface. Mugs sported witty phrases or emblems of their owners' favorite sports teams. Someone had taped the date of his service leave to the top of his screen as motivation. One desk held a photo of the worker's family: a plump, beaming wife and a bronze-haired toddler. Mitzi hoped the family had been off the station when the Cymics arrived.

The room was like a small pocket of life inside an ocean of death. Mitzi was relieved when they reached the other side of the room and faced a large, thick-paned door with a bright-yellow hazard sign posted above it.

"Through the doors?" Mitzi asked.

"Yep. You'll be in the outer circle of the reactor. You've just got to disarm the door beyond that, which gives access to the bridge crossing the reactor. Get on that bridge, drop the charge, and I can lead you out. Easy."

"Easy," Mitzi echoed, trying to sound more confident than she felt. She keyed the code into the control panel and felt the gust of cold air squeeze between the chinks in the armored suit as the gates opened.

A long steel passageway waited for them beyond. The path curved gently, so that Mitzi could see only a few dozen meters in each direction before the slope cut off the rest of the tunnel from view. The concrete walls were back, but the floor had dark-red metal grates. The interior walls were reinforced with metal brackets, and warning signs hung every twenty meters. *It must be curving around the outside of the reactor. I wasn't expecting it to be so big.*

"Okay," Nic said, "there's a staircase to your right. Go down. There should be a control panel in there. You'll need to shed the suit. We're going to play with some wires."

Mitzi turned to her right, where the metal stairwell waited. "Why's that?"

"The final door, the one that opens onto the bridge, has a billion forms of protection on it. A simple code won't work; it only opens for two forms of identification and a retina scan. You can't blast through either. The wall's reinforced, plus it'd put it into lockdown. However, Central has given me a package on how to disarm the door's locking system, and they assure me it will *probably* work."

"Probably?"

"Fingers crossed, doll."

"Wait here," Mitzi told her team as she turned toward the dark stairwell. The steps seemed flimsy and narrow, and the end wasn't visible. "Stand guard, and yell if you see anything moving."

"I'll come with you," Franc said. "You might need an extra pair of hands."

Mitzi nodded, grateful that she wouldn't be alone, and began climbing down the stairs. The metal rang with every step, and her night vision turned on halfway down.

"Can you see all right?" Mitzi asked her companion.

"So far."

Mitzi zipped open the utility pouch on the suit's hip and riffled through it until she found the lipstick-sized flashlight, which she twisted to turn on and handed to Franc. "We'll need that to see the wires anyway."

The stairs continued for what felt like forever. Mitzi soon lost sight of her crew waiting at the top of the stairwell, and the echoes built until she felt as though she were walking through a cathedral. Franc, without the assistance of his suit, started panting.

Then the door at the end of the stairwell appeared. Mitzi guessed they must have gone down at least four stories. It looked unused, even more so than the other sections of the station, and dust—true dust, not the pulverized concrete that covered other parts of the station—coated the door handle and access pad.

Mitzi typed in the code, and the light turned green. Unlike the upstairs doors, it didn't automatically open, and she had to turn the handle to get through. The door stuck in its frame, and its hinges were stiff, but the suit enabled her to shove it open without too much effort. Pipes, gauges, and crates filled what was obviously a maintenance room. Franc's torch jittered over the jumble of shapes, making the shadows dance. It wasn't a large room, and Mitzi saw their target—an electrical box—before Nic even started talking.

"Take the cover off the gray box at the back. There's a bunch of switches inside, but we want to get to the wires behind. You should have a pocketknife in your pouch to cut the plastic shield off."

"On it," Mitzi said, already digging her blade into the white plastic that held close to a hundred switches.

"Be careful. Cut the wrong cable, and our entire mission's blown."

Mitzi slowed down and focused on carving the plastic out in sections. Her knife was sharp enough to move through it fairly easily, and it took her only a minute to work the plastic out.

"Right, now you'll need to be out of the suit for this part. We're going to trace some cables."

Mitzi stepped back and pressed the button in her palm, waiting while her suit shut down and unraveled around her. She was surprised by just how different the room looked when she stepped out from behind her screen; it seemed both dirtier and darker. Franc gave her a reassuring smile and turned his flashlight toward the box, which, without the plastic cover, exposed a mess of several hundred cables, each with a different colored tag attached to it.

"Find the blue tags," Nic said, his voice sounding faint and tinny in the suit, "and trace their wires back to the plugs, then read me the numbers."

Mitzi plucked one of the blue cables away from its companions and followed it down to the bottom of the box, to a multitude of plugs. "Franc, I need more light."

He moved nearer, and Mitzi squinted at the tiny number written beside the cable.

"Uh, that's an N-one-three-three."

"Not that one. Try again."

Oh, it's going to be one of those *sorts of jobs, huh?*

Sighing, Mitzi picked out another blue tag. "P-seven-zero-four."

"Nope."

"A-five-nine-six."

"No."

As she methodically worked through the blue tags, Mitzi let her mind wander. She found herself thinking about her home planet and the tiny gray room she would never see again. She probably should've missed them, but she didn't. It was part of an old life, a very different, very drab life. If she completed the mission, maybe Central would give her another. They should; they were so low on fighters that they would probably take anyone, job history and bias disregarded.

If I get another job, will they give me a more capable, better-trained crew, or will they let me keep my current team?

She didn't like the idea of them being split up. Yes, her crew was inexperienced, and yes, most of them weren't even suited to military work, but they'd done nothing but impress her during the mission. Mir, whom Mitzi had guessed would be the biggest problem, had buckled down and done her job with minimal complaints. Skye would probably make a very capable fighter with a little more training. Adam had at least shown bravery—idiotic bravery, but bravery nonetheless—and Mitzi supposed that had to count for something. Ellen and Eoin, both quiet and shy, had each carried their burden admirably. And Franc was the most surprising; not only had he risked his life to buy his team time, but he'd actually come back.

Mitzi tried to imagine what he must have gone through, navigating the hallways in the pitch dark, suitless, with no way of knowing if he was about to walk into a Cymic, no way to contact his team. He'd had only the smallest chance of ever finding them again. It was incredible.

Her hands faltered as she traced a cable. *More than incredible. It was impossible...*

He'd found his way into the control room in under ten minutes, when he'd already told them he was kilometers away. Then he'd found the permission card almost immediately so he could let them in. And he'd been awfully quick to volunteer to accompany Mitzi to the maintenance room when he'd heard she would need to step out of her suit...

Your own brother could be a Cymic, and you wouldn't know until he attacked you.

"Mitz, did you hear me?" Nic broke through the awful fog that was filling Mitzi's mind. "That's the right cable. R-two-four-nine is the right cable. Cut it, and you can open the door."

"Right," Mitzi said, her voice so thin that she doubted Nic would hear. Her mind was buzzing. The logical side that cared about her self-preservation fought to be heard over the emotional side that was screaming in horror and fear.

All of her weapons were in the ADE, four feet away, and there was no way he would give her the chance to suit up. Her team was waiting at the top of the stairs, and even if she screamed, they wouldn't get to her in time. They might not even *hear* her. She glanced left and right out of the corner of her eyes, but the pipes were all tightly attached to the walls, and she couldn't see anything hefty that she could use as a weapon. All she had was the small pocketknife in her hand, which wouldn't even slow Cymics.

Crap, crap, crap...

"Is something the matter?" Franc asked, and there was an awful gravelly quality to his voice.

Mitzi turned, dreading what she was about to see.

CHAPTER 54

FRANC SMILED AT HER, his eyes full of gentle optimism and good humor. A crack ran the length of his face, and even as Mitzi tried to back away, it began widening, splitting his head open. His eyes swiveled oddly to continue watching her as each half of his face was pulled to the side to expose the monster inside.

Mitzi ran for her suit, but Franc was too fast. He raised an arm, and a tendril shot out of it, shredding the skin that had covered his hand. Mitzi pulled up to avoid it, and it swung toward her, hitting her in the chest and sending her reeling back against the wall. It hurt an awful lot more without the protection of her suit.

The tiny flashlight fell to the ground as Franc dropped his human disguise. The skin sloughed off, curling around behind him to be stored inside his monstrous form. Mitzi searched desperately for something to fight him with. But she was cornered, and everything that might have been useful was out of reach.

She opened her mouth to scream, hoping that her team would hear her or Nic would figure out what was happening and alert them. They'd be miles too late to save her, but at least they would be warned. A tendril hit her before she could make a noise, though, and forced her into the concrete wall. A cracking noise and searing pain across her chest told her that the impact had broken a few of her ribs.

Franc slunk closer. One tendril pinned her to the wall while a second sought her mouth, trying to push inside.

Not like this, Mitzi begged. *Let me die, but please don't let me be turned.*

She struggled, kicking, punching, digging her nails into the slimy, cold flesh, but Franc paid no attention. The tendril pushed past her teeth, and she gagged on the sickening taste.

Then she heard a crack. Franc twitched, pulling back. Mitzi gasped, suddenly able to breathe again, and spat. Franc was turning, stretching out more limbs. His body rippled as he pulled the human flesh back out so that he could see and hear. She heard another crack, and Mitzi saw something shining dimly in the doorway. Franc released her, and she collapsed to her knees, shivering and feeling sick.

It only took a second for Franc to fall too. He'd succeeded in half covering himself with the human flesh, and the result was a repulsive pile of twitching black substance and a shriveled human skin. His eyes were rolling wildly in their sockets as he shuddered, and for a second, they fixed themselves on Mitzi. They were filled with pure hatred and unadulterated fury. She turned away and saw two red darts stuck in his black skin.

Nerve toxins.

Footsteps were approaching, and Mitzi looked up, squinting in the dim light. She caught a glimpse of Mir's face behind the suit's helmet before someone picked up the flashlight and turned it on her, blinding her.

"You okay?" Skye's voice was thin and terrified.

Mitzi squinted against the light as she tried to think through her patchy knowledge about the Cymics. She knew they spread like a virus, and they infected humans by either spearing them or getting down the victim's throat. Was it enough that it had been in her mouth, though, or did she need to have swallowed it?

"Keep your gun on me," Mitzi said, her voice ragged as she pressed one hand to her burning ribs to keep them still. "If I start to change, shoot."

She was hyperaware of her body as she started counting under her breath. What would it feel like to be corrupted? Was it painful? How much of it would she be awake for?

Skye had lowered the light so Mitzi could see again, and she watched the nozzle of the neurotoxin gun Mir had pointed toward her. The girl's face was paper white, and the gun was shaking, but she kept her eyes locked on Mitzi, intense and prepared.

Mitzi counted to two minutes before she let herself slump back with a sigh. "No. I'm okay. It wasn't enough to change me."

"Prove it," Mir said, her gun still trained on Mitzi's face.

"Come again?"

"We need to be sure. Prove you're human."

Mitzi felt a tired grin grow over her face. *Good girl. She learned fast.* Moving slowly and deliberately, she reached to her right and picked up the pocketknife she'd dropped. Then she pressed the tip into her palm, in the same place she'd nicked herself that morning during the demonstration, and held her palm out so her team could see the drop of red blood.

Mir dropped the gun and threw herself at Mitzi, wrapping her arms around her torso in a hug.

"Gentle, gentle!" Mitzi gasped as the pain in her ribs flared, and Mir drew back and awkwardly patted the top of her head instead.

Skye stepped over Franc's still body and held out a hand to pull Mitzi to her feet. "You sure you're okay?"

"Yeah, if I was going to change, I'd know by now." Mitzi glanced at Franc's remains then looked away quickly. Her throat felt raw as the shock began to catch up to her. "How did you know?"

"Mir figured it out," Skye said. "A few minutes after you left. You should have seen the look on her face."

Mitzi chuckled. The sound seemed hollow. "Well done, Mir. I think I owe you a serious debt."

The girl shrugged, looking awkward and slightly pleased at the same time, and turned back to the stairs. "Can we go now or what?"

"Yeah, I've just got to cut the cable. Hang on."

As Mitzi sliced through the blue cable, she felt an ache develop in her chest that had nothing to do with the fractured ribs. She'd lost one of her team: quiet, dependable Franc, the accountant who'd come on the mission to ensure a world existed for his grandchildren.

Maybe he's done that. He died leading the Cymics away from us. His sacrifice meant we could live long enough to get to the reactors.

She felt her throat tighten, but she pushed the emotions down as she stepped back into her suit and felt it tighten around her. The pain in her ribs dulled slightly as the suit supported her body. Later, she would grieve for Franc and run through all of her poor choices, picking apart the errors of judgment that had allowed one of her team members to die, but at that moment, she couldn't afford the luxury of introspection. She had a planet to blow up.

"Nic, please tell me this is the last damn door I have to open," she said as she jogged up the stairs, gritting her teeth against the pain.

"Last one, doll." His voice was unusually soft. She wondered how much he'd heard of the scene in the maintenance room.

The stairs seemed even longer on the way up than they had on the way down. By the time Mitzi reached the brighter and more spacious passageway at the top, she would have been completely happy with never seeing another stair in her life. She turned right, toward the door. "What's next, Nic?"

"The lock's off, so you can pull the doors open. There'll be a metal walkway going across the top of the reactor, which will look something like a giant bucket half-full of fuel. Throw your charge in, and then I'll get you to the top and pick you up, and we can all go home."

"Sounds good to me." Mitzi dug her gloves into the crack in the door and began pulling. They ground open slowly and reluctantly, then a cold wind, accompanied by the heady metallic smell of fuel, crept through the helmet's seal.

They edged in, struck dumb. Mitzi had guessed the reactor must be large, but *large* felt like such an insipid word compared to the fixture she faced. She stood on the lip of an immense hole; only a waist-high concrete barrier divided her from the drop. Steam rose from the hole, obscuring the opposite side, but Mitzi guessed it had to be at least a kilometer wide.

A little to her left, metal stairs rose sharply then opened onto a walkway that stretched across the divide. It looked hilariously fragile suspended above the abyss.

Mitzi swallowed as she approached the lip of the concrete divider and leaned forward, shining her torch into it. The beam reflected off something shiny, forty feet down. Mitzi squinted at it through the steam then felt her heart freeze as the thing inside the reactor moved.

"Eoin?" she asked, mouth dry, not daring to move. "You know about this station, right? What's the fuel based on?"

"Its base?" he asked. "An altered form of poly-carbon-azatope."

"I see. And that's—"

"Water, of course."

The movement in the reactor was increasing. Shiny black

shapes rolled over each other, twisting and writhing, their moist skin glistening in the fuel.

"What's wrong?" Nic asked.

Mitzi found it nearly impossible to say the words. "There's a Cymic in the reactor."

"Just one?"

"Yes." The heaving shape rose, filling the entire width of the hole. "And also a million."

Seeking somewhere quiet and dark, the million souls lost on Station 335 had congregated in the fuel-filled reaction chamber. And they'd *consolidated*. Central had never warned her about that.

Mitzi turned off her light, but it was too late. She'd already woken them.

CHAPTER 55

A THOUSAND THOUGHTS SPED through her mind. With the Cymics diluting the fuel, would the charge still work? Would her team have time to get to the surface and be picked up? Was there even a sliver of a chance left of rescuing Adam and Ellen?

She had to try. She had to do her level best to complete the job, even if it cost her and her team—her beautiful, loyal team—their lives. Mitzi fumbled in the suit's pouch for the detonator and whimpered.

"What's wrong?" Skye's voice was tense.

"The detonator's gone."

Mir swung toward her. "What? Did you drop it?"

"Impossible." Mitzi's mind ran through the previous hour and fixed on one single moment: when she'd been tracing wires in the maintenance room. Franc's flashlight had wavered as though he'd moved.

He took it. Just in case I got away.

She thought of the four levels of stairs she needed to run down to fetch it, and a shudder ran down her back. She could no longer see the Cymics in the vat, but she could hear them, shifting and crawling upward. She began backing toward the door, ushering her team behind her. The Cymic couldn't hear in its current form, but that didn't stop her from whispering. "You three get to the surface. Pick up Adam and Ellen if you can, but don't take unnecessary risks. Get on the ship."

"What about you?" Skye asked.

Mitzi had only opened her mouth to reply when the ground under her feet shook, throwing her off balance. Dust rained from the ceiling, and the walls shook, seeming to sway, as metal squealed.

"No!" Mitzi thought of the pipes that would be running out from the reactor to feed into different parts of the stations. They were full of the Cymics, too, and if those Cymics decided to exert their full force against the pipes…"They're trying to collapse the station."

"They *are* collapsing the station." Nic was typing furiously. "Get out of there!"

"The detonator's in the maintenance room."

Nic swore. "Well, you're not getting it back. The station's being crumbled from the lowest levels up. You've gotta move before they get to you."

Mitzi could feel the intense, raw power below her feet, rising closer with a deafening rumble. The concrete floor cracked in huge black gashes, an arm-width wide and growing larger. She stepped back to be clear of them. "Door!" she hissed. "Open the door!"

Skye wrenched open the sliding doors, but she was barely in time to leap backward as the outside corridor crumbled. Then the walls and roof smashed down to block the passage. The ground under them heaved again, throwing them closer to the pit. Mitzi, who was closest, hit the concrete barrier and threw out a hand to grab Eoin before he went over the edge. She twisted to see into the pit, and sick nausea grew in her stomach. The mass of Cymics continued to rise, stretching out immense tendrils the width of tree trunks. Thousands of pale shapes loomed out of the darkness, but Mitzi didn't recognize what they were until she focused on the nearest one and stared into the blank, white eyes of a human face. The parasites were raising their skins.

"Step back!" Nic screamed, his voice hoarse.

Mitzi tried to stagger back toward the doors, but the ground had tilted, turning into a funnel, as the floors behind them rose, shooting up jagged shards of concrete and a flood of water from burst pipes. It was too steep to climb while the floor was shaking, and the plumes of dust were making it nearly impossible to see. Mitzi was thrown onto her back and felt herself sliding down the slope, toward the reaching, grasping arms of the Cymics. She tried to scramble backward, but she found it nearly impossible to grip anything while the ground tossed her about like a rag doll. Her feet hit the concrete barrier—the only thing standing between her and an inevitable plunge into the maw of the monsters below—and Mitzi bit down on a scream as the concrete began to crumble.

A boom, so loud that Mitzi thought it must have deafened her, rocked through her, and she understood why Nic had told her to move back. The roof was falling. A huge circle, directly above the Cymic pit, plunged downward, breaking into a multitude of fragments as the supports failed to hold the immense bulk together. It hit the reaching tendrils, crushing them back down into the pit. Mitzi spotted two small, shiny shapes clinging to one of the pipes jutting out of the top of the collapsed roof.

Adam and Ellen.

They'd somehow blown the ceiling into the reactor with nearly perfect precision. Mitzi squinted through the billowing dust clouds to see Adam raise an arm and wave to her. She felt frozen with shock, but her mind was galloping, digging through plans, grasping at straws.

They couldn't get through the door behind them. They couldn't go down. That left—

Mitzi glanced at the hole in the ceiling, which gave her a glimpse of blue sky. "Nic, where's your ship?"

"Not far from the reactor, doll."

"Get as close as you can." Mitzi grabbed Eoin's and Mir's arms and began dragging them left, toward the remainder of the metal bridge, ushering Skye ahead. The concrete lid Adam and Ellen had dropped wouldn't keep the Cymics down for long, but she had a plan—a crazy, stupid, recklessly dangerous plan that even *she* couldn't believe she was about to try.

The falling roof had sliced through the middle of the metal walkway, but the edges were still functional, if a little twisted. Shuffling, rolling, and pushing, Mitzi urged her companions across the horrifically steep incline and toward the bridge. "Get on. Get on!" she yelled.

The block of concrete was still pushing the Cymics downward, but it was slowing. Any second, they would be rising again.

"Climb!"

The floor had risen so steeply that that the steps leading up to the walkway were nearly sideways. Mitzi struggled up them on her hands and knees, gripping the metal slats so tightly that her suit's gloves crushed the metal, to prevent the lurching, rocking motion of the room from throwing her off. She reached the top of the stairs, where the remainder of the walkway, all twenty feet of it, stretched downward like a slide before it warped and broke off.

"Follow me," she barked to the three team members behind her. Then she threw her legs onto the walkway and let gravity drag her down it. Her gloves ground against the rails as she sought to keep herself from being knocked off, and shudders ran up her body, sending her teeth chattering. Her heart was in her throat, and her eyes were wide as she faced the end of the walkway. As she'd guessed, the Cymics were rising again, pushing the concrete up with them, but there was still a ten-foot drop from the end of the walkway into the pit. She couldn't even see if there was an intact piece of concrete where she was going to land.

She shot off the end of the walkway and stretched out her feet, bracing for impact, praying that she would land on solid ground rather than the sucking flesh of the Cymics. She heard a gasp but didn't dare look back. Concrete rose to meet her boots, and she hit it with such force that the metal suit groaned, and a spike of pain ran up the leg that had been damaged. Barely a foot behind her, the concrete ended, and the black flesh rippled, still struggling to come to terms with having a hundred tons of concrete dropped on it.

Mitzi rolled and picked herself up just in time to see that Skye had followed her—and was falling off the edge of the walkway. Mitzi threw out a hand and grabbed Skye's arm, pulling her forward, away from the edge of their precarious lifeboat. They were just in time to get out of the way; Mir and Eoin had come down together in a reckless tumble of limbs, and they slammed into the ground with a sickening crunch.

Hoping they weren't hurt, Mitzi grabbed their suits, hauling them up. "Toward the center! Move!"

Then they were running, leaping over the gaps between the chunks of concrete, darting and weaving to avoid the enraged black tendrils that were slipping through the cracks, and racing toward Adam and Ellen. The concrete was rising alarmingly quickly, and the force of the momentum made it difficult to move, even with the suits. Mitzi reached the final two members of her team just as the concrete blocks passed the jagged edges of the roof they had once belonged to. She gazed up and was shocked to see the sky, clear and bright, after so long underground. A black spot hovered not far above them, and Mitzi focused on it, praying it was close enough. "Nic, we're gonna need that pickup now."

CHAPTER 56

THEY WERE SHOOTING UPWARD so harshly that Mitzi nearly lost her footing. She stretched out her arm to Eoin, yelling, "Hold hands! Make a chain, and don't let go!"

The concrete was crumbling under their feet as the Cymic rushed them up, pushing them toward the sky, trying to purge itself of the concrete lid, just as Mitzi had hoped it would. She focused on the ship above them. The doors had been opened, and a rope ladder swung down.

The pressure was so severe that it was a struggle to stay upright. Eoin held her hand tightly enough for Mitzi to feel the pressure through the glove.

Then the momentum stopped, and Mitzi felt the horrible sensation of weightlessness. The Cymics had thrown their crumbling cover free. Mitzi spared a glance downward, but the surface of the planet was so far away that the buildings looked like children's toys.

Nic had cut the ship's engines, letting it drop like a rock in a desperate attempt to meet them. The ladder swished close to Mitzi, and she grabbed for it, missed, grabbed again, and hooked her free arm through the lowest rung.

"Up, Nic!" she yelled, and the ship's engines came back on. Suddenly, their plunge was broken as the rope went taut in the crook of Mitzi's arms. Metal groaned, the ship keeled, and white-hot pain rushed through Mitzi's chest as the fractured ribs were strained.

She clung on, eyes squinted closed as blackness swam at the edges of her vision. *Don't let go. Don't let go…* She fought to keep conscious, aware of the weight of Eoin's hand in hers. Then the ship steadied, hovering, and Mitzi finally dared to open her eyes.

The pit stretched below them, vast and seeming to bubble like a cauldron of black ooze. Her team clung to each other.

The Cymics can see us, Mitzi realized as a multitude of white specks—the human skins—began to appear on the surface. *They'll come for us.*

"Climb," she gasped, struggling to breathe despite the pain in her ribs. "Whoever's at the end of our chain, climb up and get into the ship. *Quickly.*"

Ellen gave a terrified whimper then began to scramble up them, grabbing their hips and shoulders, anywhere she could get a foothold. Mitzi closed her eyes again as nausea grew in her stomach, but she felt the girl climb over her and grab the rope ladder. She was quickly followed by a second suit, then a third, and Mitzi forced her eyes open again.

The tendrils were already rising toward them, growing like unnatural trees. Eight of them aimed for the ship. *They're too fast. We're not going to get away in time.*

Eoin, the last of their human chain, grabbed for the rope ladder. Mitzi caught a shimmer of light reflected from one of the grenades on his belt—she pulled it loose and let it drop.

Finally free of her teammates' weight, she looped both hands through the bottom rung of the rope ladder and held on tightly. She could just barely see the grenade spiraling downward before it disappeared between the vast tendrils that were seconds away from snatching at her feet.

Wouldn't it be awful if it was a dud. Delirious with pain and exhaustion, she chuckled at the idea.

Then a burst of light burned out of the shadowy pit between the tendrils, followed by a bellowing roar. The tendrils fell away, thrashing and shuddering as the fire burned them.

"Fly higher," Mitzi murmured, hoping Nic would hear her over the commotion.

The fire below her wasn't fading as she'd expected, and her eyes widened. She'd forgotten the tendrils had been basting in the reactor's fuel. They acted like fuses; the fire raced over them, flickering downward toward the reactor.

Will that be enough? she wondered groggily, feeling her grip on the ladder slacken as something shook it. *Or will the defenses kick in before the fire can spread?*

The ship was rising, and the motion of the ladder threatened to throw her off. She felt drained and didn't even have enough energy to raise her head to check that her team was safely inside the ship.

They'd better be. I got them this far. If they somehow manage to die now, I'll be so mad at them.

She relaxed her grip and felt the ropes slip out from under her arms, but instead of the gentle falling sensation she'd expected, something grabbed her hand and pulled her up.

The fresh bout of pain from her ribs cleared her head. When she opened her eyes, gasping in aching breaths, she found herself on the floor of the ship. Skye and Eoin were on each side, dragging her inside. Someone slammed the door behind them, and she heard Nic speaking, though she couldn't make out the words.

"Yes, clear!" Skye called back, and the ship's engines rumbled under them as Nic kicked it into a higher gear.

Mitzi was propped upright against the wall, and someone—Mir, she thought—pressed the buttons on her glove to open the suit. The helmet was pulled off her head, and she drew a deeper breath, relieved to taste clear air again.

"I'm fine," she mumbled as someone tried to give her a towel. She looked around the cabin. The others were climbing out of their suits. In proper lighting, the amount of damage the exoskeletons had sustained was obvious. The beautiful polished metal had been scorched, scratched, and dented. Her crew, as they stepped out, didn't look much better. They were all sweaty, disheveled, and bruised. Fresh blood ran down Adam's face from the head wound that must have reopened.

Well, at least we don't have to worry about him being a Cymic.

"Ellen," Mitzi said, trying to inject some strength into her voice, "show me you can bleed."

"What?" The girl blinked at her then gasped as she realized what Mitzi meant. "Oh, yes, of course! Hang on!"

She fumbled for the knife in her suit's pouch then pressed it to her finger, squeezing her eyes shut against the pain. A bead of blood appeared at the site, and Mitzi nodded, satisfied.

"Okay. How're you all doing? Anyone seriously hurt? Hands up if you're gonna need a lifetime of therapy."

Adam ignored her. He was bouncing around the ship's hull, beaming and flushed with success. "That was *awesome*! I bet you thought we'd be useless, huh, Cap? We sure showed you, didn't we?"

"Yes," Mitzi said drily. "You certainly showed me a predisposition to insanity. How did you manage that anyway?"

"Nic was directing us toward the place he was hoping to pick you up from, which wasn't far from the reactor. You couldn't hear us, but we could hear you, and it sounded like things weren't going according to plan. Collapsing the roof was Ellen's idea."

Ellen, clearly terrified by being associated with the plan, shook her head quickly. "No, no, all I said was—"

"She said, 'I wish we could get down to them somehow.' And that made me think of how you'd used grenades to break through the floor and get to a lower level, and I thought it might just work. So I got Nic to give us the coordinates to the top of the reactor, which was a big strip of concrete, and we threw our entire collection of grenades around to blast our way down."

"Creative," Mitzi said, cringing at how insane the idea had been. Then she remembered that she herself had come up with the plan to use the Cymic's propulsion to throw them into the ship. "Thank you anyway. And you're right—that was pretty awesome."

That was apparently what Adam had been waiting to hear. He crossed his arms and rocked on the balls of his feet, looking smugly thrilled.

The door at the back of the room opened, and Nic came out. His face looked five shades lighter than it had the last time Mitzi had seen him. He took quick stock of the room then held out his hand to Mitzi, who took it with a grateful sigh and let herself be pulled up.

"Ship's on autopilot. C'mon, let's get you a proper seat, doll."

"I want to stand," Mitzi said stubbornly, but she allowed Nic to push her into one of the plush seats that lined the room. He opened a cupboard beside them and pulled out seven water bottles, tossing five of them to the crew and handing the last to Mitzi as he sat next to her.

"I'm not going to lie—I'm pretty damn relieved to see you again."

"Same to you," Mitzi said, drinking deeply as she reclined in the chair. The pain in her ribs had subsided to a dull ache, and she let her eyes rove around the occupants of the room, watching them, assessing them. Adam had collapsed into one of the seats, legs splayed, grinning like an idiot despite the blood that was drying on his face. He'd probably come out of the experience better than all of them. She wished him luck in getting his friends to believe his story, though.

Skye had seated herself in a chair in the corner and was watching her unopened bottle. She seemed okay, if a little unsteady on her feet.

Mitzi wasn't surprised to see Eoin had his book open again. He seemed thoroughly engrossed in it. Ellen, after hovering about the room for a moment, had settled next to him, and rested her head on his shoulder. He didn't seem to mind, and Ellen, whose face looked horribly pinched and pale, was at least calm with him.

Mir sat down on the other side of Mitzi and offered her a shaky smile. "That was kind of a wild ride, huh?"

"Yeah," Mitzi said, feeling an unexpected fondness for the girl. She had to reassess all of them, she realized. As she gazed around the room, the old tags she'd given them disappeared.

Adam was no longer an idiot; he was brave, resourceful, and at least a little bit selfless. Ellen had proven that she wasn't so weak that she would collapse at the first sign of stress. Mitzi knew she would still be better suited for a calmer, safer occupation, but she'd shown that she could fight if pushed to it. Mir, the sulky teenager, had followed every command Mitzi had given, and more than that, she seemed to have incredible insight. She'd saved Mitzi's life in the maintenance room, and she'd kept her wits about her long enough to ensure Mitzi was still human.

Skye, as Mitzi had suspected, had incredible potential. Her pretty face hid a rock-solid, loyal interior. And Eoin had proven himself capable of handling the horrors of the Cymic world, and his knowledge had gotten them out of a locked room.

Franc, the only lost member of their team, had shaken off his fussy accountant appearance and made the ultimate sacrifice to save the mission. Mitzi squeezed her eyes shut against bitter tears. Losing a part of her team always stung, and Franc had been a part that she would have very much wanted to work with again. She hoped, wherever he'd gone after death, he knew just how much good his sacrifice had brought. He might have just ensured a future for his grandchildren, after all.

"Look," Nic said. He'd turned in his seat to gaze out of the window, and Mitzi followed his eyes. At first, she couldn't understand what she was looking at. It looked like an ocean in sunset; shadows and red-gold light fought for dominance on the waves. Then she realized the station was burning.

She stood up to get a better look, grinning from ear to ear. One at a time, the others came to stand beside her, peering out of the ship's windows to admire the destruction they'd created. The fire rolled and billowed, sending up huge clouds of black smoke. Every now and then, something would explode in a pop of white.

"It's spreading," Nic said, pointing to the edge of the fire, which clawed its way across the surface of the planet. The light was rippling outward, absorbing the darkness of the buildings, consuming the shadows and Cymic Parasites alike.

"That'll be enough to get rid of them all, won't it?" Adam asked.

"Should be." Nic grinned widely. "Even if the fire doesn't make it to every corner, the heat should kill them. I'll send a signal once we're back in the atmosphere, and the construction ship will leave this afternoon. By the time it arrives, the fire will have died down, and they can get that communication tower set up."

Skye, who had been standing at the end of their line, dropped her water bottle and strode toward the doors at the back of the room.

"You okay?" Mitzi called, but Skye didn't answer. Instead, she pushed inside the bathroom. Mitzi heard the door lock, followed by retching sounds.

"Oh dear," Nic sighed, and Mitzi reassessed her opinion of Skye for the third time that day. *Guess she's not so good with stress after all.*

They turned back to watch the burning planet as the ship took them closer to the atmosphere. Closer to home.

The war had only just begun, but at least now humanity had a chance.

ABOUT THE AUTHOR

Darcy Coates is the *USA Today* bestselling author of *Hunted*, *The Haunting of Ashburn House*, *Craven Manor*, and more than a dozen horror and suspense titles. She lives on the Central Coast of Australia with her family, cats, and a garden full of herbs and vegetables. Darcy loves forests, especially old-growth forests where the trees dwarf anyone who steps between them. Wherever she lives, she tries to have a mountain range close by.

VOICES IN THE SNOW

NO ONE ESCAPES THE STILLNESS.

Clare remembers the cold. She remembers dark shapes in the snow and a terror she can't explain. And then...nothing. When she wakes in a stranger's home, he tells her she was in an accident. Clare wants to leave, but a vicious snowstorm has blanketed the world in white, and there's nothing she can do but wait.

They should be alone, but Clare's convinced something else is creeping about the surrounding woods, watching. Waiting. Between the claustrophobic storm and the inescapable sense of being hunted, Clare is on edge...and increasingly certain of one thing: her car crash wasn't an accident. Something is waiting for her to step outside the fragile safety of the house...something monstrous, something unfeeling. Something desperately hungry.

SECRETS IN THE DARK

YOU CAN'T OUTRUN THE STILLNESS.

Winterbourne Hall is not safe. Even as Clare and Dorran scramble to secure the ancient building against ravenous hollow ones, they face something far worse: Clare's sister has made contact, but she's trapped, and her oxygen is running out.

Hundreds of miles separate Clare from Beth. The land between them is infested with monsters, and the roads are a maze of dead ends. Clare has to choose between making a journey she knows she might not survive, or staying safe in Winterbourne and listening as her sister slowly suffocates. At least, whatever her choice, she'll have Dorran by her side. And yet there are eyes in the dark. There are whispers in the mist. There is danger lurking in the snow, and one false step could end it all…

WHISPERS IN THE MIST

YOU WON'T SURVIVE THE STILLNESS.

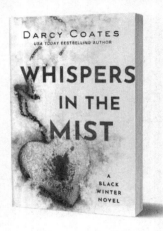

Clare and Dorran may still be alive against all odds, but relief is only temporary. Dorran is sick, and rapidly worsening. Clare fears the only way to save him lies in the mysterious Evandale Research Institute, supposedly one of the few remaining human refuges. But the research station is three days' journey away, and Clare isn't certain their small group can endure that long. Because the danger they're facing comes not only from the ravenous hollow ones…but from each other.

This terrible new world has left scars, and only some of them are physical. As Clare fights to protect the most precious people in her life, she begins to realize a horrible truth: not everyone can be saved. And sometimes the worst monsters wear a human smile.